Harun al-Rashid
and the World of the
Thousand and One Nights

Harun al-Rashid
and the World of the
Thousand and One Nights

André Clot

Translated from the French
by John Howe

NEW AMSTERDAM
New York

Library of Congress Cataloging-in-Publication Data

Clot, André.
    [Haroun-al-Rachid et le temps des Mille et une nuits. English]
    Harun al-Rashid and the world of the thousand and one nights /
André Clot ; translated by John Howe.
    p.   cm.
    Translation of: Haroun al-Rachid et le temps des Mille et une nuits.
    Bibliography: p.
    Includes index.
    ISBN 0-941533-65-4 : $19.95
    1. Islamic Empire – History – 750-1258. 2. Hārūn al-Rashīd, Caliph, ca. 763-
809. I. Title.
DS38.6.C5613 1989
909′.097′671–dc20

89-12093
CIP

© Librairie Arthème Fayard, 1986

First published in the United States by
NEW AMSTERDAM BOOKS
by arrangement with Librairie Arthème Fayard, Paris

This book is printed on acid-free paper.

Contents

1
The Horsemen of Allah

Religion taught by a prophet or by a preacher of the truth is the only foundation on which to build a great and powerful empire.

ibn Khaldun

So great were the splendours and riches of his reign, such was its prosperity, that this period has been called "the honeymoon".

Masudi

The prophet Mohammed died in Medina on 8 June 632 (13 Rabi 1), soon after his first pilgrimage to Mecca. He left no male heir and no settled arrangements for his succession; even if he had had a son, the Arabs, unfamiliar with the idea of hereditary power, would probably have rejected him. A confrontation took place between the Companions of Medina and the Companions of Mecca. Owing to the wisdom of the Prophet's close friends Abu Bakr and Omar and to the fact that Mohammed's cousin and son–in–law, Ali, was not yet in a position to impose his own candidacy, the crisis was resolved. Abu Bakr became caliph, *khalifat al-rasul*, "delegate of the messenger of God". The "election" occurred just in time to prevent armed conflict between Mohammed's first disciples, but the episode served as a warning for the future. Two years later, perceiving that his end was near, Abu Bakr named Omar as his successor and Omar acceded to power without opposition.

Lightning Raids
During his short reign, Abu Bakr led the Arab tribes in a successful attack against the northern Arabian provinces; but Omar, the most

intelligent and vigorous of the *rashidun* caliphs,[1] greatly expanded the domain of Islam with astonishing speed. In 634 the Byzantines were defeated at Adjnayn in Palestine. Damascus was taken the following year, and the whole of Syria fell after the victory at the Yarmuk. In 642, after the battles of Qadisiya, in Mesopotamia, and Nehavend, in Iran, the Sassanid empire collapsed and the emperor, Yazdiagird III, fled to Khorasan. He was assassinated in Merv in 651. Omar seized Jerusalem in 638 and Edessa the next year. Egypt fared no better. The Byzantines, who had taken it back from the Sassanids in 628, were vanquished by the brilliant Arab leader Amr al-As, first at Heliopolis and then at Babylon in Egypt (close to the site of present-day Cairo). Alexandria was finally occupied in 646. The first phase of the Arab conquest ended about 650. It was soon to continue, to east and west, without encountering any greater resistance.

In the empire of the basileus, ravaged by religious quarrels, the Byzantines were heartily detested. The Monophysite Armenians and Copts constituted a separate church. An attempt to impose monothelism had annoyed orthodox and heterodox alike and entrenched them in their rigid doctrinal positions. The Jews were outraged by an edict of the emperor Heraclius which attempted to force baptism on them; the Nestorians, banished from the empire, had sought refuge in Sassanid territory. The great majority of these populations had no difficulty in accepting their new masters, especially as their tax burden was reduced. The Sassanid empire had fallen into anarchy, and its strength was draining away. The war of conquest which had carried the armies of Khosrov III to Jerusalem and the gates of Constantinople had foundered in disaster. The official church — Mazdaean or Zoroastrian — was persecuting heretics, and the empire's exhausted, long-suffering populations were ready to welcome the first "liberator".

Facing these two weakened, divided empires, the Arabs were like the youth of the world. They possessed neither revolutionary tactics nor new weapons, but were buoyed up by their unshakable religious faith and by the prospect of prodigious booty. Their lightly armed troops were accustomed to long privation and the most hostile climates. The new occupants usually set up their camps outside existing settlements, and thus were the founders of new towns:

Kufa and Basra in Iraq, Fostat in Egypt. They did not seek to convert indigenous populations or subject them to new laws. Provided they paid a tax (the *djiziya*) Christians of all sects, Jews, and Mazdaeans were free to practise their religions and organize themselves as they wished. The chiefs of non-Muslim communities — bishops in Christian territories and *diqan* (rural notables) in Iran — collected taxes on behalf of the *wali*, the provincial chief named by the Muslim authorities. Land was retained by its owners on payment of another tax, the *kharadj*.

It was not long, however, before problems arose among the Muslims. On 16 June 656 the third caliph, the Umayyad Othman, was assassinated in Medina. Ali became caliph. The Prophet's cousin (and husband of his daughter Fatima) most probably had no hand in Othman's murder, and met with the approval of the involved parties, not only because of his close family relationship with Mohammed, but because they recognized his intransigent piety and determination to apply the Divine Law under all circumstances. But the Umayyads and their supporters left Medina accusing the new caliph of regicide and calling on him to chastise those responsible. Described as a man of mediocre intelligence, and more gifted with bravura than with skill, Ali did not know how to defend himself against this accusation. A serious division occurred within the community of the faithful. It did not disappear with the passage of time — quite the contrary — and Ali's party, the *shia*, was destined to go on expanding and to assert its separate identity by contradicting (sometimes to an irrational degree) the positions of the *sunna*, the tradition based on the words and deeds of the Prophet established in the eighth and ninth centuries by the doctors of Islam.

A few months after being named caliph, Ali left Medina — never again to be the capital of Islam — for Kufa and then Basra. In a first confrontation, he routed his adversaries in the so-called battle of the Camel (Mohammed's widow Aisha participated in it on camel-back). But Muawia, an Umayyad whom Othman had made governor of Syria, was still calling for vengeance. His position, at the head of a rich province and a powerful army, was a strong one. Ali's was less so, and became still weaker in 657 after the battle of Siffin on the Euphrates, where the Syrians rallied their wavering troops by attaching leaves from the Koran to the ends of their lances to show that only the judgment of God, embodied in *The Book*, could decide this struggle between Muslims. The decision went against Ali, and a group of his supporters abandoned his cause — the Kharidjites, "those who leave", who have reappeared at intervals throughout the history of Islam. Muawia's forces were gaining ground, but Ali refused to accept what was happening and committed the further error of trying to deal with the Kharidjites by force. The resulting massacre sealed his own fate; a Kharidjite avenged his murdered brothers by killing Ali with a poisoned sword in 661 outside the mosque at Kufa. Muawia, who meanwhile had seized Egypt and then the Hejaz, became sole caliph.

The era of rashidun caliphs had ended and that of the Umayyads[2] was beginning. The rudimentary organization of the early years gave place to a veritable empire, whose administration was at first not so much Arab as Persian and, even more markedly, Byzantine. Centred in Damascus, with a civil service largely inherited from the Greeks (Muawia himself chose a Christian secretary), the new state established the dynastic principle and incorporated the various traditions which already existed by basing itself increasingly on the *mawali*, or local converts to Islam. This irritated the earliest Muslims, for whom a state in the hands of newcomers represented neither the traditions of the Prophet nor the religious ideal for which they had fought. Ultimately this was to have serious consequences. The Umayyad empire lasted less than a century. But in that time its great caliphs — Muawia himself, Abd al-Malik, Hisham — built one of the most powerful empires mankind had ever seen, and conquered immense territories south of the Mediterranean and far into the Orient which were to remain Muslim forever.

The Umayyads threatened Constantinople several times; more importantly, however, in the space of a few years they occupied the entire Iranian plateau, which was settled by thousands of Arab families. Crossing the Oxus (the Amu-Daria), their armies took Herat, Kabul, Balkh, and, in 710 Bokhara and Samarkand. The Arab general Qutayba, whom chroniclers called a "strategist of genius", carried the Umayyad standards as far as Ferghana and Kashgar, in Chinese Turkestan. The Arabs' victory over the Chinese at Talas in 751 gave them supremacy over the region between the Iranian plateau and the Tien-Chan. They went no farther east, but to the south swept up the Indus valley and took Multan.

At the same time other Arab units were driving westwards and into north Africa. After founding Kairouan in 670, the Arabs reached Tlemcen and the Atlantic. By 710 they had conquered the tribes of the central and western Maghreb, and this put an end to Byzantine Africa. A Berber, Tarik ibn Ziyad, took seven thousand men across the strait which now bears his name (Gibralter is derived from Djebel Tarik, "Tarik's mountain") and fought a decisive battle for control of the peninsula with the Visigoth king Akhila. Cordoba and Toledo fell, then other towns. By 720 nearly the whole of Spain was Muslim.

Vengeance and Revolution

No date in the history of Islam — apart from the night when Mohammed heard Allah ordering him to preach the doctrine of the one true God — had heavier consequences than that of Ali's brutal death before the mosque at Kufa. A few years later, on 10 October 680, in Kerbela (Iraq), his son Husein also met a tragic death at the hands of Umayyad soldiers. Neither father nor son was a man of special distinction; estimable in their piety, faithful to what they saw as the Prophet's legacy, both had only the most mediocre political talents; yet their tragic deaths opened a wound in Islam which was never to be healed. The murders at Kufa and Kerbela divided the faithful forever, by colouring Shiism — the cult of Ali's party — with a passionate, mystical messianism, which has survived down the centuries to the present day.

In the eyes of Ali's supporters, the Umayyads were responsible for the martyrdom of the two most venerated descendants of the Prophet, *imams* (guides of the community) elected by God for all eternity,[3] and were guilty of abusing religion for political and personal ends. Through the turns and vicissitudes of history, from one plot to the next, their unrelenting hatred ended by achieving the downfall of the Umayyad dynasty.

Soon after Husein's death in Kerbela a group of Kufa citizens, filled with remorse for their failure to prevent Ali's murder, set out to punish its authors. To shouts of "Stand up to avenge the blood of Husein!" a thousand men launched a suicide attack on Umayyad units, and were crushed. A few months later a much larger and better organized uprising was initiated by an enigmatic character called Mukhtar, whose aim was to seize power from the Umayyads and hand it over to the Prophet's descendants through Ali's line. Suspected by the tribal aristocracy of seeking the support of the mawali, Mukhtar was killed in 687.

Another plot soon sprang up in Kufa and was successful. It was moved by the same spirit of vengeance, but this time in the name of the descendants of the Prophet's uncle Abbas.[4] It gathered force in Iran, in Khorasan, where lived some two hundred and fifty thousand Arab immigrants of Iraqi origin, under the leadership of Abu Muslim. Probably the son of an Iranian convert to Islam, this strong personality and born conspirator was to organize the revolution and lead it to triumph. His handful of men soon grew to an army of more than one hundred thousand — Muslim Arabs, but also Iranian Zoroastrians and Mazdaeans — that marched behind the black banner[5] of the Emir of the Prophet's family. Chains of beacons carried news of the insurrection from village to village. Merv, capital of Khorasan, was taken in 647. Then Nishapur. Soon afterwards Abu Muslim's supporters defeated an Umayyad army, marched into Kufa on 2 September 749, and there proclaimed Abu al-Abbas *amir al-muminin*, Commander of the Faithful, Caliph of Islam. But the first Abbasid caliph, Saffah,[6] was to reign for only a few years.

There remained the problem of Marwan, the caliph of Damascus. His armies had been beaten one after another, but so far he had left his generals to confront the enemy by themselves. After his son's defeat at the Little Zab, in Djezireh, he entered the field himself and fought against Saffah's uncle Abdallah Ali near the Great Zab. Defeated, the last of the Syrian Umayyads reached Damascus but was refused entry by the inhabitants. Fleeing from country to country, he was pursued into Egypt, where he was killed in an ambush.

Saffah was master of the Middle East. To eliminate all risk of pro-Umayyad propaganda, he had members of the disgraced family hunted down in all corners of the empire and killed. He even ordered the bodies of Umayyad caliphs to be disinterred and burned and the ashes to be scattered to the wind. The historian Tabari recounts that after assembling the last survivors, Saffah:

had them massacred and then caused a carpet of leather to be spread over the bodies, on which a meal was served to those who were present at the scene, and who ate while the death-rattle still sounded in the throats of the expiring victims.

Only one Umayyad prince escaped the Abbasid killings: Abd al-Rahman ibn Muawia, grandson of the caliph Hisham. After four years of wandering through Palestine and north Africa, where, helped by his Berber origins, he found refuge, he crossed the Strait of Gibraltar to join a group of Umayyad mawali. In the autumn of 756, in the great mosque at Cordoba, he was proclaimed *amir al-Andalus*, founding the Spanish Umayyad dynasty, which was to reign for nearly three centuries.

Saffah does not seem to have been a man of the first quality, but the words he pronounced at his enthronement leave no doubt about his — and the Abbasids' — determination to hold onto the power they had just won. "Accept with gratitude that which you have received," he is supposed to have told the inhabitants of Kufa. "Obey us, and make no mistake about the position which is now yours, for this is our affair."[7] It could hardly have been put more clearly. Syrian domination was finished forever, the Umayyads wiped out and Abbasid legitimacy proclaimed. "It was a revolution in the history of Islam, as critical a turning point as the French and Russian revolutions in the history of the West."[8]

The Abbasids began by installing themselves solidly in Iraq and abandoning Syria, which the Umayyad presence had besmirched. They deserted Damascus, traditional centre of the Middle East, and settled in lower Mesopotamia, at first near Kufa and then farther north at Anbar, which remained the capital of the empire until the construction of Baghdad ten years later.

This southward withdrawal is significant in several ways. The new dynasty had not abandoned the Mediterranean but in future would look increasingly towards the east: Persia, India, and even more distant parts of Asia. The Greek and Byzantine influence would decline, and the caliphs' state would develop into a genuine empire of the Middle East.

The Abbasids were an Arab dynasty, depending on Arabs; their language and civilization were Arabic and they employed Arabs for the great majority of important official posts. They possessed two forces whose fidelity was proof against any trial: the army of Khorasan and the family of the descendants of Abbas. The first, consisting of the loyal, generous, incorruptible, and obedient men who had carried them to power, would defend them at all critical moments. Organized on a tribal basis, they were stationed in sensitive regions such as Syria and north Africa. Favoured by the regime, rewarded with plots of land in inner Baghdad, its soldiers remained the Abbasids' "strike force" for a hundred years until they were supplanted by Turks.

The family of Abbas's descendants also gave the first caliphs, especially Harun al-Rashid, the support they needed to guide the empire through difficult periods. Loyal and united under its head, the family derived incomparable authority from its descent from the Prophet. It was sufficiently numerous to occupy all the most important posts; for example, the empire's western provinces were governed by seven of Saffah's uncles.

But the Abbasids still felt that the East was beyond their grasp: Abu Muslim, absolute master of Khorasan, now reigned there as viceroy. The thought that they owed their power to him became unbearable to Saffah, and apparently even more so to his brother Jaffar, who is said to have told Saffah, "He is a giant among giants, and you can never enjoy life as long as he remains alive."

Saffah died in 754 and Jaffar succeeded him under the name Mansour. The governor of Syria, Abdallah Ali, revolted against the new caliph, claiming that as Saffah's uncle he himself should have been the successor. Abu Muslim put down the revolt, thus rendering his last service to the Abbasids. Having no further use for the "kingmaker", Mansour summoned him to his camp, heaped abuse on him, and had him beheaded.

In the year 755 the Abbasids reigned supreme. Only eleven years later Harun al-Rashid — "Aaron the Well-Guided" — was to see the light of day and impart a glitter to his dynasty which would travel untarnished across the centuries. But before him there reigned three more caliphs. The name of one deserves only oblivion, but the vision of the other two gave the immense empire the solid political and institutional foundations it needed to survive, and created its great and glorious capital.

Mansour the Builder

An intelligent and tireless worker, but hard, violent, treacherous and miserly, Jaffar al-Mansour was in his early forties when he became master of the Abbasid empire. Intolerant of frivolous amusements, he banned music from his palace and with his own hand struck a boy who one day played a drum at his door. He rose at dawn, worked until evening prayer, and granted himself only the briefest of rests. He made all decisions, even those that involved the smallest expenditure, earning the nickname Abu al-Duwaneek (Father of Farthings), which he accepted with pride. "He who has no money has no men," he would say, "and he who has no men watches as his enemies grow great."

At the time he succeeded Saffah, Mansour already possessed much experience of men and politics. He was born around 710 at Humayma in Syria, where the Abbasid family resided while the conspiracy to place it in power was in gestation. After the generals' plot led by Abu Muslim, he should have been chosen caliph, being much better qualified than his brother. But the army chiefs favoured Saffah, ostensibly because he was the son of a legitimate wife — Mansour's mother was a concubine — but really because they thought him more malleable. Mansour's forceful personality had dominated Saffah's five-year reign; on his own accession it became even stronger, helping him to consolidate and organize the state through the twenty-one years of *his* reign.

Abdallah Ali's rebellion against the new caliph had been supported by Syrian troops who resented the Abbasids' abandoning Damascus for Iraq. His defeat removed any possibility that Damascus might become capital of the empire once again. Mansour seized this opportunity to reduce tension with the Syrians: he took no sanctions against the rebels, retained the army chiefs who had served the former dynasty, promoted some to high positions and chose Syrian units to defend his frontiers with the Byzantines. Mansour thus disarmed at a stroke the hostility of one of the empire's great provinces and established a counterweight to the all-powerful province of Khorasan, which threatened eventually to become dangerous.

The Abbasids were now secure from military rebellion, but there remained those disappointed in the new regime, with the Alids in the front rank. The family of Ali could no longer expect to see one of its members become supreme guide of the Muslims. It quickly understood, too, that its fight for a new society "founded on the Koran, justice and equality for all Muslims" had been in vain, and that the power of the descendants of the Prophet's uncle had simply replaced that of the Umayyads. As under the Umayyads, the state was a lay state. The revolution had failed.

Opposition groups soon appeared both in Iraq and in the provinces. One of the first, the Rawandiya (from the name of the small town of Rawand in eastern Iran), contested the legitimacy of Abbasid rule. Few in number but fanatical and courageous, the Rawandiya preached violent action. They tried to assassinate Mansour, who had them exterminated.

Better organized and more extensive, the insurrection of Mohammed Nafs al-Zakiya (Mohammed the Pure Soul) and his brother Ibrahim could have succeeded. In September 762, after a long period of clandestine activity, Mohammed launched an open revolt and seized Medina. "The fox has come out of his lair!" exclaimed Mansour, sending a four-thousand-man force against him. Mohammed's troops were soon defeated and he was killed. But two months later his brother Ibrahim, who had assembled a large number of supporters, launched his own insurrection at Basra. This time Mansour had the greatest difficulty putting down the revolt. His instinct for strategy and tactics being as sharp as his political cunning, however, he put an end to the only serious rebellion of his reign in February 763 at the battle of Bahrama (south of Kufa), where Ibrahim met his death. Two more names had been added to the growing list of shia martyrs.

The suppression of these revolts and the elimination of Abu Muslim had bloodily underscored Jaffar al-Mansour's determination to govern the empire alone and unhindered. The Khorasan army's acceptance of the brutal slaying of its chief, and the silence of the Alids following the executions of Mohammed the Pure Soul and Ibrahim, were proof that Mansour had made himself understood. Until the caliphate became enfeebled, the Abbasid state was to remain a centralized state ruled by a sovereign whose unlimited authority extended to the most distant provinces.

Mansour himself appointed his governors, often from the ranks of his own family, and exercised rigorous control over them (although they too enjoyed considerable power). His officials, even those closest to him, were surrounded by crowds of spies who reported back to him on their slightest deeds and decisions. Nothing could be allowed to escape the Master of the Believers, who awarded himself the title of "Mansour the Victorious", or "He who receives God's help". He was an autocrat who modelled himself on the great Umayyads and the Achemenid and Sassanid sovereigns of the ancient Orient. He used the mawali only in the role of counsellors or simple executants of his orders. One of these, Khalid ibn Barmak (doubtless already responsible for fiscal matters), bore a name that was destined to become celebrated. Mansour maintained the division between the governing elite and the mass of Muslims which had characterized Umayyad rule. Thus he secured his dynasty, but without satisfying those Muslims who wanted to see their community led by an imam under God's guidance.

It was Mansour who was actually the founder of the Abbasid empire, but his name is inscribed in history chiefly as the creator of Baghdad. Even before assuming power, the Abbasids had decided to establish their capital in Iraq. Traditionally Iraq was opposed to the Umayyads and faithful to the House of the Prophet; it was also the richest of the provinces, and yielded the most taxes to the treasury. Kufa had played a major role in the Abbasid revolution, and it was in its mosque that Abu al-Abbas — Saffah — had been proclaimed caliph. He therefore established his capital in a nearby village, al-Hashimiyah, where he had a group of buildings constructed. A little later he moved to Anbar on the Euphrates, not far from Ctesiphon, which had been the capital of the Parthians and the Sassanids.

Mansour continued to reside at Anbar after his accession, but, eventually, for reasons unknown, he moved back to al-Hashimiyah. Finding the town difficult to defend and the population of Kufa unruly and unpredictable, he began looking for a new site for the capital, finally settling on the west bank of the Tigris. The place offered many advantages. The river to the east was impossible to ford; to the south a network of canals could easily serve both as defence and supply route; the climate was temperate, mosquitoes were rare, and both banks of the river were cultivable. There is no need to add the cosmological reasons extracted from the distant Iranian past, although as a matter of fact an astronomer by the name of Nawbakht[9] gave his approval — could he have done otherwise? — to the caliph's decision. Also, Christian monks living in a nearby monastery told Mansour that old books in their possession predicted that one day a king would settle in this spot.

Mansour himself drew the plans of a circular town,[10] which were first traced on the site with ashes, so that the caliph might better visualize it. He called the future Baghdad Madinat al-Salam (Town of Peace) to suggest Heaven.[11] The circular design made defence easier by eliminating dead angles, and it reduced the cost of building the walls. Architects, engineers, masons and labourers were brought from Syria, Iran, Mosul, Kufa and Basra, to a total (it was said) of a hundred thousand men.[12] In 762, four years after construction began, all was complete.

Following Oriental practice, the main building material was sun-dried brick, with baked brick used for arches and domes, and a layer of reeds between the rows. The two concentric ramparts protecting the town were thirty metres apart and surrounded by a ditch. The perimeter wall, nearly five metres thick and thirteen metres high, was more than two and a half kilometres long.

Mansour placed his palace and the mosque in the centre of the town, with the residential area in the space between the walls and the vast palace complex. The Palace of the Gilded Gate was in the form of a square with sides half a kilometre long. The *iwan*, a vast hall open along one side only, was surmounted by a dome. On the upper storey was a second vast chamber, its roof an immense green cupola. There the caliph held court with a ceremony worthy of the Byzantines or the ancient monarchs of the Orient; there was nothing to recall the simplicity of the early days of Islam. The mosque was contiguous with the palace and communicated with it directly. A large open space separated them from the buildings housing the administrative services — treasury, arsenal, offices — and the residences of the caliph's children and high officials.

Within the walls of the administrative city, two circular streets surrounded two security zones; they crossed four avenues leading from the four city gates to the caliph's palace and the mosque. The residential quarter was divided into four quadrants, which, according to the geographer Yakubi, housed senior officers, those trusted sufficiently to be lodged close to the caliph, his principal freedmen, and, lastly, those liable to be required in a hurry for urgent business.

Along the inside of the city walls, arcades had been built for merchants' shops and stalls. But one day, as Mansour received a Byzantine envoy, a cow escaped from a slaughterhouse and caused a great tumult in the neighbourhood of the palace. After having witnessed this scene, the Byzantine was unable to resist observing to the caliph:

> Commander of the Faithful, you have raised such a structure as never existed before. But it has three faults: there is not enough water, there are no gardens, and, worse still, your subjects are with you inside your palace — and when the subjects are in the palace with the sovereign, there are no secrets.

Far from delighted, the caliph answered drily, "We have enough water to drink. As for your second fault, we were not created for frivolity and amusement. Thirdly, since you see fit to comment on my secrets, I have none from my subjects."

But the Byzantine's remarks stayed in the caliph's mind, and after a while he ordered a new water conduit to be installed. A more serious incident persuaded him that his security arrangements were inadequate. The *muhtesib*, an official in charge of the market police, took the lead in a Shiite conspiracy and tried to foment an insurrection in the town. He was quickly arrested and executed and his body exposed in front of the city gates. Mansour ordered the market to be removed to al-Karkh, outside the Round City. Because the first mosque attracted too many people to the palace environs, Mansour had another built, also outside the walls. Finally, to solve the palace's supply problems, the caliph decided to move to the palace of al-Khuld (Blissful Eternity), which had just been completed on the bank of the Tigris north of the town. On the opposite side of the river, the east bank, there rose almost simultaneously the palace of his son, the crown prince Mohammed al-Mahdi, father of Harun al-Rashid.

Mansour could expect the last years of his reign to be peaceful. He had eliminated his domestic rivals one by one. On the Caucasus frontier the Khazars had seized Tiflis but had been repelled. In Asia Minor, where the military campaigns of the basileus Constantine V had made difficulties for the empire during the Abbasid revolution, Mansour's forces had easily restored his rule. The population of Egypt had shown no reluctance to recognize Abbasid sovereignty, which now extended westwards as far as Kairouan. Spain was regarded as definitively lost, but despite the absence of formal ties to the empire, commercial and cultural exchanges continued to take place.

Mansour died on 7 October 755, in Bir Mayum near Mecca, while leading the pilgrimage surrounded by leading members of his family. He was buried in the sand of the desert. His son and heir Mahdi had stayed in Baghdad, and the grand chamberlain, Rabi al-Yunus, followed custom by keeping the news secret until Mahdi had the situation well in hand.

The succession had been settled, but not without damage. Shortly before his death, Saffah, fearing a coup d'état by Abu Muslim against the designated heir Jaffar (Mansour), had named a second heir, Isa ibn Musa, one of his nephews. Isa thus remained heir to Mansour. Mansour's son Mohammed (Mahdi), virtually excluded from the succession, tried in vain to persuade Isa to renounce his claim. Eventually, after a long struggle, Isa did give way, in exchange for financial compensation and the promise that power would revert to him on Mahdi's death. As Isa was much the older man, it seemed unlikely that this promise would have to be kept.

The Prodigal and Indulgent Mahdi

Mahdi, the son of a miser, was the opposite of his father in every way. Tabari says of him in a eulogistic portrait, "His generosity was very great, he was extremely indulgent and forgave even those guilty of the greatest crimes. No Abbasid caliph was more just, more merciful, more pious, more virtuous or more handsome." The chroniclers tell us that before leaving for Mecca, Mansour had given him some advice: "The wise man is not he who can extricate himself from a crisis, but he who foresees the crisis and prevents it." "Watch over your finances. You will be great and victorious so long as your treasury is full." And, last: "Do not permit women to interfere in politics. But I doubt that you will follow this advice."

The severe Commander of the Faithful knew his son well. He was certainly prodigal, freely spending the money his father had so parsimoniously saved. Tall, slender, and handsome, Mahdi had a dark complexion, a high forehead, and curly hair. Women liked him and he liked women. Under his reign, for the first time, women exercised a power sometimes surpassing even that of the sovereign himself.

Born in or about 745, Mahdi spent his childhood in Syria and moved to Kufa following the success of the Abbasid revolution. In charge of military operations in Khorasan from the age of fifteen, he was soon afterwards entrusted by his father with the government of this province, one of the most important in the empire. Its capital was the town of Ray (not far from modern Teheran). Mahdi lived there several years, gradually rebuilding much of the town, which was then named after him — al-Mohammediya.

Several of his children were born during his sojourn at Ray; the first was Abbasah, daughter of the concubine Rahim, who was to be involved in the most grievous events of the dynasty. Much more importantly, however, Mahdi received from his father one day — it is not known when exactly — the present of a young girl "slender and graceful as a reed", of Yemeni origin, named Khaizuran. "Take her to my son and tell him that she is made to bear children," said the great caliph, who had bought her at Mecca. He was not mistaken. Khaizuran, who had enough education to hold her own in the refined atmosphere of the court, quickly found her way to the young prince's heart. She was to bear him three sons, of whom the first was Musa, born probably in 764, and the second Harun, born two years later. Both were to become caliphs, Musa's life ending tragically and Harun going on to become the most illustrious leader of the dynasty. The third son, Isa, remained virtually unknown.

Once Khaizuran's hopes were fulfilled, her intelligence and ambition did the rest. She suddenly revealed the existence of her family, hitherto kept hidden, and her elder sister Salsal soon seduced Mahdi's half-brother Jaffar and bore him a son and a daughter. Nicknamed Zubaidah (Little Butter-Pat) by her grandfather Mansour, Salsal's daughter was to marry her royal cousin Harun al-Rashid and be immortalized in the *Thousand and One Nights*.

Indefatigably amorous, Mahdi had innumerable concubines, most of their names submerged in the flood tide of the great Abbasid century. One of them was Chiklah, a young slave taken along with the rest of the harem of the prince of Daylam (on the southern coast of the Caspian Sea) after a battle. Dark-skinned, graceful, intelligent, and an excellent musician, Chiklah gave Mahdi a son, Ibrahim. He became a celebrated musician, poet, and singer, and much later, for a very brief time, caliph. His sister, also Mahdi's child, was to be one of the great beauties of the age, a "prodigy of wit and talent."[13] Another concubine was Mamunah, of the slim ankles and high bosom, whom Mahdi had bought for the fantastic sum of one hundred thousand dirhams (an extravagance he kept hidden from his father). Speaking of her, Khaizuran confessed one day, "No other woman has ever made my position so difficult." And there were Hasanah, Hullah, Nalkah, Khaizuran's younger sister Asma... But Khaizuran, who became Mahdi's legal wife probably in 775, was far superior to these young beauties in her intelligence, her wit, her sense of humour and her skill in adapting to all situations. Little by little she acquired great influence over Mahdi, and thus naturally over the affairs of state.

By these means Mansour's court, at the heart of the empire, was rapidly transformed. The new capital's prosperity was soon reflected in the love of life, pleasure, and luxury which now prevailed there. The example of prodigality was set by the young caliph himself.

Also quite unlike his father, Mahdi tried to settle the endless conflict with the followers of Ali, the Alids, or at least with the moderates among them, by negotiation rather than by force. He pardoned the Hasanids for joining the revolt of Mohammed the Pure Soul against Mansour, and when one of them, Hasan ibn Ibrahim, gave himself up after escaping from prison, Mahdi awarded him large estates in the Hejaz. Many Alid supporters, especially in Medina, benefited from his generosity.

One decision was to have serious consequences. Probably hoping to use him against the Alids, Mahdi admitted to his inner court Yakub ibn Daoud, whose father had once served the Umayyads. Yakub was so successful in gaining the caliph's trust that Mahdi called him his "brother in God" and appointed him vizier. First holder of this office under the Abbasids, Yakub was entrusted with great power: not only was he authorized to govern the empire in the caliph's name; he appointed provincial governors and ran the central administration. Mahdi's intention was to show the Alids how magnanimous he could be to those loyal to his court.

The policy failed with the Zaidites, the most radical of the Alid supporters. When one of these, Isa ibn Zaid, refused to abandon his opposition, Yakub's continuing good relations with the Alids left him in an ambiguous position. His enemies, especially some of the mawali, started plotting against him and accusing him of encouraging Mahdi's fondness for drink and frivolity. A poet penned these verses, which were soon circulating throughout the empire:

"Awake, O sons of Umayyah! Too long have you slumbered! Yakub is your Caliph. The Caliphate, O people, is in ruins! And see, your Caliph nods between the wineskin and the lute!" Yakub's life was saved, but he spent fifteen years in prison.

The rift between the Abbasids and the Alids widened as the Abbasids increasingly presented themselves as the sole defenders of orthodoxy. Despite his conciliatory temperament, Mahdi was obliged to follow the majority view and battle heretics of all colours. His attitude hardened and he persecuted not only the Zindiqs ("those who question the revealed Faith") or Shiites, but also Manichaeans, schismatics, and atheists. The great persecution began in 782 and coincided with the struggle against the followers of al-Muqanna, an Iranian who veiled his face and cited the memory of Abu Muslim. In the Caspian region the caliph also had to deal with the Muhammira,[14] who flew red standards.

During Mahdi's relatively short reign, a turning point in the history of the Abbasids, the rival pressure groups within the ruling class became so intense as eventually to endanger the regime. In the front rank of these groups were the Iranians, soon to be headed by the powerful family of the Barmakids. Since time immemorial the Barmak[15] (or Barmakids) had occupied a prominent position in Bactria, probably as high priests of the Buddhist temple at Balkh, where, according to the pilgrim Huang-Tsang,[16] there were nearly three thousand monks in the seventh century. Converted to Islam probably in the last years of the Umayyad dynasty, they joined the Abbasid revolution, in which one of them, Khalid, seems to have played a crucial role. Their influence was to increase almost beyond measure, until the moment of their resounding fall. A legend grew up around this family, which for many years enjoyed a power unequalled in the history of the Orient.

Khalid ibn Barmak passed on his admirable qualities to his children. Masudi praises "his deep wisdom, his energy, his learning and his forcefulness", while the historian Yezdi describes him as "generous, true to his word, pious, humane, firm and clever".[17] His learning, especially in medicine, was profound. He was famous for his generosity to scholars and poets and is said to have given one poet ten thousand dinars for writing his eulogy. With his son Yahya at his side, Khalid became one of the dominant personalities in Mahdi's entourage.

The Barmakids relied on the *kuttab*, or "secretaries", in building up their formidable influence on the caliph and on the state. These men, mostly of Iranian origin, had not forgotten the illustrious past of the Sassanid empire — itself equipped with a strong bureaucracy — and their presence steadily "Iranianized" the government.

The kuttab and the mawali were overlapping groups. Indigenous Muslim converts, the mawali were by now cooperating with the conquerors in the administration of the country. With the passage of time they had managed to become assimilated, and some had joined the ruling elite. To the great displeasure of their rivals, several had been appointed provincial governors and heads of the post office (*barid*), which meant that in effect they were senior intelligence officials.

Mahdi was not a man to neglect his duties as head of government. In every ministerial department he placed a controller reporting to him directly, in order to separate the powers of the military from those of the administration, especially where the setting and collection of taxes was concerned.

The third pressure group, a faithful ally of the regime, was the *abna*, the Khorasan army, the Abbasids' most solid support. Installed in Baghdad where it enjoyed special privileges, it remained united in protecting the Abbasids against the mawali and the kuttab. But tensions between the military and civilians and between different civilian groups were to lead to conflicts that, thirty years later, placed the empire in peril.

The emergence of a bureaucracy, competition between pressure groups, and the increasingly dominant role in politics of the court and its women, had carried the dynasty beyond the stage of struggling to secure its power. There remained no serious threat from within, and the caliph's title, "Guided by God", suggested that the Abbasid revolution had been successfully completed. With a bit of juggling (not the first time in history), the Abbasids linked themselves directly to the Prophet and his uncle Abbas who, they now claimed, had been named by Mohammed himself as his successor. At the same time, the caliph was withdrawing into a majestic isolation more reminiscent of the Acheminid and Sassanid emperors than of Mohammed's first successors or even the Umayyad caliphs.

Ten years after his accession, Mahdi could rejoice in the (relative) peace that prevailed within his empire and in the humiliation he had inflicted upon the infidels of Byzantium. Only forty-three years old, the just caliph, so fond of life and its pleasures, had reason to look forward to a long and happy reign. But destiny took a hand and death ambushed him as he travelled to Gurgan, in Khorasan, to visit his son Hadi. According to some, he died in a hunting accident, striking his head against a low portal when pursuing a deer on horseback among ruins. Other accounts attribute his death to poison accidentally administered by his favourite concubine, Hasanah. The young slave is said to have poisoned a pear that was meant to be eaten by a rival for the caliph's affections but that Mahdi, seated nearby, plucked the fruit as it was carried past in a bowl.

Hadi the Brute

The succession was arranged with little difficulty. Mahdi had named Hadi as heir presumptive and Harun as second in line: only the two children of the slave Khaizuran were considered, so great was her influence on the caliph. Hadi had been placed in charge of the government of the eastern half of the empire, Harun of that of the west and Armenia. Mahdi later had second thoughts about the succession; indeed, the reason for the fateful visit to Gurgan was to persuade Hadi to defer to his brother Harun. This led to claims that Hadi may have been involved in his father's death.

On receiving the news, the empire's new master set out for Baghdad, which he reached twenty days later. Harun had already granted, in his brother's name, an accession gift of eighteen months' pay to the capital's troops, and accepted on Hadi's behalf the oath of allegiance from dignitaries and soldiers. All Hadi needed to do was take possession of power. He named as vizier Rabi al-Yunus, who kept the post of chamberlain; Yahya remained his chief adviser.

Hadi, the caliph "with the short lip" (his mouth was permanently open), was bad-tempered, vindictive, and unscrupulous: "Hard, coarse in his habits, difficult to approach, the first Caliph to be preceded by bodyguards carrying naked swords, clubs and bows ready-strung," were Masudi's words. His short reign confirmed his bad reputation in the empire and justified the fears of his family — his mother and his brother Harun, in particular.

At first there was nothing serious to disturb relations between

Khaizuran and her son. The honours and privileges granted her by Mahdi were maintained, and Hadi showed her respect and affection; he visited her regularly from his palace of Isabadh, on the outskirts of Baghdad. When prevented from doing so by his duties as sovereign — which he performed scrupulously, receiving high officials and petitioners in person — he would send her a note accompanied by a present.

Harun, for his part, accepted the situation philosophically on Yahya's advice. Caring more — in appearance at least — for poetry, music and other pleasures, deeply in love with his young wife, the stunning Zubaidah, he was little disposed at this stage to provoke a fight with a man whose cunning and brutality he knew better than anyone.

Storm clouds began gathering over the regime with the death of Rabi al-Yunus, who had aroused Hadi's resentment by collaborating closely with Khaizuran in the difficult period after Mahdi's death. Relations between the men took a turn for the worse over a woman, the young slave Amat al-Aziz, who, before becoming the caliph's favourite, had been Rabi's. Hearing a rumour that the vizier had told a courtier he had never loved a woman so much, Hadi was seized by jealousy and attempted to have Rabi murdered. The plot was exposed, but a few days later the vizier died suddenly after drinking a cup of honey. This murder made a profound impression on Harun and Khaizuran.

Khaizuran intended not merely to retain the influence she had enjoyed in Mahdi's lifetime but to increase it, in the Oriental tradition that places the queen mother in the very front rank. She was fabulously rich, and Hadi became exasperated by her large court and the crowds of petitioners which filled her antechambers. He wrote a letter ordering her to stop interfering in affairs of state. Khaizuran was not a woman to give in meekly, and the threatening storm soon broke. The young caliph one day refused a favour she was requesting for the chief of police. When she insisted, Hadi said loudly:

Remember this well: I swear by Allah and by my children that if I hear one of my generals or officials has been knocking at your door, I will have him beheaded and confiscate his property. What is the meaning of these daily processions in front of your house?

Have you no spindle to occupy your hands, no Koran to pray to God, no housework to do? Take care! And open your door to nobody, be he Muslim, Christian or Jew.[18]

Hadi had little affection for the handsome, brilliant brother who had been on the point of replacing him as crown prince. Once in power, he soon conceived the idea of replacing Harun in the order of succession with his own son Prince Jaffar. He raised the subject with Yahya the Barmakid, who dissuaded him by pointing out that the precedent could be used against Jaffar himself. Hadi agreed, but later raised the matter again. This time Yahya argued that should the caliph die while Jaffar was still a child, he would not be accepted by the people either as a war leader or as a religious chief, and this might induce other members of the Abbasid family to claim power. He advised him to wait until Jaffar was old enough to be caliph, and then ask Harun to give up his right to the succession. Once again Hadi assented but, encouraged by certain of his generals, he finally swept aside all objections.

Harun was not at all eager to confront his redoubtable brother and first appeared ready to agree to everything. But once the prerogatives of crown prince had been taken away from him, his position became extremely threatened. All had abandoned him except Yahya, who for some time had defended his interests (one of Yahya's sons was Harun's foster brother) and who managed by degrees to stiffen his resistance to the caliph. An anecdote retailed by several historians illustrates Harun's new stance towards his brother. Their father had given Harun a priceless ring that Hadi greatly desired for himself. He sent Yahya to obtain the ring, threatening to cut off his head if he returned without it. Despite Yahya's entreaties, Harun would not give up the jewel, but said that he himself would carry it to his brother. As he crossed the bridge over the Tigris, however, Harun tossed the ring into the river, saying, "And now let him do what he likes." With Yahya thus cleared of responsibility, nothing further happened. But the incident fed the caliph's anger.

Hadi next tried to kill his mother. He sent her a dish of rice with a letter saying that he had found it so excellent he wished to share it with her. Khaizuran gave some to her dog, which died a few minutes later, then sent word to her son that she too had found the dish excellent. Tabari tells us that Hadi replied, "You did not eat it, or I should by now be rid of you. Never before has a sovereign watched his mother reign in his place." Hadi also tried several times to have Harun poisoned; Harun tried to flee but was caught by Hadi's men and imprisoned in Baghdad with Yahya.

Harun's fate was all but sealed when Hadi suddenly fell gravely ill, perhaps with a stomach ulcer, a malady to which the family was susceptible. But it seems more likely that he had consumed a poison his mother had managed to have mixed in a drink. The doctor who examined him said that he would be dead in less than nine hours. The doctor was not mistaken; but it is said that Khaizuran hastened Hadi's end by arranging for young slaves to smother him with cushions.

No sooner had the caliph expired than Khaizuran ordered Yahya's release and then sent General Harthama with the news to Harun, whom he found asleep. "Awake, O Commander of the Believers!" boomed the general. "What are you saying?" cried Harun. "Don't you know what will become of me if Hadi learns that I have been thus addressed?"[19] On hearing that his brother was dead, however, Harun lost no time setting out to take possession of the seals of state. As he left he received another message, one announcing the birth of a son to his Persian concubine Marajil. The boy, who was named Abdallah, was to become the caliph Mamun, one of the most illustrious figures of the Abbasid dynasty. "Thus, this night of destiny, predicted by Khaizuran, saw the death of one caliph, the accession of a second, and the birth of a third."[20]

At virtually the same moment as Abdallah entered the world, the young Jaffar was awakened and compelled to renounce publicly his rights as crown prince. None of the generals who had helped persuade Hadi to disinherit his brother made a move. Together Yahya and General Harthama had guided the changeover with a masterly hand. The provinces received the news as calmly as Baghdad. On 15 or 16 September 786 (15 Rabi 170) Harun al-Rashid — the Well-Guided — was proclaimed caliph. He was a little over twenty years old.

The poets celebrated the new sovereign's accession in customary fashion:

Live long, O Caliph, to thy heart's content,
In scented shade of palace minarets.

Let all about thee, through the golden days,
Strive hard to satisfy thy slightest bent.
But on that day when laboured breath, and pain,
Signal at last thy body's near demise,
Then shalt thou know, alas! that all thy joys
Were but illusory, and thy triumphs vain.[21]

2
Youth and Splendour
of the
Well-Guided One

*Did you not see how the sun came out
of hiding on Harun's accession and
flooded the world with light?*

Mosuli

*The Caliph Harun al-Rashid was the
most generous prince of his time and the
most magnificent.*

Thousand and One Nights

Little is known of the early years of most Oriental sovereigns. It
was only after the event, when a caliph or sultan was already on
the throne, that his formative years became of interest to chroniclers.
The childhood of Harun the Good is no exception.

Childhood and Tranquil Life
Born in February 776 in Ray, in Khorasan, Harun spent his earliest
years in the castle overlooking the town. Defended by a ditch and
a thick wall pierced with five gates and well-irrigated by two rivers,
Ray was soon to become one of the glories of the countries of Islam.
Harun, it was said, always remembered with pleasure his native
town, where the wives of notables had competed for the honour
of suckling him.

When Harun was three or four years old, Mahdi moved to
Baghdad and settled in the palace he had built on the banks of the
Tigris. There the young prince received the education given to royal
children — very nearly the same as that reserved for other children
of the upper classes. Caliphs raised their sons with extreme care;
did not Mohammed rank educated men after God and the angels?

They entrusted the task to scholars, as well as to hand-picked poets and musicians, and monitored their sons' progress regularly, testing them in private or in public. The education of princes began at age five or six — "to instruct the young is to carve in stone", people would say — and it ended when they reached the age of fifteen or so and received their first official mission.

While the Umayyads, still close to their Bedouin roots, favoured arms and sport over religion and intellectual pursuits, the Abbasids held the study of the Koran, philosophy and law in the highest regard. A young Umayyad prince had only to learn to read the Koran, but an Abbasid was expected to know something of exegesis and the science of tradition. The high intellectual level of the Abbasid civilization, which preserved the heritage of antiquity for the West, undoubtedly owed much to the fact that princes of the dynasty were taught to respect matters of the mind from their earliest youth.

Masudi gives us an account of Harun's instructions to the grammarian Ahmar on the education of his son Amin:

Ahmar, the Prince of the Faithful is entrusting you with his most precious blood, the fruit of his heart. He gives you full authority over his son, whom he charges with the duty of obeying you. Be therefore equal to the task the Caliph has given you: teach your pupil to read the Koran, instruct him in the traditions; adorn his memory with classical poetry; teach him our sacred customs. Let him weigh his words and know how to speak to the point; regulate the amount of time he devotes to amusement; teach him to receive with respect the elders of the family of Hashim who come to see him, and to be considerate with the officials and officers who attend his receptions. Let not an hour pass in the day without turning it to account for his instruction; be not so severe that his intelligence withers, nor so indulgent that he becomes accustomed to idleness. Correct him, while he depends upon you, by employing friendliness and gentleness; but if these have no effect on him, then use severity and employ rigour.[1]

This programme for the training of an *adab* (a gentleman) is doubtless very similar to that followed in Harun's own education. Mahdi, who was himself quite cultivated, gave his son several tutors, each specializing in a different branch of learning. Kitai, a celebrated intellectual, was his "governor" and had authority over these teachers. But his "tutor" was Yahya the Barmakid, whom Harun called his "father". One of the most remarkable men to govern the Arab world in the first centuries of the Hegira, Yahya remained close to Harun until his disgrace.

The close links joining the Abbasid family with the descendants of the Barmakids since the earliest years of the dynasty[2] had thus been further strengthened. As in the previous generation, the children of each family were suckled by the women of the other. Later, Harun's baby son would nuzzle at the breast of Jaffar the Barmakid's wife, and a daughter of Jaffar would be nursed by the caliph's wife.

When Harun reached the age of thirteen, Yahya was appointed "Special Secretary", a title that gave him considerable power. He was not restricted to a supporting role; when the young prince took command of a major expedition against the Byzantines, Yahya went with him. Later, when Harun was sent to govern the western provinces of Azerbaijan and Armenia, it was Yahya who actually managed these immense territories. Yahya was politically gifted and able immediately to demonstrate administrative talents and a strong sense of responsibility. Harun, who was more interested in military issues, left him free to act as he thought fit. Yahya was an ideal companion for the young prince, who liked to enjoy life; for Yahya, the years in the provinces became a valuable apprenticeship for the role required of him in the future.

Harun's first act on ascending the throne in September 786 was to name Yahya vizier, as echoed in the *Thousand and One Nights*:

Al-Hadi's demise and the accession of al-Rashid to the Khalif's throne were known to the people of Baghdad before daybreak. And Harun, amid the pomp of his kingship, received oaths of obedience from the emirs, the notables and all the assembled people. And on the same day he raised to the Vizierate El-Fadl and Giafar, both sons of Yahya the Barmecide. And all the provinces and lands of the Empire, and all the Islamic peoples, Arab and non-Arab, Turks and Daylamites, hailed the authority of the new Khalif and swore allegiance to him. And he began his reign in prosperity and magnificence, and sat shining in his new glory and in his power.[3]

Adviser to the sovereign and head of the secretariat with responsibility for government, foremost personage of the state after the caliph, the vizier exercised different functions in different periods. Usually of mawali origin — non-Arab, often Iranian, but always a Muslim convert — he was a cultivated man and generous patron. In Harun's time his role was essentially one of personal service to the caliph. In the next century, as viziers became more important, the caliph's responsibilities were gradually reduced to the point whereby he could only endorse his minister's decisions. Many viziers were born into "dynasties" of viziers and secretaries (kuttab), and more than a few were men of considerable achievement, especially in the financial, political, and military fields. Often these great servants of the state found themselves obliged to supplement the deficient personalities of caliphs who were incompetent or ill-prepared to rule the empire; inevitably some were tempted into decisions that favoured their personal interests over those of the state.

Harun conferred on Yahya powers that had previously belonged exclusively to the sovereign; they included the right to appoint secretaries of the *diwan*[4] and to judge cases of abuse of authority. Masudi goes so far as to claim that Harun handed Yahya his own crown, saying, "My dear father, it is you who have placed me upon this throne through your Heaven-blessed help, your happy influence and your wise management: so do I invest you with absolute power."

Nevertheless, Yahya had still to contend with the redoubtable queen mother Khaizuran. The vast wealth of the former Yemeni slave only magnified her power still further. Until her death in 789, Yahya would sometimes need all his agility to mediate between Harun and a woman determined to enjoy every bit of her authority. The vizier, who in any case could not argue directly with the caliph or his mother, had to make his points by "progression and allusion" and through symbolic anecdotes. "With Caliphs," he used to say, "to argue against something is the same as inciting them to do it, for if you try to prevent them from acting in a certain way, it is as if you were spurring them on."[5]

Yahya was powerfully aided in his task by two of his sons, Fadl and Jaffar, who shared the functions of the vizier and sat at his side during public audiences, most unusual in the Orient. Jaffar later received the seal of office, which then returned to Yahya before being passed on to Fadl. Thus the seal of the sovereign remained in the same family, and for the first ten years of his reign, Harun's history was interwoven with that of the Barmakids. His government was run by these three men, competent, adept, and of uncommon intelligence.

After Hadi's dramatic death and the series of betrayals that preceded it, heads might have been expected to roll. Those who had renounced their oath to Harun, the crown prince, to swear allegiance to his nephew Jaffar — and they were many — probably spent some restless nights. It was Yahya who saved them, along with the internal peace of the empire (for a time at least). He somehow managed to persuade Khaizuran, who wanted the immediate massacre of all traitors, that they could be more usefully employed fighting the enemy.

His advice was followed and two scapegoats were chosen to pay the penalty for all the others. One high dignitary, the chief of police, escaped punishment in an ingenious way. He managed to nullify his broken oath to Harun by promising to walk all the way to Mecca. He kept his promise, but walked on carpets his servants unrolled before him. Ali ibn Isa ibn Mahan, a leading officer of the abna, and Yazid ibn Mazyad, one of Hadi's military advisers, both of whom had urged Hadi to replace Harun with Jaffar, were simply exiled, to be recalled years after Khaizuran's death. Harun's reign began in joy.

Soon after God — with a little help from Khaizuran and Yahya — had carried him to supreme power, Harun made his first pilgrimage to Mecca. History gives us no details of the journey, which he was to repeat several times and to which the Abbasids attached the greatest importance; undoubtedly it was an occasion for the new sovereign to demonstrate his generosity. More is known about the pilgrimage made by Khaizuran a few months later: a triumphal procession from which alms flowed, it was said, like the waters of a river. Nearly every day the queen mother ordered a shelter, a fountain or a mosque to be built along the pilgrims' route. She found the house in which Mohammed was believed to have been born and had it converted into a mosque, along with the house in which the Prophet and his Companions used to meet. For many years the latter was known as Khaizuran's House.

By such means the Abbasids strove to emphasize the religious

37

character of their regime. For Mansour and Mahdi, the motive had been to justify, so to speak, the conspiracy among the descendants of Abbas leading to the seizure of power in 750, by suggesting that the Abbasids had driven out the Umayyad caliphs in order to lead the faithful back to the true path of Islam. Harun surpassed his father and his illustrious grandfather in his profound conviction that God had chosen him as Commander of the Faithful and imam. On all solemn occasions he would don the Prophet's cloak (*burda*) and carry the staff (*kadib*), symbolizing respectively the qualities of "successor to the messenger of God" (caliph) and "God's power on earth", a title Mansour had assumed. The caliphate was viewed primarily as an institution whose first duty was to defend religion. The Abbasid caliph was there to ensure the maintenance of strict orthodoxy and enforce obedience to rules and commandments laid down for all time.

Towards these ends, Harun al-Rashid surrounded himself from the beginning with men of religion with whom he would debate points of dogma and canon law. His reign gave a renewed importance to the holy places, and the pilgrimage to Mecca soon acquired a spectacular quality of devotional propaganda, further enhanced by Harun's extreme generosity: he spent a million dinars during one pilgrimage alone.

Above all, for religious as well as for political reasons, Harun fought against heresy in all its forms. The immense empire, composed of a mass of diverse peoples in which Arabism was dissolving, could be permitted only one faith and only one law — its cement and its raison d'être. The caliph was obliged to ensure that they were respected. He was going to fight the Alids and struggle, as we shall see, against the Zindiqs.[6]

The danger to the first Abbasids came solely from religious and social agitators. No external enemy posed a serious threat. Their only formidable neighbour, Byzantium, absorbed in its own plots and crises, was in no position to bother them. Nevertheless Harun, whose father had sent him campaigning beyond the Taurus, never took his eye off the empire of the basileus. Never forgetting that the fight against the infidel is prescribed as a duty by Islam, and probably drawn, like so many kings and emperors after him, by the mirage of taking Constantinople, he prepared to march against Byzantium. Along with the battle for religion, this war was to become the major concern of his life. Reserving military matters for his personal control, he took the army in hand immediately after his accession. In certain frontier regions, he ordered the construction of a new line of defence to reinforce or replace the *thughur*, chains of forts built by Mahdi.

The Commander of the Faithful in his Palace

Khaizuran died, probably of natural causes, in the autumn of 789. She was just fifty years old. Making no effort to hide his grief, Harun, barefoot in the mud, followed her coffin to the Rusafa cemetery on the east bank of the Tigris which to this day bears Khaizuran's name. Entering her tomb, he recited the last prayers, as well as the famous eulogy of ibn Nuwairah, which Mohammed's wife Aisha had pronounced over the tomb of her father, Abu Bakr, the Prophet's first successor. Then the silence of eternity descended on the great Khaizuran. But even when all the players in her life's drama were long dead, the chroniclers, historians, and poets were recalling the romantic destiny of this Yemeni slave who became the wife and mother of caliphs and did not shrink from criminal acts to place her favourite son on the throne.

As soon as his mother was dead, Harun took the seal of state away from Jaffar the Barmakid and gave it to another of his favourites, Fadl ibn al-Rabi. (Khaizuran had always been opposed to this wish of Harun's to curb the influence of his vizier's great Barmak family.) He also ordered the arrest of Ibrahim al-Harrani, Hadi's former vizier, and the confiscation of all his property. Yahya succeeded only in softening this measure.[7]

Harun, at twenty-three, presented a fine figure: he was tall, well-built, light-complexioned, and curly-haired; his face was handsome, according to Tabari, and is described in the *Thousand and One Nights* as having "a very small mouth and large puffy cheeks". In this period he usually lived in Baghdad at the palace of al-Khuld, built by his father on the banks of the Tigris. In front of the palace was a large esplanade dominated by the headquarters of the chief of police. On high days and holidays, reviews and parades were held there before the large crowds that came to admire the spectacle of imperial pomp and the caliph's serried regiments.

We have no precise information on the interior design of the palace of al-Khuld, but we know that it was of imposing size, like all palaces of the Orient from earliest times. The first of a series of palaces erected along the Tigris, al-Khuld[8] answered the caliphs' concern with security by combining on one site their residence and the political and administrative centre of the empire. In addition to the vast audience and reception chambers, the palace contained innumerable rooms and private apartments for court dignitaries and secretaries. Like the Round City itself, al-Khuld was built in traditional Oriental style of mud brick reinforced with baked brick and covered with stucco work. Strong outer walls punctuated with large towers gave it the appearance of an enormous fortress.

Mansour had arranged about the palace a series of delightful gardens inspired by those of the Sassanids and by the various "paradises" planted by Umayyad gardeners, enchanted settings for court life which Mahdi and especially Harun further sweetened and embellished. Banks of flowers carefully grafted and transplanted to reproduce the words of famous Arabic poems; trees banded with precious jewel-studded metals, their leaves gilded and silvered; ponds and waterfalls; little bridges of rare wood from far-off places; dreaming pavilions; yews and cypresses mirrored in still water; dragonflies tracing the characters of a couplet to the caliph's glory... These gardens owed little to nature and much to an art carried to perfection. Tabari tells us that inside the palace was a small garden planted with pink-flowering trees surrounding a room carpeted in pink fabric, which was manned by servants dressed in the same colour. Some of these gardens are described in the *Thousand and One Nights*:

> The garden at whose gate they had fallen asleep was called the Garden of Delights, and in the middle of the garden was a palace called the Palace of Marvels belonging to the Caliph Harun al-Rashid. Whenever the Caliph felt his chest constricted he would come to this garden and this palace to breathe freely, to amuse himself and forget his cares. The entire palace was formed of one immense chamber lighted by eighty windows. This chamber was opened only when the Caliph came; then all the lamps and the great chandelier would be lighted and all the windows flung open, and the Caliph would sit on his great divan, covered in silk, velvet and cloth of gold, and cause his singers to sing and musicians to delight him with their music... And thus, in the

calm of the night and amid the warm air sweetened with the scent of the flowers in the garden, the Caliph could expand his chest, in the city of Baghdad.

Even within the immense rooms of the palace, there grew the rarest and most beautiful flowers: "In the meeting room a small garden was reflected in a pond of alabaster in which a small fountain tinkled, a cool delight and an enchantment in its miniature perfection."

There are numerous lyrical and picturesque descriptions of these magical places of both Harun's time and the next century. One of the most famous is the account of the reception[9] of the Byzantine ambassadors John Rhadinos and Michael Toxaras, sent by the emperor Constantine Porphyrogenitus to negotiate an armistice with the caliph Muktadir and to ransom Greek prisoners:

The number of the hangings that had been placed in the palace of the Prince of the Believers, as to curtains of gilded brocade ornamented with fine gold embroidery, representing the outlines of elephants, horses, camels, lions and birds, and of great tapestries, plain and decorated with designs and also embroidered, was thirty-eight thousand curtains, among which curtains of gold brocade were to the number of twelve thousand five hundred. The number of oblong carpets in the corridors and courtyards, trodden by the cadis and the envoys of the King of Greece from the outermost gate called Bab al-Amma al-Jahid to their arrival in the presence of al-Muktadir, without counting what was in the private apartments or audience chambers by way of rugs of Tabaristan and of Dabik intended to be seen but not trodden upon, was twenty-two thousand pieces.

The envoys of the Greek emperor were led through the vestibule of the great Bab al-Amma gate to the palace called Khan al-Khail, composed largely of porticos with columns of marble. In this building, on the right side, were five hundred mares bearing five hundred saddles of gold and silver without blankets, and on the left side five hundred mares wearing blankets of brocade with long hoods... They were next taken to the wild beasts' enclosure, then to a palace where there were four elephants caparisoned with motley of brocade and silk; on the back of each elephant were eight men from Sind with artificers armed with fire-throwers, which struck terror into the hearts of the envoys. Next they were led to a palace containing a hundred lions, fifty on the right, fifty on the left, each held on the leash by a guardian and wearing chains and irons at head and neck.[10] After this they were taken to the modern pavilion; it was a palace between two orchards, in the middle of which was a lake of pewter surrounded by a channel of pewter more brilliant than polished silver. The length of the lake was thirty cubits and the width twenty. On it were four delicate boats, gilded and bedecked with embroidered cloths of dabik and covered with gilded dabik. Around this lake was an orchard in which palm trees grew; these were said to number four hundred and their height was five cubits. Each tree trunk was entirely encased in carved teakwood and banded with gilded red copper... The ambassadors were then taken from this palace to the palace of the Tree, where there was a tree in the centre of a great circular basin of clear water; the tree had eighteen limbs, each carrying many branches on which were perched large and small birds of all species, gilded and silvered. The greater part of the tree's branches were of silver, but some were gilded. At certain moments they bent and shook, and the leaves of many colours which they carried trembled, as when a wind shakes the branches of trees, while all the birds sang and cooed.[11]

The *Thousand and One Nights* also describes a great room in the palace which probably resembles the one in which the envoys of the basileus were received by the caliph:

Then she opened a door and introduced them into a great hall having a dome held up by eighty pillars of transparent alabaster, whose bases and chapters were sculptured with gold birds. Upon a golden background inside the dome, lines of living colour repeated the designs of the wide carpets which covered the floor. Between the columns were vases of flowers, and empty vases too beautiful in their bright flesh of jasper, agate and crystal to contain anything. The hall gave straight upon a garden, whose entrance path was ornamented with pebbles in the same colour and symmetry as the carpets and dome, so that all three made a harmony beneath the naked sky.[12]

Let us visualize these carpets, immense but intricately worked, shot through with gold threads, pearls and precious stones; the silken hangings also encrusted with jewels; the ornate golden chandeliers; the walls painted with scenes from the lives of earlier caliphs — all the rarest and most beautiful creations of man and nature brought together in the dream palaces and fabulous gardens of Baghdad.

It was here, in these majestic halls and in the seclusion of his private apartments, that the caliph lived with hundreds of other people. Centre of the empire's official life and private dwelling of the Commander of the Faithful, source of all decisions of state and the point on which all its activities converged, the palace was a closed, almost mythical universe, a forbidden city to which nobody was admitted unless he lived or had business there. It was in the palace, far more than in the mosque, that the art of decoration flourished, making it the main showcase — albeit reserved for privileged eyes — of a state then reaching the apogee of its power and wealth. The caliph usually received visitors and dignitaries while seated on a sort of couch, the *sarir*, beneath a canopy. He was hidden from the multitude by a curtain, which served to emphasize the sacred character of the amir al-muminin, the title all visitors were obliged to use when greeting him.

Palace life was regulated by strict etiquette. It was to become even more rigid in the next century when the Iranian influence increased with the arrival of the Buyids.[13] The Buyid Adl al-Daula, during a ceremony that invested him with broad powers taken from the caliph, prostrated himself nine times before reaching the *sidilla* (state canopy) and then, when given permission to enter, kissed the floor twice more. As the caliph's real power declined, so the protocol would become ever more elaborate.

In Harun's day the chamberlain (*hatib*) led the visitor behind the curtain into the caliph's presence. After kissing the latter's hands and feet, he would await permission to be seated; if the caliph wished to humiliate him, the wait might be a long one. None could speak before the caliph had spoken. During large public audiences, dignitaries and courtiers were called one at a time in a precise order. Descendants of the Prophet's Companions and the first converts took precedence over ordinary believers, while dignitaries and officials were called in order of rank and salary. All Muslims are equal, of course, but some more so than others even in God's eyes.

Hundreds of people gravitated towards the caliph: princes, sons and grandsons of earlier caliphs; scions of the family of Abbas; and then chamberlains, secretaries, guards, and all the staff necessary for everyday life — cooks, water carriers, carpenters, saddlers, valets — without forgetting doctors, muezzins, astronomers, and jesters. The palace was a town within the town, destined to become even larger in the next century with the proliferation of servants and non-Arab guardsmen (Turks, for the most part).

The Harem

The caliph's women and children lived in the harem.[14] Harun was reputed to have two hundred women in his harem, twenty of whom gave him children — not so many, compared with the twelve thousand women of Mutawakil's palace some fifty years later. This part of the palace, which has so long inflamed the Western imagination, was not the place of debauchery so often and so enviously described. The caliph's wives, and those concubines who had borne him children, had their own apartments. Many other women — concubines and servants — also lived in this small world organized and controlled by yet other women and by eunuchs.

Most of the women in the harem would have been purchased from specialist slave merchants or would have been presented to the caliph by members of his family or dignitaries wishing to get into his good graces. In Harun's time they were of the most diverse origins: Arab, Circassian, Turkish, Greek (the latter a by-product of the innumerable skirmishes and raids between Arabs and Byzantines).

Mahdi had been the first to open the Baghdad court to culture, luxury and refinement. From the very beginning of his reign, Harun sought to surround himself with cultivated men and women. He chose his wives and concubines — perhaps especially the latter — from among the most intelligent, as well as the most seductive, women. Some were sent to Taif or more likely Medina, where there were long-established schools of singing and music. Even in Baghdad there were teachers of music and other arts, some of whom had as many as eighty "students". Thus the great singer Ishak was engaged to train several palace women, according to the *Thousand and One Nights*:

Harun had given him, in pure love, the fairest of his palaces, and Ishak's duty there was to instruct the ablest of those girls sought in the markets of the world for his master's harim in the arts of music and singing. When one of them excelled her companions in mastery of song and of the lute, Ishak would take her to the Khalifah, and she would sing and play before the throne. If she gave pleasure, she was raised straight away to the harim.[15]

These slave artistes could cost as much as two thousand dinars; a century later one of them was sold for thirteen thousand. The possession of cultivated slaves or concubines was a manifestation of imperial luxury. Often the caliphs themselves, including Harun, were the sons of slaves — Arabs and, later, other races. Abbasid blood, like that of the Ottoman sultans from the end of the sixteenth century, was mingled with the blood of peoples from outside the Arab world.

Of the four legitimate wives permitted to Muslims, Harun had three soon after his accession: Azizah, daughter of Khaizuran's brother Ghitrif; Ghadir,[16] who had been Hadi's concubine; and Zubaidah, another cousin, whom he married in 781 or 782 (she was the daughter of Jaffar, one of Mansour's sons, and Khaizuran's sister Salsal). Beautiful and intelligent as she was, it was not easy for Zubaidah to make her way among the harem's dozens of women, each lovelier than the next, or to negotiate as she did the treacherous byways of politics. She was the only woman for whom Harun felt a deep attachment.

After the death of his first two wives, Harun later married three women of noble lineage — Umm Mohammed, Abbasah, and a girl from the family of Othman — but none of them really counted. Despite his innumerable amours, in his heart it was always Zubaidah who held pride of place.

Islam is a polygamous society that encourages lovemaking: "O ye who believe! interdict not the healthful viands which God hath allowed you" (Koran, Sura V). "When you perform the act of love, you are giving alms" (Hadith). "Sensual pleasure and desire are as beautiful as the mountains" (Hadith, according to Zaid ibn Ali). There is considered nothing wrong, therefore, in a wife's sending a beautiful woman to her husband's bed, and Zubaidah did so on several occasions, one of which had unexpected consequences.

One day, at the palace of Yahya the Barmakid, Harun heard the song of a brown-skinned slave called Dananis, who had received excellent musical training. For reasons that were not exclusively artistic he showered her with presents, including a necklace worth thirty thousand dirhams. To persuade the alarmed Zubaidah that he had been rewarding Dananis only for her talents as a singer, Harun asked her to listen to a performance, which also won the enthusiastic admiration of the assembled Abbasid princes. Zubaidah was convinced, and by way of an apology sent Harun a present of ten magnificent female slaves.

Several of these women gave Harun children. Marajil, from the Herat region, bore him a son, Abdallah, on the famous Night of Destiny: his destiny was to become the great caliph Mamun and to order the assassination of his rival Amin, son of Zubaidah. Harun fathered five children of another slave, Maridah, from distant Sogdian; one of these, too, was a future caliph, al-Mutasim, successor to Mamun. Harun was passionately in love with Maridah, and their lovers' quarrels and reconciliations were immortalized by the poets in a number of anecdotes.

Many other women passed through the life of the Commander of the Faithful and gave Zubaidah restless nights. Flustered by one gorgeous rival's success in catching Harun's eye, one day she went to ask the advice of the caliph's younger sister Ulaiyah, who undertook to get the fickle fellow back for her. Ulaiyah was a respected poet, and set to work on a song of reconciliation — "They can tear out my heart, but it will never let him go" — with which the young slaves of the two princesses surprised Harun one evening as he took his usual stroll in a cool courtyard. Touched and captivated, the caliph returned to Zubaidah, and the young performers were half buried under an avalanche of dinars and dirhams.

Dhat al-Khal (Beauty Spot), Sihr (Charm), Diya (Splendour), Hailana (probably Helen, a Greek)... Beauty Spot cost the caliph thirty thousand dinars. In a quarrel once with another woman of the harem, jealous of her success with Harun, she lost her temper and cut off the tip of the other's nose, whereupon her rival tore from her cheek the precious ornament that had given her her name; all ended in elegant verses and the golden voice of Ibrahim al-Mausili. There was Inan, a beauty from central Arabia, whose exorbitant price even the great caliph could not afford, and another Greek from Heraclaea, captured during the battle for possession of the town.

Amid the throng of young and appetizing rivals Zubaidah, although aging, always managed to retain the affection and esteem, the love, of Harun. He admired her taste, her imaginative mind, the splendour of her house, but also her piety: a troupe of a hundred slave women worked in shifts of ten to recite the Koran all day long. It is true that she spent freely on clothes and cosmetics and on the most extravagant fantasies; she even owned a monkey that was looked after by its own staff of thirty men until one day a choleric general, irritated by the ceremony surrounding the animal, drew his sword and sliced it in two. However, her generosity and charity knew no bounds. Masudi, in the long passages he devotes to the activities of Abbasid princes and princesses, writes of Zubaidah's:

> serious works, foundations without precedence in Islam... The nobility and magnificence of this princess, in grave matters as well as in pleasurable things, placed her in the front rank. She spent thousands of dinars on the hostels, reservoirs and wells which she gave to the Hejaz and the frontier areas of the Empire... and all this without neglecting her other generosities, the help and well-being which she spread among the needy classes.

By the end of the eighth century Harun, greatest sovereign of the Orient, was also the richest and most powerful man in the known universe, his renown reaching the ends of the earth. In his palace overlooking the Tigris, he lived amid hundreds of women, princes, officials, and servants, in unheard-of luxury and ostentation. All these people worked, plotted, or sought pleasure in an atmosphere of refinement and cruelty reflected — almost certainly faithfully — in contemporary writings and stories. Thousands of dirhams, sometimes thousands of dinars, might be lavished on the author of a felicitous couplet. A pretty singer, bought in the slave market for the harem of the Commander of the Faithful or that of some other prince, could see the instant fulfilment of her wildest dreams. The most delicate love, and the crudest, blossomed among treasures of beauty and rarity. And Masrur the executioner, "blade carrier of his vengeance", always followed a few paces behind Harun during his nocturnal expeditions around Baghdad — behind Harun the Good, who once asked one of his sons to behead a prisoner in front of him to show whether he had learned to handle a scimitar.

Millions of Dirhams

On ordinary days visitors were admitted to the palace dressed in white, but on solemn occasions all were required to wear black, the Abbasid colour. The *qabaa*, a sort of calf-length jacket with sleeves, was obligatory wear, as were the *qalansuwa*, a high-crowned skullcap of fabric or fur, and a sabre and sash. During these ceremonies Harun himself wore the *duraa*, an ample, sleeved garment, buttoned down the front, of silk or wool heavily embroidered in gold, and the qalansuwa with a turban. He wore the Prophet's cloak (burda) on his shoulders and carried his staff and sword. Audiences were held to invest people with new responsibilities or with honours, or to welcome a victorious general on his return. But the most stately and sumptuous audiences were reserved for the reception of ambassadors whom the caliph particularly wanted to impress, that they might take back to their sovereigns a fitting description of the power of the Commander of the Faithful.

Of all the feasts that took place in the palaces of Baghdad, none was more splendid than the marriage of Harun's son the caliph Mamun to Buran, daughter of the vizier Hasan ibn Sahl. It was still being talked about in the Orient several centuries later. The wedding cost the bride's father the fantastic sum of fifty million dirhams, but Zubaidah spent thirty-five million and another princess twenty-five. Contemporary chroniclers report that Hasan had balls of musk the size of melons scattered over the guests, each ball containing a slip of paper bearing the name of an estate, a male or female slave, or some other piece of property. The guests had only to present the paper to the designated official to take possession of these gifts, some of which were worth a fortune in themselves. Handfuls of fine pearls were strewn round the bridegroom's feet — the guests had only to stoop to gather them up — and a big dish of them poured over the bride by her grandmother, Mamun refilling the dish with still more pearls and offering them to Buran. Zubaidah gave the bride a famous jacket that had once belonged to Abdah, wife of the Umayyad caliph Hisham. Its buttons were made of diamonds and rubies. During the festivities, which lasted seventeen days, gold and silver pieces and balls of musk and ambergris were scattered among the crowds outside.

The celebrations marking Mahdi's accession had cost so much that the royal treasuries were completely exhausted for some time. Also remembered are the feasts given a few decades later by the caliph Mutawakil to celebrate the circumcision of one of his sons. The chairs and the trays of drinks were encrusted with jewels, and trays heaped with gold pieces were carried among the four thousand guests by servants crying, "The emir of the faithful invites you to take what you want." A million dirhams were distributed among the caliph's servants and household; three sets of court attire were presented to each guest, and a thousand horses and donkeys were placed at their disposal to carry off the presents they had received. This celebration cost the caliph eighty-six million dirhams.

Everyday life in the palace, especially in Harun's time when the caliph's treasury had benefited from the fiscal policy of the Barmakids, was characterized by the same luxury. "And to him who is of kin render his due, and also to the poor and to the wayfarer; yet waste not wastefully... let not thy hand be tied up to thy neck; nor yet open it in all openness." (Koran, Sura XVII). It was some time since these strictures had been observed. Drink came in golden goblets, and Zubaidah would only eat from plates of precious metal. Spoons were of gold or crystal; the very tables were plated with gold and silver. Inside the harem only the most beautiful and costly objects were to be seen — Chinese pottery, vases of gold and crystal.

The accounts of chroniclers and the many descriptions of Baghdad life in the *Thousand and One Nights* give us an accurate reflection of reality:

She brought them a golden jug and basin filled with scented water for their hands, which she rinsed for them with a marvellous ewer enriched with rubies and diamonds... then brought them scent of aloes in a small gold pot... Wine was brought and served in goblets of gold, silver and crystal... young boys sprinkled the guests with musk and rose water from jewelled gold sprinklers.

Zubaidah, whose slippers were sewn with precious stones, literally staggered under the weight of her jewels, sometimes requiring the support of two slaves to stand upright. She was carried about in palanquins of silver, ebony, and sandalwood, lined with silks and sable and fitted with gold handles. Ambergris burned in censers within. When poets sang her praises with skill, she would fill their mouths with pearls. Khaizuran lived in similar splendour, and was said once to have bought a piece of cloth for the fabulous sum of fifty thousand dinars; after her death, eighteen thousand dresses were found in her chests. It was not unusual to pay one thousand dinars for a fine piece of cloth,[17] and even princes, who accumulated quantities of them, could easily pay five hundred dinars for a piece.

As well as these silks, brocades, and delicate wool fabrics embroidered with pearls and gold thread, there were rare perfumes, each used according to precise rules and only with the garments thought appropriate. Powdered musk was mixed with rose water, aloe, and pinks; Bahrain ambergris and attar of roses were sprinkled on the person or even on the floor. The dead were anointed with perfumes; scented smoke curled from censers of precious metal whose forms reflected the artistic variety of the empire. At banquets the guests drowned in scent; clothes, food, houses were impregnated with perfumes of every sort. The air inside the palace was saturated. "Incense, balm and perfumes to burn in the chamber, and rose water and water of orange blossom to sprinkle on our guests... nor shall I forget aromatic essences or silver censers of fragrant water."[18]

Everyone in the palace, man or woman, was covered with jewels. They wore them on their fingers, hung them around their necks, decorated their clothes profusely with rubies, diamonds, turquoises, and chunks of amber. On their heads they wore circlets encrusted with pearls and precious stones. Courtiers and concubines, dignitaries, princes and princesses vied with one another in elegance and extravagance. The Barmakids set an example of the most unbridled luxury; Jaffar showered handfuls of gold on poets and musicians, and his palace[19] almost eclipsed that of the caliph. He did not hesitate to give fabulous sums for a cloth or an *objet d'art* pleasing to his eye. The grandees and rich merchants of Baghdad imitated him to the extent that their means allowed.

The Privileged Inner Circle

Kept apart from the caliph by rigid protocol, most of the palace men and women never addressed him unless, bent humbly before him, they were required to answer his questions. Only a small group was privileged to live close to him, to converse, and even to argue with the caliph. These were the *nadim*, the caliph's companions.

Already the Umayyads, and before them the Sassanids of Persia, had formed the habit of surrounding themselves with men of talent. Saffah, the first Abbasid, often sent for such men but spoke to them through a curtain. Mansour did the same. Mahdi was the first to mix with them, but he forbade his sons Hadi and Harun to socialize with commoners on pain of a beating. On becoming caliph, however, Hadi chose his drinking companions from among the talented; Harun institutionalized the custom by deciding to summon those men he considered outstanding in letters, the arts and sciences, and theology. To each he gave a rank and a salary; equal in status to high dignitaries of the state, the nadim's sole responsibility was to interest and amuse the caliph. In addition to their high titles and appointments, Harun would give them presents of money as a sign of particular approval. The singer Ibrahim al-Mausili received four thousand dirhams for one composition.

The nadim had to be amusing without being vulgar, instructive without being pedantic, serious without being humourless. They were expected to be able to converse on any subject, even cookery, and also to display practical ability on occasion.[20] They also had to excel at ball games, hunting, marksmanship, and, above all, chess.[21] Harun, according to Masudi, was the first chess-playing caliph: "It is impossible to live without distraction, and for a sovereign there is none better than chess." Harun also played backgammon with his nadim, and it is said that on one occasion he staked the clothes on his back, lost, and had to strip naked.

The nadim would gather for the evening several times a week in the palace gardens, or indoors during the winter. They wore special garments: a duraa over the shirt and a turban of silk woven or embroidered with gold thread. Seated near the caliph, four or five on each side, they answered his questions, told stories, and recited verses, while refreshing themselves with wine.

When the king's narrators and evening companions are about him, none may be the first to move his lips, nor may they interrupt or contradict him even when they have rare and interesting things to tell; the sole purpose of each must be to listen well and give his whole attention to the sayings of the king... When addressing the king he must not speak hastily, but with words measured and well chosen; nor must he gesticulate with his hands or with movements of the head, nor change position or fidget in his seat, nor look towards anyone but the king.[22]

One of Harun's favourite nadim was Ishak, son of Ibrahim al-Mausili, also a nadim and a renowned musician. In addition to his artistic talents, Ishak was famous for his knowledge of history, grammar and poetry. Harun is reputed to have said to him one day, "Had you not been a singer, I should have made you a judge." Ishak makes several appearances in the *Thousand and One Nights*:

It is related, O auspicious King, that in Baghdad, the city of peace, the home of joy, pleasure's dwelling, and the garden of wit, the Khalifah Harun al-Rashid, Vicar of the Lord of the Three Worlds and Commander of the Faithful, had, as his cup-companion and perfect friend, a man whose fingers were wrought of harmony, whose hands were loved of lutes, whose voice was a lesson for the nightingale, the marvel of music, the king of singers, Ishak al-Nadim of Mosul. Harun had given him, in pure love, the fairest of his palaces.[23]

The witty repartee of the poet Abu al-Atahiya also amused Harun. Many other nadim celebrated for their talents helped lighten the caliph's evenings, some for many years, others for only a few months. Among them were the illustrious Abu Nuwas, one of the greatest poets of the Arabic tongue, and Abbas al-Ahnaf, Salm al-Kashir, Marwan ibn Abi Hafsah, who were also poets and musicians.

Harun's half-brother Ibrahim[24] occupied a special place in the sovereign's entourage. Touched by destiny, he would later sit on the caliph's throne, although not for long. Ibrahim and his sister Ulaiyah, who had been educated with great care, had become singers and musicians "such as have never been heard either before or since the preaching of Islam". Harun, a few years their senior, was very fond of them both. He made Ibrahim governor of Damascus, but missed him so much that he brought him back to Baghdad and introduced him into his intimate circle. He never tired of listening to Ibrahim, but did so only in private, as it would have been unseemly for a prince of the blood to perform for any audience other than his own family. Lyric poetry aroused as much enthusiasm in the aristocracy as in the other classes of Baghdad society.[25] Public opinion would support one singer against another, as it did in Vienna or the small Italian capitals during the nineteenth century. Great musicians like Ishak were the equals of the most important personages of the country. Harun adored music and had a passion for the poems of Abu Nuwas and Abu al-Atahiya, which his half-brother would sing accompanied by his women singers and by oboes and lutes. One day Harun gave permission for Ibrahim to sing a poem by Ahwaz to a small group of intimates who had never heard him before. Overflowing with admiration, Harun ordered that he be given a million dirhams without delay, which Ibrahim, whimsical and extravagant, probably spent before the day was over.

Harun al-Rashid is not remembered as a miser, but his prodigality was outclassed by Ibrahim's, so much so that on one occasion Harun became annoyed. Dining with Ibrahim one day, the caliph was served fish that seemed to have been cut into tiny pieces. "What is this fish?" he asked. "The pieces you see are in fact fishes' tongues," came the reply. "And how many are there?" The servant indicated that there were at least a hundred and fifty. "How much did all that cost?" "More than a thousand dirhams, sire." Harun refused to eat any more and asked Ibrahim for a thousand dirhams. Ibrahim obeyed. The money would be used for alms, explained the caliph, adding a request for another thousand dirhams. "That is to redeem your extravagance," said the caliph, "and not only the money but the dish on which the fish was served will be given to the poor."[26] The dish was worth at least three hundred dirhams.

Exceedingly vain, Ibrahim was jealous of other artists' talent and intolerant of their success, treating as enemies those poets and musicians who earned public admiration; for Ishak and his father, among others, his feelings were not far removed from hatred. On becoming caliph, however, he took no advantage of his ephemeral power to exact artistic vengeance. Having spilled no blood, this highly coloured personality was able to resume his place in the palace as a nadim in the entourage of Harun's son Mamun, who forgave his short-lived usurpation.

Very different from Ibrahim, Jaffar the Barmakid was the Well-Directed Caliph's closest companion and the best loved — with a more than normal affection, according to some stories, although the evidence does not support these. While Ibrahim was gigantic and far from comely, Jaffar was slight and extremely good-looking, with a beauty Ibrahim one day described in song:

> To find words for his beauty, think of the purest gold coin of ancient Egypt; the pearl which, glowing from the shell's depths, breaks the diver's heart; or gold leaf floating from the craftsman's hand to gild the pages of a wondrous book.

Jaffar, it is said, was enraptured by these verses.

Jaffar was a leader of fashion, always dressed with extreme care and with a sharp eye for elegance. He started the mode for high collars to hide his own neck, which was a little on the long side. The storytellers made him Harun's companion in the caliph's nocturnal wanderings around Baghdad when his "chest was constricted" — with boredom — or when he wanted "to learn of the actions of governors and walis in order to dismiss those against whom complaints were made".[27]

As the right hand of a caliph who symbolizes a period of justice and prosperity in the empire, Jaffar — with his father, Yahya — was closer to Harun than any other man, and exercised more influence, until the Commander of the Faithful distanced himself from the Barmakids. Very cultivated, a gifted calligrapher and jurist, author and orator, he was of a gay and lively disposition. His taste for pleasure matched Harun's own at the beginning of his reign, and the two men formed a close personal friendship. Jaffar had apartments in Harun's own wing of the palace of al-Khuld and shared the evenings of the Commander of the Faithful with other nadim and the singers of the harem. Both men were fond of the grape — Harun drank wine twice a week[28] — and their parties often ended in drunkenness. But Jaffar, who had an uncommon appetite for work, which he dispatched with unusual speed, was always bustling about his multiple tasks from early morning.

Later Harun was to make Jaffar governor of Egypt and send him to Syria to keep the peace. But Jaffar's most important functions were at court, where he held several posts and sat, often with his father, Yahya, and his brother Fadl, to hear the people's complaints and appeals and to punish abuses of authority. For a number of years he held the great seal of state, commanded the caliph's guards, headed the intelligence service (barid), controlled the textile factories (*tiraz*) — which held a virtual imperial monopoly on luxury fabrics — and directed the mint (which even struck some coins in his name). Acting in all of these capacities, he gave ample proof of his exceptional ability, intelligence and sense of responsibility. Ibn Khaldun says that he was actually called "sultan", an indication of the general extent of his supervisory powers and control of the empire.[29] Eventually Harun entrusted him with supervising Mamun's education when the latter became second heir to his elder brother Amin (Zubaidah's son). "Rich as Jaffar", they used to say in the streets of Baghdad.

There is a story that the singer Ibrahim al-Mausili once came across a fine garden when in the company of Harun and Jaffar, fell in love with it, and discovered that it was for sale at a price of fourteen thousand dinars. He quickly composed some couplets about the garden's beauties and recited them to Harun; the caliph granted the price of the garden, and Jaffar added five thousand dinars of his own. His proverbial generosity was equalled only by the opulence in which he lived. But, more prudent than Fouquet, he took Ibrahim al-Mahdi's advice and presented his sumptuous, newly built palace to his pupil Mamun. A great lover of music and poetry, himself a musician, he gathered about him the best poets and singers of both sexes, rewarded them spectacularly, and, when necessary, defended them against the attacks of rivals. One of them, Abu Zakkar, was so devoted to Jaffar that he could not bear to survive him, and asked to share the sufferings that followed his eventual disgrace.

His good humour and largesse, combined with the influence he was known to have on the caliph, made Jaffar one of the most popular men in Baghdad, acclaimed as he passed through the streets. This renown among the populace probably contributed to his downfall.

Jaffar's brother Fadl, according to Tabari, had more experience and showed himself more "adept in business". Less hedonistic than Jaffar, he drank no wine and stayed away from the more debauched evening sessions. But he too was very generous, rewarding poets and paying annuities to several of them. To an Indian who had written a poem about him he gave a thousand dinars, a racing camel, and a robe; the interpreter got five hundred dinars.

Fadl was a serious, hardworking, intelligent man. For a time he replaced his father at the head of the government, and held the seal of state before Harun gave it to Jaffar. He remained one of the caliph's most trusted helpers, usually in the roles of governor and commander of military expeditions. Thus he was governor of western Iran — and perhaps earlier of the province of Ray[30] — but most notably of Khorasan, where he achieved remarkable results in pacifying that troublesome province. He was popular there; it was said that during his mandate twenty thousand children were named after him in recognition of the benefits he had bestowed on the population.

Harun's foster brother (suckled by Khaizuran), Fadl, had a wilful, imperious character, which made him difficult to handle. More conciliatory than Harun in his attitude towards the Alids, he fell into disgrace following the escape of a member of this family whom he had protected. But he remained tutor to Prince Amin, whose proclamation as heir to the throne he had helped engineer. He and Jaffar were lifelong rivals, and the fact that one was tutor to the heir to the throne, and the other to the next in line of succession, did nothing to ease relations within the Barmakid family, nor between the Barmakids and Harun.

Yahya the Barmakid had two other sons, Musa, who became governor of Syria, and Mohammed. Both, but especially Mohammed, were long numbered among the caliph's intimates. They bore the title of emir, passed on in due course to their children and cousins. One of Yahya's brothers, Mohammed ibn Khalid, was the caliph's chamberlain for nine consecutive years.

It was in Harun's entourage that the Barmakids met their great rival, Fadl ibn al-Rabi, whose star was to brighten as theirs slowly dimmed. After their downfall, in which he was involved, Fadl ibn al-Rabi would become Harun's right arm. His father, Rabi al-Yunus, was a man of humble origins whose intelligence and talent had enabled him to obtain important posts, including that of chamberlain in Mansour's court. He won the caliph's trust and was appointed comptroller of the purse, then vizier (at the time more an honour than a working post), while his son Fadl took over the job of chamberlain. Fadl, too, was to be a trusted intimate of caliphs, first Mahdi and then Harun. He was given the seal of state, appointed chamberlain in 795, and in 803, when the Barmakids fell from favour, he was named vizier. As Harun's intimate adviser, greatly respected by Zubaidah, he remained a dominant figure in the palace at a time when political, military and administrative functions, seldom precisely defined, were often combined with the more delicate tasks of a companion in pleasure of the Commander of the Faithful.

Other dignitaries and grand personages frequented the palace, led by the Abbasid princes, Harun's half-brothers, uncles, nephews, and cousins: Allah ibn Mohammed; Ali; the illustrious Abd al-Samad who served five caliphs; and many others. General Harthama, Ali ibn Isa, the future governor of Khorasan, other generals, Jibril (the caliph's doctor), and the theologian and *cadi* (town judge) Abu Yusuf also inhabited this small, cloistered world of restless intrigue and scheming, where currents of influence swirled unpredictably back and forth.

3
First Shadows
on the State of Grace

*The peasants themselves maltreated the
poor who were among them.*
Denys de Tell-Mahré

The Price of Extravagance

The munificence of caliph and princes, the luxury in which men
and women led their lives, and the construction of heavenly palaces
and gardens all required money. Before an empress can have her
slippers sewn with precious stones or ladle pearls into a poet's
expectant maw, she must find the astronomical sums such lavishness
demands. But the Muslims had made their major conquests and
little booty came from the raids on the Byzantine frontiers. The
profits and taxes on trade — despite the stimulus provided by the
court's running expenses — were far from sufficient. In the Abbasid
empire, as elsewhere throughout history, there was but one source
from which the state could always extract something more — the
purse of the subject, whose name today carries an explicit
connotation of subjection.

The tax system was pretty straightforward. Muslims were
expected to make a voluntary contribution (*zakat, sadaka*) at the
same time that they paid a tithe (*ushr*). In this they were obeying
one of the five commandments of Islam. Non-Muslims paid a poll-
tax, the djiziya, in addition to a land tax, the kharadj. The wish to

avoid these taxes produced mass conversions among local populations, but the land tax was soon extended to cover all land that was held by Muslims as well as by non-Muslims. Estates acquired by conquest (*fay*) of various groups — states, churches, absentee owners — often became public property. Such property could either be exploited directly by the state or conceded to an individual, who then became responsible for the taxes on it. This system, called *katia* or *iqta*, was also used by the Byzantines and amounted to a long lease on a public property. Later, in the eleventh century, the *wakf*, or *habou*, made its appearance: a sort of permanent foundation with named beneficiaries (either private individuals or public institutions such as mosques, caravanserais, and hospitals). The wakf still exists today.

The kharadj was paid either in kind, in which case, depending on the crop grown, from a quarter to a half of the harvest would be taken; or in money, the amount calculated according to the land area, the crops being cultivated, and, above all, the quality of irrigation. The Sawad, the area around Baghdad, was taxed mainly in kind, but the money system was used almost everywhere else. Taxes were collected either by a civil servant responsible for the district or by a tax farmer. For the latter, the tax authorities would fix the sum payable by the "farmer" somewhat below the potential tax yield of the district. The difference represented his profit. This time-honoured system — still in use today — probably gave rise to the worst abuses. In addition to their taxes, the peasants (or taxpayers) were expected to bear most of the cost of collection and give food and shelter to the collectors.

There were other taxes, each giving rise to its own abuses and extortions: unwarranted fines, the confiscation of estates or fortunes claimed to have been illegally acquired, special taxes to secure police protection. Denys de Tell-Mahré, a Monophysite patriarch in upper Mesopotamia, in his *Syriac Chronicle* gives a sombre account of the common people's lot in this region shortly before Harun's accession. The situation is unlikely to have been very different in other parts of the empire. Denys mentions one collector who decided on his own authority to appropriate for the state a band about twenty metres wide around any building that could be considered public. Another imposed a levy on all merchandise in shops and private houses. Everything was taxed, Denys says, "including bees, pigeons and hens", at wholly arbitrary rates. The plight of the lower classes did not improve under Harun, quite the contrary.

Taxes calculated in money had to be paid in money. This usually obliged peasants to sell their harvest immediately after it was gathered, often to dealers in league with the tax office who offered about half its real value. Late payment was heavily penalized, sometimes by the use of torture. The least punitive method was to imprison the taxpayer until he paid up. To avoid selling their grain for a fraction of its real worth, peasants would often borrow to pay their taxes and might later need to take out a second loan to pay off the first. Ultimately, the peasants might be forced to place themselves and their property under the "protection" of some notable, thereby losing both their freedom and their land, the latter being absorbed into their "protector's" estate. Others would flee the tax collector, joining the ranks of the landless unemployed. Sometimes, after travelling hopelessly from village to village, they turned to thievery for survival. The authorities would pursue these fugitives, who, when caught, were obliged to repay all their back taxes to their community, the villagers of which were held collectively responsible for their default and thus had reason to track them down on their own. To add to the tensions in such communities, the flight of peasants from the land had dire effects on the economy and the authorities tried, not always successfully, to repopulate abandoned villages.

During this period the same misery prevailed throughout the Orient — north Africa, Syria, Iran, and Egypt (where a system of compulsory passports was instituted). In Khorasan and Transoxania, where ideas of agrarian egalitarianism were well established, the frequent revolts had much to do with social issues. They also converged with a variety of messianic movements,[1] such as those of Sanbad the Mage, of Ustadis, of al-Muqanna the Veiled Prophet, or the movement in the name of Abu Muslim the Assassinated.

Not all peasant revolts had their origins in social issues (those that erupted in Egypt in 785, for example, were the result of an Umayyad insurrection against the Abbasid authorities), but the misery of the population always aggravated political or religious conflicts. From the second half of the eighth century, the contrast between the poverty of the common people and the dizzying luxury of the court and privileged classes became ever more marked.

Mansour was notably hard on the taxpayer. "The most miserly of all the caliphs of the family of Abbas", as Tabari calls him, did not modify the Umayyad tax system. Based essentially on the rural economy, it varied considerably from one province to another. Furthermore, as a result of rapid urbanization, towns were taxed proportionately much less heavily than the countryside. Rich merchants, whose contribution was left to their consciences, often paid nothing at all. Duties on imported goods were very light, and many traders evaded them altogether. Mansour tried to balance the system, but without much success: the peasant, who was easy to find and easy to coerce, continued to bear most of the tax burden.

The prodigal Mahdi, whose enormous financial requirements have been described, withdrew from the army its right to collect taxes. Excellent in itself, this measure nevertheless opened the way to a more rigorous system. Despite the steady development of agriculture, the peasantry's standard of living declined.

Neither did the Barmakids do anything to remedy the situation. Yahya was a remarkable administrator, but his first priority was to augment the wealth of the state and the caliph (not forgetting, of course, his own and that of his family). He never hesitated to confiscate land on behalf of the caliph or of one or another Barmakid. Properties abandoned by their owners or not yet occupied by their inheritors, as well as shops, houses, and land belonging to "enemies" of the state or of Islam, were thus seized under a more or less legal pretext. In this way the caliph and his family acquired immense properties[2] producing enormous revenues; for example, an agent was appointed solely to manage Zubaidah's estates in Egypt.

In these matters Yahya behaved strictly as a financier, with little regard for the effects on the population. He never considered adopting the tax reforms suggested by the more far-seeing members of the caliph's entourages. He increased tax collection by reorganizing the system and requiring tax to be paid whether the harvest had been good or bad. He also appointed special officials to collect tax arrears. These officials exhibited particular severity in the Mosul region, where all farm animals were taxed and all arrears demanded and even the Arabs, hitherto able to claim certain exemptions, were taxed to the full. Some peasants revolted; others fled, notably to Azerbaijan, where they swelled the numbers of those who had taken up arms to protest against the withdrawal of privileges granted to the Arabs. Uncontrolled elements soon joined them in this sensitive frontier zone frequently raided by the Khazars.

Social and Religious Agitation

In Egypt and north Africa, social movements were accompanied by anti–Muslim rebellions. In 767 the Copts had defeated the Muslim troops sent from Fostat to restore order. The Abbasids, who were busy at the time fighting the Berbers, were not able to recapture Kairouan and end the rebellion until five years later. Under Harun, the Arabs living in the Hauf region east of the delta rose in their turn when the authorities reinstituted taxes on cleared land. When the local prefect was defeated and killed, fresh troops — commanded by Harthama ibn Ayan, one of Harun's preeminent generals — were sent from Syria to deal with the rebels. In 789, ten thousand more troops were assembled and marched against the peasants, who had revolted again when the prefect declared an increase in land tax. Another tax increase in 793 led to new fighting, more serious this time, and reinforcements had to be sent to restore the precarious peace. A few years later Harun was obliged once more to dispatch troops from Baghdad to put down yet another revolt, which had broken out in southern Sinai and then in Fostat itself. Fostat was sacked and burned by mutinous soldiers: they were protesting against the "adjustment" of their wages, which the government wanted to pay in equal parts of money, wheat, and fabric![3]

In Khorasan and western Iran the discontent caused by such abuses was reinforced by other factors. In these provinces which had nurtured the Abbasid revolution and given the new empire its most remarkable men, agitation had never ceased. The Umayyads' adversaries had started the trouble and continued it, winning the support of the masses by making all sorts of promises — notably in the area of social justice — which they were incapable of keeping. As these illusions evaporated, resentment turned against the Abbasid authorities, although the peasantry also blamed its local chiefs, the diqan. The messianic propaganda generated during the revolution had become confounded with local beliefs and thus, for many people, with the rejection of Islam. Nothing was easier for self-styled "messengers of God" or "reincarnations" of Abu Muslim and other dead rebels than to whip up mobs of malcontents ready to believe absolutely anything provided they were promised an improvement of their lot. All movements received a welcome, whether they were associated with Manichaeism or with the ancient Persian culture, although these desperate revolts were undoubtedly foreign to Iranian national feeling.

Thus, at the time of Harun's accession, authority was being contested in most of the Persian provinces. In Khorasan and Transoxania the most dangerous movement, that of al-Muqanna the Veiled Prophet, had been crushed with difficulty, only to be replaced by the ideologically similar Muhammira. The Khurramiya, close to Mazdaeism, were also rebelling, along with many other groups. Harun's armies did not restore order until 796, after several years of intense fighting.

In Tabaristan and Daylam, coastland regions of the Caspian Sea, the agitation was primarily Alid and Kharidjite in form. Yahya ibn Abdallah, a descendant of Hasan (one of the sons of Ali) led an open revolt against the Abbasids, supported by indigenous tribal chiefs and a broad segment of the population. Events quickly took a disquieting turn: the inadequate local garrisons — apparently less than eager to hunt down a descendant of the Prophet's nephew and son-in-law — had no success against the rebels, whose numbers continued to increase.

In 792 Harun al-Rashid put Fadl the Barmakid in charge of the western provinces of Iran. It was the best possible choice. Fadl used the winter, which hampered military operations, to negotiate, and Yahya ibn Abdallah agreed to surrender in exchange for a guarantee of safety. The document was signed by the caliph himself and countersigned by the doctors of law and the Hashemites[4] of Baghdad, Yahya retired to Medina bearing rich gifts; however, the promise of *aman* (mercy) nothwithstanding, he was murdered not long afterwards (adherence to his given word was never Harun's strong suit). Having ended the rebellion without bloodshed, Fadl then went on to construct caravanserais and mosques, notably in Bokhara, and to excavate a canal in Balkh.[5] Finally, he waived the tax arrears owed by local populations, thus restoring calm throughout the country as far as the region of Kabul and Bamyan, conquered for the first time.

Fadl then raised in Khorasan an army of fifty thousand men, twenty thousand of whom were sent to the western regions of the empire under General Harthama's orders, and the rest to Baghdad.

Intended to reinforce the units sent against the rebellious movements, and more favourably disposed to the Barmakids than to the abna, this army was called the *abbasiya*. We shall hear of it again.

The crushing of Yahya's revolt did not dispel Harun's suspicion of the Alids, which was now focused on Musa al-Kazim,[6] a direct descendant of Husein, the son of Ali killed at Kerbela. This holy man, respected by all, had been arrested by Mahdi, then released; now, although he was not engaged in any political activity, Harun had him arrested again. His death in captivity was probably from natural causes, although Harun has been accused of having him killed.

Other religious movements influenced by social issues were still jolting the empire.[7] Most were inspired by the Kharidjites, the Islamic sect formed in 657 after the battle of Siffin. Kharidjite doctrine advocated free will and human responsibility, and its followers demanded the right not only to choose the head of the community, Arab or other, but also to rise against him if they thought fit. They were divided into several sects, all of which opposed the unitary caliphate.

In the first years of Harun's reign a Kharidjite insurrection broke out in the Nisibe region of Djezireh, led by a tribal chieftain named Walid ibn Tarif. With an army of thirty thousand men Tarif marched on Azerbaijan and Armenia, conquered them in short order, levied his own taxes, and for two years flouted the central authority. Ultimately, Harun was forced to send General Yazid ibn Shaybani, one of the men who had strongly opposed his accession to the throne. A fine military commander, at whose side Harun had fought the Byzantines, Shaybani succeeded in killing Walid.

Another revolt, stemming from the same religious and social causes, broke out in the Herat region of Khorasan when a Kharidjite called Hamza ibn Adrak assumed the title "Emir of the Faithful" and killed the governor. After suffering a bloody defeat, he fell back to Seistan, then to Kirman. It took years to put down this rebellion, which was based on terrorist action and preached that every believer had a duty to oppose the authority of the caliph or that of anyone recognizing him. An outstanding organizer, with a good army and an astonishing propaganda service, Adrak was defeated only in 820, by the self-defence groups formed by the inhabitants of Nishapur.

In all these regions, exactions by the authorities and the harsh behaviour of some governors heightened social discontent and exaggerated rebellious divergences. Human misery always engenders rebelliousness. So does tyranny, especially when accompanied by outrageous demands. Religious hatred can also be a powerful force; it is no concession to superstition or the irrational to accept that religious sentiment may partially motivate human actions.

It is quite obvious that to explain the events of the seventh and eighth centuries in terms of an alleged conflict between Aryanism and Semitism is to be less than serious. Is it necessary to point out that the men of Khorasan and the shores of the Caspian, of the Yemen and the Hejaz, would never have viewed the problem in these terms? Or that "Persian nationalism" and "Arab nationalism" are meaningless in the context? By the same token, it is inaccurate to regard Shiism and its associated heresies as specifically Iranian in origin. Shiism, "a fundamentally Arab movement,"[8] started in Mesopotamia and northern Syria and was later taken up by certain Iranian townsmen.

> It was Arabs who first brought Shiism into Persia, where the Arab garrison city of Qum, a colony from Kufa, was one of the main Shiite strongholds. The opposition expressed by Shiism was a social revolt against the Arab aristocracy, along with their Creed, their State and their hangers-on, rather than a national revolt against the Arabs.[9]

Thus, not long after the beginning of Harun al-Rashid's reign, the political, social, and religious troubles discernible since the first years of the Abbasid regime took a turn for the worse. Behind its dazzling facade, the colossal structure left by the first two Arab dynasties was beginning to show small cracks, presaging the heavier damage soon to endanger the integrity of the whole empire. The extreme centralization of the regime — furthered by Harun and the Barmakids — made the empire vulnerable by subjecting all decisions, even those concerning the most remote provinces, to the Baghdad government. That remarkable intelligence organization the barid supplied the central authorities with information on all events of importance, even happenings in small towns on the fringes of the empire. But communication took weeks, even months; the caliph's and the vizier's decisions were far less effective than they might have been if taken promptly by a governor on the spot. Furthermore, governors, even when invested with full powers, might not be competent and loyal. In times of crisis the caliph sometimes had to send a man of ability to restore order, as he sent Fadl al-Barmaki to Iran and Jaffar to Syria.

Nevertheless, these centrifugal currents had not yet assumed truly alarming proportions. The army was not always large enough to keep order everywhere, but recruitment had yet to become a serious problem. Although Arabs were increasingly reluctant to sign on, contingents could still be raised in Iran and Khorasan. The time had not yet come for the caliphs to place their own security, and that of the state, entirely in the hands of mercenaries.[10]

The Caliph Takes Charge

The first chapter of Harun's reign was drawing to its close. The inexperienced young sovereign had gradually become aware of his almost limitless power. Not that the Commander of the Faithful had ever been a mere plaything in the hands of women and Barmakid ministers: he was already known to have ignored Yahya's advice and had even defied the imperious Khaizuran. Irritable, self-confident, and alert to the slightest threat to his power, he had personally ordered the arrest of the pious and inoffensive Musa al-Kazim and the death of Yahya ibn Abdallah, whose safety he had guaranteed. He was neither an amiable puppet nor the "Good Harun" of Oriental legend but a man intolerant of opposition and even of argument. Like many other heads of state, he was beginning to favour malleable men over clever ones, as Fadl al-Barmaki discovered.

Highly competent both as minister and general, Fadl had never hesitated to argue with the caliph and had even ignored certain of Harun's decisions. This independence was one of the causes of his disgrace; another was the "little vizier's" success in Khorasan, which made Harun jealous. Fadl was accused of protecting the Alids, whom the Barmakids had always tolerated despite Harun's fear of an Alid conspiracy. On his return from Khorasan, Fadl received fulsome praise from the caliph, but he was never given another important job and lost his administrative functions a few years later.

67

The task of governing Khorasan was now given to Ali ibn Isa ibn Mahan. He committed error after error, but he belonged to the faction opposed to the Barmakids. He also commanded the abna, which had shown its disapproval when Fadl levied the rival abbasiya in the eastern provinces; the army's Syrian and Iraqi units had also been less than pleased by the creation of this new corps. Yahya opposed the appointment of Isa ibn Mahan, whom he regarded as incompetent, but in vain. It seems likely, in fact, that the caliph gave Isa the job precisely because he knew it would annoy the Barmakids.

In addition to Fadl's decline and the simultaneous promotion of Isa ibn Mahan, Yahya's brother Mohammed lost the important office of chamberlain and was replaced by Fadl ibn al-Rabi, who came from a rival family and around whom a sort of opposition to the Barmakids now took shape. All the signs were that the caliph, after ten years on the throne, was ready to bring the powerful family's dominance to an end.

Raqqa

Harun was also preparing to move out of Baghdad. The caliph, it was said, had never really liked this prestigious town, created by his grandfather. The air was bad there, he complained. And the proximity of the abna, with its feuds and privileges, disturbed him, as did the continual growth and discontent of the capital's already huge population. Deeply concerned, like his predecessors, for his personal safety, Harun felt ill at ease there. He had already tried to leave Baghdad on at least two occasions. He is thought to have toyed with the idea of building a palace at the foot of the Zagros in western Iran, but, on falling ill, had dropped the project. Two years later he built a residence in the Mosul region, but never moved into it. In 796 he finally decided on Raqqa in the Djezireh, on the left bank of the Euphrates, in the town of Kallinikos,[11] which had been there since antiquity.

Raqqa was a long way from Baghdad and from the empire's political, commercial, and intellectual centres in lower Mesopotamia. If questions of security had been uppermost in Harun's mind, he would surely not have left his women, children, and treasures behind in the palace of al-Khuld. It seems probable that military considerations played a large part in the decision to move closer to the borders of the Byzantine empire.

It will be remembered that Harun, as a very young man, had been given command of an expedition against the Byzantines by his father; he had reached Constantinople and "leaned his lance"[12] against its walls. And we have seen him, barely settled on his throne, ordering stronger defences for this frontier. These measures hardly seem warranted, as crisis-ravaged Byzantium did not pose the slightest threat. More likely, from the very beginning of his reign Harun was planning not just to raid and plunder the Byzantine frontier but, if God willed it, to get as far as Constantinople. War against the Byzantines was the great project of his reign. His systematic construction of powerful bases at the foot of the Taurus, and his decision to move his residence there, cannot be explained in any other way.

Populated by Christians but held by the Arabs since 639, Raqqa had been awakened from its torpor by Mansour, who built a new town, al-Rafika, nearby. The two settlements soon merged. The town was in the shape of a horseshoe with its flat end lying along the bank of the Euphrates, today a kilometre distant. The gates, the double walls, the street layout all recalled the Round City but on a smaller scale (the diameter of the town being about fifteen hundred metres). The crenellated outer wall of dried-mud brick, four or five metres thick, was strengthened at intervals by twenty-eight towers (built of baked brick) housing defence posts. Water was supplied through channels made for that purpose. A big rectangular mosque, ninety-three by one hundred and eight metres, was built in the town's centre.

Southeast of the mosque, within the city walls, rose Harun's palace Kasr as-Salam (Palace of Peace). Sumptuous and very large,[13] it consisted of buildings separated by courtyards and gardens scattered over a wide area. There was no external decoration; all that could be seen from the outside were featureless walls of mud brick (the foundations were of stronger baked brick). The luxury was on the inside: moulded stucco, tapestries, gilding, paintings, carpets. Amid this glittering decor lived hundreds of people, even more cut off than they had been in Baghdad from the local population, which supplied manpower and other necessities to the gigantic court.

The influence of Sassanid Persia, which was to become even more apparent during the next century, could be felt increasingly in every domain. In imitation of the King of Kings, the caliph withdrew into his palace and surrounded himself with ceremony that grew more and more ornate. Religious leader, Emir of the Believers, soon to become "shadow of God on earth", he was the most powerful sovereign of his time; his palace was like the holy of holies, and he only emerged from it amid enormous pomp to dazzle the eyes of his people. The jumble of ruins scattered over the plain to the east of the Euphrates still helps us to imagine him surrounded by his court, in this vast palace among the "paradises" created for him by his gardeners and architects, his game parks[14] similar to the many established in the desert by the Ummayyads for hunting and amusement. Very fond of field sports and an excellent horseman, Harun built a racecourse at Raqqa on which he would run horses from his stables. The chronicler Jashiyari has described the delight shown by the caliph when a race was won by a horse belonging to him or to one of his sons. The course was also used for playing polo, or *cawgan*.[15] It seems likely that this game (of Iranian origin) was introduced by Harun when he lived at Raqqa, but the caliph himself preferred a variant of the game, *tabtab*. He also introduced *birjas*, archery from horseback and tilting with a lance at a cylindrical target. Harun took part in these games on a equal footing with his companions. He also participated in archery competitions. He was one of the first caliphs to keep a permanent company of archers.

The Well-Guided spent the last thirteen years of his reign, and of his life, in Raqqa. His visits to Baghdad were brief and became more and more infrequent. Eventually it would happen that, returning from the south, he would pass by the capital without entering it. The administration of the empire necessarily became divided between the two towns, serving only to complicate matters. The caliph's interest was directed above all towards the frontier zone, and he gave more attention to the preparation of campaigns beyond the Taurus than to the government of the empire — one reason, perhaps, for the government's deterioration in the years that followed the decision to move out of Baghdad.

4
The Difficult Years

*In this way, the life of a dynasty
corresponds to the life of an individual;
it matures and passes into an age of
stagnation and thence into retrogression.*

ibn Khaldun

The years following Harun's accession had their measure of turmoil
and crisis, though nothing severe enough to endanger the empire.
But there is every indication that the caliph's move from Baghdad
to Raqqa coincided with the ending of the state of grace. He did
not seem, as yet, to have made any conscious resolve to rid himself
of the Barmakids. But various members of his retinue had noticed
that he was growing impatient with them and that the star of their
great rival, Fadl ibn al-Rabi, was in the ascendant.

Apart from his military plans against Byzantium (the main reason
for his cultivation of Charlemagne), Harun's central preoccupation
at this time was the succession to the throne. He thought about it
incessantly, discussed it with his confidants, and eventually came
to a decision that did little or nothing to settle the matter.

The time spent in Raqqa by the Well-Directed — more than half
his reign — was a period of heightened activity as, following the
decade-long "honeymoon", the problems of the empire began to
appear in their true, sometimes tragic colours. The signs of
disintegration already discernible in various parts of the empire
became more marked. Indeed, some provinces gained almost
complete independence.

Unity of the Empire Threatened

At the end of the eighth century the Abbasid empire was at its peak. Economic prosperity without precedent in that part of the world, the best military forces of the age, and a refined civilization combined to make the caliph of Islam the most powerful sovereign of his time. His possessions stretched from the Atlantic to the Tien-Chan and the Indus delta, from the Taurus to Bab al-Mandeb and the Blue Nile. His enemies were weakened by internal discord. The empire of the basileus was struggling through a series of crises, the latest of which, brought about by the rise of iconoclasm, had done much damage and was not yet resolved. Charlemagne, soon to wear the crown of the Romans, could not begin to rival the caliph, still less become a serious enemy. And he was so far away! No one in the known world could equal the commander of millions of believers — Arabs, Africans, Egyptians, Berbers, Turks — who five times a day said the same prayers, prostrated towards the same sanctuary, and who were also united by the Arab tongue, the language of the Koran, which had become the language of administration and culture from one end of the empire to the other.

Master of a centralized state based on that of the Sassanid empire, the caliph was there to maintain order in this varied collection of countries. He had to deal with local particularisms, feudal magnates great and small, a wide assortment of heretics, and political movements fuelled by poverty and resentment. Hardly a year passed without the appearance of one or more rebellions successful enough to demand urgent military action by governors and generals.

The Umayyads had established Arab control over the provinces by subjecting enormous masses of people to the authority of a few. The Abbasids ran the administration largely through the agency of non-Arab Muslims, people with a much more intimate understanding of local populations but who may have been empowered too late to allay the resentments of those conquered. Or was it inevitable that some of the latter would try to recover their freedom at the first opportunity? In any case, the social and religious movements born during the first decades of the Abbasid dynasty would, by the end of the century, make irreparable rents in the political fabric of the empire. Excessive centralization and the empire's enormous size made control of the distant provinces difficult. Governors no doubt found it hard to resist the temptation to assert a measure of independence.

First conquered at the end of the seventh century, north Africa had been Islamized largely through the agency of Kharidjism, a widespread heresy at that time. Born out of the refusal of a group of believers to accept arbitration between Ali and Muawia, its doctrine had an egalitarian character very acceptable to rural populations in the Maghreb. Its missionaries had found sanctuary with the Berber tribes, probably after being driven out of Iraq by Umayyad persecution. The "liberating heresy" spread very fast among peasants and montagnards unimpressed by the Arabs' glamour and alienated by their arrogance. Around 757, during Mansour's reign, a group of Kharidjites seized Tripoli and made it their capital; the following year another group took Kairouan, holding it for three years before the caliph's governor recaptured the town. Despite the ensuing massacre, the position of Baghdad's representative remained precarious. When an anti-caliph was proclaimed at Tlemcen, the governor, Ibrahim ibn Aghlab, did not even try to remove him. At the end of Mansour's reign the situation looked distinctly shaky, with yet another holy war ravaging the country; the Abbasid governor, Omar ibn Hafs, was besieged in Kairouan and killed. Large reinforcements, under the command of Yazid ibn Hatim, were sent to put down the insurrection — sixty thousand men from Iraq and Syria and thirty thousand from Khorasan, well equipped and heavily armed. Weak spots were fortified with new *ribat*,[1] and old Byzantine citadels were restored and garrisoned with elite troops. These measures got results, and in 772 the Kharidjites were defeated in Tripolitania and their leaders killed. Yazid retook Kairouan, then ruled with a successfully heavy hand for fifteen years. The governor was succeeded by his son, then his brother — the beginnings of a dynastic system of governorship, an effective one, certainly, but not without disadvantages of its own.

On this occasion, however, Yazid's family failed to hold on to power. The Barmakids did not wish to see provincial governments passing from father to son and tried to remove from office anyone they thought likely to give trouble. After a long struggle between the two parties for influence on Harun al-Rashid, the Barmakids succeeded in arranging the appointment of the illustrious Harthama ibn Ayan, the general closest to them. He continued the pacification of the region with the support of some of the abbasiya, the army recruited in Khorasan by Fadl al-Barmaki. He also built the ribat at Monastir, which is still to be seen there today, one of the most majestic and best preserved in north Africa. Harun may have personally ordered its construction to block the route to Spain.

Harthama was recalled at his own request as new storm clouds gathered over the region. A confused period followed. The governor Mohammed al-Mukatil, appointed by the Barmakids, was deposed by the *jund* (army) and the people. Restored by the governor of the Zab,[2] Ibrahim ibn Aghlab, he was again expelled by his subjects, who began pressing Aghlab to take over the province. After some hesitation Harun agreed. In July of the year 800 the future Ibrahim I, emir of Ifriqiya, was invested as governor of the great western province of the empire.

A new era had opened for Ifriqiya[3] and, undoubtedly, for the empire itself. The first agreement had just been signed between the caliph of Islam and the governor of a province; under its terms the governor not only lost the one hundred thousand dinar subsidy paid by Egypt for the upkeep of occupation troops but also undertook to pay the caliph forty thousand dinars every year. Ifriqiya now enjoyed financial autonomy, most likely the precursor of autonomy in other fields, although no idea of independence was implied. The emir of Ifriqiya administered and governed the province without any supervision from Baghdad. He was not an official, who could be recalled or dismissed from his post, although he remained a vassal of the caliph, with his investiture subject to renewal on the accession of a new caliph. But there was no interference in the local order of succession; the Aghlab family kept power for more than a century.

It was almost impossible for the central government to exercise much influence in a province distant from the capital and rich enough to manage without financial aid, and so there was a steady erosion of links between Baghdad and Kairouan. Ibrahim acted quickly to secure his near-independent position. He formed a five-thousand-man "black guard" devoted exclusively to his personal protection and thus placed himself out of reach of the jund. The internal peace maintained by his wise administration, along with the country's level of economic development, ensured loyalty on the part of the population.

To demonstrate that he was not just a transient governor but a virtually independent sovereign whose prestige rivalled the caliph's,

Ibrahim built near Kairouan a magnificent residence,[4] Kasr al-Kadim, which he called Abbasiya in deference to the ruling dynasty. He moved there with his black troops, some of the more loyal Arab units, and his court and servants; and it was at Abbasiya, perhaps, that he received the envoys sent by Charlemagne to ask for the body of St Cyprian. One of his successors, Ibrahim II, constructed the great castle of al-Raqqada (of which traces still exist), set among immense gardens not far from Kairouan.

Like the caliphs, the Aghlabids used their resources for religious and utilitarian building. They extended the Sidi Oqba mosque in Kairouan, one of the oldest and most venerated in Islam, and also the Great Mosque of Tunis, as well as those of Sousse and Sfax. They built or improved various fortresses and waterworks. This transformation of the country was accompanied by an intense religious and intellectual life. Kairouan under the Aghlabids became a great centre of learning and Koranic literature, where followers of the different Oriental schools of thought soon created an atmosphere as stimulating as that of Baghdad, Fostat, or Basra.

By the end of Ibrahim I's reign, which almost coincided with Harun's, Ifriqiya was partially outside the empire. The caliph was reduced to reminding its people of his existence by giving aid to the victims of natural disasters and helping pay for religious monuments. Harun's role in this region, hardly more than that of constitutional head of state and spiritual figurehead, prefigured the loss of executive power by his Abbasid successors in Baghdad itself a century later.

The Kharidjite heresy had been rooted out of Ifriqiya, but not from the adjoining region to the west (now the central part of Algeria). Conquered in the middle of the seventh century, the Berber population of this region had also been Islamized by Kharidjites (the sect is to be found there to this day, most notably in the M'Zab). The caliph's armies had not been able to reconquer them. Ifriqiya was therefore obliged to tolerate as neighbours populations that almost all practised a heterodox form of Islam.

The most important of these Berber emirates had been founded in 761 at Tihert (Tiaret) by Abderahman ibn Rostem, a Persian expelled from Kairouan during the struggles to restore orthodoxy in Ifriqiya. He was elected imam by the local Kharidjites, who chose his successors from among the members of his family. The

Rostemids' authority was both supreme and hereditary, and they acquired prestige and influence in a large area of north Africa. Their theocratic regime, in which Berbers were, naturally, influential, paid close attention to economic matters. The Rostemids, who ruled until the early tenth century, gave priority to trade exchanges between the coast and the interior, a policy that was extended even to countries south of the Sahara. This "hereditary republic" of merchants, in which Persians remained influential, kept up relations with the nomads and cultivators of the interior, gave protection to caravans, and by these means extended its influence — flavoured with Kharidjism — as far as Spain and Iraq. Travellers and immigrants were attracted from all quarters by the prosperity of Tihert, while Rostemids were given court appointments by the emirs of Spain.

As always in medieval Islam, economic prosperity was accompanied by learning. Mathematics, astronomy,[5] literature, poetry, and of course religion were all studied by this rather ascetic population. A certain distance was maintained from the dissipations of Kairouan, which Tihert considered a negative example. Baghdad was even more remote from the outlook of these Berbers and Persians, who disagreed with the doctrines professed by the caliph and his entourage and disapproved of what they saw as the dissolute morals of his court and his capital. But the whole central Maghreb had drifted apart from the Baghdad government long before the coming of the Aghlabids. Harun had no authority there and his name was no longer even mentioned.

Farther west, Islam had arrived at what is now Morocco at the end of the seventh century and the beginning of the eighth; a heretical element was immediately added to it by the local montagnard populations. Here, too, excesses by tax collectors, the abuses of governors, and the general weakness of the administration soon disillusioned peoples whose adherence to orthodox Islam was recent and usually superficial. Kharidjite and Mutazilite doctrines were favoured, mainly because their disciples opposed official authority and seized every excuse for rebellion. Around 740, in a revolt that originated in the far west, the tribes seized Tangier and then overran a large part of the country. The resulting widespread rejection of Umayyad power continued under the Abbasids. Virtual anarchy reigned among the tribes; principalities formed and disintegrated;

occasionally they became kingdoms. One of these, founded by a member of the Prophet's family, was to give Islam one of its most glorious centres of civilization, the beautiful city of Fez.

In 786, the year of Harun al-Rashid's accession, an Alid revolt broke out in Medina. Husein ibn Ali, a Hasanid, barricaded himself in the mosque and proclaimed himself amir al-muminin. Supported by only twenty-six Alids, a handful of converts, and a group of pilgrims, Husein's rebellion had no chance of success, and the authorities allowed him to withdraw and set off for Mecca. That would have been the end of the story, had not army units escorting the pilgrimage intercepted Husein's escort. In the following engagement, Husein was killed and his troops scattered. Pursued by the caliph's men, the Alids fled in all directions; one of them, Yahya ibn Abdallah, reached Iraq, then Ray. Although the newly enthroned Harun put a price on his head, he continued his flight through Khorasan and Transoxania and finally reached Daylam, from where he issued a call for rebellion. Fadl ibn al-Rabi managed eventually to persuade him to surrender. His death sometime later contributed to the break between Harun and Fadl, the caliph unjustly accusing his minister of engineering it.

Idris, another member of the family, had a more glorious destiny. Accompanied by one of his freedmen, Rashid, he managed to reach Egypt, where he kept out of sight for a while to evade Harun's vigilant police before leaving for the Maghreb. There he found sanctuary with a Berber tribe at Volubilis (Oualila). His prestigious descent from the Prophet helped him to found a dynasty that lasted more than a century; and, above all, he created Fez.

Idris I soon conceived the ambition of possessing a capital that would rival Kairouan or Tihert. Situated beside a river, at the crossroads of two main trade routes, Fez was a considered choice. Surrounded by Berbers, Idris sought to attract Arab migrants to the spot. From Fez, he was also able to pursue the Islamization of the peoples of the interior, who were by no means cured of Christianity, Judaism, and even idolatry. From 801 his son was minting coinage. He himself died in 791 — poisoned, it was said, on the orders of Harun al-Rashid, whose fear and hatred of the Alids increased with the passage of time.

Idris II continued his father's work. He moved Fez upstream to the opposite bank of the gully and built the mosque of the Cherif and a palace. In 814 the town experienced an influx of eight thousand Arab families expelled from Spain after an unsuccessful revolt against the Umayyads. The section they built is still called the Andalusian quarter.

The kingdom of the Idrisids remained at its peak for another thirty years. A centre of commerce, travel, learning, and religion, it cast its light as far away as Egypt. The non-sectarian Idrisids[6] tolerated all religious currents, even the least orthodox, and had no desire to turn their capital into a Shiite centre. At such a distance from the court of Baghdad and the religious centres of the empire, the caliph's influence was extremely limited; this part of the Maghreb would never again fall under Abbasid control.

Neither would Spain. Abderahman I, the Umayyad prince who survived the massacre of his family to be proclaimed amir al-Andalus in 756, never recognized the Abbasids or allowed the caliphs of Baghdad to interfere in his domains. The colour black was banned from his states, and he and his entourage dressed in white, the Umayyad colour. For a time the Friday sermon was given in the caliph's name, but even this was abandoned following the submission of the Abbasid governor. Later the very name of the Abbasids became accursed. The emirs tried on several occasions to foment seditions against the caliphs; Abderahman I may have gone as far as preparing an expedition to drive the Abbasids out of Syria. By Harun's time no political links remained between the new Arab kingdom and the empire of the Commander of the Faithful.[7]

Ifriqiya, Spain, and Tihert were so far from Baghdad that their secession hardly affected the destinies of the empire, while the movements agitating Egypt and Syria had not yet become either serious or profound. The Yemeni revolt of 795 was easily put down; its leaders were sent to Baghdad and strangled, on Harun al-Rashid's orders. The governor was recalled and peace restored.

Things were very different in Khorasan (eastern Iran and parts of Afghanistan and Transoxania). Everything that happened there resounded though Baghdad and the empire — through the administration, whose personnel was largely of Persian origin, and the army (both abna and abbasiya). It was becoming evident that the appointment of Ali ibn Isa to govern the province had been a mistake. Thinking only of exploiting Khorasan, he massacred the diqan who opposed him and exacted huge sums from the population to send to Baghdad. The oppression became so unbearable that complaints even began to reach the capital. A leading notable, Hisham ibn Farkusrau, fled to Baghdad and asked for the caliph's protection; another feigned paralysis to escape ibn Isa's anger. Yahya raised the matter with Harun and asked him to call ibn Isa to order, but without success. For one thing, ibn Isa had powerful and devoted military forces at his disposal; for another, Harun was reluctant to give in to pressure from the Barmakid, whatever the cost. And besides, his governor kept appeasing him with sumptuous presents.

Harun saw only that the power of the local notables, formerly associated with the Barmakids, was being reduced and that money and presents kept flowing into Raqqa. The situation was so tense, however, that several revolts erupted, prompting the caliph to send troops to Iran. Their losses alarmed him enough to pay a visit to the province. Interrupting his campaign against the Byzantines and leaving the large forces on the frontier of Asia Minor under the command of his son Qasim, he left for Khorasan.

It was the first time that a reigning caliph had travelled so far to the east. He stopped at Ray and never reached Merv, the capital; but the short visit to his birthplace did little to improve matters. The results of agreements signed with tribal chiefs from the Caucasus and the Caspian region were insubstantial. Ali ibn Isa arrived loaded with presents to see the caliph; he gave a glowing account of the general situation and left after being confirmed in his post. Harun probably wanted only to be convinced. He took no decisive action with regard to Khorasan, reaffirmed his confidence in ibn Isa, and went back to Raqqa. A few years later he set out again for the eastern provinces, this time never to return.

The Succession Problem

The rules of succession in the Muslim empire had never been clearly defined, let alone codified. Ali's elevation to the caliphate unleashed a drama whose consequences are still being felt today. The Umayyad century was one long struggle with the Alids. With the Abbasids in power, Mansour in his turn had to wage a difficult campaign, against his uncle Abdallah. It will be recalled that on the Night of Destiny Harun assumed the throne upon his mother's assassination of his brother, who had threatened her life. The size of the Abbasid family, ever-increasing by virtue of the equal rights enjoyed by children of legitimate wives and those of concubines, favoured the development of factions and feuds. Succession problems were a constant worry to caliphs, the more so as both men and women tended to die relatively young.

Harun al-Rashid had fourteen sons, but it was soon accepted that only the two eldest, Abdallah (the future Mamun) and Mohammed (Amin) counted in the succession. The first, born on the Night of Destiny, was the son of the Persian slave Marajil, who died the same night. The second was born several months later to Zubaidah, a legitimate wife of royal blood. Harun's affection for them and the care with which he supervised their education feature in numerous tales. He himself chose their teachers, among whom was his own former tutor, the illustrious sage Kitai, who has left his own description of a graceful interview between the caliph and his two young sons:

> The two little princes appeared looking like two stars from the firmament, charming with sweetness and gravity. Eyes lowered, they advanced with stately paces to the threshold of the room, from where they addressed their father with the royal greeting and the most eloquent good wishes. Rashid told them to approach and invited them to sit on either side of him, Mohammed on his right and Abdallah on his left. He then asked me to make them recite passages from the Koran and to ask them some questions: all of which they answered in the most satisfactory manner, passing the test with entire success. Rashid was enchanted and did not hide his happiness.

The princes then recited poems.

> I had never seen among the children of a caliph [Kitai continues] two young princes so quick in repartee, so elegant in their language or so skilled in showing what they knew, as Rashid's two sons; and I wished them a thousand blessings, to which their father agreed by saying *amen*. Pressing them to his heart, he held them in a long embrace; and when he released them I saw that his chest was wet with his tears.

Harun's love for these two sons did not blind him to the grave defects of the boy born to his legitimate royal wife or to the promising qualities of the Persian concubine's child. The first, he said one day:

> is enslaved by his passions, his whims which alone rule his conduct... the freedom with which he dissipates his fortune and involves women, even slaves, in his affairs. Abdallah, on the other hand, deserves nothing but praise; his judgment is sound and he can be entrusted with the most important business... In Abdallah I find Mansour's energetic wisdom, Mahdi's piety and al-Hadi's pride.[8]

"Praise be to God," said Harun on another occasion on the subject of the future Mamun, "who has given me a son who sees even better with the eyes of his spirit than with those in his head."

Deeply concerned with the long-term stability of the empire and the power of the Abbasid family after his death, Harun was haunted by the fear that his successor might not be equal to the task. In 791 he had made everyone take the *bayah* (oath of allegiance) to Amin, then five years old, though not without encountering resistance from some quarters. Certain members of the family, with an eye to their own prospects should the throne fall suddenly vacant, objected on grounds of the prince's extreme youth. Amin's "tutor" Fadl al-Barmaki managed to overcome the objections, and the Khorasan authorities took the oath first.

As Amin grew older, however, Harun could not help realizing that he would be a mediocre man. He confided his worries to Yahya al-Barmaki: "I want to be sure that I am succeeded by a man whose conduct I approve and whose actions I respect, a man I know will govern skilfully, without any hint of pusillanimity or weakness. I refer to Abdallah. But the family prefers Mohammed, so if I show preference for Abdallah, they will turn on me."[9] This was precisely the problem; the divisions now starting to appear were going to shake the Abbasid family, and the empire itself, once Harun was gone. His decision was that after Amin the crown would pass to Abdallah, who soon afterwards was given the *laqab* (title) of Mamun and the government of Khorasan; Amin received the western part of the empire. The bayah ceremony was held first at Raqqa, then in Baghdad.

With the passage of time, the defects of one prince and the virtues of the other became, if anything, more apparent. Perhaps even more seriously, each had acquired a party of supporters who made no secret of their views. Amin's party consisted of the royal family, headed, of course, by Zubaidah. A realistic woman, she too could see that her son's laziness and indifference to affairs of state would make him a poor caliph. Harun had given Mamun enough armed forces to keep the province of Khorasan under control, and Zubaidah feared that this posed a threat to her son. But her anxieties angered the caliph. "If there is any cause for one of them to fear the other, it is Mamun who should beware of your son, not the other way around," he said coldly. In fact Zubaidah's fears were not entirely imaginary, as Harun seems to have contemplated promoting Mamun from second in line of succession to heir apparent. Finally, however, he decided to give a more solemn and binding form to the arrangements he had already made, so as to make any posthumous tinkering with the succession more difficult.

For a ceremony affecting the whole future of the Abbasid family, and the "Successor to the Prophet" at its head, Mecca was the only suitable setting. Harun set out in December 802 accompanied by the princes, many high dignitaries, and the entire court, including Yahya al-Barmaki and his sons Fadl and Jaffar. The high chamberlain Fadl ibn al-Rabi was also present. The palace jurists had prepared a text setting out the details of the succession and the pledges to be given by the two princes. The young brothers swore in the name of Allah not to transgress its clauses, on pain of the most severe punishments possible — seizure of goods for distribution to the poor, pilgrimage to Mecca on foot, compulsory divorce from all wives, and the liberation of all slaves.

After observing the rites of the pilgrimage, in the presence of the assembled dignitaries, Mamun and Amin, at Harun's request, with their own hands attached the text they had just approved to the sacred walls of the Kaaba. Of concern to believers in omens, the document came loose from the wall and fluttered to the ground. Harun ignored the incident, and letters were sent to all the provinces detailing the arrangements for the future of the empire. He ordered them to be read out even in the most obscure towns; the documents themselves were entrusted to the wardens of the Kaaba and set in precious-metal frames studded with pearls, rubies, and emeralds.

The documents thus signed and made public went far beyond settling the problem of the caliph's succession. Amin undertook to respect his brother's right to the succession; but, more importantly, he recognized Mamun's sovereignty over Khorasan — the whole eastern part of the empire from Hamadan to Transoxania, including Kirman, Fars, and Seistan. Mamun's powers over this vast territory were greater than those of a governor or those accorded a prince of the blood on one of the royal visits sometimes used to stiffen state authority in one part or another of the empire. Army, treasury, taxes and tithes — Mamun saw to them all. Tax revenues were to be spent on the spot, not sent to Baghdad; administration, defence, and barid were under his exclusive control. The caliph had no right to send any official or inspector and could ask for no tribute; his authority was reduced to a vague receipt of obedience and fealty. The Arab empire of the Abbasids was still at its glorious peak; but this arrangement prefigured the concept of the caliph as a purely spiritual authority which was soon to prevail in Aghlabid, Idrisid, and Tahirid territories and later to spread to the rest of the empire.

Despite the solemnity of these ceremonies in Mecca, few people thought that the two princes would honour their undertakings. On leaving the Kaaba, Jaffar al-Barmaki is said to have approached Amin and made him repeat three times, "May God desert me if I betray my brother!" To contemporary observers, Harun's solution was notable mainly for its defects. The poets, as usual, gave elegant voice to public opinion:

The most perfect sovereign has been given the worst of advice: to sunder the caliphate and divide the land.
If the one who conceived this idea had reflected upon it, his hair would have turned snow-white.

And Masudi writes that a camel driver was heard humming the lines, "An election of broken promises; a conflagration of war awaits the flame..." Questioned on the meaning of these remarks, the man replied, "Swords will come out of their sheaths, discord and division will tear the empire apart." Although probably dreamed up long afterwards, these anecdotes describe the doubts and fears aroused by the oath at Mecca.

Three years later Harun decided to name another of his sons,

Qasim, third in line of succession. He gave him authority over northern Mesopotamia and the provinces to the south of Anatolia. The empire had been dismembered a little further.

The Well-Guided never gave his reasons for parcelling out the Abbasids' heritage in this way and returning to the pre-Islamic concept of the collective ownership of goods. Apart from the mediocrity of his son Amin, he had doubtless begun to understand how unwieldy his extremely centralized empire was. Governors were able to get away with excesses of all sorts. Closer supervision was needed; and it was sound policy to keep control in the hands of members of the royal family, especially in Khorasan, where Mansour had once been obliged to send his son Mahdi, giving him much power over the east. Perhaps Harun al-Rashid also believed that entrusting his sons with direct authority over the two halves of the empire would help to contain the centrifugal forces developing there.

As it happened, the division served only to increase the risk of open conflict. In truth, there was little that could be done to prevent it: the immense extent of the caliph's possessions, the conflicting interests of different provinces (masked but not diminished by the common religion), and the disappointments and resentments dating from the Abbasids' arrival in power all tended to disrupt the empire. The oath at the Kaaba may not have been the direct cause of the civil war that was soon to divide the Abbasid family and the Arabs; but it did nothing to prevent it.

The Tragedy of the Barmakids

> *Here then, O auspicious King, is that sorry tale which mars the reign of the Khalifah Harun al-Rashid with a bloodstain which not even the four rivers shall wash away.*
>
> **Thousand and One Nights**

Harun stayed in the holy city for several days more, making his devotions; then, in January 802 (Muharram 187), he set out with his court on the return journey to Raqqa. The caravan halted for a few days' rest at al-Umr, near Anbar. On the fourth day, recounts Tabari, the caliph summoned the Barmakids Yahya and his sons

Fadl, Jaffar, and Musa, and, "after discussing affairs of state with Yahya, presented them with robes of honour as if to contradict the rumours then current that they were in disgrace. This pleased them and they were greatly reassured."

Just a few hours later, there broke one of the bloodiest storms in the history of Islam:

At the hour of prayer Harun said to Jaffar: "I would not allow you to leave, but that I have a mind to spend the evening drinking among my slaves; go then and amuse yourself also among yours." And he went to his harem and began drinking. After a while he sent someone to see whether Jaffar was doing the same. On learning that Jaffar was sunk in melancholy he sent to him again saying: "It is absolutely essential, I swear on my head and my life, that you order a banquet and abandon yourself to enjoyment; for I will have no pleasure in my wine unless I know that you are drinking too." His heart troubled and heavy with fear, Jaffar ordered the banquet to be prepared. There was in his service a blind musician named Abu Zakkar. After drinking for a while he said to the musician: "My spirit tonight is beset with the most restless fears." Abu Zakkar replied: "O Vizier, never has the Prince of the Believers shown such benevolence towards you and your family as he did on this day." "But I am oppressed by sad forebodings," said Jaffar. "Have done with such foolishness," replied Abu Zakkar, "and give yourself up to pleasure." At about the time of evening prayer a servant came from Harun bringing Jaffar sweetmeats, dried fruits and perfumes. And at about the hour of the final prayer Harun sent more of them, and later a third time. The Caliph left the tent of his women at about midnight. He called Mesrur [Masrur] the eunuch and said to him: "Go immediately and find Jaffar, take him to your tent and cut off his head, then bring it to me." When he saw Mesrur, the Vizier Jaffar started trembling. "The Prince of the Faithful is calling for you," Mesrur said. Jaffar asked where the Caliph was. "He has just left his women," Mesrur replied, "and returned to his own tent." Jaffar said: "Let me go first into the tent of my women, to make arrangements." "That is not possible," said Mesrur. "Make your arrangements here." Jaffar did so and left with Mesrur, who drew his sword when they reached his own tent. Jaffar asked him what his orders were and Mesrur replied: "The Caliph has ordered me to take him your head." "Take care," said Jaffar, "it is possible he gave the order while in his cups, and may think better of it later." Recalling their former friendship, he begged Mesrur to go back to the Caliph, and Mesrur agreed. Harun, seated on his prayer carpet awaiting the eunuch, asked immediately: "Where is Jaffar's head?" "Prince of the Faithful," Mesrur replied, "I have brought Jaffar." "It was not Jaffar I wanted, but his head!" exclaimed the Caliph. Mesrur went straight back to where he had left Jaffar and cut his head off, then presented it to Harun, who said: "Keep the head and the body until I ask for them. Now go straight away and arrest Yahya, his three sons and his brother Mohammed, son of Khalid, and take them to the tent where you will load them down with chains. Then take possession of all their property." Mesrur carried out these orders. At daybreak Harun sent the head of Jaffar to Baghdad. The following day he set out for Raqqa.[10]

Jaffar's body and head were handed over to General Harthama and other officials, with orders from Harun to take them to Baghdad. The head was exposed on the Middle Bridge, the town's main street, and the body, cut into two pieces, on the Upper Bridge and the Lower Bridge. The grisly remains stayed there for two years until Harun had them taken down and burned.[11]

All the members of the Barmakid family were arrested, along with their clients and servants. Yahya was at first placed under house arrest but later joined Fadl in prison in Raqqa. He refused Harun's offer of house arrest in the place of his choice, saying he did not care where he lived, so long as he was not reconciled with the caliph. Treated sometimes well and sometimes harshly, Yahya died in prison in 805, when he was about seventy. Fadl, ill with hemiplegia, died in 808 at the age of forty-five, about the same age as Jaffar at his death. Harun is said to have had him tortured to force him to disclose the whereabouts of some of his own and his family's possessions; he was given twenty lashes and would have died then and there but for the devoted nursing of a fellow prisoner. He left these verses: "It is to God that we address our supplications in the hour of our misfortune, for He alone has the remedy for our sufferings and affliction. We have left this world, and yet we inhabit it still: we do not count ourselves among the dead, nor yet among the living."

Fadl's funeral was the occasion for a demonstration of sympathy with the Barmakids; Zubaidah attended it in person, along with the crown prince Amin and a large gathering of dignitaries. On hearing that he had died, Harun al-Rashid is supposed to have said, "My destiny is close to his!" Astrologers had predicted that he would follow his foster brother to the grave; and so it turned out.

Musa and Mohammed, Yahya's two surviving sons, stayed in prison until the accession of Amin, who set them free. The possessions of all members of the family in Baghdad, Raqqa, and elsewhere were confiscated, as were those of their relations, friends and servants. Zubaidah was arrested along with Dananir[12] (Yahya's famous freed slave singer) and other women slaves and concubines; but the children of Fadl, Jaffar, and Mohammed — and Yahya's mother and Fadl's mother — were spared. More than a thousand women, children, freed slaves, and followers of the Barmakids were killed. Their houses were ransacked and their possessions seized by the treasury.

The fall of the Barmakids and the brutal treatment of the family's leading members had an immediate and resounding effect in Baghdad and throughout the empire. Apart from their enemies, very few rejoiced. "Harun's conduct aroused general disapproval," writes Tabari soberly. "The memory of it will live on until the day of judgment, when it will not escape notice that the punishment inflicted on the Barmakids was not an act of political wisdom." Poets echoed the general emotion; they left a large number of eulogies which still survive, all expressing regret at the disappearance of such wise and generous men, whose names were associated with a vanished epoch:

Let us stop and rest our horses: there are no benefactors now, nor supplicants for their largesse. Tell Generosity: you died when Fadl died; and call to Adversity: come, flaunt yourself each day. *Achdja*

Fortune has cast down the sons of Barmak, leaving no one for us to love. All riches had they, none more worthily possessed; now they are gone, their riches are no more. *Achdja*

The sun of generosity has set, the hand of beneficence shrivelled, the tide ebbed in the ocean of munificence: the Barmakids are no more. This family's star, which showed the straight road to the guide of our caravan, no longer glimmers on the horizon. *Salm al- Kashir*

They who embellished the earth like a bride now leave it widowed. Jaffar was Vizier to God's chosen deputy on earth; he shone with wisdom, merit and glory. The whole world obeyed him, on land and on the surface of the seas. His genius ruled the empire and made his will respected everywhere... He had the world under his wing, and looked forward to an exceptionally long life until fortune dragged him into the abyss. May Heaven preserve us from a like disgrace. *Mansour Nemri*

The time of the Barmakids was quickly identified with the Abbasid golden age, which was later to be confused with the reign of Harun al-Rashid. In a famous passage, the *Thousand and One Nights* colours these years with nostalgia:

After that the Barmakids were an ornament for the brow of their century, and a crown upon its head. Destiny showered her most favourable gifts upon them, so that Yahya and his sons became bright stars, vast oceans of generosity, impetuous torrents of kindness, beneficent rains. The world lived at their breath, and under their hands the empire reached the pinnacle of its splendour. They were the refuge of the afflicted, the final resort of the comfortless. The poet Abu Nuwas said of them:

Since earth has put you away, O sons of Barmak,
The roads of morning twilight and evening twilight
Are empty. My heart is empty, O sons of Barmak.

They were admirable viziers, wise administrators, they filled the public treasure. They were strong, eloquent, and of good counsel; they surpassed everyone in learning; their generosity equalled the generosity of Hatim Taiy. They were rivers of happiness, they were good winds bringing up the fruitful clouds; it was through them that the name and the glory of Harun al-Rashid clanged from the flats of Central Asia to the northern forests, from Morocco and Andalusia to the farthest bounds of China and Tartary.

The renown of the Barmakids was still strong in the Orient several centuries later. The expression "time of the Barmakids" was long used there to signify "all that was good", "the highest degree of good fortune and abundance". Even as late as the seventeenth century Makkari, the historian of Spain, used the adjective *barmeki* to signify "that which was worthy of the time of the Barmakids".[13]

The disgrace and fall of the Barmakids has been the object of intense speculation for twelve centuries. Many explanations have been put forward for Harun's brutality to these men to whom he owed so much — one his "father", one his foster brother, and the third his closest friend. The whole family had served the Abbasids for three generations with competence and devotion. Harun himself never disclosed the reasons for their chastisement. When his sister Ulaiyah one day asked him why he had had Jaffar killed, he replied, "My child, my life, my one remaining happiness, how would it advantage you to know the reason? If I thought that my shirt knew, I would tear my shirt in pieces." On another occasion he said, "If I knew that my right hand knew the reason I would cut it off."

There is a good deal of evidence that more than a sudden fit of temper lay behind the execution of the man closest to Harun's heart. Djahiz[14] writes that an intimate of the caliph — probably Masrur the sword-bearer — recounted that in Mecca, "from close to al-Rashid, our garments touching as he held the cloths veiling the Kaaba," he had heard Harun "addressing the Lord directly: 'O God, I ask as a favour that Jaffar ibn Yahya may perish.'" There are many other indications that the decision was reached slowly over a period of years, probably under the influence of persons hostile to the Barmakids. "All those who had grievances against them watched their every move and reported their mistakes to the caliph, and these reports accumulated in his mind," Tabari writes. Long before their downfall, a climate of insecurity began to envelop them. One day, for example, the caliph scolded Yahya sharply for entering his presence without permission, although this was their established daily practice. On another occasion he complained to his doctor that Yahya was not consulting him on affairs of state but simply acting on his own authority. Fadl's responsibilities were withdrawn piecemeal over a long period; Jaffar became aware long before the tragedy that Harun's feelings for him had changed. All of this supports the conclusion that the Barmakids' disgrace was not the result of a potentate's whim but of a weighed decision Harun gradually reached regarding these men who had served him well but, inevitably, made decisions of which he did not approve and sometimes behaved as if he did not exist.

The popular imagination seized on the appalling manner of Jaffar's death and quickly invented romantic explanations arising more from sentiment than from accuracy. These were adopted by contemporary historians and have been echoed by writers and storytellers ever since.[15]

Both Tabari and Masudi tell us that Harun al-Rashid held his sister Abbasah in great affection and loved to spend his evenings in her company. But his favourite companion was Jaffar. It was quite unsuitable for a man from outside the family to be admitted to the company of a young woman, but Harun found a way to arrange things: he decided to marry them to each other but with the proviso, he explained to Jaffar, "that you see her only in my company, that your body never approaches hers and you have no conjugal relations with her. You may thus share our evenings of pleasure without risk." Jaffar accepted and swore solemnly before witnesses never to visit his young wife, stay alone with her, or even spend a minute under the same roof unless Harun was present. Thus, whenever Jaffar saw his wife, "he avoided looking at her and lowered his eyes."

Jaffar was handsome, however, and according to Tabari, "There was no woman in Harun's palace, either among the free-born or among the slaves, more beautiful than Abbasah." The inevitable occurred. The instrument of destiny was Jaffar's mother, Abbada, "a woman of small sense and restricted outlook". Abbasah showered her with presents and trinkets and then, realizing that Abbada could deny her nothing, persuaded her that Jaffar would gain a great advantage if he united himself with the daughter and sister of caliphs. Abbada told her son that she had come across an educated young slave, graceful and charming — "incomparable beauty, a ravishing figure" — whom she intended to buy him as a present. After keeping him waiting for a while, Abbasah arranged to be present one night when Jaffar went to see his mother. His head "still affected by the fumes of wine", he failed to recognize Abbasah until, the marriage consummated, she asked him archly what he thought of the wiles of royal princesses. "Who are you talking about?" "About me, the daughter of Mahdi." Jaffar was horrified. "You have thrown me away for nothing and brought me to the edge of the abyss," he told his mother.

Abbasah was pregnant and gave birth to a son, who was whisked to Mecca in the care of a eunuch and a maidservant. Nothing might have come of the matter had Zubaidah not learned of it. Complaining to Harun one day that Yahya al-Barmaki, as steward to the caliph, was officiously locking the doors of all palace apartments every evening, she added, "If he really looked after the harem, he would have prevented his son from committing a crime!" Pressed to explain, the caliph's wife told the whole story, including the existence of the child. In Mecca soon afterwards, Harun had the child tracked down, then did away with both him and his sister.

In another version,[16] Abbasah organizes a series of great feasts for Harun in a garden beside the Tigris. On the first night she sends a beautiful slave to Harun and another to Jaffar, then another pair on the second night, and so on, until she substitutes herself for Jaffar's slave. According to this version the couple had two children, Hasan and Husein, aged ten and eight respectively when the drama of al-Umr took place. (Harun spared their lives.) A eunuch of Zubaidah's household, however, claimed that Harun punished his sister by having her nailed up in a chest with all her jewels, and then had the chest buried in a trench under a mass of bricks and rubble. Her steward and ten servants were massacred and her children thrown into a furnace as Harun cried, "Better steel than shame!" Their executioners, Masrur's henchmen, were said to have been sewn into sacks and thrown into the Tigris.

Romantic notion, bazaar rumour, or truth? Masudi and Tabari give credence to the tragic story of the two beautiful lovers, but ibn Khaldun[17] suggests that Harun would never have given the princess Abbasah in marriage — even an unconsummated one — to Jaffar, whose ancestors had been Persians and idolators. Most modern historians are sceptical, pointing out that the sources for this story are too late for credibility. If this is accepted, however, doubt must be cast on everything reported by Masudi, Tabari, and the other leading chroniclers of the period. What we find

unconvincing today is mainly the improbable character of the story
— its moralizing, tales-from-the-Orient flavour, the nature of the
punishment of the guilty — and all the wonderful details
embroidered into it over time. Nor should we forget that Abbasah,
older than Hadi and Harun, was nearly forty and had already been
married twice. It is difficult to imagine this woman, well past her
first youth, inventing naive and tortuous stratagems to inveigle into
her bed a handsome man who would have had to be completely
drunk to fail to recognize her. Just as Harun would have had to be
extremely myopic — something of which history makes no mention
— to fail to notice the pregnancy of his sister, whom he saw
frequently. Perhaps the origins of this marvellous and frightful story
should be sought in a different kind of sentimental episode involving
Jaffar, through a transposition of male to female.[18]

What, then, were the reasons behind Jaffar's execution, a deed
that arouses strong emotion in Arabs down the long centuries?
Jaffar, it had been asserted, was a Muslim only in appearance; he
built mosques for his own amusement and found readings from the
Koran infinitely tedious. In his heart of hearts, he remained a
Mazdaean.[19] Supporters of this view cite in evidence his alleged
advice to Harun al-Rashid to burn incense in the Kaaba day and
night, as if he wished to turn it into a temple of fire. How lukewarm
were his Muslim convictions showed also, it was claimed, in his
tolerance of Alids, heretics, and other enemies of orthodox Islam.
He was accused of arranging the release of Yahya ibn Abdallah, the
Alid rebel leader in Daylam.

This explanation too is unconvincing. It was Fadl who settled
the Daylam rebellion (and suffered Harun's reproaches). Jaffar, on
the contrary, may have ordered the execution of another Alid,
Abdallah ibn Hasan, against the caliph's orders. He was also accused
of drawing a large sum from the treasury on behalf of an Abbasid,
Abd al-Malik ibn Salih, whom Harun suspected of wishing to
dethrone him. The ever-watchful caliph is said to have been furious.

Jaffar's wealth and extremely luxurious lifestyle, exhibited in the
palace he had built overlooking the Tigris, irritated Harun. There
are a number of stories about the caliph's resentment of Jaffar's
ostentation. Out hunting one day with a large, splendid entourage,
Harun asked, "Has there ever been so sumptuous a train?" "Nothing
can compare with Jaffar's," answered a tactless courtier... As the

procession passed villages that had lavish pavilions set among magnificent gardens, the caliph wondered aloud to whom they belonged. "Why, to the Barmakids, of course," came the reply. Harun then said, "We played ourselves false by doing so much to augment the power and opulence of these Barmakids. Look at them now, at the pinnacle of grandeur! Who could ever estimate their riches?"[20]

Probably more decisive than the caliph's occasional fits of jealousy and irritation — which in any case may have been invented long afterwards — was the chamberlain Fadl ibn al-Rabi's hostility towards Jaffar. The two men detested each other. Jaffar was an obstacle to Fadl's ambition and knew that the chamberlain would stop at nothing to destroy him. Fadl nurtured in Harun's mind a feeling of distrust towards Jaffar, then fanned it into hatred. Opposition to the Barmakids crystallized around him.

Fadl ibn al-Rabi was not alone in his hatred of Jaffar and his family. The handsome favourite's pride and often insolent manners had earned him some formidable enemies. Zubaidah, for example, had never much liked the caliph's intimate friend, who, apart from his other faults, was "tutor" to Mamun, her son's rival. It was known throughout the palace that Harun admired Mamun's gifts and was thinking of promoting him over Amin in the order of succession. The new arrangements made in Mecca did little to settle matters or calm Zubaidah's anxieties. There is every reason to suppose that in the last few weeks before the drama her considerable influence was probably exercised against Jaffar.

Harun's relations with Fadl al-Barmaki were of an altogether different character. The caliph respected the ability of the oldest of the two Barmakids but felt little sympathy for him. Fadl had twice been governor of Khorasan and each time had succeeded admirably. As capable in military matters as in politics and administration, he was envied for his success, not least by his brother Jaffar (who denigrated him in front of the caliph). Other high dignitaries were jealous of the popularity he had won despite his cold manner and vanity.

Fadl al-Barmaki also showed himself to be very tolerant of the Alids; like Jaffar, he was blamed for letting Yahya ibn Abdallah go free. He may have disobeyed the caliph by saving the life of Musa al-Kazim (not for long, however; his father, Yahya, later did away with Musa, doubtless on Harun's orders). The caliph also complained of Fadl's indulgence towards another Alid, the Hasanid ibn Tabataba. Despite his unlimited power, Harun was seized by a kind of panic whenever he imagined the possibility of rebellion. Fadl, on the other hand, believed it wiser to leave the Alids in peace, as they were not actually a threat. Accused of weakness in dealing with the caliph's enemies, on bad terms with his own brother and almost every high dignitary outside the Barmakid group (Fadl ibn al-Rabi leading the pack), Fadl al-Barmaki was the first to be relieved of his functions by Harun. He kept only the post of tutor to the crown prince Amin.

As for Yahya, by the time Harun brutally terminated his family's "reign", his very existence had become an affront to the caliph. From being his entirely trusted guardian angel during the early years of Harun's reign, Yahya had become first a tiresome mentor, then an obstacle. Very different from the caliph in character and temperament, favouring flexibility and conciliation where the other leaned towards impulsive, often brutal decisions, the old man gradually became an intolerable burden to the maturing Harun. It was probably inevitable that an anxious sovereign, jealous of his prerogatives, would dismiss such a man sooner or later. Harun was far from stupid and could surely see that the real danger lay in his loss of power, leaving him eventually with only the trappings of sovereignty. Several historians quote the story told by Harun's doctor, Jibril, who was in the palace one day when a distant murmur was heard. Harun asked what it was and someone replied, "It is Yahya sitting in judgment on cases of abuse." "May God bless and reward him!" exclaimed the caliph. "He has relieved me of this burden and is my substitute." When the same thing happened several years later, Harun said, "May God strike him with misfortune! He deals with business entirely as he sees fit, ignores my opinions and follows his own inclinations rather than mine." Zubaidah was present and seized the opportunity to launch a savage attack on Yahya.[21]

Yahya certainly had no ambition to supplant Harun, although he has been accused of it. But might not he or one of his sons, or even another member of his family, sooner or later become involved in an intrigue to replace Harun with another Abbasid, or even (confirming Harun's worst fears) with an Alid? From the viewpoint of the Commander of the Faithful, the destruction of the Barmakids can be seen as a logical and inevitable sequel to the decisions taken at Mecca. Would the division of the empire be possible if the Barmakids remained in power? The tragedy of al-Umr should perhaps be seen in the context of the succession problem and not as the outcome of a struggle between Arab and Iranian influences.

The Barmakids came from Khorasan, but their roots were Buddhist, not Zoroastrian; they do not appear to have been overenthusiastic about spreading Persian culture and influence. Their tolerance for the Alids — who were Arabs, not Iranians — had nothing to do with their origins. There was no shame in coming from Khorasan, where the Abbasid revolution began: its people were one of the regime's firmest supports. The Barmakids were wholly assimilated into Arab culture, even if, like everyone else at the time, they were receptive to Iranian influences in everything from philosophic doctrines to cookery and sartorial fashion. Of all the complaints Harun made about them, not one had to do with their Iranian background.

The Barmakids' many descendants had diverse fortunes. Those who had been spared or managed to hide resumed normal life when Mamun became caliph. Mohammed ibn Yahya and Abbas ibn Fahd were both made governors, one of Basra and the other of Khorasan. Musa was governor of Sind, and his son Imran later governed the same province. Musa's grandson Abd al-Hasan, a poet and historian, was a nadim of the caliph Muktadir. Among other illustrious descendants of the family we can list the celebrated biographer ibn Khallikan (a descendant of Jaffar who died at Damascus in 1282), as well as a vizier of the Samanids, an ambassador of the Ghaznevids, and a jurist in tenth-century Spain. Men were sometimes called "al-Barmaki" because they were descendants of followers of the great family. Certain peoples have claimed descent from the Barmakids — for example, the Boramik (Bormata) who settled first in Tripolitania, then in the Touat. Finally, Gerard de Nerval writes at length in his *Voyage en Orient* about some female dancers, the Chawasies, who claim to be called Baramikeh (Bormeke) and to be descended from the Barmakids.

5
Harun and the Outside World

Charlemagne's relations with Aaron king of Persia, who ruled all of the Orient except India, were so cordial that the latter placed more value on Charlemagne's friendship than on that of all the kings and princes in the rest of the world.

Eginhard

You shall surely conquer Constantinople. Excellent indeed shall be the army and the amir who take possession of it.

Mohammed (Hadith)

The closest world to the Arabs, and the only one with which they maintained relations, was the world centred on the Mediterranean. Foreign policy — to the extent that it existed at all — was directed towards the countries washed by this sea. For the Caliph of the Faithful was so powerful, his possessions extended so far, and he had such contempt for all that did not belong to *dar al-islam* ("the land of Islam") that foreign sovereigns in his eyes were no more than vassals from whose ambassadors he would occasionally, under exceptional circumstances, deign to receive homage.

Foremost among these countries was Byzantium. The Mediterranean was no longer a "Byzantine sea". All its oriental and north African possessions had been seized by the Arabs; its dominion over Italy was fading into memory; and in the north the Slavs had long ago crossed the Danube and were battering at the walls of Constantinople. For centuries the fate of Byzantium hung on the refusal of its enemies to work together, on its technical superiority ("Greek fire"), and on its series of exceptional personalities who always appeared just as all seemed lost, to save once again the legacy of Constantine and Justinian.

So it was in the eighth century. Seven emperors were proclaimed and overthrown, one after another. Two of Justinian II's ministers were burned alive. Disaster followed disaster. Revolts and insurrections broke out on all sides. The empire awaited a saviour, and he appeared in the form of Leo III the Isaurian, the "strategist" (one who holds supreme military and civil power), from Anatolia. Rising against the emperor, Leo III was soon acclaimed by the senate, the army, and the people.

The new emperor's first task was to stop the Arab advance. He managed this through a cunning intrigue with Maslama, a general at the head of a powerful army sent against Byzantium by the Umayyad caliph. The siege of Constantinople was lifted, but attacks began again a few years later. The Muslims even reached Nicaea, not far from the capital. The city protected by God seemed indeed to be the one Islam meant to conquer.

However, the issue that dominated the reign of Leo III and that of his son Constantine was the quarrel they started over religious images. Were the reasons religious or political? Did the emperors want to curb the growth of the landed wealth of monasteries and at the same time reduce the number of monks? Probably Leo III and his dynasty, with their Oriental background, were influenced by Jews and Muslims, to whom the use of images was forbidden. Citing the Arab peril, Leo III ordered the destruction of a statue of Christ, greatly venerated, which stood over the imperial palace in Constantinople. The mob rose in fury and iconoclasm became a violent issue — another step towards the break with the papacy and the dismemberment of the Roman empire (to the profit of the Frankish kingdom, whose power was dawning in the West).

No pope recognized the iconoclast doctrine. Gregory II decreed excommunication for any person accepting the authority of the basileus. Leo III responded immediately by ordering that Illyricum (Dalmatia, virtually the whole of the Balkan peninsula, Sicily, and Calabria) be separated from the Roman patriarchate and joined to Constantinople. The division of Italy and the empire was complete. Soon afterwards the pope placed himself under the protection of the Frankish king Pippin, who in 754 promised Stephen II that he would "take up the cause of the Blessed Peter and of the Roman republic". The basileus had hoped to unify the Byzantine empire but had not been able to prevent the emergence of a rival. Less than half a century later in Rome, Charlemagne was crowned Emperor of the West. After a long eclipse and invasions by the barbarians, the West was about to force its way onto the cramped world stage.

At the eastern end of the Mediterranean an empire in crisis but still large and powerful; in Europe another empire beginning to form; in the far west the emirate of Cordoba, western successor to the caliphate of Damascus, where the last of the Umayyads had established a power admired even by its enemies... what other states would the Abbasids meet in pursuit of their diplomacy and commerce?

Only those at great distances could be compared with theirs. Japan was at one of the high points of its history. The Nara epoch was unifying the country and opening it to the sea, but its exchanges were limited essentially to the Far Eastern world. In China the Tang dynasty, beset by uprisings and revolutions, vacillated between anarchy and absolutism. After their defeat at Talas in 751, the Chinese left Central Asia for good. China's loss of this last chance to influence the destiny of countries between the Tien-Chan and the Mediterranean helped determine the future of the Middle East and perhaps that of Europe.

The Turkic tribes maintained and strengthened their position — Oghuz westwards, Karluk towards Lake Balkach. An Uygur khanate of Manichaean religion prospered in northern Mongolia, then settled in the oases of the Tarim. The Khazars came to rest on the steppes between the Urals and the Don, where some converted to Judaism; they extended their influence to the north, and the Byzantine emperor used them against the Arabs.

In northern Europe, Scandinavian and Anglo-Saxon princes — the Heptarchy — were beginning to exchange their products for those of the Mediterranean and the Orient. They used eastern routes (Kiev, the Russian rivers, Maiz) and western routes (the Rhone valley, the Meuse, the Baltic ports). Within a few years, exchange between the Islamic world and northern and western Europe expanded from a trickle to a great river, while relations with south-east Asia and the islands of the Indian Ocean also became more common. In all these countries, especially in India, where powerful dynasties reigned, merchants travelled from place to place, and they passed on their knowledge of distant lands. Once established, the Abbasid empire underwent prodigious economic development. Like that of Europe in the fifteenth and sixteenth centuries, Islam's Renaissance was a time of encounters.

The Commander of the Faithful and Charlemagne

At a time when the hearts and minds of men were afire with religion, would the battle between Christ's faithful and the Muslims be pursued everywhere, unceasingly, with neither side distracted by other considerations? Certainly not. Wars were being waged increasingly for political reasons. Diplomatic relations were carefully maintained and alliances formed wherever an advantage could be seen. The Byzantines were willing to support the Umayyads of Spain against the Abbasids, who themselves used any and every means in the effort to overthrow the regime founded in Spain by the offspring of the hated Umayyads. The Frankish kingdom, which supported the pope in his conflict with the basileus of Byzantium, looked with favour upon any defeat the basileus might suffer at the hands of his great Abbasid enemy, whose troops gnawed periodically at the frontier like the tide of a restless sea. Carolingians and Abbasids shared an interest in struggling against the Spanish Umayyads. Pippin had taken the pope's side against the basileus in the quarrel about images and so found himself a virtual ally of the caliph. Above all, the raid on Poitiers (732) was still remembered; the Arabs had not been driven out of Narbonne until 751. Some collaboration between the Franks and the Abbasids was therefore only to be expected.[1]

The Franco–Abbasid "collaboration" started around 765 with an exchange of diplomatic missions between the two sovereigns Pippin the Brief and Mansour. In that year, the Carolingian monarch sent ambassadors to Baghdad, who returned accompanied by the caliph's own ambassadors bearing "sumptuous presents" for Pippin. According to chroniclers, Mansour's envoys were respectfully received by Pippin at Metz and returned home by sea loaded with new gifts: "... the diplomatic mission of 765 to Baghdad served to complete a circle of alliances ranging the Pope, the Abbasid Khalifah and the King of the Franks against the Umayyads and Constantinople."[2] *Alliances?* The word is surely an exaggeration. It would perhaps be more accurate to say that following the principle "my enemy's enemy is my friend", the three heads of state had established a community of interest which would lead them to support one another under certain circumstances. Did Mansour, then, recognize Pippin's sovereignty over Zaragoza and Barcelona? The governor of the latter had become a vassal of Pippin, probably in 752. Even before the Umayyads arrived in Spain, the Carolingians were looking towards the peninsula. It was quite logical, given the right circumstances, for the Abbasids to use the Frankish interest in the countries south of the Pyrenees against the Umayyad usurper. That was probably all there was to it. But such mutual recognition by two states so remote from each other in every way was remarkable in itself.

, Pippin died in Saint-Denis on 24 September 768, and was entombed in the abbey in accordance with his wishes. A few days earlier he had divided the empire between his two sons, Charles and Carloman. Charles was given the north and the west of the kingdom, Carloman the southeast. Charles was crowned at Noyon, his brother at Soissons. The arrangement did not last long. Fate intervened and Carloman died three years later; his followers rallied round Charles, the future Charlemagne, "the living expression of the final success of a fusion between the Roman, Gallic and Germanic elements of what was to become Europe".[3] It was as a Christian — and European — emperor that a few years later he revived the "Oriental policy" outlined by his father.

Several years passed before the young king could give his full attention to such distant horizons and the complicated policy they demanded. The Italian question and the conquest of Saxony were of far more immediate concern. He settled the first problem by sending away his wife, daughter of Didier, king of the Lombards, and then defeating Didier in battle. He used the title "King of the Romans", which had been conferred on his father, as a pretext to intervene in the affairs of the papacy. Later he had his son Pippin crowned king of Italy, which became in large part a dependency of the Frankish kingdom.

With the Saxons, Charles largely eschewed policy in favour of force, sometimes brutal. Slowly and methodically, he set about making a conquest. Pacification of Saxony was not achieved until 804, but most of the elders and a large part of the people submitted at Paderborn in 777.

In the same year, probably coincidentally, the governor of Zaragoza, Suleiman ibn al-Arabi, arrived in Aix-la-Chapelle; in revolt against the emir of Cordoba, he had come to persuade the Frankish king to mount an expedition to northern Spain. Charles crossed the Pyrenees at the head of two armies in the spring of 778. But al-Arabi's promised support did not materialize, and the expedition was disastrous. Charles did not manage to take Zaragoza; during the retreat, the entire Frankish rearguard was massacred in the defile of Roncevalles.

It was a hard lesson for Charles. Expeditions across the Pyrenees seemed to be more difficult than he had thought. The local population of booty-hungry montagnards were not very reliable. Worse still, alliances with Muslim chiefs seemed fragile, almost always dependent on the ever-changing relations between the chieftains themselves. The people hated the idea of joining forces with an infidel sovereign against fellow Muslims. Charles gave up the idea of adding to his possessions south of the Pyrenees. Better for the security of his kingdom would be to establish along the frontier a buffer state, equipped with substantial military forces, which could stop the Arabs if they tried to advance northward. This was the kingdom of Aquitaine, on whose throne Charles placed his son Louis (later known as Louis the Pious).

Years passed. Charles had become prudent; when Gerona, a Frankish possession, was taken by the Arabs, he did nothing to get it back. He made no answer to the appeals of the governor of Barcelona, despite assurances that the town would surrender to him without a fight, but limited himself to mounting a more modest operation in the region north of the town. It was at this time that he decided to send a mission to Baghdad to the Commander of the Faithful, Harun al-Rashid.

Charles's First Mission to Harun

The caliph was then at the summit of his glory. News of his splendour and of the prosperity of his empire reached across the seas. Everyone knew that as a young prince he had led an expedition as far as the Bosphorus. Every year his armies penetrated deep into the territories of the basileus. Charles knew this, and knew also that despite the scandals and weaknesses of the Byzantine court and the menaces that assailed its leaders on all sides, the emperor of Byzantium was his only great rival. The Frankish king had been irritated by Greek intrigues in Italy; he was indignant about events in Constantinople, where power was in the hands of a woman who had put out the eyes of her own son. The papacy was held by Leo III, a weak and discredited man accused of degrading acts (Charles had written exhorting him to "live decently"). In this troubled situation the Emperor of the West and the Caliph of Baghdad were the two pillars of the world. It was quite natural for Charles to want, if not an alliance with Harun, at least an established relationship giving insight into the caliph's opinions and intentions.

Charles's plenipotentiaries were probably given specific instructions, but no details have survived, so that we can do little more than discern their broad lines in the general context of the two monarchs' policies.

The question of Spain was certainly one on which Charles would have desired clarification. The Franks had long been worried by the Muslim presence in the peninsula. Charles had not forgotten his defeat there, and in recent years his troops and those of the kingdom of Aquitaine had again been operating in Spain. The Abbasids for their part may have given up hope of overthrowing the Spanish Umayyads, but they considered themselves in a permanent state of war with the usurper emir. To the extent that distance permitted, Baghdad kept an eye on events in Cordoba. Since enemies of Abderahman I and his successors could hardly escape being friends of the caliph, the Abbasids had friends among the Arab chieftains in Spain who might be inclined to collaborate with Charles against the Umayyads.

Charles's relations with Byzantium were naturally more subtle. Aix-la-Chapelle and Constantinople, the two Christian powers, were engaged in a struggle for imperial supremacy. The pope was soon to place the crown of Rome on Charles's head, which was to create tension between those empires. The Frankish mission left for Baghdad only three years before that crucial event, the coronation of 25 December 800. The state of relations between the basileus and the caliph was certainly not a matter of indifference to Charles. Nor was he unaware that the caliph had every interest in accentuating divergences between the two great Christian states.

Finally there was Jerusalem, holy city of the Christians, with its churches of the Holy Sepulchre and St Mary of Calvary; the basilica raised on the spot where Helena, mother of the emperor Constantine, had found the True Cross; and the Church of the

Ascension at the summit of the Mount of Olives, from which Christ ascended into Heaven. Pious foundations, convents, and monasteries filled the city, housing a swarming clergy — mainly Greek but also Latin — governed by the prestigious patriarch, the third most powerful and respected title of Christendom (after the pope and the patriarch of Constantinople). Christians poured into Jerusalem from all over Europe. Sacred to Muslims as well as to Christians, it was a town where pilgrims could perform their devotions peacefully, except for the kinds of incidents which occur in all places of pilgrimage and are the doing of vagabonds and thieves.

Just as Charles was about to send his envoys to Baghdad, disquieting news reached Aix-la-Chapelle. Some Bedouins, whom the Muslim authorities had evidently treated laxly, had raided Jerusalem, pillaging Christian communities and killing eighteen monks. Despite personal excesses, Charles was a very pious man and this news upset him. He instructed his envoys to discuss the matter with the caliph and urge him to curb misdeeds of this sort. He also charged them with winning the favour of Muslim princes and with distributing money to needy Christians, in Egypt and north Africa, as well as in Syria and Jerusalem.

A great deal has been written about the famous elephant brought back by the envoys, a present to Charles from Harun al-Rashid. Some historians have even suggested that the sole purpose of the Frankish mission was to enhance the imperial menagerie with this fabulous animal. But the great king of the Franks had many other reasons for sending ambassadors to the caliph. It is more likely that Harun made the gift spontaneously to show friendship for Charles and emphasize the exceptional importance he accorded both to Charles personally and to his state.[4]

For his mission to the Orient, which left towards the end of 797, Charles had chosen two laymen, Lantfried and Sigismond (probably an interpreter), and an Israelite named Isaac. The route to the Orient at that time was by sea to Egypt, then overland to Jerusalem and Syria; or by sea to Beirut or Antioch, then overland via Aleppo and along the Euphrates to Raqqa and Baghdad. The Frankish envoys appear to have taken the latter route.

Isaac returned alone three years later, the only survivor of this long, arduous journey; Lantfried and Sigismond had perished, probably on the way home.[5] It was thus the Israelite who brought back Harun al-Rashid's handsome gift, the elephant Abulabbas. Arriving with his cumbersome companion on the African coast, Isaac sent to Charles asking for a ship to transport him. Charles dispatched the notary Ercibald (Ercanbald) to help on the journey back to the Rhineland. Abulabbas was landed at Porto Venere in Liguria in October 801, wintered in Vercelli, and on 20 July 802 entered Aix-la-Chapelle in the presence of the emperor, to the sort of popular reception one would expect. Charles gave a personal audience to Isaac, "an unheard-of honour for a Jew of that time".[6] Abulabbas died in 810.

Between the departure of Charles's three envoys and Isaac's return, several things had happened which affected relations with the Orient. Towards the end of 799 a monk arrived in Aix-la-Chapelle who had been sent by George, patriarch of Jerusalem. He carried relics from the Holy Sepulchre as a gift to the emperor to thank him for the dispatch of the three envoys to the Holy City and for the alms they had brought. Charles sent the monk back a few weeks later in the company of Zachary, a priest from the palace, bearing gifts for the holy places. Zachary returned with two monks whom George had sent to Charles from Jerusalem — a Greek from Saint-Saba and a Latin from the Mount of Olives. Charles received them on 23 December 800, two days before his coronation in Rome; they brought him "the keys of the Holy Sepulchre and those of the City and the Mountain [Mount Sion] with the holy standard".[7] The emperor kept the two monks by him for a while and sent them back to Jerusalem the following April.

Contemporary annalists and later historians have read more meaning into the gesture of the keys than they actually had. Handing over the keys of a city was even then a routine ceremony. Popes had long before established the custom of giving small "keys of St Peter's" to people they wished to honour; those of the Holy Sepulchre and Mount Sion were undoubtedly offered in this spirit. The Holy Standard was almost certainly a finely wrought gold casket containing a few pieces of the True Cross.[8] These presents gave proof of the Jerusalem clergy's gratitude to Charlemagne, not just for his gifts of money, but probably also for his ambassadors' present and future efforts on behalf of Oriental Christians. The keys were thus purely symbolic. In any case, they did not (as some have maintained) make Charles governor of Jerusalem, any more than they made him a vassal of the caliph, who in all likelihood never heard that they had been sent.

Muslims at Charles's Court

More significant than the presents from the clergy of Jerusalem or the elephant Abulabbas was the arrival, at the same time as Isaac, of two Muslim dignitaries. One was a member of Harun al-Rashid's entourage; the other came from the emir of Kairouan, Ibrahim ibn Aghlab — the most powerful emir in north Africa — whose role in Ifriqiya will be recalled. Ibrahim had not sent his representative to the great Western sovereign on a mere whim; he wanted to initiate formal relations with someone who, from across the Mediterranean, looked very much like the man of the new era.

Charles received the two ambassadors near Vercelli in northern Italy. They brought him presents from the caliph and the emir: several monkeys, balm, spikenard, assorted unguents, spices, various perfumes, and every sort of medicine "in such quantity," wrote Notker, the monk of Saint-Gall,[9] "that they seemed to have emptied the East and emptied the West." All the signs were that Harun's mission was in response to the one sent by Charles in 797 and indicated that the approach was welcomed. It was one of those moments that decide the destiny of empires. The papacy and the Eastern empire were in a state of extreme crisis. Charlemagne's coronation aroused fears in Byzantium that the all-powerful emperor might decide to march on Constantinople and drive the usurping Irene from the throne of the Caesars. Harun, who, like all the great sovereigns of Islam, dreamed of one day taking Constantinople himself, was especially interested in Charles's plans: was he going to marry Irene or send his armies against her? We do not know what Charles said to the two ambassadors or what message they brought him. Did they have proposals for the Emperor of the West from Harun and Ibrahim? No record has survived.

Given the political context, however, there is every reason to believe that the future of the Eastern empire of Christendom ranked high among the concerns of the caliph, whose military preparations on the frontier were continuing. Ibrahim, also a neighbour of Byzantium (with which he shared a maritime frontier), was extremely interested in Byzantine affairs. His ambition was apparent; less than three decades later his successors landed in Sicily — a

Byzantine possession — and in southern Italy. For the moment the Aghlabid emir was watching, learning, and preparing. And there was Spain, on which Charles, Harun, and Ibrahim had thoughts, certainly had information, and probably had designs. This double diplomatic mission sent by Harun and Ibrahim deserves more attention than it is usually given.

The two Muslim envoys spent a few months at Charlemagne's court, stupefied (according to the monk of Saint-Gall) by the splendours they witnessed. They attended the religious service in the cathedral on Easter day, after which the emperor did them the unusual honour of inviting them to his table, where "the extraordinary things they had seen took away their appetites". They left before the end of 802.

Second Frankish Mission

At the end of 802, only weeks or at most months after the Muslim envoys' departure, Charlemagne sent another embassy to Harun. This second mission was entrusted to one Radbert, probably a court dignitary. The *Annals of the Kingdom* tell us nothing about his journey or his stay in Iraq, except that Radbert and his companions had the good fortune to pass unrecognized through the Greek fleet that was attempting to conquer Dalmatia under the command of the patrician Nicetas.

Radbert died so soon after his return to Italy that he was unable to give a proper account of his embassy. But two other missions arrived with him: one from Harun al-Rashid, headed by a certain Abdallah; the other from Thomas, who had succeeded George as patriarch of Jerusalem. Thomas's mission was composed of two monks, Felix and George, the latter of German origin and abbot of the community on the Mount of Olives. They brought the emperor the new patriarch's letters of enthronement and a request for subsidies for the upkeep of Christian communities in the Holy Land. Abdallah, by way of contrast, was loaded down with magnificent presents from Harun: a tent with multicoloured linen hangings of great beauty, many bolts of silk fabrics, perfumes, oils, balm, two grand candelabra of gilded bronze, and, most wonderful of all, a clock, also of gilded bronze, which "left all who beheld it wholly stupefied."[10]

The Jerusalem religious mission was in no way out of the

ordinary. Abdallah's embassy, on the other hand, was most unusual, as Harun's earlier mission had been. It was probably Abdallah who confirmed for Charlemagne the granting of concessions that he had requested — or that Harun had proposed — during their earlier contacts. The only text to be trusted on this matter is that of the *Annales Regni Francorum*. Eginhard, in his *Vita Caroli*, blends the various exchanges in such a way that from his account it is impossible to identify the concessions granted to Charles by the caliph or to date them. Charlemagne's historian writes briefly that "not only did the caliph, once aware of Charlemagne's desires, grant him all that he asked, but he also placed in his power the sacred place whence the salvation of mankind had come" or, in other words, "the very Holy Sepulchre of our Lord and Saviour and the place of His resurrection." Writing his *Gesta Caroli* some sixty years later, the monk of Saint-Gall invented a speech of Harun al-Rashid to Charlemagne's ambassadors in which the caliph affirms that he is placing the promised land in Charles's power and that he himself will administer it as the emperor's "attorney".

These short passages from the two chroniclers have led modern historians to believe that Harun granted Charles a "protectorate" over Palestine. Without entering here into any detail on this controversy,[11] we can hardly doubt that the word "protectorate" is an anachronism. The notion of a protectorate was unknown in either Western or Oriental law in the ninth century; nor does it correspond to the reality of the case. What is the meaning of the Holy Sepulchre's being placed in Charles's power? No doubt Harun granted him "power" — but what power exactly? — over the precise spot where Christ was buried, the tomb itself: "the place where the Lord was laid, wrapped in bandages, and which Arculfe measured with his own hand as being seven feet long... and whose area taken all together might serve as a bed for a man lying on his back."[12]

Nothing in the surviving Western texts supports anything beyond this interpretation. Over the tomb itself — nothing more — the caliph may have granted some power to the Emperor of the West. Did this power extend to the rest of the building, the Church of the Holy Sepulchre? Whatever Harun's political interest in satisfying Charles's wishes, it is unlikely that the caliph could have gone beyond very limited, even symbolic, concessions. We know that Harun was extremely attached to his religion, which had served as a pretext for driving out the Umayyads and justified, in a sense, the reign of his dynasty over the Muslim state and the community of the faithful. The power of the Commander of the Faithful was politically absolute but limited by strict observance of Islam, more so perhaps during the century of the first Abbasids than at any other period. To hand over to an infidel sovereign a building containing the tomb of his God — albeit an empty tomb — would therefore have been dangerous: one obvious risk, among others, would have been that the Alids would exploit what might be considered a religious violation. Fearful and anxious, and often with good reason, Harun was not a man to take chances of that sort. It is most unlikely that Harun offered Charles a protectorate over Palestine, and no text seems to confirm it.

Thus the "gift" of Christ's tomb, which itself can hardly be doubted despite the absence of confirmation from Arabic texts, was essentially symbolic. But in Charles's eyes and in the eyes of all Christians, the tomb of the Saviour had inestimable value; the idea, however fictitious, that it had become Charlemagne's "property" could only excite the imaginations of men and women who dreamed of going to pray in Jerusalem. Charles's prestige has profited from it down the centuries. It became part of his legend. Apart from the (wholly invented) stories of the monk of Saint-Gall, an imaginary journey to the Orient by Charlemagne was described, complete with the emperor's arrival in Jerusalem, Harun's gift of manger and sepulchre, and Charlemagne's return with the body of St Andrew. A twelfth-century poem, "Charlemagne's Journey in the Orient", depicts the emperor's progress in driving pagans from the Holy City at the head of an army of pilgrims. By such means Charlemagne was transformed into the first Crusader — a role that everyone, until the end of the Middle Ages, believed was his.

Apart from the symbolic gift of the sepulchre, the Muslims probably granted Charlemagne the right to "protect" religious establishments in Jerusalem by extending, maintaining, and restoring their buildings and by helping pilgrims with their travel and living arrangements. Stories of the period hint at the presence in the Holy City of seventeen nuns of Frankish origin. Charles's subsidies, it seems, were used to build a hostelry, a market, and a library for the use of pilgrims. The emperor may have subsidized the purchase of vineyards and gardens in the valley of Josaphat, and legend has it that he bought the "Field of Blood" in which Judas was supposed to have invested his thirty pieces of silver.

Through these diplomatic contacts, Charlemagne may well have helped to improve the situation of Christians living in Muslim-dominated countries. Following Harun's death in 809, the empire underwent a period of disorder, lasting nearly ten years, during which Christians endured the tribulations suffered by all minorities in troubled times.[13] Afterwards their life returned to normal, with only temporary difficulties occasioned by local conditions or the "peculiarities" of certain officials. Of the concessions granted by Harun to Charlemagne, there remained essentially the buildings and restorations to which his subsidies had contributed; probably for a certain length of time an increase in the number of Frankish clergy in the Holy Land; and a tradition that lasted long after the two great emperors.

Less than two years after the visit of Abdallah and his companions to Charlemagne's court, Harun al-Rashid died in Khorasan. Did Abdallah arrive in time to give an account of his discussions with Charlemagne, or had the caliph already left Raqqa by the time his ambassador returned? No Arabic text makes any mention of Harun's relations with the Emperor of the West. The caliph's death and the subsequent civil war interrupted the exchange of diplomatic missions, and the upheavals that followed in the Abbasid empire created a new situation. Harun's successors, Amin and Mamun, were not interested in foreign affairs;[14] the war with Byzantium ended, despite a last campaign by Mamun shortly before his own death. Charlemagne had died in 814.

It is always risky to try to rewrite history. What would have happened if Harun's reign had not ended suddenly and the caliph had been able to carry through the aggressive policy he was planning against Byzantium? It has been assumed that the two emperors concluded formal agreements, some historians going so far as to posit an "Aix-la-Chapelle/Baghdad axis". This is to ignore the gulf separating the two men and the two empires, a distance that was psychological as well as physical. Their collaboration would certainly not have been as close as that. But they were nowhere in direct competition, and their shared hostility to Cordoba and distrust of Byzantium made them see the "international situation", around the Mediterranean at least, in a similar light. Both of them, Harun especially, wanted a weakened Byzantine empire. Could the Commander of the Faithful also have been trying to prevent a possible collaboration — not very desirable from his point of view — between the Frankish and Greek empires? Possibly, although the danger seemed less than immediate at that moment in history. And despite its physical remoteness, Harun also feared the new Muslim Spain, whose development had been rapid and brilliant. During these first years of the ninth century, with the unity and cohesion of the Abbasid empire under threat in several provinces, Harun knew that the other great emperor was not an enemy and might become a friend. Probably the whole significance of the relations between the two men and their respective states lay not in diplomatic alliance or specific military projects but in the certainty that they had nothing to fear from each other and, further, that they could count on each other if their adversaries should start to look dangerous.

The Two Eyes of the World

Prayer, pilgrimage, fasting, and charity comprise, with the profession of faith, the five pillars of the Muslim religion. There is a sixth, "a duty which is communal, not personal", and an imperious necessity for the man God has placed at the head of the community of the faithful: *jihad*, or holy war against infidel countries to extend the world of Islam and convert conquered peoples or hold them in subjection in the status of *dhimmi*.[15] Carried to power "on the crest of a religious wave", calling themselves "messengers of God", the Abbasids took this obligation even more seriously than did the Umayyads (who defined themselves more modestly as "messengers of God's Prophet").

By the end of the eighth century, however, the Arabs had reached their limits. The Sassanids had vanished, erased from history forever. In the East, although agitation was to last several decades more in the countries of the Oxus, the battle of Talas had ended Transoxania's pretensions to independence and blocked Chinese expansion into central Asia. The empires of the Far East were out of reach. That of the Carolingians was also too far away — fifteen hundred kilometres separate Gibraltar from the banks of the Loire — to be seriously considered. The attack on Poitiers, always regarded by Muslim historians as no more than a setback suffered by "a band of soldiers raiding beyond their most remote frontiers",[16] was never to be repeated. The Arabs had run out of conquerable territories in the East as in the West. New peoples awaited the message of Islam.

There remained the empire of the basileus and the dream of conquering Constantinople. It was to haunt the imagination of Muslim emperors for centuries; later, when one of them at last succeeded in conquering the city,[17] it was the turn of Christian kings and emperors to dream of recapturing it, an obsession lasting almost to the present day. Had it not been for Leo the Isaurian and "Greek fire"[18] (significantly aided by Bulgar attacks on the Arabs), Maslama's expedition might perhaps have succeeded. This campaign marked the high point of the Arab expansion. The Abbasids at the pinnacle of their power — first Mahdi, then Harun al-Rashid, and, last, his son Mamun — came up against Byzantine land and naval forces that, reorganized on a territorial basis,[19] were soon able to demonstrate a new effectiveness.

Sentenced to Meet
The Arabs of the early Middle Ages had no immediate neighbours apart from the Byzantines. Other peoples lived at enormous distances, journeys measurable in months; to deal with them at all involved something rather like exploration, for next to nothing was known about them. Under Muslim law, travelling in infidel lands was a reprehensible act, permitted only if its purpose was to ransom captives. Trading was not regarded as a justification for visiting an infidel country.[20] None but the hardiest travellers did so, usually with the intention of making a quick fortune. Most people were ignorant of Asia and had only the vaguest ideas about Europe. As for Africa, they knew only the Maghreb and part of the east coast. The rest of the world belonged to myth.

The Byzantines were somewhat less vague about the countries to the west and north. They had relations, mainly commercial but also political, with the Carolingians, among others; and central and southern Italy had been part of the Greek empire until the middle of the eighth century. They too seldom ventured outside their frontiers, even less since the Arabs had occupied the southern Mediterranean coastline and gained partial control over trade with distant lands.

Having only each other as close neighbours, the Arabs and Byzantines were condemned, so to speak, to maintain reciprocal relations. These were often interrupted by wars, but they existed in the form of exchanges of every sort. The two peoples also showed curiosity about each other, even if the difference between their religions and customs was too great to allow for mutual understanding. Each of the great neighbours was convinced of its own superiority, while accepting the division of the world — on a strictly temporary basis — between the two empires. The Muslims believed that they were the elect of God, that theirs was the only true religion, and that one day it would be the faith of the entire world. They held the Byzantines to be guilty of imposing colleagues on God (through the Trinity); among the lesser faults of these miscreants, the Arabs listed their miserliness, their habit of breaking their word, their dirty and shameless women, and their appalling cuisine; apart from all this, they supplied the Muslim world with eunuchs whom they themselves castrated.[21]

The Byzantines, for their part, believed that only their kingdom — the kingdom of God — embodied the religious, intellectual, and moral ideals a man might wish for here on earth. "Who lives within the Empire belongs to the people of God; who lives outside has not attained to full humanity. Byzantium is the civilized world, the *oikoumene*; the regions beyond are *eremos*, desert."[22] The Muslims had destroyed an immense empire that prefigured the empire of God. They had broken the unity of the world even as it was being achieved. And they were impious; there was nothing more to say.

Byzantines and Muslims regarded each other as barbarians. The attitude of superiority was even stronger among the former than among the latter. Nevertheless, there they were, facing each other across common frontiers. Trade relations had existed between Arabs of the peninsula and Greeks of the Christian empire since pre-Islamic times. The Prophet himself, also the caliph Omar, knew from experience that duties were payable on entry to Byzantine territory. Under the Umayyads, goods were exchanged mainly by sea routes: Egyptian papyrus, among many other products, was shipped to Constantinople. This trade was increased during the economic expansion of the Abbasids. It was still routed through Constantinople, where a mosque had been built for Muslim traders, but also now through Trebizond and the frontier town of Lamos, to the west of Tarsus. Fairs were held in Lamos periodically, and it was there that exchanges of Greek and Arab prisoners took place. The export of certain goods was forbidden; foreign traders were not allowed to leave Arab countries carrying balm or copies of the Koran, while the Byzantines forbade exports of oil.

Arab and Byzantine sovereigns sometimes exchanged presents. Muawia sent the basileus fifty thoroughbred horses, whose export was strictly controlled; Mamun sent civet-cat furs and musk. Harun al-Rashid sent the emperor Nicephoros perfumes, a tent, and dried fruits; in return he received two hundred garments of precious fabric, falcons and hounds. The empress Irene later presented Harun with thirty thousand pounds of goats'-hair cloth. Diamond-encrusted gold belts, garments of rare silk, and slaves of both sexes were exchanged. The *Thousand and One Nights* contains more than one mention of presents from the emperor of Byzantium to the Commander of the Faithful:

> Now these are the presents which Afridun, lord of Constantinople, sent to Uman al-Numan: fifty of the fairest virgins in all Greece, and fifty of the most glorious boys from Rome, dressed in gold-embroidered silken full-sleeved robes, with coloured pictures in needlework upon them, and silver damascened gold belts holding up double skirts of brocaded velvet which fell in unequal lengths, gold rings in their ears from which depended single round white pearls each worth a thousand pound weight in gold. The girls, too, were sumptuously decked.
>
> These were the two principal presents, but the rest did not fall short of them in value.[23]

Such presents, always precious, sometimes strange (one emperor sent Muawia one man of gigantic size and another of Herculean strength), marked occasions like the signing of a treaty, an exchange of prisoners, or the accession of an emperor or a caliph. The gifts were escorted by ambassadors, who also received presents that they were allowed to carry away with them. They enjoyed diplomatic immunity. Some, curious to learn as much as possible about the country they were visiting — always for a limited time, since permanent embassies did not exist — missed no opportunity to associate with members of the caliph's entourage and travel about the country, or at least the capital. The caliph or emperor would invite these envoys to his table; the envoys would reciprocate with banquets designed to impress their guests with the wealth of their sovereign. Baghdad and Contantinople tried to outdo each other in display. Jean le Syncelle, who met Mamun in Damascus in 831, distributed large sums of money among dignitaries, courtiers, and even the people in the street. Constantinople was extremely pleased; he had "revealed the Empire to the Saracens".

The caliph and the basileus corresponded by letter. When one of them was asking for an exchange of prisoners or proposing a truce, the letter would be courteous, almost friendly; when the letter contained a declaration of war, its tone would be violent, sometimes insulting (as in the letter from Harun to Nicephoros). They also wrote letters that had nothing to do with politics. The emperor Nicephoros asked Harun to send him the poet Abu al-Atahiya in exchange for as many hostages as the caliph wanted. Despite Harun's insistence, the poet refused to go. Earlier, the Umayyad caliph Walid had written to Justinian asking for Greek artisans to build a mosque in Damascus (and threatening to destroy churches in the event of a refusal). Some time after Harun, the caliph Mutawakil, one of the Abbasid dynasty's more extravagant builders, sent to Byzantium for painters to decorate the walls of his palace at Samarra. One of their murals depicted a church and some monks.

Many historical facts and anecdotes — often heavily embroidered — attest to the relations between the supreme authorities, as well as between intellectuals, of the two empires, their attention drawn across the frontier as if by reciprocal mirages — what Louis Massignon calls "a mirage reflected in a blazing mirage."

In Arab thought of the eighth and ninth centuries, Byzantium was very much the heir of the ancient Greeks, whose culture was revealed to the Arabs through translations of Greek works. Caliphs avid for these works of antiquity, both to fill their libraries and to spread learning, sent Arab intellectuals to Constantinople to seek out Greek texts. A Byzantine monk brought to the emir of Cordoba a treatise by Dioscorides, which he explained to the emir. Mamun asked the emperor Theophilus to send him the geometrician and astronomer Leo.

In his letters, the caliph always invited the emperor to convert to Islam. Replies in kind sometimes led to lively theological arguments, like those between Omar II and Leo III and between Harun al-Rashid and Constantine VI. In the middle of the ninth century, with the permission of Michael III, the caliph Watiq sent a scientific expedition to Ephesus to examine the remains of the Seven Sleepers.[24] The same caliph later organized an expedition to central Asia to find the wall built by Alexander to keep out the peoples of Gog and Magog.

Clearly, relations at the very top were not always unfriendly despite the almost permanent state of war between the two empires. Byzantium, according to the historian Vasiliev, even gave a sort of precedence to the Arabs over representatives of the West: Byzantine protocol placed Saracen "friends" higher up the imperial table than Frankish "friends". Oriental ambassadors took precedence over Westerners.[25]

Individuals from both empires crossed the frontier to live in exile. Arabs were sometimes tempted by the freedom to drink wine and by other liberties permitted in Byzantium. Others were fugitives who had committed some crime. There are numerous examples of Byzantine political refugees who secured important posts with the caliph; some were converted and settled down, while others tried to return home. Sometimes whole tribes would defect to escape an authority they found intolerable. Prisoners of war might choose to stay among their captors; they would convert, then be given land. Byzantium recruited interpreters from among them.

Of the Byzantines who passed into the service of the Arabs, the most illustrious was undoubtedly the strategist Tatzates, who fled in 784. Elphidios, another strategist, left apparently because he was accused of being the empress Irene's lover. Euphemios, commander of the Sicilian fleet, had a different reason: he had married a nun. When the strategist Andronic Doukas went over to the Arabs, he became a convert to Islam.

Many caliphs had mothers of Greek origin: Qaratis, mother of Harun al-Rashid's grandson Watiq; Habashiyya, mother of Muntasir; Qurb, mother of Muhtadi; Dirar, mother of Mutadid; and, a little later, the famous Shaghab, mother of the caliph Muktadir, whose court was overrun by men and women of Greek descent. Shaghab is remembered among imperial concubines for her greedy love of luxury and wealth.

The two empires learned something of each other's customs and civilizations through the prisoners and captives who lived among the population. Public figures were kept under a form of house arrest and could receive anyone they wished. The others, who were made to work, often in factories, were brought by force of circumstance into daily contact with those among whom they lived. There was even more contact in frontier regions, where almost everyone spoke both languages and where the main occupations were smuggling and espionage. Incessant fighting, exchanges of prisoners, war in all its aspects could not fail to occasion reciprocal influence.

For the Christians, finally, pilgrimage to Jerusalem was an opportunity to glimpse the inside of the Arab world, about which so much was said and so little known. Although only fragmentary information has survived from the Abbasid period, it seems that subjects of the basileus were free to enter the Holy Land without hindrance, probably after they paid dues and obtained a visa. These contacts, too, would have helped to inform Muslims and Christians about one another.

Obliged by geography to live in two neighbouring worlds, looking across the frontier with mingled contempt and admiration, Arabs and Byzantines were both attracted and repelled by one another. Their mutual hostility was somewhat reduced by the monotheism each professed and by their common conviction that apart from themselves — and to a lesser extent the Persians and the Indians — there were only peoples wallowing in the gloom of ignorance and savagery. "There exist but two eyes to which the Divinity has entrusted the task of illuminating the world: the powerful monarchy of the Romans and the wisely-governed community of the Persians," the Sassanid Khosrov had once written to the emperor Maurice. Now the Persians had gone and it was the Arabs' turn to "illuminate the world".

Harun al-Rashid at War with the Basileus

Saffah and Mansour had both treated war with Byzantium as a matter of limited importance. The first two Abbasid caliphs were so busy consolidating the regime and resisting attacks by the Khazars that war against the infidel was still a secondary concern. The same thing applied to the infidel, who had more pressing worries: fighting the Slavic tribes in Thrace and Macedonia and, above all, warding off attacks by the Bulgars, which were far more dangerous than anything the Arabs could manage. Large battles seldom took place between the armies of Mansour and Constantine V, but they raided each other's territory, sacked towns (Melitene, Massisa, Adana, and Marach among others), and deported the inhabitants. In 771 the Arab fleet mounted a raid on Cyprus and captured its Byzantine governor.

With Mahdi's accession to power, the offensive on Byzantium took on a new vigour. After 778, following the conquest of Samosata by Leo IV, the caliph raised a powerful army, led by his uncle Abbas ibn Mohammed, which seized Marach. The Byzantines reoccupied the town and moved the Monophysite population to Thrace; the following year, with Marach again in Arab hands, Hasan ibn Qahtaba assumed command. With thirty thousand men and some additional volunteers, he penetrated as far as Dorylea (today called Eskichehir), three hundred and fifty kilometres from Constantinople, burning and sacking the countryside without meeting any opposition: the emperor had ordered his troops to withdraw without fighting.

By 780 the Arab threat to Byzantium was becoming serious. Mahdi first extended the line of fortifications dotted along the frontier which served as strongpoints for his troops. After the Byzantine attack on Marach he improved the town's defences by building Hadath, between Marach and Melitene (Malatya), so as to block out any attack mounted from the north. A continuous line of thughur thus took shape, running from Syria to the borders of Armenia. They were garrisoned by regulars and volunteers who lived on pillage and tributes while waging a permanent "holy war" on a shifting front against Byzantine volunteers, who used the same raiding and pillaging methods in defence of Christianity — *gazi* and *murabitun* against *akritai*, still to be found on the edges of the two worlds centuries later. Out of touch with the authorities, virtually isolated from all contact except with local populations, they fought one another, sometimes fraternized, and occasionally deserted to the enemy with arms and equipment. These relations contributed to the formation of the Muslim dervish mystique, which is immortalized in Greek, Arabic, and Turkish chivalric literature.

Having secured his frontier defences — Harun was to develop them further — Mahdi launched his first major expedition in 779.

Overall command was entrusted to Harun, who was probably already being considered for succession to the throne. Mahdi wanted to train his son for command, as his own father had trained him, by putting him at least nominally in charge of an army. The young prince, not yet fifteen years old, was surrounded (not surprisingly) by generals and advisers; prominent among them were Khalid the Barmakid and his sons Yahya, Hasan, and Suleiman, as well as the chamberlain Rabi al-Yunus. It seems that for practical purposes command was exercised by Yahya. Mahdi and the Abbasid princes accompanied Harun through the passes of the Taurus as far as the Ceyhan,[26] where the caliph picked the site for a town that was to be called al-Mahdiyya. Harun kept the honour of leading the army into enemy territory. The army was composed of contingents Mahdi had levied from the Khorasan regiments, plus what were probably volunteer units. With so many troops the risk of defeat was small, and the indications are that the expedition was meant as an exercise for the young prince rather than as an actual war.

The Byzantines, deep in another of their dynastic quarrels, had more pressing tasks than making war on the Arabs; in any case, the greater part of their army was in Sicily trying to put down a revolt led by the island's strategist Helpidius. Harun's main action was the siege of the fortress at Samalu, whose parched and starving occupants surrendered after thirty-eight days. Although many Muslims had been killed during the siege, Harun agreed to the conditions posed by the inhabitants: none should be executed and their families should not be split up. They were taken to Baghdad. Harun had been given his baptism of fire.

Two years later, after several of these raids into enemy territory, the first full-fledged expedition set out. This time a great army was raised to strike deep into Anatolia, perhaps as far as Constantinople. Did Mahdi really mean to capture the "Middle Town", as the Umayyads had attempted to do on four previous occasions?[27] If this had been his intention, surely he would have taken personal command of the army and even more certainly sent his fleet — admittedly quite small at the time — to give maritime support to the land forces? This was not done. But the *idea* of seizing Constantinople was definitely present in the mind of the caliph Mahdi, "He Who Is Led by God".

The throne of Constantinople was occupied by the formidable

Irene, an "obscure provincial",[28] who had seized power from her ten-year-old son Constantine on the death of her husband, the emperor Leo IV. As all major state posts were held by her enemies the iconoclasts, her power was fragile; she dominated officials with her strong personality, but was still obliged to manoeuvre with skill and caution. In the face of external threats the army, based on the proven system of Themes perfected by Leo III, stayed loyal to her.

Once again Harun was given supreme command of the expedition. As in his earlier campaign, he was flanked by al-Rabi and one or more Barmakids. His commander-in-chief, Yazid ibn Mazyad (one of the shrewdest generals of the period), was leading forces of considerable size — according to Tabari, 95,793 regulars backed by numerous volunteers. The expedition left at the end of winter, on 9 February 781, and entered enemy territory during the first days of spring. The crucial fortress at Magida, at the exit from the Cilician Gates, fell to the Arabs, who stood firm against the attacks of Byzantine cavalry. Following ancient Oriental custom, Yazid met in single combat the Byzantine general, the "Count of Counts", Nicetas, who abandoned the field. Nicetas's troops fled and were chased by the Arabs across Anatolia as far as Nicomedia (Izmit). "And Harun," Tabari says, "advanced until he reached the channel (the Bosphorus) at Chrysopolis (Usküdar)," while other units continued operations at Baris (Isparta) and in other parts of Anatolia.[29]

Once again the Arabs were at the walls of Constantinople; and once again they went no further. Could they have taken the town if they had been willing to pay the price in men? They were far from their bases, and the "Well-Guarded" was strongly fortified. But — if we are to believe the poet Marwan ibn Hafsah — they came very close to succeeding: "You strolled round Constantinople prodding it with your lance, and its walls were covered in humiliation. But you did not choose to take it, deigning only to receive tribute from its kings as the cauldrons of war boiled."

Byzantium was long past the peak of its power. Irene had had to send troops to Macedonia, Greece, and the Peloponnese to deal with a revolt by the Slavs, and the region around Constantinople was poorly defended. Fearing that her shaky hold on the throne might not withstand a long siege, she sued for peace, and Harun agreed to open negotiations through emissaries. The talks were briefly compromised when Harun had three Byzantine envoys arrested, but the empress finally agreed to pay an annual tribute of 70,000 dinars and to release the 5,643 Arabs who had been taken prisoner. According to Tabari, the Greeks lost 54,000 men in this campaign, and Harun needed 20,000 beasts of burden to carry off the riches left to the Arabs after they had burned lesser booty. There was so much of it, say the chroniclers, that the price of a horse dropped to one dinar, a sword could be bought for a dirham and a breastplate for even less. The armistice was for three years only.

Harun marched back into Baghdad on 31 August 782, to loud acclamations; the chroniclers regarded his entry into the capital as one of the events of the year. It was now that Mahdi named him as successor after Hadi and that he was given the name Rashid, "the Well-Guided". Still under twenty, Harun had twice made war on Byzantium, and the experience marked him for life: war against the Greeks, the enemy of Muslims and Arabs, was to remain a priority throughout his reign.

Fortifications and *Razzias*

The truce with Irene held for some time — thirty-two months, in Tabari's estimation. It was first broken by the Greeks — "with perfidy", in the chronicler's words — during the month of Ramadan 785; Arab raiding resumed almost at once, with Arab horsemen "taking booty and returning victorious". The following year a new Byzantine offensive reached Adathe (Hadath), a town built by Mahdi in the vicinity of Germanicaea (Marach). The governor had to flee, along with the garrison and the merchants. The Arabs took it back the same year and occupied Ushna (Ushnu), on the Armenian frontier. The Greeks meanwhile seized other towns in Arab territory, which were later destroyed and rebuilt by the Arabs; one of these was Tarsus, rebuilt by Abu Suleiman Faradj, known as "the Turk", in the year of Harun's succession. Razzias and the taking of loot and prisoners thus marked Mahdi's last years and the beginning of Harun's reign. The new caliph made sure that raids took place at least every summer, but he launched no major expeditions. His main effort was concentrated on completing and improving the fortified line defending northern Syria in the direction of Armenia and Azerbaijan.

As a military system the thughur did not function well: the forts were held by men mostly from Syria and the Djezireh, who were rewarded with land in addition to their wages, and had quickly become centres for smuggling and all sorts of contraband traffic with the Byzantines, to the detriment of the treasury. More importantly, the slack discipline in the forts seriously compromised defence. Without wholly doing away with the thughur, which were retained as advanced outposts, Harun revised the defence system and established the main fortifications south of the Taurus, on the borders of the Gulf of Alexandretta, as far as Aleppo and beyond. Tarsus was given a strong garrison. The term "thughur" was replaced by *awasim*. For a long period that name was attached to the region itself, which included Cilicia and Syria as far as the Euphrates. Garrisons pulled back from the thughur, with other reinforcements, were stationed in a large number of fortified towns, including Hadath, Missisa (on the Ceyhan), Ainzerba, Zibatra, Haruniya,[30] and Membidj (the ancient Hierapolis), where Abd al-Malik, an Abbasid, was placed in command at the centre of this "hedgehog-like" defence system.

The Byzantines did nothing to prevent this development, which was to pose a perpetual threat to the basileus. It is true that they were going through a crisis. As the conflict between Irene and her son approached its climax, the empire reeled under the impact of bloody intrigues and palace revolutions. Irene exercised iron control over Constantine, and broke off his engagement with Charlemagne's daughter Rotrude — perhaps changing the course, if not of history itself, at least of the eastern and western Roman empires. Forced to relinquish power, she regained it through the treachery of the emperor's entourage after he had dared to divorce his wife Mary the Armenian and marry one of his mother's ladies-in-waiting (an adultery that aroused the indignation of the all-powerful Church). Ministers fought among themselves, Irene had her enemies' eyes put out, and the empire continued to fall apart until a coup d'état one day brought in a new emperor able to resume the offensive against the Arabs.

These days were still far in the future. By 790 Harun's line of defence was strong enough to serve as a base for new sorties, and the caliph's generals sent expeditions every year. They seized Urgüp in Cappadocia, laid waste to Amorium (Phrygia), and advanced as far as Samsun, on the Black Sea. In 797, a year after moving to

Raqqa, Harun himself crossed the frontier with his armies, while other columns went to Ancyre (Ankara); Ephesus, on the Aegean; and the Sea of Marmara. Repeated Byzantine counter-attacks had no success; nobody could resist the Arabs, who went where they wanted in Asia Minor, destroying and pillaging and leaving permanent traces on the country. The disturbances caused by the Arab invasions and the resulting mixing of populations altered forever its demographic, ethnic, and economic geography. Prosperous regions were impoverished while others, left relatively unscathed, were able to develop.[31] Voluntary and forced movements of populations gave Anatolia a composite aspect that the later arrival of the Turkish peoples did not wholly efface.

Combined with Byzantium's breaking of its links with Italy, the wars against the Muslims helped put an end to Byzantium's universalist pretensions. After expansionist beginnings, the Hellenic Roman empire was forced on the defensive from the eighth century onwards, a reversal that is revealed in the reform of its army: the Themes had the military organization of a resistance movement in which the whole population was required to take part. The Byzantine army was no longer a conquering one, and still was not in the tenth and eleventh centuries, even though some of the provinces taken over by the Arabs were then delivered from "Muslim tyranny".

The Caliph's Anger

Irene was overthrown by a conspiracy in 802. Nicephoros, the *logothetos* (minister) of the treasury, was crowned emperor and Irene was locked up, first in the monastery of Prinkipo on the Sea of Marmara and later at Lesbos. She died the following year.

Nicephoros, who was of Arab origin, wanted to wash away immediately the humiliations that had been heaped on the empire during the empress's reign, and believed the restoration of morale in the weakened state and army to be a matter of urgency. In dispute with Charlemagne over the Frankish ruler's title of (Holy Roman) Emperor, which the Byzantines refused to recognize, and over possession of Venice, Nicephoros rejected the proposals brought to him by Charlemagne's ambassadors, which might have assured him of peace in the West at least for a while. At the same time, he let Harun know that the tribute Irene had undertaken to pay would no longer be forthcoming. On this occasion Nicephoros's letter was studiously insulting:

> Nicephoros, King of the Rum, to Harun, King of the Arabs:
> The queen who reigned before me treated you as a rukh while herself assuming the posture of a mere pawn. She paid you sums of money which in reality you should have paid to her. This was due to woman's weakness and foolishness. When you have read my letter, send back the money you received from her and ransom yourself out of trouble by paying the sums you are required to restore to me. If you do not, the sword shall decide between us.

Nicephoros erred badly in sending such a letter to Harun. Using these terms to the Commander of the Faithful and God's Messenger on Earth was worse than a declaration of war; it was the sort of insult that only a monarch with immense military power could hope to get away with. Harun fell into such a rage, Tabari reports, that "nobody dared look at him, let alone speak to him... so great was the fear that a word or gesture might increase his anger still further. The Vizier himself could not decide whether to offer some counsel or leave him to take the decision alone." The caliph called for ink and scrawled in his own hand on the back of the emperor's letter:

> In the name of Allah, the clement and merciful.
> From Harun, Emir of the Believers, to Nicephoros, Dog of the Rum:
> I have read your letter, O disloyal son. My answer will reach you sooner than you wish. Greetings!

Then he ordered the army to get ready.

Two columns marched across the frontier. One, led by Qasim, Harun's son by the concubine Kasif, drove towards Cappadocia, where it besieged Kurra (Korran), seat of the province's governor. One of Qasim's lieutenants, Abbas ibn Jaffar, took another column towards the fortress of Sinan (Sinasos, in the region of Urgüp). After a few battles, both withdrew in exchange for the release of Muslim prisoners.

Harun led his own army towards the Cilician Gates, near Heraclaea (Eregli, northwest of the gates). He seems not to have occupied this fortified town, but his troops pillaged and burned the countryside around it, taking prisoners and much booty. Nicephoros, who had certainly not expected such a quick response, indicated that he was willing to sign a new treaty and pay an annual tribute. The caliph agreed and withdrew to Raqqa, leaving his generals in Anatolia, where they continued to make war. One of them, Ibrahim ibn Jibril, took the fortresses of Safsaf and Thebasa, near Ancyre, and razed them. Nicephoros riposted by leading an attack on the Arab army at Krasos, in Phrygia, where, wounded and surrounded, he owed his survival to the bravery of his officers. Muslim historians claim that he lost nearly fifty thousand men and four thousand beasts of burden in this engagement, but this must be an exaggeration. Both sides then observed the truce.

Nicephoros was the first to break it. The news arrived in winter; Harun's entourage feared that he would take to the field without delay, and nobody in the palace dared tell him that Nicephoros had broken his word a second time. Eventually the poet Abu Mohammed gave him the news by reciting a tirade composed for the occasion:

> Nicephoros has violated the peace you granted him, but the wheel of fortune will turn against him;
> Rejoice, O Emir of the Faithful, for God brings you a fine windfall.
> Your subjects rejoice at the arrival of the messenger bringing the good tidings of this violation,
> And hope that from your hand without delay will speed an expedition, such as to soothe men's souls and make a famous battlefield.
> Nicephoros, when you fall into acts of treachery because the Imam is far away, you show your ignorance and blindness.
> [. . .]
> We may be careless, but the Imam is not; he never forgets the duty of his immovable will to govern and administrate.
> He who would mislead his Imam has nothing useful to say; but his sincere counsellors give good advice.

Despite the season, the caliph decided without hesitation to go to war. There is no detailed account of this campaign, but Arab chroniclers indicate that it was very difficult and subjected the men to "the most painful exertions". How far did the Abbasid troops go? We know only that they were victorious and that Nicephoros once again agreed to pay a tribute. The poet Abu al-Atahiya gives us this cryptic account: "The world has declared its assent to Harun, and Nicephoros has become a dhimmi to the Imam... The Caliph did not come back until he was satisfied and had gone as far as he wanted."

Harun had triumphed over his enemies, but the price had been the dead and the captives left behind in Anatolia. Their numbers are unknown, but Arab historians mention that "tall prisons had been built" to house the captives subsequently exchanged. Expeditions to the Anatolian plateau, with its extremes of climate, were always full of hardship and always left prisoners, sometimes in very large numbers, in the hands of the enemy.

Although he had come off badly in almost every encounter with the caliph's troops, Nicephoros did not disarm. Did he hope to resolve his empire's internal difficulties by achieving successes against the Muslims? Or was he afraid that the Abbasids, then at the peak of their power, might launch a major offensive on Constantinople, this time with decisive results? The naval expansion programme ordered by Harun[32] must have been deeply disturbing to the basileus, who recognized the threat to his capital from combined land and sea attacks.[33] The Abbasid empire could afford to arm and equip as many men as it deemed necessary to fight the infidel. From his frontier fortresses, Harun could at any moment send out units to devastate Anatolia and afterwards pull them back to the shelter of the impregnable awasim. It must have been tempting for the most powerful sovereign in the world to crown the glory of the Abbasids by taking the most coveted city in the universe, a fact not lost on Nicephoros. Hence his repeated harassing attacks on the Abbasid troops, even though his own armies were in far from perfect condition: he wanted to remind the Arabs that forays into harsh and hostile Anatolia were nearly always risky and that his locally recruited forces would probably inflict heavy losses on them. Almost certainly his objective was to discourage the caliph from mounting a major expedition to the west and the north, or at least to delay it as long as possible.

This analysis was surely not far wrong, but for the moment at least the basileus's worst fears were not realized. Serious disturbances in Khorasan, resulting from maladministration by the governor, Ali ibn Isa, distracted Harun from his design on the Propontidis and the Bosphorus. Interrupting his campaign in Asia Minor, he left for the eastern provinces, where his presence settled nothing. Nicephoros used the respite to repair fortresses destroyed by the Arabs during their recent marauding expeditions.

The Well-Guided in the Field

By May 806 the caliph was ready to go to war again. This time the size of the force assembled was considerable: one hundred and thirty-five thousand regular troops from the abna and the abbasiya, soldiers from provincial units, volunteers, and irregulars. Was Harun hoping to draw out the largest possible number of enemy units, wipe them out, and then drive towards the Bosphorus? Or was his intention simply to lay waste to Anatolia once more and turn it into a desert?

After mustering around the awasim, the army crossed the frontier on 11 June 806, in its usual marching order: the vanguard in front, followed by the right wing, the centre, the left wing, and the rear guard. Scouts reconnoitred the surrounding countryside and signalled every suspect movement. Campsites were fixed in advance in places that were defensible and where water and supplies could be obtained; by the time the bulk of the army arrived at the site, the vanguard would have made the necessary arrangements. Each day the army would decamp and move on to the next site, chosen in the same way, until it reached the battlefield. This too would have been chosen in advance if possible, with an eye to the contours of the ground, the presence of watercourses and other features, and the direction in which the men should face so as not to be dazzled by the sun (the astrologer invariably present in the sovereign's entourage was often consulted).

The army was organized into large units (*khamis*), each commanded by a senior officer responsible to the commander-in-chief, the *amir*, appointed by the caliph. The amir was absolute master of the army. Smaller units of between ten and a hundred men were answerable to their own officers. The officer commanding a khamis, like a modern regimental or divisional commander, was free to make his own tactical decisions on the battlefield provided, of course, they fit in with the amir's battle plan. Sometimes the army would fight drawn up in a continuous line; other times, in small groups.

In the front rank were the archers and crossbowmen, their weapons of variable size and power. Used since earliest antiquity in both war and the chase, especially by the Persians, the longbow was a foot soldier's weapon until the cavalry adopted it under the influence of the peoples from the steppes. Pioneered by the Turks, on whom it conferred a long-lasting military superiority, archery from horseback spread via the Persians to the Arabs (who never completely mastered the technique). The crossbow was in use from the beginning of the ninth century. Apart from these light weapons, carried singly by infantrymen, artillery consisted of darts projected from a tube or channel, and ballistas capable of hurling heavy projectiles as far as three hundred metres. In the second rank were other foot soldiers, armed with spears or sabres of so-called Damascus steel and protected by small shields, usually of wood or leather.

Behind the infantry waited the cavalry, armed with heavy lances, javelins, or sabres, and later, under the Turkish influence, with bows that were used to fire demoralizing showers of arrows at the enemy, with an effect chroniclers likened to "a hailstorm or swarm of bees". Both horse and rider were protected by light armour, coats of mail, and breastplates made from thin strips of steel, far less heavy than Western armour would be. The mace, the broadsword and other weapons were also used; this weaponry, variable in weight, form, and effectiveness, saw no essential changes until the Crusades and the arrival of the Mongols. The Orient in general favoured light weapons.

Cavalry had the decisive role in battle and was to retain it far into the future, until the use of firearms became widespread. The groundwork would be laid by archers and infantry, who would charge repeatedly until the enemy line was broken; other troops would stand ready to repel the enemy's attacks; then the cavalry would go into action, drawing the enemy cavalry into pursuit, only to turn and scatter it. This tactic, learned from the Turks, worked well against the Byzantines, who were unskilled in dealing with it.

Killing was kept to a minimum. The first objective was to take prisoners, who could then be either ransomed for money or goods or exchanged for Muslim captives held by the enemy. Pillage was the rule of war and perhaps its main attraction for the troops. Each man would seize anything he found which had value, especially young boys and girls who could be sold as slaves. Great massacres were rare, except when the enemy had displayed a desire to kill; then there would be little quarter on either side. In principle the sovereign had the right to a fifth of the booty, but assessment was difficult and in practice everyone captured and carried off whatever he could. Both Muslims and Christians marauded almost with the sole aim of piling up plunder to swell the wages of the regular troops.[34] Nomads tended to destroy whatever they could not carry off; regular troops would burn crops and destroy livestock to weaken the enemy, but usually refrained from damaging plantations of trees or irrigation works.

Wars seldom lasted long unless the circumstances were exceptional — usually one season, sometimes two. Supplies were always a difficult problem, and winter is long and harsh on the plains of Asia. The men were reluctant to spend more than a few months away from home, and their booty could not be dragged around indefinitely. The army would withdraw, after winning its victory or negotiating a truce with the enemy, in return for the payment of a tribute in coin or merchandise (Irene, for example, paid Harun partly in wool). On the rare occasions when the caliph's army was defeated, a victory would be announced anyway. Feasts were given to celebrate victory, especially when the caliph had been in personal command. Rewards would be distributed, the streets of Baghdad illuminated, and the population invited to rejoice.

Siege and Capture of Heraclaea
The Greeks were expecting a new war: even before the Arab army entered Byzantine territory, it had taken the offensive and attacked Anazarbe and neighbouring settlements (805–806). As Harun headed towards Tyane, where he established his headquarters, one of his leading generals, Abdallah ibn Malik, was besieging Dhul-Kila (between Tyane and Caesaraea) while another, Daud ibn Isa, with seventy thousand men, laid the region to waste and wiped out any Byzantine squadrons that showed themselves. Other units were taking Hisn al-Sakaliba (now Anasa Kalesi) and Thabasz in Cappadocia. Evidently Harun intended to clear the whole region between the awasim and Cappadocia.

The caliph suffered an early delay, however. Masudi writes that on reaching Heraclaea, on the road to Iconium, Dorylaea, and the north, he asked two of his awasim generals whether they thought the place was worth besieging. The first, Mokhalled ibn Husein, answered, "It is the first fortified town you come to on Greek territory, and also the strongest and best defended. If you attack it and, with God's help, take it, no other place will be able to stop you." The other general, Abu Ishak, told Harun:

> Emir of the Believers, this citadel was built by the Greeks to dominate strategic routes and bar access to them. Its population is small, so small that if you conquer it there will not be sufficient booty for all the Muslims to have a share; if on the other hand it resists you, the delay will harm your plan of campaign. The wisest course in my view is for the Emir of the Believers to go and attack one of the great towns of the Greek empire. If he takes it, then the whole army will have its booty; should he fail, then the excuse is ready.

Events proved Abu Ishak right. Harun probably thought that Heraclaea would not long resist the powerful means at his disposal, but the reverse was the case; the siege turned out to be extremely difficult. We have no details of the fortifications surrounding Heraclaea, but they commanded a valley and were completely surrounded by a ditch, which suggests that they were quite strong. Harun, of course, possessed all the available equipment for taking a well-defended town: siege engines, enormous battering rams, catapults, naphtha ("Greek fire"), and long scaling-ladders. But seventeen days passed without a single breach made in the walls; Heraclaea did indeed seem the "strongest and best defended" of towns. The Muslim army's losses were mounting, while shortages of food and animal fodder began to cause Harun serious anxiety.

It was clear that the caliph had made a bad decision, and he consulted Abu Ishak again. This time the general advised against abandoning the siege: "A withdrawal would be damaging to the royal authority, weakening the prestige of our religion and encouraging other towns to close their gates on us and resist." He suggested building a town outside Heraclaea "while we are waiting for God to grant us victory."

Harun took this advice and had some building work started to make it clear to the town's defenders and to his own troops that he would keep the siege going as long as necessary. One of the single combats characteristic of ancient and medieval warfare now took place. As Masudi recounts:

> The town gate opened and a man of remarkable beauty, wearing magnificent armour, was disclosed to the attentive eyes of the Muslims and cried in a resounding voice: "Arab soldiers, we have looked at one another long enough. Let one of you, or ten or twenty, come and measure themselves against me!" But Harun was asleep, and none dared wake him that he might give permission for one of his men to fight. The next day the Greek came again and issued the same challenge. Several generals offered to fight with him, but Harun chose a simple soldier instead so that, if he should be vanquished, the army would not be cast down in spirit.

A long tussle began between the Greek champion and a soldier from the frontier, ibn al-Djurzi, a gazi famous for his courage. After the two had rained blows on each other — several of which on either side seemed severe enough to have proved decisive — ibn al-Djurzi looked to be on the verge of defeat and turned as if to flee. But he was only using the standard feint of the horsemen of the steppes. The Greek chased and caught him, but as he raised his arm to strike, ibn al-Djurzi managed to land a heavy blow that unhorsed him; then, with a second stroke of his broadsword, he struck off his adversary's head. "This victory exalted the Muslims and threw the infidels into consternation."

The Arabs now stepped up the pressure by "throwing fire". "Set fire in the mangonels and put that in action," ordered the caliph. "There will be no resistance from them."

> They did as he had ordered: they wrapped stones in flax and naphtha, set fire to them and hurled them against the ramparts. The fire stuck to the walls and disintegrated the masonry so that stones burst and fell down. When fire had enveloped every part of the town those who were besieged opened their gates and asked for quarter.[35]

The poet ibn Djami describes the burning of the town in two vivid verses:

Heraclaea surrendered when she saw this surprising thing: heavy machines hurling naphtha and fire.

It was as if our fires on the flank of the citadel were coloured stuffs drying on a fuller's lines.

Nicephoros was under threat from the Bulgars and promised not to rebuild Heraclaea or the fortresses of Dhul-Kila, Samalu, and Hisn Sina. He sent fifty thousand dinars to ransom the inhabitants of the region. Sentimental concerns often marked affairs of this sort, and one day two of the basileus's top dignitaries arrived in the caliph's camp with a letter from Nicephoros asking Harun to release a young girl from Heraclaea, a patrician's daughter engaged to be married to his son. "This request," the letter said in part, "can do no harm to your religion or to you. If you see fit to agree, then do so." Harun immediately had a throne placed for the girl in her tent. When she came up for sale, he arranged to have her bought for a very high price, then sent her to Nicephoros, along with the tent, its eating and drinking vessels, and all the other objects in it. Sometime later he is supposed to have built a fortress in her memory — Heraqla, on the Euphrates near Raqqa. Nicephoros had also requested perfumes, dates, *khabis* (a sort of pastry made from flour, milk, and honey), raisins, and treacle. Ambassadors carried these goods to the basileus, who sent Harun in return fifty thousand dirhams loaded on a bay horse, a hundred brocade robes and two hundred of embroidered silk, twelve hawks, four hounds, and three horses.

The capture of Heraclaea was treated by the Arabs as a great event: better even the capture of a small town than none at all. The event passed virtually unnoticed on the Byzantine side. (They would have reacted quite differently if Ancyre or Dorylaea had fallen.) Great celebrations were organized in Baghdad for the return of the army. Contests brought the best poets flocking to Raqqa. Abu al-Atahiya declaimed these lines:

Did not Heraclaea intone her death-song once under attack by the king whose designs are Heaven-favoured?

Harun's threats crash like thunder. His chastisements are terrible and quick as lightning.

His banners, oft visited by victory, float like clouds on the breeze.

You have triumphed, O Emir of the Faithful; see and taste your triumph: here is all the booty; and here, the road home.

The Greeks promised not to rebuild the fortresses that had been destroyed on the far side of the Taurus during the previous campaign. No sooner had the Arabs withdrawn across the frontier, however, than Nicephoros once again ordered them to be repaired. Early in 807 Harun prepared for a new campaign. A few months later he set out once more towards the frontier and set up his camp at Adata.

He went no further. The caliph sent Harthama and thirty thousand men against Nicephoros, whose harassment tactics were increasing. Harun also ordered that the thughur be readied to strengthen frontier defences; but he suddenly returned to Raqqa, and the great campaign was put aside for the moment. Harun was once again worrying about Khorasan.

6
Death in Khorasan

O God, King of the Kingdom, thou givest power to whom thou wilt, and from whom thou wilt, thou takest it away! Thou raisest up whom thou wilt, and whom thou wilt thou dost abase! In thy hand is good; for thou art over all things potent.

Koran, Sura III, 25

Harun's visit to Khorasan in 805 little altered the situation there. Ali ibn Isa had continued his exactions and the masses were becoming increasingly restive. A worrying new rebellion had broken out, bringing to public notice one Rafi ibn Layt, whose family had been powerful under the Umayyads. A large number of malcontents quickly gathered about him.

The revolt had interesting origins, which Tabari recounts as follows:

Rafi ibn Layt, a distinguished officer of the Samarkand garrison, of agreeable appearance and very fond of wine and women, pursued a life of pleasure. He became amorously entangled with the wife of Yahya ibn Achatli, who was attached to the court of Harun al-Rashid. Following Rafi's advice, the woman annulled her marriage by apostatizing, then re-entered Islam; after the delay prescribed by the law, Rafi married her. Yahya complained to Harun and laid the facts before him. He in turn wrote to Ali ibn Isa ordering him to punish Rafi by imprisoning him, and to make an example of him by parading him through the town mounted on an ass and with his face blackened, and finally to force him to separate from the woman. Ali told the governor of Samarkand to carry out these orders; the governor forced Rafi to send his wife away and put him in prison, but otherwise treated him with respect. He escaped from prison and fled to Balkh, where he lived in secret, and sent to Ali asking for *aman* [mercy]. Ali granted the discharge and sent him back to Samarkand. As it was still impossible to live publicly with his wife, he assumed the leadership of Samarkand's adventurers and seized control of the town; then he resumed living with his wife. He was acclaimed by the inhabitants, who had become very tired of Ali and his agents.

The charge of adultery brought against Rafi by Ali was obviously only a pretext to get rid of someone who, as grandson of the last Umayyad governor, still possessed great influence. Rafi was supported by much of the population, who had had more than enough of Ali's abuses of power, and by tribal chiefs in Sogdian, Tokharistan, and Transoxania. Ali sent forces against Rafi under the command of his son, but the son was killed and the troops routed. Ali then intervened in person, but he too was defeated and fled to Merv. The inhabitants of Balkh now rose up and killed the governor's representative. The problem was becoming acute: the entire eastern half of the empire was going up in flames and threatening to secede. Ali called on the caliph for help. Harun was at last realizing that his governor was incompetent. But Ali still had considerable power and it would have been foolhardy to dismiss him summarily.

The task of dealing with Ali was entrusted to Harthama, who had experience in such situations. He was to give Ali a letter from Harun which began: "O son of a whore, whom I have heaped with benefits... you tyrannize the Muslims and turn my subjects away from me. Now I send you Harthama, who is to arrest you, take away your treasures, and call you to account for your actions..." Harthama arrived in Merv with twenty thousand men and went straight to the palace. There, after a hurried meal, he gave Ali Harun's letter, arrested him, and made him restore to the rightful owners the property he had appropriated; he then sent Ali to Baghdad.

Ali's arrest relieved Khorasan of a bad governor but did not bring the rebellion to an end. The insurrection stretched from Azerbaijan to Ferghana, showing how superficial was the tie of the peoples of Khorasan to Islam — and the extent to which they had retained their own national characteristics. Indeed, some of these populations were to acquire political emancipation just a few decades later.

Harun saw the danger and realized that he had to act quickly. Harthama, for all his excellence, was only a representative. Fadl ibn al-Rabi, Yahya's replacement as vizier, lacked the abilities of the great Barmakid, and he had been given fewer responsibilities. Only the caliph could make the necessary decisions, and Harun resolved to go to Khorasan in person.

The caliph was suffering stomach pains and knew that he was seriously ill; but his acute sense of responsibility as leader of Islam, and his wish to keep intact the heritage of the Abbasids, gave him the courage he needed to make the long journey on horseback.

He left his third son, Qasim, who had been made governor of Syria-Awasim, in charge at Raqqa and passed through Baghdad, where he entrusted power in his absence to his heir, Amin. Mamun, for his part, observing that his father was not well, feared that the governorship of Khorasan granted to him in the succession agreement might be withdrawn if he was not present, and insisted on going too. Was he not, after all, governor of the eastern provinces? The vizier Fadl ibn al-Rabi and his principal secretaries also accompanied the caliph.

The journey was arduous. Each of Harun's sons had placed a spy in the caliph's entourage to report on his illness: the faithful Masrur — the swordbearer of the *Thousand and One Nights* — was working for Mamun, the doctor Jibril for Amin, and a third agent for Qasim. Those about Harun wished to hasten his end, and the Commander of the Faithful, the Caliph of Islam, was made to suffer atrociously by the intractable horses he was given to ride.

Hearing that there was a celebrated doctor at the court of one of the kings of India, Harun sent for him by the quickest means possible. The treatment gave him some temporary relief and he was able to make a number of decisions, including one to send Mamun to Merv immediately, so that his son would be in the capital with his troops in the event of the caliph's death. Harun spent a few days at Ray, moved on to Gurgan, and then, seeking better air, went to

Tus, where he took a turn for the worse. He stopped, unable to travel any further. There, after being captured in a battle, the brother of Rafi ibn Layt was brought to the caliph one day. "Enemy of God," said Harun, "you and your brother have wrought such havoc in Khorasan that I have been obliged to make this long journey in my present weakened state. Now, by God, I am going to make you suffer the most terrible death ever inflicted."[1] And the caliph awarded himself the dreadful satisfaction of having the man slowly cut up by a butcher, who detached his finger and toe joints one by one, then the larger joints, and finally cut his body into four pieces.

Despite his own sufferings and those he inflicted on others, Harun was still moved by poetry. He had these lines copied in beautiful calligraphy:

> Where are the kings, and all the others who lived before you?
> They are gone where you will go when your time comes.
> O you who have chosen the world and its delights, whose ear is ever open and avid for flattery,
> Drain all the pleasures of this world; they always end with death.[2]

"Could it not be said that these words are especially appropriate to me?" he asked.

On 24 March he called together all the Abbasids present in the army and addressed a few remarks to them:

> All that lives must perish. All that is young must grow old: you see what destiny has made of me. I give you three recommendations: keep religiously to your undertakings; be faithful to your imams and united among yourselves; and watch over Amin and Mamun: should one of them revolt against his brother, stifle his insurrection and condemn his perfidy and faithlessness.

Then he distributed some of his possessions and, since his death was already rumoured:

> he had an ass brought to him and attempted to mount, but his legs would not obey him and he could not hold himself in the

saddle. He inspected a number of winding-sheets and chose one for himself, saying as he gazed upon it these words from the Koran: "My wealth hath not profited me! My power hath perished from me."[3]

Harun died the same day (3 Djuma 193), in the presence of his son Salih, the vizier Fadl ibn al-Rabi, and his favourite servants. They buried him at Tus, in the garden of Sanabad. The place later came to be known as Meched, "Tomb of the Martyr", in memory not of the caliph but of the eighth Shiite imam, Ali al-Rida, who died at Tus in 818 and was buried near Harun. The imam's remains rest in a handsome mausoleum visited by Shiites from all over the world. Nothing survives to mark the resting place of Harun al-Rashid.

The Well-Guided
Thus ended, far from Baghdad, the reign of the caliph whose image came to be identified with the golden age of the Abbasids and of Arab civilization. Posterity always takes account of those things that add lustre to happy periods of history, allowing those that would tarnish them to fade into the shadows. Contemporaries of Harun who were still alive as the empire fell apart could remember it virtually intact, united under the remote but almost unquestioned authority of the Commander of the Faithful, whose opulent court reflected a prosperity without precedent.

As we shall see, the prosperity of townspeople was at its peak, enormous inequalities notwithstanding, during the twenty-three years of Harun's reign and the next few decades. Barely thirty years after its first brick was laid, Baghdad had become the economic centre of the known world. Men and goods flooded into Mesopotamia, which was full of new and expanding towns and had raw materials and finished goods flowing in and out in all directions. It was undoubtedly at the end of the eighth century and the beginning of the ninth, in the time of Harun the Good and his immediate successors, that the benefits of this prosperity reached the broadest cross-section of the population.

It was a period of fervent intellectual activity, which began during Mamun's reign. The flowering of poets, translators, and men of science (the new poetry) and the appearance of the first great prose writers, the luxury of the court, and the philanthropy of Zubaidah and the Barmakids, as well as that of the caliph himself, combined to paint a picture whose colours have only grown richer with the passage of time. The *Thousand and One Nights* gives us its reflection — often embellished, perhaps distorted, but exact in the overall effect when viewed not as a source of historical fact but as a portrait of the decor and texture of a society. This is how the period looked to the men who composed these stories about Baghdad and the towns of Mesopotamia. Masudi was describing memories of the Well-Guided Caliph when he wrote, more than a hundred years after Harun's death: "So great were the splendours and riches of his reign, such was its prosperity, that this period has been called 'the honeymoon'."

The half-legendary image of Harun al-Rashid's reign owes much to the contrast with the misfortunes that struck the caliphate and the Abbasids immediately afterwards. It is almost impossible to arrive at a clear assessment of the man or the sovereign. Lightweight hedonist and pitiless despot? Rigorous and faultless Muslim? Political genius? Crowned dolt? Praised to the skies and dressed in every virtue by some, denigrated by others, this man who might have been corrupted by absolute power was, in fact, a sovereign seldom given to excess and able to use authority without weakness or scruple — not pointlessly cruel, but without pity when the occasion demanded it. As Suleiman the Magnificent ordered his dearest friend, Ibrahim, to be killed before his eyes, so Harun had Jaffar beheaded and imprisoned his "father" Yahya and his most able minister, Fadl. These brutal deeds, carefully prepared for in absolute secrecy, show him to have been easily offended, treacherous and vindictive. He was also insecure and nervous, which is revealed in his attitude towards the Alids, whom he kept under constant surveillance, eliminating any who looked dangerous. He had some Yemeni rebels strangled, and on the very eve of his death condemned to the most dreadful tortures a brother of the rebel Fadl ibn Sahl. But we should not forget the spirit of permanent revolt which existed among his religious and political enemies — the Alids, Kharidjites, Zaidites, followers of Muqanna, and innumerable others — all of whom could count on social discontent to provide them with supporters.

There can be no doubt that Harun was deeply religious. For proof we have his nine pilgrimages to Mecca, in no way like pleasure trips despite the relative comfort in which he travelled; his hundred daily prostrations; and the charities that confirm his reputation for goodness. His love life, neither more nor less turbulent than those of other princes or even of rich commoners, violated none of the precepts of Islam.

He was touchingly devoted to his beloved Zubaidah until the end of his life, although her influence was not always a positive one. His fondness for drinking wine with his nadim was hardly exemplary, but there is no evidence of the excessive drinking supposedly indulged in by several other caliphs. The care he devoted to the education of his sons shows him to have been an attentive father. Seen in this light, he appears a worthy and affectionate man, epicurean but not given to excess — he would occasionally indulge in cookery as a hobby — God-fearing but even more afraid of anyone posing the slightest threat to his power or tarnishing it in any way. "He sometimes brings Louis XIV to mind" (Gaudefroy-Demombynes), and also Suleiman the Magnificent.

Opinions differ on Harun al-Rashid's political skill, as they do on the Sun King's. On the debit side must be listed Harun's obtuseness in supporting the Khorasan governor Ali ibn Isa despite the constant stream of unfavourable reports on him. The caliph's fiscal policy, in practice the work of the Barmakids, was unfortunate. It only worsened conditions for the rural populations and was a principal cause of the constant social unrest that troubled the empire. His foreign relations, conditioned almost exclusively by his plans against Byzantium, demonstrate a desire to broaden the empire's horizons and seek outside support in a long-term policy — with Charlemagne especially — which came to an end with his premature death.

Harun al-Rashid has been accused by contemporary and later commentators of hastening the disintegration of the empire by dividing it. The assessment is not entirely convincing. The immensity of its territories made them hard to rule or administer from Baghdad, and a measure of decentralization was not a bad idea. It was not Harun's fault that his two heirs turned out to be very different in ability. In any case, the centrifugal stresses were so strong that such a vast and disparate body could not long remain united under a single authority. Local particularisms and local interests were certain sooner or later to overcome the binding forces of language and religion, the two components of Arab–Islamic civilization. These were simply not strong enough to hold the empire together against steady political erosion.

This portrait of the great caliph, whose personality (like that of other men) exhibited one or two contradictions, would not be complete without mention of the fondness for arms he had acquired in his youth. Harun was a soldier all his life. From the moment he ascended the throne, he devoted a good deal of effort to consolidating a military system on the frontier with the Byzantine empire; later, to be nearer this work, he left wives, children, and possessions in Baghdad and moved to Raqqa, where he spent the last thirteen years — more than half — of his reign. We have seen that one of the great concerns of his life was to enlarge the domain of Islam through war. Exceptionally for an Abbasid caliph, he took part personally in expeditions into Byzantine territory, at least one of which was meant to seize Constantinople. His approaches to Charlemagne were made with these plans of conquest in mind; he delayed them to deal with the urgent problems in Khorasan, and his early death there left them forever unfulfilled.

Harun's Dispositions Vindicated

Zubaidah was in Raqqa when she heard of the caliph's death. She immediately organized a funeral ceremony at which Harun's daughters, his sister Ulaiyah, and the court dignitaries were present. The poet Ishak al-Mausili, asked to compose a eulogy, finally had the palace choir sing a funeral dirge from the time of the Umayyads. Other matters were already occupying people's attention. A few months later Zubaidah left Raqqa for Baghdad and moved into her palace of al-Karar, where she lived for the rest of her life.

Two days after Amin learned that he had become Commander of the Faithful, on a Friday, the bayah was taken at a ceremony in the mosque of the Round City. From the *minbar* the new caliph pronounced a eulogy of the deceased and summoned his subjects to obedience. Afterwards princes of the blood and high dignitaries filed past him one at a time, reciting the prescribed words. Other courtiers and officials, under the close surveillance of Amin's uncles, then took the oath of loyalty. The troops were given a bonus equivalent to two months' pay.

At Merv, Mamun himself announced the caliph's death and received the oath of loyalty on Amin's behalf and also in his own right as second in line to the throne. He paid his soldiers a year's salary. A few days later a number of political prisoners were released, including, at Zubaidah's request, the surviving Barmakids.

When he tried to settle the succession in advance, Harun had been aware that it would not be negotiated without difficulties. The oath at Mecca was intended to prevent the worst from happening. What followed, however, went beyond the most pessimistic forecasts and brought the empire to the brink of total collapse.

Harun had hardly drawn his last breath before people started tampering with his arrangements. At Karmasin (Kermanshah), during his last journey, he had given orders that in the event of his death the troops with him should be sent to Merv and placed under Mamun's command. On the day Harun died, however, an emissary of Amin who had arrived at Tus some time before, delivered some letters secretly given him in Baghdad by the heir to the throne (Harun, suspecting something, had had him searched, without success). One of them ordered that the caliph's family and court be placed under the authority of Fadl ibn al-Rabi and sent to Baghdad and that the army be put under the command of a named group of generals. These orders flagrantly contradicted those left by Harun, and the generals held a council to discuss them. Fadl ibn al-Rabi tipped the balance by saying, in substance, that he would sooner obey a live sovereign than a dead one. The officers did not take much convincing.

Mamun made no protest and busied himself repairing the damage caused by Ali ibn Isa's maladministration of Khorasan. Tax reductions, demonstrations of piety, and a more equitable justice system soon won over the masses; their support for the rebel Rafi ibn Layt melted away and he surrendered to General Harthama. Fadl ibn al-Rabi and Ali ibn Isa managed to get the governorship of Syria-Awasim withdrawn from Qasim. Mamun riposted by suspending postal communications between Khorasan and Baghdad and by replacing the governor of Ray, who was too easily influenced by Amin. Emissaries now arrived from Baghdad telling Mamun that Amin's own agents would be collecting the taxes in Khorasan in the future and that a representative of the post office, appointed by Amin, would be sending the latter daily reports on the province.

As these measures amounted to a request that he give up Khorasan, Mamun refused to allow them to be carried out.

Learning from the Abbasid revolution, which had begun in Khorasan with a conspiracy and an intensive propaganda campaign, Mamun kept the frontier under surveillance. Roadblocks were set up and caravans searched as they entered and left the province. He invested Ray with a conspicuously inadequate garrison, twenty thousand men commanded by one Tahir ibn Husein (who was to play a major role in the years to come). The brothers continued to exchange requests and refusals for several months. Mamun asked Amin to send him his wife Umm Isa and his children and to pay him the hundred million dinars bequeathed to him by his father. Amin refused, and took away by force some valuable jewellery Mamun had given his wife. But Mamun's active adviser Fadl ibn Sahl watched over his interests in Baghdad. Amin had already delegated power to his vizier and returned to his life of pleasure and amusement, giving himself up to the most extravagant fantasies.

Neither Mamun nor Amin doubted that their quarrel would end in armed confrontation. The break became inevitable when Amin displaced Mamun as heir to the throne in favour of his own two-year-old son, Musa. Mamun's name was no longer pronounced at Friday prayer and was replaced by Musa's on coinage and on the embroidery of the royal cloak. Amin also had the Mecca charter, which Harun had placed on the wall of the Kaaba, taken down and torn up. Mamun responded in kind. He removed Amin's name from his coinage and the Friday sermon and he dropped the title of heir presumptive and assumed that of imam. By November 810, less than two years after the death of Harun al-Rashid, nothing remained of his efforts to ensure family and political peace. The civil war was about to begin.

Amin chose Ali ibn Isa, the former Khorasan governor, to lead a force of about 40,000 against Mamun's army, defeat it and take him prisoner. Amin gave Ali a present of 200,000 dirhams and advised him to rule Khorasan justly and reduce the level of taxation. "If Mamun falls into your hands," he said, "send him to me in silver chains." Ali led his first-rate army towards Ray, where Tahir awaited him with 20,000 men. The two armies met outside the town where, after a fierce battle, Tahir broke the Iraqi centre and scattered his adversary. Ali, unhorsed and wounded, had his head cut off, and

Tahir sent it to Mamun, who on the same day assumed the titles Caliph and Commander of the Faithful.

There were now two caliphs. Amin, the caliph of Baghdad, immediately sent another army against Mamun, this time twenty thousand men of the abna led by a competent general, Abderahman ibn Djabalah. The engagement took place between Ray and the town of Hamadan, in which Abderahman took refuge after his defeat. Two months later he capitulated, but broke his word and was eventually killed. Tahir's way to Baghdad was clear.

Victory was now within Mamun's reach. He had demonstrated his superiority over the wretched Amin and the Baghdad government. But two more years, and a number of dramatic events, were to pass before he would enter his capital as a conqueror.

Amin sent new troops to replace his beaten armies, but his remaining generals were reluctant to risk the fate of their predecessors and he had trouble persuading anyone to lead the armies. Two of those who did agree to go, Ahmed and Abdallah, saw their troops routed before battle had even commenced by the rumour that the troops still in Baghdad had been given two years' pay as a bonus. This enabled Tahir to capture the important fortress of Holwan without spilling a drop of blood. Mamun ordered Harthama, who had now arrived with twenty thousand men, to hold the terrain so that Tahir could advance on Baghdad.

The capital was in a state of total confusion. The commander-in-chief of Amin's troops, General Husein ibn Ali ibn Isa, had tried to start a rebellion by proclaiming to his soldiers: "How can we bear the humiliation of being under the command of one who is neither man nor woman? Amin lives only for his pleasures and neglects both army and government." He was arrested, but the army was split. The caliph, unable to restore order, made the situation worse by distributing arms to the population, which he believed would fight for him. Mamun's two generals arrived outside the walls of Baghdad on 25 August 812, and besieged the city.

The "Commune" of Baghdad

Baghdad was well fortified and not an easy prize. Amin had had the gates strengthened and distributed money to the troops, some of whom were quartered by the Khorasan gate, where they faced Harthama's army. Tahir was camped before the Basra gate, and a

145

third general (in charge of Mamun's siege engines) was encamped to the south of the city. The town quickly fell into the hands of the populace. "Peaceable and enlightened people were lying low," Tabari writes. "Brigands thieves and vagabonds were masters of the city, killing and looting with impunity." The historian Kennedy compares Baghdad during the siege with Paris at the time of the Commune. "The collapse of authority among the traditional ruling class had given some popular elements, hitherto without influence, the opportunity to make their entrance to the political scene." All authority ended with the desertion of the commander of the caliph's guards. "Conduct of the war fell into the hands of adventurers and the dregs of the populace," Tabari writes. "Destruction and ruin continued until the splendours of Baghdad were no more." Masudi quotes these dramatic lines:

> It is for Baghdad that I weep, having lost the sweets of a life of riches... Some are cast brutally into the flames. Here a woman weeps for one of her own trampled by the mob, there a man with loud cries calls for his family, another for his cherished friend. A black-eyed girl calls for a brother who is no more; he is fallen beside his friend, a stranger from afar, a headless cadaver in the middle of the street. The massacre reaches into every corner. The son defends his father no longer, the friend abandons his friend. All that we cherished has gone, and I weep. The markets of Karkh are deserted, wandered by vagabonds and passers-by. The war has made the rabble give birth to wild lions with cruel teeth.

Ali the Blind, another poet, writes similarly:

> Our wars have raised up men who are not of Qahtan or of Nizar [Arab tribes], troops in woollen armour who fling themselves into battle like devouring lions... They do not know retreat. One of them alone, without even a breechclout to cover him, attacks a force of 2,000, crying as he strikes: "Take that from the vagabond warrior!" ... None remain in Baghdad but unfortunates doomed to misery, and escaped convicts... The mother is no longer safe in the harem; no uncle or other protector remains to defend the door. Nor are we willing, lately, to die for our faith. Lord, Thou who canst do all, may Thy name be invoked!

These naive and grandiloquent tones accurately reflect the disaster that had overtaken the great city, whose inhabitants were paying the price of the most enormous urban concentration of the age. The siege lasted a year and the fighting was extremely violent. Armed with staves and slings, helmets of palm leaves on their heads, and shields of plaited rushes tied to their forearms, the people of Baghdad fought with extraordinary bravery against Mamun's ironbound cavalry and its swords and lances. Destitute of everything, even clothes, they have been written into history under the name "The Naked". Masudi tells us that one day:

> The Naked, 100,000 in number, armed with spears and staves, wearing paper crests and blowing into reeds and bullhorns, joined Amin's other defenders and through several of the city's gates charged upon Mamun's supporters. A very bloody engagement followed; The Naked had the upper hand until midday, then, attacked by the whole of Mamun's army, gave ground. About 10,000 were drowned or perished by fire or steel.

The revolt of The Naked, who wanted Baghdad to remain the capital, was the forerunner of the frequent rioting that was to shake the great city at intervals long afterwards. On a rumour or sparked by a brawl, for political or economic reasons, the mob would take to the streets, looting, burning, destroying, and killing. These popular tornados became part of city life and were called *fitna* ("violation of the unity of the community of the believers"), their perpetrators becoming *al-amma* ("nameless and faceless mob"), brought onto the streets by hunger.

Amin had lost all control over the situation. Having no money left to distribute, he gave permission for those so inclined to break into the houses of his officials — something that had already been occurring for some time. He cried out in despair, "May God destroy both sides! For I have only enemies, those who are with me as much as those who are fighting me: the first want my goods, the second my life."

Events began moving faster towards the end of 813. With communications between the east and west banks cut, and the Karkh quarter occupied by enemy troops, Amin's territory was reduced to the Round City and its immediate surroundings. The caliph and

147

Zubaidah had left their palaces of al-Khuld and al-Karar and taken refuge in the Kubbat al-Khadra, in the heart of the town. Amin's few loyal generals advised him that his best course was to assemble a few hundred of the best soldiers of the abna and attempt a night sortie from one of the city gates. He could escape to Syria or Mesopotamia and from there try to recover his throne. He was dissuaded from following this plan by his entourage, which included agents of Tahir. Why not surrender, they suggested, but to Harthama, whose hot blood had been tempered by age and whom he knew, rather than to the overzealous Tahir? Amin contacted the old general secretly with this proposal, and an agreement was reached that Amin would surrender to Harthama, while the insignia of the caliphate — the cloak, staff, and ring — would be handed over to Tahir. Accompanied by only a handful of men, Harthama would bring a boat to a spot near the palace and the caliph would flee with him. At the last minute Harthama, who had observed suspect movement on the riverbank, suggested putting the operation off until after dark. Amin refused.

Arriving at the appointed time with his few men, Harthama threw himself at the caliph's feet, crying, "O my lord and master! O son of my lord and master!" The little group boarded the general's barge, but as it left the bank, armed men attacked it. They put so many holes in the boat that it sank under its occupants. Harthama was saved by a soldier who grabbed his hair, while Amin leapt into the water and swam to the opposite bank, where he was recognized, surrounded, and taken on a donkey to a nearby house. Promptly informed of the caliph's departure, Tahir sent several slaves, including a certain Koraich. Upon seeing them, Amin knew that his end was near, and showed great dignity. When his police chief, Ahmed, who had been arrested with him, said, "Accursed be the ministers who have placed you in this situation," he replied, "Speak nothing but good of my ministers. They are innocent. As for myself, I am not the first to have tried and failed to do something." He fell to praying. When armed Persian soldiers entered at about midnight, the caliph tried to sell his life dearly but was struck down by two blows to the head. Koraich, who had delivered them, cut Amin's head off and took it to Tahir, who observed the custom by exposing it on the main bridge of Baghdad.

So perished, on the night of 24 September 813, the eldest son of

Harun al-Rashid and the only caliph descended from the Prophet through both parents. His last words are supposed to have been: "We belong to God and to God we return! I am the Prophet's cousin, the brother of Mamun!"

Mamun was now the sole caliph, but there was a long road still to travel before he could establish authority over the empire. The aftereffects of the civil war were not to be effaced overnight, and a number of events delayed his return to the capital.

When Amin died, Mamun was still in Merv with his vizier and "protector" Fadl ibn Sahl, who hoped to make Khorasan — where he had great influence and powerful friends — the centre of the empire.

Either because Mamun wanted to put an end to the eternal squabble with the Alids or because he favoured their cause — probably for both reasons — in the spring of 817, surprisingly, he decided to name as heir presumptive Ali ibn Musa, better known as Ali al-Rida, eighth imam of the Duodecimian Shiites. Black, the colour of the Abbasids, was abandoned for the Alid colour, green. Ali was married to the caliph's daughter Umm Habib, and another of Mamun's daughters, Umm al-Fadl, was given in marriage to his son Mohammed. The Abbasids were not cut out of the succession, but the throne was to be occupied provisionally by the man thought most worthy, specifically the one likeliest to heal the quarrel between Alids and Abbasids, until peace was restored and it was possible for the caliphate to return to Abbas's line. Mamun's intention was to consolidate the caliphate by affirming the unity of the Prophet's family. What happened was the opposite.

Once again confusion reigned in Baghdad. Eventually the Abbasid princes who were at hand decided to depose Mamun and substitute as the new caliph someone who had been close to Harun. Their first choice was Mansour, a son of Mahdi, but he refused. Another of Mahdi's sons, Ibrahim, was then proclaimed caliph, and prayers were said in his name in the great Baghdad mosque on 24 July 817. Mamun's was no longer mentioned. Ibrahim received the name al-Mubarak, "The Blessed". Once again the empire had two rival caliphs.

Ibrahim was a strange choice. He was better known as a singer and musician than as a statesman. A great artist, close companion of Harun, pleasure-loving and quite prodigal, he was in no way suited to direct the empire, especially in its current circumstances. The treasury was empty, and Ibrahim soon had to draw on his own fortune to pay the troops. When this proved insufficient, he gave permission for officers to pay themselves out of the harvest of the Sawad (the Baghdad region). They appropriated crops and looted villages, which did little to increase the new caliph's popularity. Fresh riots broke out in the capital as Ibrahim's supporters clashed with the Alids.

Ibrahim's cause was plainly lost, and Mamun's solution to the Alid problem had failed: everyone but Mamun himself realized it. Ali al-Rida opened the caliph's eyes by explaining that the people opposed his nomination as heir presumptive because of Fadl ibn Sahl's presence at the head of the government. Most of the Muslims in the empire were against Mamun's passing power into Alid hands, and it was for this reason that Ibrahim had been proclaimed caliph. Mamun should therefore return to Baghdad, for only his presence could restore peace. The generals confirmed this analysis, and at the beginning of 818 Mamun left Merv. A few weeks later Fadl ibn Sahl was assassinated, probably on Mamun's orders. The caliph moved towards Iraq in brief stages; after six months he reached Tus, where he prayed at the tomb of Harun al-Rashid. It was there that Ali al-Rida died after "eating too many grapes" — poisoned, some said, at Mamun's request. Whatever their causes, these two deaths were very useful to the caliph: he was rid of the hated vizier and could abandon his Alid policy.

Tahir, who had stayed discreetly in Raqqa with his army, was ordered to march on Baghdad, which he reached at almost the same moment as the caliph, on 10 August 819. Harun al-Rashid had been dead for more than ten years.

7
Baghdad

Baghdad which has no equal either in the Orient or in the Western world.

Yakubi

Baghdad, in the heart of Islam, is the city of well-being; in it are the talents of which men speak, and elegance and courtesy. Its winds are balmy and its science penetrating. In it are to be found the best of everything and all that is beautiful. From it comes everything worthy of consideration, and every elegance is drawn towards it. All hearts belong to it, and all wars are against it.

Muqadassi

"What is the name of this place?" asked al-Mansour.

"Baghdad," came the answer.

"By God," replied the caliph, "this is the very town which my father, Muhammad ibn Ali, said that I should found and have as my dwelling place, and that my descendants would reign over after me. Since before the days of Islam no prince has been aware of its existence, in order that God's expectations and commands might be accomplished through my efforts: thus are the traditions proved true and the signs and portents made clear. Assuredly this 'island' bordered to the East by the Tigris and to the West by the Euphrates will become the crossroads of the universe. It will be the mooring for ships sailing up the Tigris from Wasit, Bassorah, Ubulla, Ahwaz, Fars, Oman, Yamama, Bahrein and other places. Goods will arrive here along the upper Tigris from Mossul, Diyar Rabia, Rakka, Syria, the Marches (of Asia Minor), Egypt and the Maghreb. The town will also be accessible to the peoples of the Djabal, of Ispahan and the provinces of Khorasan. Praise be to God, Who has kept this capital for me by leaving all my predecessors ignorant of it! By God, I will build it and dwell in it for all of my life, and it will be the residence of my descendants; and it will surely be the most prosperous town on earth."[1]

The Most Prosperous Town on Earth

Virtually no trace remains of this glorious prodigy of urban success. The site owed nothing to the contours of nature: there were no hills like those of Rome and Istanbul, no cool oasis like the one at Damascus, and no acropolis on which to build a citadel like those of Athens and Jerusalem. Other big towns — Babylon, Seleucia, Ctesiphon — had been built relatively nearby. Like Baghdad, all were on the route joining the Iranian plateau with Mesopotamia and Syria. For thousands of years men, crops, and merchandise had been moving between the Mediterranean and central Asia, India, and the Far East along the old road that crosses the Zagros between Khaniqin and Hamadan to reach the Mesopotamian plain not far to the north. The land around Baghdad is seldom flooded, and the Tigris is close enough to the Euphrates for linking canals to be built without difficulty. This nexus of communications, easy to defend, was perceived on sight to be an exceptionally well-endowed spot. An enormous urban concentration swiftly developed there.

Mansour's original plan was to build a city-fortress in which he could centralize power: a political and administrative capital without gardens or gymnasiums. What took shape day by day was a metropolis whose splendour and riches attracted multitudes of men from all corners of the empire and beyond. Begun as a palace and government complex, Baghdad was a large town before a dozen years had passed; less than half a century later Harun al-Rashid's capital was the biggest city in the world, with a population of perhaps a million. This was at a time when the biggest cities in northern Italy and Flanders were inhabited by at most forty thousand souls. The Paris of that time seems minuscule by comparison with Baghdad's hundred square kilometres. Only Constantinople, or perhaps Damascus or Cairo, which would soon have populations of three hundred thousand to five hundred thousand, could stand the comparison.

This kind of phenomenal expansion has occurred at various points in history — for example, in Europe during the twelfth and thirteenth centuries and in the Balkans and Anatolia during the fifteenth and sixteenth centuries. Its causes are always the same: peace, political stability, efficient administration, and new resources or economic currents widely exploited by active populations. For these reasons the Arab Orient of the eighth and ninth centuries was the scene of one of the most impressive bursts of urban development the world has ever seen.

Baghdad offered all the conditions necessary for this growth, and Mansour's stroke of genius was to have recognized and exploited them. The agricultural economy was in full expansion following development work carried out under the Sassanids: the draining of marshes and the irrigation of dry tracts; the introduction of sugarcane, the date palm, the orange tree, and various textile plants (especially cotton). Situated in a fertile area needing only the attention of gardeners and farmers to make it productive, Baghdad, like an island between its two rivers, was made even more amenable by its canal network. As people poured into the town, its incessant construction and growing needs called in their turn for ever-increasing supplies of manpower and capital. The feverish speculation that resulted is illustrated by this anecdote reported by the historian al-Khatib al-Baghdadi: A Byzantine ambassador to the court of Mahdi stopped suddenly during a tour of the city and said to the great chamberlain accompanying him, "Here is a spot which is ideally suited to a business investment. Would you be so kind as to ask the caliph to lend me half a million dirhams? I am sure I can double it in a year." The ever-generous Mahdi answered, "Give him the half-million dirhams he demands and add another half million. When he goes back home, be sure to send him each year the earnings of this money." This was done, and the Byzantine used the caliph's money to build a flour mill at the confluence of two rivers close to the town. Every year until his death, the profits of his business were forwarded to him.

Like the basileus's ambassador, everyone — starting with the Abbasid family and all the officials of the state, great and small — went in for speculation. Land was bought and sold, shares were taken in business ventures, and the religious prohibitions concerning the lending and handling of money were less than scrupulously observed.

Those who had been granted land by the caliph were the first to settle close to the Round City. They were led by the regime's most loyal subjects and, in particular, the members of the Abbasid family. Did not Mansour say of them when instructing his son, "Respect them, put them in the forefront, be generous in your dealings with them, place them above others; for their glory is also yours, and the praises addressed to them are also addressed to you"? Mahdi's sons settled on the east bank, while the caliph built his palace at al-Rusafa, on the other side of the Tigris, where his entourage and high officials joined him.

The Sahaba also established themselves on land given them by the caliph. Belonging to the most faithful tribes (Koraish, Ansar, Yemen), they were the caliph's closest companions. There were many of them at his court, where they kept alive the literary and poetic traditions of the pre-Islamic past. Mansour had encouraged them to teach his heir, Mohammed (Mahdi), Arab literature and history, and Mahdi did the same with his own sons Hadi and Harun. Many other Arabs were also given land. The Abbasids did not forget the debt they owed to tribal chiefs whose influence had yielded towns like Mosul, Wasit, Basra, and Kufa into their hands during the revolution.

Nor did they forget the decisive support of the troops of Khorasan, those Persianized Arabs settled in Iran who formed the spearhead of the army that carried them to power. Returned to the Arabic tradition, reorganized on a tribal basis, and said to be "loyal, generous and uncorruptible", they were the most dependable units in the armies of the first Abbasid caliphs. In Harun's time they owned whole neighbourhoods just outside the Round City, grouped in accordance with their places of origin in Persia.

The mawali occupied a quarter of their own. After Mansour's death, Mahdi had increased their prestige by giving them a role in the administration (especially in the barid), which expanded still further in Harun's time. Only later, after the dramatic quarrel between his sons, did they begin to dissolve as a group and mingle gradually with the general mass of Muslims. In the early days many were counted among the caliph's closest advisers, and some even became viziers. Their intervention was sometimes decisive in settling problems with the succession. Outside their residential district, in all parts of the town they owned pieces of land granted them by caliphs.

Mansour's original plans contained no provision for extending the metropolis, but expansion became necessary to accommodate the flood of immigrants who started arriving as soon as the caliph took up residence under the Green Dome. Mansour was doubtless as surprised as anyone. The newcomers, of widely varied origins, were neither disciplined nor trustworthy, and the authorities were wholly unprepared for the scale of the problem. The first immigrants came from Khorasan, the Yemen, the Hejaz, Wasit, Kufa; they were followed by a flood of people from every part of the Orient and of all social classes — intellectuals, craftsmen, merchants, smugglers, unemployed vagabonds — who crowded into the town and its environs. The market had already been moved to al-Karkh, southwest of the city, and this section quickly became the main commercial centre. Yakubi describes it as follows: "A sizeable market, about two parasangs[2] in length by one wide. Each trade had its own allotted avenues arranged in shops, stalls and courtyards, so that the trades and professions would not be mixed together." This division of markets into separate areas for different activities was not new, and still exists today in the Orient.

Al-Karkh grew quickly until, in Yakubi's words, "there was no larger or more splendid quarter in Baghdad". Elegant houses were built, jumbled in with more modest dwellings, in the disorder to be found in almost every Oriental town. But some neighbourhoods became more fashionable than others because of a sort of snobbery resulting from the social stratification that characterized big towns in the Abbasid period. Al-Shamassia was one of these sought-after addresses: judges lived on some streets, rich merchants on others, shopkeepers on still others. Of course, the character of neighbourhoods often changed as a result of political and social events; even markets were sometimes moved from one part of the town to another.

In a very short time the right bank of the Tigris, where the Round City and the Karkh quarter were situated, became overcrowded, and the town overflowed onto the east bank of the river close to the camp Mansour had built for his son Mahdi. This new quarter, al-Rusafa, sprang up around the caliph's palace. Mahdi's generosity and the buildings constructed by his officers and staff attracted more and more people into the district. The Barmakids moved there and added to its prosperity. Yahya and Jaffar each built a luxurious palace; later Amin and Mamun did the same. For superstitious reasons or for love of building, no caliph seemed willing to live in his predecessor's house and built a new one for himself more luxurious than the last. Harun, who had several palaces in different regions of Iraq, moved from one to another accompanied by his enormous household and staff. Settlements sprang up around these palaces: built of dried-mud brick and occasionally of baked brick, they collapsed as soon as maintenance ceased.[3] The local people would then help themselves to secondhand materials, reducing these dwellings to the sort of formless ruins that still cover the Mesopotamian landscape.

By the end of the eighth century, there were twenty-three palaces in Baghdad, each covering a substantial area. Most of them were in the southern part of the city known as Dar al-Khalifa. Baghdad now sprawled on both sides of the river. In Harun's day the banks were linked by three pontoon bridges, one close to the Khorasan gate, another at al-Karkh, the third further south. As the town was intersected by a network of canals, both goods and passengers were transported largely by water. According to Muqadassi, "The people of Baghdad come, go and move about on water. Two-thirds of properties in the town give onto the river." As in Venice, the waterways were crossed by numerous small bridges and crowded with thousands of barges and pinnaces. It was said that every inhabitant "should have an ass in the stable and a boat on the river". Caliphs possessed extravagant processional barges; Amin had six, each in the form of an animal: eagle, lion, horse, elephant, dolphin, and serpent.

Egalitarian but Structured

The town was immense, octopus-like. The most ostentatious luxury — and the most refined — existed alongside misery of a frightfulness known only in the Orient. Fanatical religious sects frequently engaged in bloody outbursts. Fires and floods ravaged the buildings, and epidemics the population, without warning and at hurricane speed.

> Baghdad is a marvellous place for the rich
> But for the poor a place of misery and distress.
> Long will I wander, confused, through its streets,
> Lost like the Koran in an atheist's house.[4]

All Muslims belong to the *umma*, the community of believers whom God judges without distinction. There is no hierarchy of birth in Islam, no nobility, apart from that formed by the Prophet's family: this is divided into Talibids (Talib was the father of Ali) and Abbasids, the former called Sharif and the latter Sayyid. The regime made sure that these relatives, who numbered several thousand, enjoyed a decent standard of living. But, according to *sharia* (Muslim law), every believer, whatever his place in society, is the equal of any other. Such, at any rate, is the juridical ideal.

The realities of daily life in Baghdad were more complex. Abbasid society was clearly structured into a hierarchy, which was based mainly on money.

The Slaves

At the bottom of the social scale were the slaves, who were numerous in the towns (few were employed on the land).[5] The institution of slavery in the Orient dated from prehistory and had become a characteristic feature of Oriental societies. It is mentioned several times in the Old Testament.[6] The Babylonians even made it legal for parents to sell their children who had behaved badly towards them, and a husband was entitled to sell his wife. In this matter the Prophet Mohammed was a reformer: the Koran instructs that slaves be treated like other men.[7] The Hadith include these words attributed to Mohammed: "And your slaves! Make sure that they eat the same food and wear the same clothes as yourselves. And should they commit an offence you are unwilling to forgive, sell them; for they are God's servants, and should not be tormented."[8]

The majority of the eunuchs who watched over the caliph's harem were white, either Slavs (hence the word "slave"), or Greeks from Syria and Armenia (several originally destined for the clergy). Although they had been castrated before being put up for sale,[9] some took concubines and even wives. Blacks were trimmed "to belly level" to prevent them from procreating. Of the many slaves in the entourage of caliphs, some were entrusted with official missions; they included generals, admirals, and high court dignitaries.

During Harun al-Rashid's time the fashion for eunuchs degenerated into sexual perversion. Amin had such a passion for eunuchs that his mother, Zubaidah, used to dress the prettiest girls in her harem in boys' clothing to tempt him away from them.[10] The fashionable world followed suit, and pretty girls at court who were slim enough to get away with it began disguising themselves as boys. The Junoesque figures hitherto preferred fell out of favour and small-bosomed, narrow-hipped women became the beauties of the day. "She was tall and slim, with marvellous outpointing breasts... a bee's waist... and all her body wavered like the tender shoot of a willow," says the *Thousand and One Nights*.[11] This taste for the *ghulamiyyat* (*ghulam* means "slave") swept through the aristocracy and the moneyed classes, although men with an exclusive passion for boys seem to have been unusual. Pederasty, rarely practised by Arabs before Islam, may have come from Khorasan and caught on during the first few centuries with the importation of young white slaves from Europe. There are innumerable poems addressed to boys; but were these verses expressions of genuine sexual passion or merely a fashionable exercise, similar to those cropping up later in Persian and Ottoman society?

Slaves also worked in business and commerce (either directly for their owners or autonomously on the owner's behalf), as builders and craftsmen. Big enterprises employing large numbers of slaves were rare. Generally the slaves were treated with the moderation prescribed by the Koran. It was considered a pious act to set slaves free, and this was very often done in fulfilment of a vow or oath. The slave would then be totally free but usually remained tied to his former master as a "client" or follower.

Slave women were used primarily for domestic work, and every well-off household possessed several. Young and pretty slaves might become the master's concubines. The edict against using concubines as prostitutes was seldom infringed; more often their master would have them trained in singing, music, and poetry. The concubines of imperial princes — Khaizuran, for example — had often been bought after receiving instruction in accomplishments and good manners provided by their owners, who regarded them as an enormously profitable investment. When a concubine bore a child, it was compulsory to set her free, while the child, if recognized by the father, had exactly the same rights as his legitimate children.

Numberless children were born to concubines of every origin and of all races, with extensive ethnic mixing the result. From the eighth century onwards almost all caliphs were the sons of slaves;

Harun himself was no exception. The same equality existed among the offspring of aristocratic or wealthy families.

The People

Above the slaves in status but often below them in living standards were the plebs of Baghdad, a class that included barefoot ragamuffins and small shopkeepers, as well as a whole range of porters, bath boys, peddlers, handymen, idlers, and seasonal labourers who made up the motley street mob of all colours, races, and tongues so characteristic of the capital of the Abbasid empire. Beggars and cripples without work or fixed abode wandered the city by day looking for work or a crust to eat, and by night sought shelter in mosque courtyards, under bridges, or in some other remote corner.

They supplied the rank and file of the bands of semi-brigands which looted rich neighbourhoods and pillaged the shops and warehouses whose owners refused to pay protection money. In times of crisis, as during the war over Harun's succession, these outlaws (*ayyarun*), armed with slings and cudgels and protected by palm-leaf shields and helmets, took part in uprisings and were capable of confronting the caliph's cavalry. Some joined the police (*shurta*), either for the wages or — surprisingly often — to neutralize the forces of order when there was trouble. Sometimes confused with the *fityan* — organizations of young men seeking to live without working — the shurta were the fityan's allies in struggles against the authorities. When led and organized by the fityan, they were a formidable fighting force.

The large class of peddlers and small shopkeepers, though seldom poverty-stricken, had very limited means. If Baghdad had been known as a place where it was easy to starve to death, it would not have attracted the numbers of people it did from the fringes of the empire. The expansion of commerce raised the population's standard of living to a level most European towns would have envied in the early Middle Ages.

The Bourgeoisie

The middle class was composed mainly of traders and merchants, doctors, landlords, and officials. Buildings and landed property were profitable when not excessively taxed. (According to al-Tanukhi,[12] the tax on the revenues of a granary was equivalent to more than half the profit — one of the many bitter complaints recorded by chroniclers of the time.) The range of incomes was evidently very broad, both among the owners of gardens and cultivable land around Baghdad and among shopkeepers. Although business was always good for restaurant owners, butchers and sellers of cooked meat, fruit, vegetables, and so on, the ubiquitous small street sellers did not make an easy living. Petty officials did not earn enough to buy land close to Baghdad, which successful traders had been acquiring since the beginning of the ninth century. Teachers and poets lived on what they could get from their pupils and patrons; the latter could be generous in the extreme, some poets living almost like lords.

Many of these traders, landlords, artisans, and small businessmen were descended from men who had been given land by the first caliphs as a reward for their loyalty; these estates (iqta) surrounded the town. Some prospered, while others lived more modestly on decent incomes. A cloth merchant or modest landowner might leave an estate of eight hundred to one thousand dinars. Those possessing a garden from one of Mansour's iqta could rent it out for a high sum.

The middle class also included craftsmen, who sold the articles they made in their own shops. Utility and household objects were almost all made by these private artisans. State-owned or state-controlled workshops monopolized shipbuilding, arms manufacture, and much of the textile industry. Craftsmen were subject to strict price and quality controls imposed by the state; for some products, especially textiles, a government stamp was required.

The transformation of the half-agrarian, half-pastoral Mesopotamian economy into a commercial economy created giant centres of commerce, of which Baghdad was the first; and from about the end of the eighth century these changes led to social upheavals on a vast scale. The most important of the changes was undoubtedly the appearance of a "bourgeoisie", which in a short time became essential to every aspect of life in the empire. The bourgeoisie was one of the main supporters of the Abbasid regime.

The profession of merchant is highly regarded in Islam: "The trustworthy merchant shall be seated at the foot of God's throne," as the Prophet is supposed to have said. Or, in the words of the caliph Omar: "I would rather die in the saddle of my camel during a business trip than be killed in some holy war." A hero of the battle of Qadisiya against the Sassanids declared: "One dirham earned by trade means more to me than ten paid to me for soldiering." Theologians emphasize the fact that Abu Bakr, the first caliph, was a cloth merchant and Othman, the third, a grain importer. The display of wealth is not frowned upon; quite the contrary according to this Hadith: "When Allah gives riches, He wishes them to be seen."

Ostentatious display had been widely discussed at the beginning of Islam. Seldom have so many men scented themselves, dyed their hair, covered themselves with jewels, and worn costly clothing as in Baghdad. Luxurious habits were not regarded as terribly shocking, although some fastidious spirits were more critical of flamboyance than, for example, of the habit of buying and maintaining harems of young slaves. Had not the Prophet himself and his son-in-law Ali many concubines in addition to their legitimate wives?

The accumulation of wealth was not condemned, either. Mohammed is supposed to have said, "Poverty is next to apostasy." But financial and commercial transactions were expected to be fairly conducted: promises were to be kept, customers were not to be misled, defective merchandise was not to be passed off as good, and debtors were not to be treated brutally. Honesty, even delicacy, was required of a trader who wished to please God.

The Equals of Princes...

In Baghdad, people often took the name of their profession in place of the traditional tribal name, especially if the profession was an honoured one: cloth manufacturers and merchants, for example, called themselves Bazza(s) after their trade. The cloth market, separate from the other trades, was based close to the mosque, along with banking and jewellery. The power of big merchants — importers, exporters, shipowners, jewellers, dealers in grain and oil — was considerable. Some did an enormous volume of business, and lent money to caliphs and viziers in exchange for protection (which might include turning a blind eye to practices of dubious legality). Their pressure groups brought influence to bear on the government and the state. Outside the court itself, they were the ones who lived in the greatest luxury, possessing the finest houses and gardens, the most beautiful slaves, and the largest household staffs. For such advantages, they compensated by building mosques and fountains, maintaining charitable institutions, and giving liberal alms. Traders and bankers, like princes, protected and supported writers, poets, musicians, and singers; they invited the artists to their homes, where the latter would form a "court" to flatter the patron's intellectual and artistic "expertise".

Like everyone else in Baghdad, the bankers and big traders were of very diverse ethnic origins. Persians and men from Basra and southern Arabia were considered the most skilful in business; but the people of Kufa could hold their own in every way. Greeks (found everywhere in the empire), Levantines, and Indians were also regarded as clever businessmen. The Jews were redoubtable rivals to all of them; many lived in Baghdad, where their strength was in money-changing and banking. They too lent money to viziers and to the state.

The time when generals and secretaries (kuttab) had taken precedence over everybody else was over. When the wars of conquest ended, the regime had as much need of rich men versed in business as it did of civil servants and officers to maintain its armies. Neither princes nor high dignitaries turned up their noses at merchants. A Persian maize dealer was on intimate terms with Mamun's vizier Fadl ibn Sahl; Mamun's successor, al-Mutasim, appointed as vizier one Zayyat, the oil merchant whose father supplied the court. Rare under the first Abbasids, Arabs of bourgeois origin swarmed around the caliph by Harun al-Rashid's time.

Many of these merchants were also religious men and intellectuals. It has been noted that the majority of theologians were merchants or merchants' sons — more than 60 per cent in the ninth century — and especially textile dealers. Muslim merchants had always been protected by Islamic law, which set customs duties of 10 per cent for foreign merchants, 5 per cent for the non-Muslim subjects of an Arab state, and only 2½ per cent for Muslims.

Clergymen and Judges

Ulemas (clergymen) occupied an envied social position. They were counted among the *ayan* (notables) and played an essential part in the daily life of the people of Baghdad. Everyone, princes and paupers, consulted these pious and learned men on all occasions and treated them with the greatest respect.

A great many men devoted their lives to the branches of Koranic science: commentators on the Koran associated with the different sects and juridical schools; "collectors" of the Prophet's words who spent their time examining sayings attributed to Mohammed; jurists who answered all sorts of questions put to them by cadis or perhaps by the caliph; preachers whose Friday sermons gave them such power that they were often appointed by the caliph himself; street orators who guided public opinion in not only spiritual but also political matters and who had therefore to be kept under close surveillance; muezzins... All these men were important to the life of the capital. Islam was still less than two centuries old, its dogmas had yet to be established, and there were frequent and fervid controversies. Religion and politics were closely entwined, and the Alid problem in particular was still far from being settled.

Cadis also belonged to the ulema class. Arbitrators in disputes between individuals, they had the heavy responsibility of judging their neighbours and with it much power and prestige. Not every jurist would accept the job; some felt it weighed too heavily on their conscience. Others refused to receive any salary, maintaining that sitting in judgment on their neighbours could not be treated as a trade. Many lived in conspicuous poverty, like the two Baghdad brothers who possessed only one turban and one garment between them, so that when one went out, the other had to stay at home; or the chief justice who dressed in the cheapest cotton. So fiercely independent were some cadis that they refused to stand up in the presence of the caliph. When the caliph Mamun appeared in court one day as a simple citizen and sat down in the presence of the judge, the latter ordered a cushion to be brought for Mamun. And the philosopher al-Kindi reports that when in Egypt a representative of Queen Zubaidah had the impudence to sit down during a hearing, the cadi sentenced him to ten strokes of the whip. During the eighth and ninth centuries, judges sat in mosques, always dressed in the Abbasid colour black, with the plaintiffs seated round them in a circle. Only witnesses of good reputation were heard, and those who were not well known were investigated before being allowed to give evidence.

In this way Islam continued the tradition born in the empires of the ancient Orient that nothing, not even religion, is more important to a people than justice. It survived intact in the Ottoman empire, one of whose most glorious and respected sovereigns, Suleiman the Magnificent, was nicknamed "the Legislator" by his subjects.

Apart from religious differences, which sometimes led to violence between Muslims, these peoples from the four points of the compass lived in harmony, without the slightest trace of racial segregation. There was a normal healthy pride in one's origins, but there was no question whatsoever of treating a man with contempt for the colour of his skin. In any case, at all levels of society people's origins were so mixed that nobody could claim racial purity, the caliphs, as has been noted, included. Racism was unknown in Islam; also unknown was hatred for Christians, Jews, or others not sharing faith in the Prophet. In Baghdad no distinction was made between Muslims and followers of the Bible.

The majority of Christians were Nestorians. It was in their monastery of Dayr al-Attiq, a little to the south of what was to become the Round City, that Mansour was received when he came to choose the site of his capital. The Christians had a number of churches and convents, especially in the Karkh quarter; and there were many Nestorians in al-Shamassia. Monophysites were less in evidence. But neither group was troubled in any way, and Baghdad under the first Abbasids was an important centre for Nestorian missions to central Asia.

Nor did the Jews have much to complain about at that time. Settled in Mesopotamia for more than twelve centuries, farmers, townspeople, and craftsmen, they had not been disturbed during the Muslim conquests or the Abbasid revolution; indeed, these upheavals had somewhat improved their situation, as they had been persecuted by the Zoroastrian Sassanids. The chiefs of the community moved into the Round City as soon as it was built, and Baghdad became their judicial and administrative centre. Under Harun certain Jews were very influential in politics and especially in finance. On the religious and intellectual fronts, the Talmudic school of Baghdad sent its rays far beyond the frontiers of the empire: "academies" of what has been called Babylonian Talmudic scholarship spread the rabbinical tradition as far as southern Europe.

Life in Baghdad

This is the famous city of Baghdad, the home of sweetness! She lies beyond the assaults of winter, sleeping in the shade of her roses in an eternal Spring, with flowers and gardens and the murmur of many streams.

34th Night

From the sumptuous mansion of the court dignitary or great merchant to the porter's hovel and the shop doorway sheltering the beggar for the night, Baghdad contained every imaginable sort of dwelling.

The climate is torrid for part of the year, and most of what we would call middle-class houses possessed a garden for air and coolness, with a pond shaded by palms and cypresses. Roses were grown, also narcissus, anemones, violets, jasmine, lilacs, and pinks; lotus floated on the ponds. The tulip had not yet arrived from central Asia, but orange trees, brought from India, were beginning to appear. Gardens became a passion, as they did later among the Ottomans, who expended vast sums to buy tulip bulbs. Numerous poets sing of the sweet evenings spent in their cool fragrance, with poetic competitions, songs and music, and the enjoyment of innocent — and not so innocent — games.

Following the ancient Babylonian techniques, houses were built of sun-dried or kiln-fired brick — for the poorest dwellings, pounded earth — cemented with clay or mortar and with rushes laid between the layers of bricks. The bricks were plastered over, often in panels placed to create effects of form and colour. Ceramics were used for the same purpose — tiles with a metallic glitter (called *kashani* after the town of Kashan), hexagonal or square in outline, blue or turquoise, green or yellow. Baghdad was the world centre for glazed ceramics. Stucco decoration in the form of linear or arabesque patterns or stylized flowers was widely used, mainly for door and window embrasures; this style was brought to perfection at Samarra. Doors were often made from ebony or other precious woods and decorated with gold leaf.

Roofs were flat, as everywhere in the Orient, and people slept on them during the hot summer nights. Multi-storeyed houses were rare in Baghdad, but in other towns at this time — in Fostat, for example — houses of up to eight floors existed. Rich dwellings were entered through an ornately decorated passage (*dilhiz*) leading to an internal courtyard, around which were arranged the rooms reserved for the men and for entertaining guests. Another passage led to a second courtyard, which was the centre of the harem. A third section contained servants' quarters. A house might have fifty rooms, nearly all giving onto internal courtyards; those opening onto the street would have corbelled bays or windows. Light was admitted through round windows twenty to fifty centimetres in diameter.

Water for domestic use was brought from the Tigris on the asses or the mules of water carriers, but there were also channels carrying water from the reservoirs. Some houses had wells in their courtyards (building a drinking fountain has always been regarded as a pious deed in Islam). The people of Baghdad used all sorts of means to make their houses cooler: rooms set in the basement with ventilation conduits arranged to catch the wind;[13] running water over the walls; a piece of water-moistened cloth shaken to and fro by a servant (*punkah*); blocks of ice placed in the cavity of a double wall. The very rich also placed pieces of ice in the dome covering one of the rooms. Heating was easier: charcoal burned in braziers of iron (for common mortals) or of silver or silver gilt (for the rest). The cold season in Baghdad is unpleasant but mercifully short.

There was little furniture. People lived on the floor, although beds were not unknown in rich households. "Climb upon this bed, my lord...," a young person says to a king in the *Thousand and One Nights*. In Harun's time the sarir was used as a sofa; it was long enough for at least two people to sit side by side in the Oriental manner. At night people slept on a mattress (*firas*), whose stuffing would be more or less comfortable according to the owner's means. The thickness of cushions depended on the stature of the persons expected to sit on them; people of refinement had them stuffed with down and with the fur and feathers of exotic animals and birds.

The wealth of a household could also be measured by the number and quality of its carpets. The most prized came from Tabaristan and Armenia; red in colour and woven from fine wools, they had been valued since the time of the Umayyads. Harun's wives sat only on carpets and cushions from Armenia, the only ones thought worthy of the caliph's court. Also desirable were carpets from

166

Isfahan and Mazenderan, which could be found in all colours and patterns. From Hira (southern Iraq) came carpets admired for their decorative birds, horses, camels, stylized flowers, and geometric designs.

There were no large items of furniture in a house of the eastern Middle Ages; only low objects, such as storage chests — for eating-vessels, clothes, books, money, jewellery — made from metal, wood, woven fibres, and precious metals. Some, like the *sunduq*, were so long and wide that a man could sleep on top of them; others, small enough to slip into a sleeve. Objects were also arranged on shelves in wall niches which might be more or less decorated. Heavy furniture — cupboards and the like — did not exist.

Large private houses had bathrooms, equipped in the same way as public *hammams*. Opposed at the beginning of the Hegira because of its foreign origins, the use of the bath caught on during the eighth and ninth centuries (daily ritual ablutions are prescribed by Islam). But a tenth-century caliph still called the hammam "the Grecian bath". By Harun's time, baths were to be found in every town. Baghdad had between fifteen thousand and sixty thousand (depending on the period and the authority cited). The true figure in the eighth century must certainly have been closer to the first than to the second. The buildings were designed without architectural pretensions; some were coated with asphalt, which made them look as if they were fashioned of black marble. Masudi notes that they were often decorated with images of the fabulous bird Anqa, an Oriental angel with a man's head bearing a bird's beak, four wings on each side, and talons in place of hands.

During this period the hammam acquired a social role that still survives in Muslim countries. Men and women used it on different days, and friends would meet there to exchange news and gossip. Bath houses were not always safe, as one Mohammed Sakara points out: "I shall not be returning to the baths of ibn Musa, despite their incomparable perfume and heat. There are now so many thieves there that prudent bathers arrive naked and barefoot. Like Mahomet I arrived, only to depart like Bishr [a famous Sufi]."

The hammam was a sort of annexe to the mosque,[14] which itself was the vital centre of Muslim life, the community's meeting place, where believers would gather to pray and hear the imam. The Abbasid revolution was claimed to have been carried out in the name of a religion neglected and distorted by the Umayyads. Their successors wanted to stamp the regime with the mark of Islam, and to spread religion through propaganda and the multiplying of places of worship. Caliphs and princes therefore built mosques all over the empire, especially in Baghdad.

Arab historians make extravagant claims about the number of mosques in the capital during the ninth century, some even suggesting as many as sixty thousand. The earliest of the Great Mosques (*djami*) — those used for midday prayer on Fridays — was the one in the Round City. Harun al-Rashid rebuilt it almost entirely in 807; another Great Mosque was built later in al-Rusafa and a third in 901 near the new Tadj palace. Government proclamations were read out from the pulpit (minbar) at the time of the Friday sermon (*khutba*); also, during the first centuries of the Abbasids, the Great Mosque was the setting for the oath of loyalty to new caliphs on their accession. These mosques were also used as assemblies where supporters and opponents of the regime could meet (and often come to blows). Demonstrations and revolts sometimes broke out there; the imam might be attacked and the pulpit overturned.

There were also countless small mosques — neighbourhood oratories or chapels. These were small buildings where the local inhabitants gathered for prayer five times daily. They were actually frequented at all hours, because mosques served as shelter for travellers and the homeless. The cadi heard his cases there, and the sage would teach his pupils, who sat around him on mats or carpets. Above all, the neighbourhood mosque was a place for the exchange of news, got at some slight risk of being robbed, as thieves hung about there in search of prey. In the courtyard, stallkeepers would set up their displays and sell everything from books to food and cool scented water. Meetings were held there; in the evening especially, after a day of oppressive heat, the mosque and its surroundings would present a scene as lively as that of a forum. Jugglers, conjurors, and the *qusass*[15] (storytellers), who played an important role in Muslim life, practised their skills in the courtyard.

It was not until the end of the ninth century that caliphs ordered the merchants to be turned out of the temple. At about the same time, the mosques were embellished with chandeliers of precious metal and glass lamps, hung from chains of silver or gilded copper. Also at this time mosques began to be illuminated in the evening on Muslim feast days; they thus became reflections of the caliph's power.

Dress

The variety of clothing worn in Baghdad gave its streets a colourful and picturesque appearance difficult to imagine today. Every ethnic group had its own traditional dress, and any busy street would have contained styles of Arab, Persian, Turkish and Berber origin, with a good sprinkling of Greek and Slavic costumes worn by slaves from across the Mediterranean.

Some items of clothing were worn by almost everybody. The *izar* was a cloth worn draped around the body, which women also used to cover their heads. The populace wore a shorter, knee-length version, the *mizar*, while the poor covered themselves with a sort of robe, usually woollen, called a *shamla*, which also served as a blanket. Bedouins wrapped themselves in a heavy woollen *aba*. Next to the skin, both men and women wore a *ghilala* and a *sirwal*, like a pair of trousers held up by a cord. The *qamis* (hence *chemise*, shirt) might be made with wide sleeves that could be used as pockets. The duraa (sleeved garment), mentioned earlier, was obligatory dress at the palace. The caliph and other high dignitaries would adorn theirs with diamonds and other precious stones. All persons in the caliph's service wore black; to refuse to dress in the Abbasids' colour was equivalent to resigning. Cadis and lawyers were obliged to wear a *taylasan*, a long piece of cloth covering the shoulders and hanging down behind like a sort of hood.

Nobody went bareheaded. To take away a man's headdress was a punishment. The commonest was a skullcap, a sort of fez, with a turban wound round it. Mansour had adopted a tall headdress, probably of Persian origin, which resembled a wine jar; tall hats were then adopted by cadis. But these were just passing fashions. A man's most distinctive sign was his turban, and all men wore one. According to one contemporary author, a turban was "a shield on the field of battle, a distinction in an assembly, a protector against vicissitudes, and it makes a man look taller." Obviously the length and type of material in a turban would vary with the means of its owner; some princes decorated theirs with diamonds. Certain colours were reserved for high-ranking officials and generals.

In summer the people of Baghdad wore sandals, in winter high leather boots (roomy enough to contain a knife and a handkerchief). Long or short stockings, either of wool or some fine fabric, were also worn; they too were used as pockets and might contain books or writing materials. At some periods the non-Muslims (*dhimmi*) were required to dress differently from Muslims; Harun al-Rashid ordered the dhimmi dress regulations, which had fallen into disuse, to be brought back into force. His doctor is said to have opposed the measure, and the order was cancelled sometime later. In general, non-Muslims did not have the right to wear swords. Their women were obliged to wear yellow or blue clothing out of doors, and to wear red shoes. In the middle of the ninth century the caliph Mutawakil ordered the dhimmi to wear yellow hoods and turbans and their wives, on leaving the house, a yellow dress. None of these regulations was observed for long.

Ordinary women, who went twice a day to fetch water from the nearest canal with their children tugging at their skirts, dressed as best they could; but for the rich women of Baghdad nothing was too extravagant. Dresses of all kinds were made for them, and blouses with or without sleeves, in fabrics of different colours, perhaps of silk and cloth-of-gold. Furs were added in winter. Harun's singers wore qamis and sirwal in pink, green, or red. Zubaidah started the fashion for shoes encrusted with precious stones; Ulaiyah, Mahdi's daughter, was the first to wear jewelled headbands:

I bathed and perfumed myself, chose the fairest of my ten new gowns and, dressing myself in it, put on my noble pearl necklace, my bracelets, my pendants, and all my jewels. I wound my brocaded belt round my waist, threw my large veil of blue silk and gold over my head and, after continuing the direction of my eyes with kohl, put on my little face veil and was ready. (17th Night)

Here are two other beauties from the *Thousand and One Nights*:

In order fittingly to receive her sisters, the eldest princess had put on a fair robe of red silk on which were gold birds with emerald beaks and claws; she sat, heavy with jewels, on her audience throne... (611th Night)

Zain al-Mawasif went indoors and bathed in the hammam. Her girls tended her as for an extraordinary occasion; they depilated what there was to depilate, they rubbed what there was to rub, they perfumed what there was to perfume, they made long what there was to make long, and they made short what there was to make short. Then they put a robe worked in fine gold upon her and set a silver fillet about her head to hold a circle of rich pearls, a circle which fastened at the back, and dropped two knots of rubies upon the virgin silver of her shoulders. They tressed her black hair, perfumed with musk and amber, into twenty-four braids which fell to her heels... (656th Night)

Eating

> *O ye who believe! Eat of the good things with which we have supplied you, and give God thanks if ye are His worshippers.*
>
> **Koran, II, 167**

The ostentation of the rich of Baghdad was nowhere more pronounced than in the realm of gastronomy. The nutritional value of a dish hardly mattered, nor did people much care whether it was tasteless or overseasoned, so long as it was original. The essential thing was that after a dinner given by a rich merchant or senior official, the whole of society should be talking about it the next day. If the host's cook had managed to produce a new dish, ideally from the recipe of some great foreign personage's chef, the reputation of the household would be enhanced. The search for novelty led to the introduction of dishes from Iran and even from the Byzantine empire, despite the latter's enmity with Islam. Turkish cuisine was soon to exercise its own influence.

Cuisine is an aspect of a society's manners, of its culture. The Romans had a passion for it; so did the Greeks in the Hellenic period, and the Sassanids. The Abbasids became interested in the culinary arts almost from the beginning of their empire, as soon as the growth of commerce made it possible for a relatively large minority to indulge its gastronomic imagination. There were books on the art of living. One, an Arabic translation of a Persian original, is mentioned by Masudi, who quotes a Sassanid king testing his son on his general knowledge:

> What are the best dishes, the most beautiful birds, the most agreeable meats, the coolest jellies, the best kinds of meat stock, the most delicious fruits, the most pleasant musical airs, the seven best ingredients for soup, the sweetest-smelling flowers, the loveliest women, and the best racehorses?

In the *Thousand and One Nights* Harun al-Rashid cooks a fish:

> Harun took the pan, put it on the fire, placed butter in it and waited. When the butter was bubbling well he took the fish, which he had first thoroughly scaled, cleaned, washed, salted, and covered lightly with flour, and put it in the pan. When it was well cooked on one side he turned it over, with infinite skill, and when the fish was cooked to perfection withdrew it from the pan and laid it on broad green banana leaves. Then he went into the garden to gather lemons, which he cut and arranged on the banana leaves, then took the finished dish to the guests in the hall.

Several court dignitaries wrote books on cooking: Ibrahim al-Mahdi[16] (the musician and poet prince who was caliph for a few months), General al-Harit ibn Bashir, and many others, including the great historian Masudi. There were also books on dietetics, one of which, the *Kitab al-Agdiya* (*Book of Foods*), by the Jewish doctor Suleiman al-Israili, was translated into Latin and used by the school of Salerno until the eighteenth century.

Poets wrote lyrically about marvellous unique dishes, unknown and unequalled delicacies provided by their munificent hosts. An eighth-century savant, Salih ibn Abd al-Quddus, writes mockingly of the flood of gastronomic poems: "We live among beasts, who wander around looking for new pastures but have no wish to increase their understanding. In their eyes, he who writes on fish and vegetables has superior merit; while he who teaches true science is tiresome and boring."

Costly spices from Southeast Asia and Africa were used by those who could afford them: pepper, nutmeg, cinnamon, musk, ginger, cloves. Many aromatic plants — usually available from local sources — were also used for cooking: parsley, mint, poppy, devil's-guts, rose leaves and rosebuds, pistachios, garlic, onion, mustard, and so on. The more different ingredients a dish contained, and the longer it took to prepare, the more successful it was thought to be.[17]

Chicken was the most popular meat among the better-off classes, as it could be cooked in an infinite variety of ways. The *Kitab Wuslaila al-Habib*, written in the Ayyubid period, included more than seventy-four recipes for chicken with pistachio, rose jam, mulberry jelly, parsley, orange, etc. Chickens were raised in the surrounding countryside and even in Baghdad itself, to ensure supplies of fresh eggs. The fowl was usually marinated overnight, boiled, then cut in pieces and fried in sesame oil. Quantities of goat, beef, lamb, and mutton were also eaten. Doctors recommended chicken and mutton but were less enthusiastic about beef, which they believed to be a dry meat; they encouraged the raising of cattle for milk, however. Meat was prepared by washing it in hot water, then browning it in oil. Large fish from the Tigris or the Euphrates were also in demand (small ones, being very cheap, were generally left to the poor). They were eaten fried, pickled in vinegar, or made into soup.

"A table without vegetables is like an old man without wisdom," ran an Arab proverb of the time. Another proverb held: "Vegetables are the ornament of a table." Peas, kidney beans, and broad beans were served most often. They were made into soup or boiled in salted water and served with sesame oil, nuts, or breadcrumbs. Egg plant was also popular — stewed, fried, pickled in vinegar, or cooked in milk. Persons of distinction avoided carrots and leeks (because of their odour), but used garlic and onion. Asparagus was greatly prized in high society, the Damascus product being regarded as the best; poets sang its praises. Watercress, radishes, spinach, beetroot, and lettuce were not ignored, although people of refinement avoided anything "which stains the teeth or gums".

The Orient of twelve centuries ago was already a land of sugary confections, for rich and poor alike. Most were based on almonds, sugar, sesame oil, milk, and syrup, scented with rose water, musk, and cinnamon. Cultivation of sugarcane had spread throughout the Near East not long before the Hegira. The sugar consumed in Baghdad usually came from Khuzestan. Harun al-Rashid received

large quantities of it from Seistan each year in payment of taxes.
Isfahan used to send him white honey.

Presentation was important to the reputation of a good table, and
several recipes from the Muslim Middle Ages include pertinent
advice. Saffron was widely used for its handsome golden colour,
and some dishes (like "omelette in a bottle" or "mock brains") had
a highly original appearance. Even when the guests were few the
dishes were plentiful and elaborate. At one dinner given by the
celebrated singer Ishak ibn Ibrahim no fewer than thirty fowls,
prepared in different ways — not to mention the other dishes and
the hot and cold desserts — were served to a total of three diners.

Cooks with good reputations fetched extremely high prices in
the slave market. Black women were thought particularly gifted as
cooks; Indians, too, were highly regarded, and Djahiz thought there
were no better cooks than those from Sind.

The art of the table began with the letter of invitation, such as
the following:

> We are in a company which is blessed by everything save thee.
> Besides thee we have everything we need for our contentment.
> The eyes of the narcissus are open; the cheeks of the violet are
> ablush; the censers of lemon and orange trees are spreading their
> perfume — eloquent are the lutes, fragrant the cups. The fine
> market-hall is open — the herald is there to announce you. The
> stars of the carousing companions have risen and well outstretched
> is the amber sky. By my life, when thou comest we will be in a
> heavenly paradise and thou wilt verily be the very centre of the
> pearl string.[18]

Before the meal, a servant would pour water over the guests'
hands from a ewer, starting with the master of the house: "The
slave waited on them herself, gave them a golden vase holding
scented water when they had eaten, poured a rose scent for their
faces and beards from a ewer enriched with rubies, and perfumed
their clothes with aloes burnt in a small gold brazier." (152nd Night)
The master of the house or the oldest of the guests would then
begin to eat. The dishes were brought either one after the other or
all together and set on a cloth, an animal skin, or palm leaves spread
on the floor. In wealthy circles a low table (*maida*) might be used,

nearly always round and made of wood or stone (usually onyx) inlaid with ebony, jade, or mother-of-pearl. Small and portable, it might be nothing more than a tray placed on the floor or on supports (*kursi*) of wood or chased metal. People did not eat at the table, which was simply a platform to hold the dishes. Knives and spoons were used, but eating was done with the fingers. Polite people cut their food into the smallest possible pieces, did not allow their hands to become greasy, did not try to get the marrow out of bones, and never took for themselves the brains, kidneys, or liver or white meat of a fowl, as these were considered the best parts of a dish. It was considered rude to lick one's fingers, stuff one's mouth, put too much salt on one's food, or use a toothpick in public.

Wine was never drunk at table; guests were offered sweetened iced water, scented with musk and rose water. Iced water was a great luxury in summer. Wine was reserved for evenings spent in the company of friends with musicians, poets and women singers, and sometimes a lot was consumed. People usually entertained in the evening, and a dinner would be given for a limited group: "In addition to the host and the musician, three makes an agreeable company. Once the number reaches six, it is a crowd," goes one proverb, while another notes pithily: "Less than five is solitude, more than five, the *souk*."

High Days and Holidays
In Baghdad, as elsewhere, anything could serve as a pretext to take a rest from the monotony of daily life, and regular feast days were important. Islam is very broad-minded in this respect, and in addition to their own, the people of Baghdad celebrated feasts inherited from Oriental antiquity, the many Christian holidays, and others that were survivals of practices whose origins were lost in the mists of time. The cosmopolitan Abbasid empire tolerated everything.

There were two main Muslim feasts, id al-Fitr (or id al-Saghir), at the end of Ramadan, and id al-Adha (or id al-Kurban) — the feast of sacrifice, or the sheep feast. All Muslims, even the least fervent, observed the daytime fast during Ramadan, allowing no water to pass their lips no matter how hot the weather might be. The whole population would then joyfully celebrate the end of the fast. The feast was prepared long in advance; children would make collections in the street to buy decorations and sweetmeats; food would be prepared and new clothes acquired. On the day itself, in mid-morning the caliph would lead officials, escorted by armed troops, in procession to the mosque, where he would put on the Prophet's cloak and lead the prayers. The devotions over, everyone would trade visits and good wishes and embrace their friends and loved ones. They would feast for three days. In the evening, with palaces illuminated and the vessels on the Tigris strung with lights, Baghdad glittered "like a bride in her beauty and finery".

Id al-Adha marks the day on which pilgrims to Mecca, reaching a point that is called Mina, throw pebbles against a rock to drive off the demon and then sacrifice a sheep and a camel. At the time of the Abbasids, during the three days of the feast, sheep were slaughtered in the public squares. The caliph would attend sacrifice in one of the palace courtyards and send the meat first to people he wished to honour, distributing the rest to the poor. People would dress in new clothes and give one another presents, but mainly they gorged themselves on meat.

Shiites, for their part, celebrated the birthdays of Fatima and Ali, and some Sunnis the Prophet's birthday (to the intense disapproval of zealots who regarded it as an affront to the purity of Islam). Marriages and births in the imperial family were observed by everybody: Christians and Muslims would decorate and illumine their houses, the caliph would scatter money, and the poets would compose verses for the occasion. But the most extravagant rejoicing was reserved for the circumcision of princes. One caliph, Muktadir, had five of his sons circumcised on the same day, for which he spent six hundred thousand dinars. Almost invariably, caliphs would arrange for orphans and poor children to be circumcised at the same time, and their relatives would leave the palace after the ceremony loaded down with money and presents. On these occasions several hundred boys would often be circumcised at the caliph's expense.

Other occasions for festivities were the accession of a new caliph, the naming of an heir to the throne, or the caliph's return to Baghdad after a victory over the infidel or some group of hostile Muslims. The announcement that one of the caliph's sons could read the Koran fluently, an acquirement known as the *tahdir*, would also be greeted with a celebration; the caliph would distribute robes of honour, pour pearls and gold pieces over his guests, and give slaves their freedom. For Harun's own tahdir, Mahdi had freed five hundred slaves and distributed generous gifts. The poets would sing of the happy event and receive their rewards; the people would light torches and hang garlands.

Of all the feasts imported from foreign calendars, the one most celebrated in Baghdad (many of whose inhabitants were of Persian origin) was Naurouz, heralding the arrival of spring. It was originally introduced by the troops who carried the Abbasids to power. The day began early, with people going to the nearest well or canal and sprinkling water over themselves. Women would make special cakes based on rose water, almonds, and sugar, and the poets would versify. Presents would be exchanged, and a register was kept of the masses of gifts sent to the caliph by all classes of society. The palaces of the caliph, princes, and dignitaries would be alight for six days with lamps burning scented oils and costly ingredients; the air would be thick with incense.

Other Persian feasts were Mihraj, marking the onset of winter (on this occasion drums would be beaten), and Sadar, during which crowds would gather along the banks of the Tigris to see the glittering barges of princes and viziers. For Sadar, houses were fumigated[19] and people would drink wine, sing, and dance around bonfires.

Baghdad Muslims celebrated Christian feasts with equal enthusiasm, not even bothering to discover their significance; the rejoicing of their Christian neighbours was perceived as another opportunity to have a good time. The environs of Baghdad were crowded with Nestorian and Monophysite convents, and their patron saints' days occasioned all sorts of ceremonies and celebrations. Anyone could join in, and some of the large monasteries, with their many gardens, drew big crowds. Good wine was available. "On a rainy day, what a pleasure it is to drink wine with a priest," wrote one appreciative chronicler. The convents of Baghdad were also reputed for their games, notably backgammon.

On Easter day a procession of Muslims and Christians together would wind its way to the Samalu monastery, a magnificent edifice in the middle of a large park on the northeast side of town. Shabushti recounts that he feasted there "until I mistook the earth for a boat and the walls danced about me." On the last Saturday in September people went to the monastery of the Renards, also surrounded by gardens, and on 3 October the feast was at the Ashmana monastery. People went there by boat "with wineskins and girl singers" to spend three days in tents "with wine and pretty faces". On the first Sunday of Lent the Muslims would join the Christians at the monastery of Ukbara — a village known for its excellent wine — where men and women together would "drink, dance and amuse themselves". On the fourth Sunday several more days of feasting would begin, this time at Durmalis. On Palm Sunday young slaves carrying palms and olive branches would walk in procession through the caliph's palace. The feast of St Barbara came on 4 December and Christmas three weeks later. Bonfires were lighted and nuts cracked open because "Joseph lighted a fire to keep Mary warm while she was in labour and fed her with nine nuts which he had found in the saddle-bag."

Games

> *The angels endorse three games: the play of a man with a woman; racing; and archery contests.*
>
> **Hadith**

People played a great deal in Baghdad, both at home and in places like clubs, to amuse themselves but also to make money (despite the Koranic prohibition against certain forms of gambling). Horse racing and polo were popular. In Harun's time, races were held at the track built by his father, Mahdi, which also served as an exercise and parade ground for the army. Later other racetracks were opened, some within the perimeter of the caliph's palace and those of other princes. These tracks had gardens, hammams, apartments, dining rooms, and so on.

The horse enjoys high status in Arab culture, which used to hold the animal to be of supernatural origin. It was on his horse al-Burak that the Prophet Mohammed went to Jerusalem and made his ascension to Heaven. The modern Arab horse is relatively recent, its bloodline established about the seventh or eighth century, out of crossed Yemeni and Syrian strains with an injection of different blood from the Caspian region.

The Prophet himself liked horse racing, worked out a set of rules for it, and organized races at Medina with donated prizes. His example could only encourage equestrian sports and competition — polo, jousting with lance or sabre, equestrian archery, etc — all of which were, of course, excellent training for jihad.

Dogs, mules, camels, and asses were also raced and bets wagered. Pigeon racing, however, was so popular in Harun's reign that it became a social problem: some would spend their whole fortune buying a racing pigeon or lose it in betting. A pigeon could be worth as much as five hundred dinars, a pigeon egg one dinar. Training these birds took time and patience but could be very rewarding. According to Djahiz, a pigeon could earn as much for its owner as a farm. Harun al-Rashid loved pigeon racing and, with fellow enthusiasts also attracted by the beauty of the spectacle, used to eagerly await the arrival of the "runners", while gamblers simply hoped for a big win.

Archery was another favourite sport of skill which doubled as useful military training. People would lay bets on the outcome, and these competitions, generally held in the autumn, were best attended when renowned archers took part. Both fixed and moving targets were employed. The archer had to keep his feet still and move only his torso. Crossbow archery also attracted large crowds; the weapon had first appeared at the beginning of the Umayyad period and could fire stones or lead projectiles, as well as steel bolts.

Wrestling events were also very popular, and caliphs encouraged them. Harun's son Amin in particular used to watch competitions and reward the victors. Some caliphs were wrestlers themselves and it is claimed that Mutadid, at the end of the ninth century, proved his strength by fighting a lion which he dispatched with two strokes of his sword. Weight lifting was practised in all classes of society; Harun's son al-Mutasim, eventually Mamun's successor, one day lifted an iron door weighing more than three hundred kilograms. Fencing was a familiar sport, running races were held, and swimming contests and regattas were organized on the Tigris.

Animal fights were one of the greatest entertainments; special markets sold rams, dogs, cocks, and quails suitable for fighting. Betting on these fights was forbidden, but gamblers still managed to go home without their shirts.

8
The Economic Miracle

From the eighth to the tenth century the Muslim world exercised an uncontested economic supremacy over the Occident as well as the Orient.

M. Lombard

I bought goods which I knew would sell quickly at a good and reliable profit... I set out with them... We sailed for days and days, from island to island and from sea to sea...

Sinbad the Sailor

The Abbasid empire was such a big and powerful state that no enemy could seriously threaten it or even approach its urban and political centres. In consequence, it became the most prosperous economy of its time.

Persians, Byzantines, Egyptians, Syrians, and the peoples of upper and lower Mesopotamia had always exchanged goods and merchandise, but these were mainly luxury products in limited quantities. The Islamic conquests opened up far greater volumes of exchange, and the Abbasids expanded these on a prodigious scale. Trade within the empire increased as Arabic became a *lingua franca* and Islam a common religion that gave everyone the same laws and the same pattern of life. A society getting bigger and richer by the day attracted bold traders, who travelled across oceans and continents, and goaded the more audacious investors into speculative trading in those exotic products that would return enormous profits.

The soaring prosperity of the caliph's empire, the improvement of living conditions, and the arrival of large numbers of slaves, resulted in rapid demographic growth (the same thing happened in the France of St Louis, in Europe after the Hundred Years' War, and in the Ottoman empire under Suleiman the Magnificent). Similarly, both in the Near East and in Khorasan, some towns became enormous centres. Increasingly complex relations developed among these towns, even though "the whole world kept Baghdad time".[1]

Vast Rural Populations

More than eighty per cent of the empire's population lived in the countryside and cultivated the land. The Near and Middle East are not exclusively deserts. Egypt had been the granary of antiquity; Mesopotamia was scattered with fertile oases; Syria had fertile plains and valleys; and Iran had its fertile rim of mountains and many oases surrounded by irrigated fields. There were hundreds of thousands of hectares of cultivated and sometimes irrigated land, more than enough to feed the local populations and the inhabitants of the towns.

Housing stayed virtually unchanged until very recent times. In Mesopotamia, people lived in huts of reeds or palm branches; in parts of Khorasan and Syria, houses were built of stone, while in forested areas, such as the southern shores of the Caspian, they were built of timber. Some houses had an upper storey, the ground floor reserved for stables and storerooms; in others, people and animals were jumbled together on the beaten earth floor. Isolated dwellings were rare, and most villages were surrounded by a palisade for protection against wild beasts and human intruders.

Unlike the medieval peasantry of western Europe, that of the Arab countries was free; the peasant, in principle at least, was not a serf. Numerous texts carry references to "fugitive peasants", but most of these were men in flight from the tax collector. The result seems to have been a fairly high shifting or floating population. Sometimes a peasant would engage a richer villager as his protector, who in exchange for a regular fee (the *taldjia*) would negotiate with the tax authorities on the peasant's behalf. The *himaya*, another form of "social security", usually ended with the merging of one property into another; land might also be confiscated directly by the tax authorities or by richer landowners.

These practices, dating from before the Arab conquests, meant a steady absorption of small properties into larger ones. When the process was accelerated, there were social shocks and upheavals.

More and more the cultivator living on his land was replaced by the big, town-dwelling landowner who lived on the remittances sent by his agent or bailiff, the *wakil*. In consequence of the Barmakids' fiscal policies and the multiplication of huge properties belonging to the caliph and his family, these large estates appeared in greater numbers after the reign of Harun al-Rashid. Khaizuran owned villages and vast estates all around Baghdad and throughout the empire, and kept adding to her properties, especially those in Egypt and Mesopotamia. Many other Abbasid princes and princesses were great landowners, and high dignitaries imitated them. In the next century the military aristocracy was increasingly to take over land, at the expense not only of small peasant farmers but also of medium landowners and (quite often, in Iran) of the diqan.

This development had no adverse effect on production, which continued to grow. Neither did nomadism; its expansion after the Arab conquest encouraged the pastoral economy without weakening agriculture in any way.

The prime source of wealth was, of course, the cultivation of land. But — during a period when the West was developing the countryside rather than the towns — the Muslim world was becoming urbanized. There were reciprocal benefits; agriculture was stimulated by the trade between urban centres, while the towns depended on the countryside for food and other products.

The staple food of the medieval Muslim Orient was white bread; only ascetics and the poor ate the rye bread widely consumed in the West. Wheat had been the most widespread crop since time immemorial, followed by barley, which was fed to animals. Wheat was grown in upper Mesopotamia, barley in the lower Tigris valley; Egypt (especially the Fayoum region), Syria, Ifriqiya, and the central Maghreb were major wheat producers.

Rice, brought from India to lower Mespotamia before the Christian era, reached the Mediterranean after the Arab conquest; it may have been introduced to Iraq by the Persians. It was grown in Fayoum, around the Dead Sea, and increasingly in Muslim Spain. In Harun's time, there were large rice plantations in Mesopotamia. Olives were widely cultivated in Syria, Ifriqiya, Spain, and the central Maghreb.

The Koran's discouraging attitude towards wine did not result in the wholesale destruction of vineyards, despite efforts by various caliphs to have this done; nor was the Fatimid Hakim, later, any more successful in this endeavour. After the conquests, the vine continued to be cultivated in the Nile delta, Syria, Mesopotamia, northern Palestine, and southern Spain, where Malaga and Jerez were already being produced (the latter made from plants originally brought from Shiraz). The date palm, native to lower Iraq, spread with the Arab conquest into southern Syria, Cilicia, the western Sahara, and the south of Tunisia and Algeria. Another product grown in great quantities was sugarcane; a recent arrival from India via Susiana and Khuzestan, it now grew in Mesopotamia and Egypt (its biggest Mediterranean producer and consumer) and was soon to be found in Sicily. Other fruits and vegetables that the Arabs spread around the Mediterranean were the orange (from India) in Sicily, Morocco, and Spain; the banana; the lemon; artichokes; and spinach.

The cultivation of industrial crops became relatively common. Cotton was the most important: another plant native to India (from where it had reached the Near East through Turkestan in the time of the Sassanids), it was grown in Transoxiana, Iran, and southern Iraq, but principally in Palestine and Syria; the Aleppo region would soon be supplying the entire Mediterranean world. Almost unknown in Egypt during the ninth century, cotton later caught on there and has remained to this day a determining factor in the Egyptian economy. The main Egyptian textile was linen, made there since early antiquity, as we know from fabrics found in the pharaohs' tombs. Flax was cultivated all over the Nile delta but especially in the region of Damietta and Tinis; in Tunisia it was grown primarily in the region around Carthage and Tunis; in Spain it grew in Galicia and the far south; in Iraq on the lower Euphrates; and on the Caspian seaboard of Iran. One of Egypt's traditional sources of income, papyrus, was gradually supplanted by paper and disappeared about the middle of the ninth century. Hemp, widely used for making ropes, ships' sails, and coarse clothing, was cultivated in central Asia, lower Mesopotamia, and Spain. Camel hair was used to make felt (central Asia and Armenia) and thick woven fabrics (Khorasan, Egypt).

Wool was by far the most important textile fibre. At this time the countries of Islam, led by north Africa, were the world's only large wool producers. The plateaus of the Maghreb, the mountains of the Atlas, the high Tell and the Aures, and the plains on the Atlantic coast bred sheep of the best quality with thick, fine wool. The Berbers introduced the new breed into Spain simultaneously with the custom known as *mesta* (still followed), whereby the flocks of several villages are entrusted to a single shepherd for their seasonal migration. Other pastoral techniques were brought into the Spanish peninsula by the Berbers at about this time. The Merino sheep also appeared, the result of crossbreeding with rams from the Maghreb. The growing desire of the expanding towns for textiles led to more production and trade, and flocks multiplied in every region. Sheep were raised on a large scale in Egypt, Syria, and Palestine, northwestern Iran, Fars, and Khorasan. The growth of flocks and the practice of seasonal migration caused much deforestation.

Silk was long known to the Arabs but did not reach the Mediterranean until after the sixth century. There is a well-known anecdote about a group of monks who are supposed to have brought silkworm eggs hidden in their pilgrims' staffs to Byzantium during Justinian's reign. From the time of the Arab conquests, silkworms were cultivated wherever the climate was suitable. This too was favoured by economic expansion, and for some time production was barely sufficient to satisfy the ever-growing demands of the court. From the eighth century onwards the major silk-producing regions included Khorasan, the Caspian seaboards, western Iran, and Armenia, along with the plain of the Orontes and Spain, especially Andalusia (where silkworms had arrived with the Syrians accompanying the Umayyads). By the ninth century enough silk was made to satisfy the desires of the whole empire and even to export a good deal to Byzantium, which depended almost entirely on the Muslim world for supplies of raw silk.

Agricultural productivity was much higher than in western Europe: Egypt, for example, yielded on average four or five times as much wheat per hectare — more in some areas — as did Europe in Charlemagne's time. Comparable yields were not achieved in France until the eighteenth century and were unusual even then. The Arabs were not born cultivators but made good use of methods that had existed before their conquest and often devised improvements.

Apart from durum wheat and barley, which are relatively easy to grow in semi-arid conditions, all products of the earth require water. Irrigation systems have existed in the Near and Middle East since antiquity, conduits, dams, and dykes that retained water or diverted it from rivers and watercourses bringing additional alluvial nutrients. The works were arranged so that water flowed by itself without needing to be pumped or lifted, often through systems of underground galleries (*foggara*; in Iran, *qanat*) with wells dug into them at regular intervals. The first caliphs developed these irrigation systems. After the conquest of Iraq, the caliph Omar ordered a dam to be built to supply the new town of Basra with water. The early Abbasids undertook substantial irrigation projects.[2] The construction of Baghdad and the development of the surrounding farmlands required an enormous investment in canal building; Harun al-Rashid had several dug around the capital, in the Raqqa region, and in Samarra. Canal upkeep and the sharing of water supplies were strictly regulated in Iraq as well as in Spain, Ifriqiya, and Khorasan. The director of the Water Bureau in Merv, an official employing more than ten thousand people, enjoyed higher rank than the chief of police. In Egypt, the Nile floods were measured on the famous Nilometer at Fostat, which enabled the Egyptians to calculate the area of flooded land and thereby make tax assessments.

Various kinds of equipment were used for lifting water; the simplest was an earthenware or hide pail attached by a rope to one end of a counterweighted pole, but buckets mounted on a wheel or along a rope belt (*daliyah*, *noria*), usually powered by animals, were also used (and up till recently in the Orontes valley). Flour mills, presses, and other such equipment were usually driven by waterwheels; windmills were found only in Spain.

Livestock-raising provided not only food but also a variety of other products and raw materials for industry. New pastoral techniques originating mainly in central Asia led to an unprecedented development of pastoral areas and to variety in the kinds of animals raised. In the eighth century the buffalo arrived in lower Mesopotamia. Brought from India by migrating Gypsies, it was soon to be found in Syria, then in Anatolia.

Because of the role the horse played in Muslim expansion, it heads the list of domesticated animals. There were several breeds. The short, stocky Turkish-Mongol horse was a pure product of the

Asian steppe. The heavier Iranian beast, able to carry the weight of armour, was later exported to India, where it became the steed of the Mahratta cavalry. The Barb (Berber) horse, interbred with other strains after the conquest of Spain, became the ancestor of the western European horse. The Arab horse proper came from Syria, where the horse born of crossing a Barb stallion with an Iranian mare was then crossed with a horse from the high pastures of Arabia. It was bred mainly in Egypt, Arabia, and Spain.

The camel played a capital role in the economy of the Arab and Oriental world during the Middle Ages. With the disappearance of the wheel at the end of antiquity,[3] the camel became the preferred pack animal. Its rivals were either too slow (the ox) or too small (the horse). Tough and relatively fast, the camel could carry a load of more than two hundred kilograms, and ferried heavy loads throughout the Near and Middle East. In the east and in central Asia, the two-humped Bactrian camel, raised mainly in Iran and Khorasan, was used; in the Arabian peninsula, Syria, and Egypt, donkeys worked alongside the single-humped dromedary.

As a result of the growth in consumption and the development of trade — not just within the empire but world wide — production reached hitherto unknown levels during the reign of Harun al-Rashid. Basra (the greatest port in the Muslim world), Kufa, Wasit, Fostat, Merv, and other towns became giant markets. Contemporary writings hardly ever mention a glut of any product or a fall in price which might, in such an event, follow.

The improvement of communications favoured technical progress. Men had never travelled so much between the Atlantic and the Hindu Kush. Never before had ideas and goods circulated so freely. The heaviest foodstuffs as well as the lightest, wheat as well as spices, were transported over thousands of kilometres. Raw materials were easily carried from the places where they were produced to the places where they would be processed. Damascus obtained its steel from India. Silver came largely from mines in Afghanistan. Baghdad ate (as it does today) Syrian asparagus and Lebanese apples. Clothes of Egyptian linen were worn in Iran. Despite the hostility between the two governments, Baghdad fashions were instantly copied in Cordoba. Paper-making, which reached Samarkand by the middle of the eighth century, was being practised in Baghdad a century later. Irrigation systems used in

Ferghana reached Spain in the same length of time. Movements of populations, exchanges of prisoners, and wandering pilgrims diffused the available techniques, methods, and procedures; brought them into competition with each other; and exposed them to outside influences. Never had men exchanged so much in the way of products and knowhow as in the years following the collapse of the great Sassanid empire, the loss of its Hellenic domains by Byzantium, and the accession of a new dynasty of caliphs in the Muslim world.

A Textile Civilization[4]

Textiles were the great industry of the Muslim world. They were the most evolved product of the Middle East, the most refined and diverse: heavy, thick woollen stuffs from north Africa; light fabrics from Iran; gauze, voile, and linen from the Nile delta; luxurious foulards from Khorasan and Kabul, which were sent to China itself; silk hangings from Antioch and Baghdad; lush Armenian carpets, and many others. From *washi* (luxurious embroidered material) to the cotton fabrics of Syria and Egypt, not forgetting the coarse materials in which the Baghdad poor swaddled themselves, the Muslim empire made everything imaginable to clothe human beings.

So great was the demand that spinning and weaving were carried on almost everywhere — first of all for the benefit of palaces, where enormous sums were spent on decorating their many rooms. Then there were the elaborate costumes donned by princes, princesses, courtiers, and high civil and military officials, whose fashions were imitated (to the extent of their means) by other classes of society, particularly by the mercantile grande bourgeoisie.

Men dressed according to their profession and their rank in society. Merchants wore a shirt and *rida* (cloak). Preachers wore a sort of waistcoat with a belt. The dress of officials was precisely regulated: cadis wore the *dahniya* (high-crowned cap) and the taylasan; the vizier and secretaries, the duraa. Poets were noted for colours, singers for the elegance of their attire. Army officers tried to outdo one another, some adopting silk tunics and trousers edged with fur. Furthermore, the same costume was not worn all day.

Caliphs attached great importance to dress. Harun's grandson Mutawakil was once pleased by a garment made from a sort of silk interwoven with another fibre. "This fashion," writes Masudi, "was followed by all members of his household and spread out among the people. All desired to copy the sovereign, and this kind of fabric reached a very high price, the technique of making it being improved to follow the fashion and to satisfy the taste of the prince and his subjects." Caliphs' wardrobes were stored in special buildings and placed in the care of a senior official. The size and scale of these wardrobes can be gauged from this conversation between the caliph Muwaffak (second half of the ninth century) and his vizier Hasan:

"O Hasan, this stuff pleases me," said the caliph. "How much of it have we in store?" I immediately took from my boot a small scroll on which were noted the totals of all the goods and fabrics in the stores, and found that there were 6,000 pieces of the garment in question. "O Hasan," Muwaffak then said to me, "see, we are naked! Write to the country from which it comes that they must send us 30,000 pieces of this stuff, and that as quickly as possible!"[5]

We might also mention the Umayyad Hisham, who took so many clothes on a pilgrimage that 700 camels were needed to carry them; after his death 12,000 washi tunics and 10,000 silk sashes were found in his wardrobe. We know the contents of the wardrobe left by Harun al-Rashid: 4,000 gold-embroidered silk robes; 4,000 silk robes edged with sable, mink, or other furs; 10,000 shirts; 10,000 caftans; 2,000 pairs of trousers; 4,000 turbans; 1,000 robes of different fabrics; 1,000 robes with hoods; 5,000 handkerchiefs; 1,000 gilded sashes; 4,000 pairs of shoes, mostly edged with mink or sable; and 4,000 pairs of hose.

One indication of the importance of dress was the caliphal custom of honouring people by presenting them with robes (as if awarding decorations). "Robes of honour" were of different fabrics and of greater or lesser value depending on the recipient's rank and the level of honour being conferred on him. These *khila* consisted of the robe itself, a shirt, a pair of trousers, a taylasan, and a duraa. The caliph would award them at times of religious festivals, on such important family occasions as marriages and circumcisions, after victories, or simply to show approval of the work of a particular dignitary. Sovereigns exchanged robes of honour. Mamun sent five hundred brocade robes to an Indian prince; the basileus Leo sent three hundred to Harun al-Rashid, and in the next century Queen Berthe sent twenty gold-embroidered robes to Muktafi Billah. Charlemagne is known to have received a tent from Harun al-Rashid, as well as a large number of silks and linen hangings.

Caliphs also distributed fabrics to their servants and their families twice a year, in winter and summer. As this meant clothing several thousand people, the palace's demand for fabric was great indeed.

Carpets of course played an essential part in daily life, serving as beds, cushions, or seats. Some were immense: one carpet belonging to the caliph Hisham measured 54 by 27 metres. Sometimes their patterns were so fine they constituted works of art. When travelling, caliphs and dignitaries lived in grand tents — portable palaces, in fact. The caliph Mustansir owned a marquee 70 metres across, supported by a central pillar more than 30 metres high. A pavilion belonging to another caliph was woven entirely from gold and held up by silver poles. Yet another, with its accessories, weighed more than 17 tons.

During state ceremonies, or when a powerful foreign ambassador arrived, fabrics and hangings were stretched along the processional route and the ground was covered with mats. Brocade curtains, gold embroideries, carpets of silk woven with gold thread and encrusted with pearls and precious stones, state livery for horses and camels — all these miles of precious fabric were turned out for the court and the palace by the various workshops and factories of the empire.

Fabrics were basic tools of a policy founded on prestige. They were distinguishing signs between social classes and within the state hierarchy, means of reward or payment, treasures passed from one sovereign to another. They remained for centuries one of the great successes of a civilization whose textiles have rarely been surpassed.

The most luxurious stuffs were woven in the caliph's workshops, the tiraz. This Persian word originally meant a robe or fabric bearing embroidered inscriptions, but was later extended to cover the factories themselves. These were scattered throughout the empire: in Baghdad, of course, and, among other places, in Samarra, Khorasan, Dabiq (in the Nile delta), and Kairouan. Owned personally by the caliph, they were regarded as a state service and were directed by high-ranking civil servants assisted by departmental heads, controllers, and their staffs.

It is part of royal and governmental pomp and dynastic custom [explains ibn Khaldun] to have the names of rulers or their peculiar marks embroidered on the silk, brocade, or pure silk garments that are prepared for their wearing. The writing is brought out by weaving a gold thread or some other coloured thread of a colour different from that of the fabric itself into it... Royal garments are embroidered with such a tiraz in order to increase the prestige of the ruler or the person of lower rank who wears such a garment, or in order to increase the prestige of those whom the ruler distinguishes by bestowing upon them his own garment when he wants to honour them or appoint them to one of the offices of the dynasty... In the Umayyad and Abbasid dynasties the greatest importance was attached to the tiraz.[6]

In the time of the Abbasids the tiraz inscriptions were in Kufic calligraphy.[7] They generally included an invocation to Allah, the caliph's name and title (e.g. al-Rashid), and a short religious tag. They could also be painted, embroidered, or worked into a carpet or tapestry.

The tiraz were very far from holding a monopoly on the textile industry. There were also many private workshops, and their output was certainly greater than that of the tiraz. At Tinis, for example, weaving was the sole industry and employed the entire working population; the same was true of other towns and villages in the Fayoum. Women and children worked in these factories, mainly on spinning. Wages in general were extremely low.

Spinning was done with the aid of a distaff or spindle, weaving on a horizontal or a pedal loom. Both were of Chinese design. Other complex techniques, doubtless also of Far Eastern origin (especially the one known in France as Gobelin), enabled workers to weave pearls and precious stones into the fabric and were used in working gold or silver threads. Gold first appeared in fabrics at the end of the eighth century, usually in the form of a thin leaf of metal rolled around a thread. Fabrics enriched with silver came mainly from Spain and Persia, where there were silver mines.

In Harun's time, weaving techniques made it possible for any animal or plant form to be represented.[8] Techniques continued to improve, but the beauty and harmony of the products of Middle East workshops in the Middle Ages have never been equalled.

Spinning, weaving, and dyeing were carried on almost everywhere in the Arab world: cotton and wool in Morocco, silk and wool in Spain, wool and cotton in Ifriqiya, cotton in Syria and Cilicia, silk and cotton in Khorasan. In Iraq itself, Baghdad and its suburbs Baqdara and Hafirah contained factories working cotton, silk, and wool in all their forms; Kufa was reputed for its shawls; Basra and Ubulla produced tent fabrics and a kind of high-quality serge; muslins were made in Takrit, Hira, and, especially, Mosul There were eighty carpet workshops in Ahwaz; in Abadan several dozen factories turned out mattresses and cushions. Baghdad and Numaniah, Armenia and the Bokhara region were renowned for carpets, Transoxania (especially Merv and Nishapur) for cotton fabrics, Syria for carpet silks, and so on.

But the three main textile-producing areas were Fars, Khuzestan, and the Nile delta. In Fars around thirty centres, particularly Fasa, Qurqub, Kazarun, and Tawaj, produced silk brocades, furnishing fabrics, and woollen hangings, knotted-pile and needlepoint carpets, and cotton clothes. Khuzestan specialized in linen, brocades, and various silks. As for the Egyptian delta, its twenty-odd towns supplied the whole empire and the export market with everything from the heaviest to the lightest fabrics: linen brocaded with gold, gauzes, voiles of all colours and qualities, patterned cloth — "all sorts of materials", according to Yakubi, who adds that in Tinis "are made costly fabrics, thick or fine, like the materials of Dabiq, gauze, striped velvet cloths with fringes, flower-patterned stuffs."

Other Industries

Compared to the textile industry, paper making by the Arabs was still a small-volume business in the time of the Abbasids. It is hardly necessary to dwell on the consequences of the introduction and development of this technique or on those of its transmission to the West.

Until the eighth century, people wrote either on parchment (dried sheepskin) or on papyrus (narrow strips of papyrus reed stuck together with starch paste). The Umayyads used papyrus, but the Abbasids preferred parchment, "because it was desired to make them [documents] more respectable and to ensure their authenticity and longevity."[9] But in 751 the Arabs defeated General Kao-Sin at Talas and took Chinese prisoners who knew how to make paper from flax and hemp. These captives were sent to Samarkand, where a factory was built for them. The technique, like others borrowed from the Chinese, then spread westward. It is thought that Jaffar the Barmakid, following the advice of his brother Fadl, who was then governor of Khorasan, opened the Arab world's first paper factory in Baghdad in 794–795. Within a few years others were built, in Andalusia, Morocco, Sicily, Damascus, and Tiberias; but Samarkand remained the source of the best paper for many years. Soon Egypt abandoned papyrus and started making its own paper. Foreign countries, led by Byzantium, bought paper from the Arabs.

Metals were worked, although the shortage of wood restricted exploitation of ore deposits. Some raw metal was imported from Africa, but greater quantities came from the West and from India. Domestic objects of iron and copper were produced by small workshops whose output was usually sold locally by the makers. There were forges in most areas which turned out chains, tools, fortress gates, and the like. Harran in Syria specialized in the manufacture of scales and other scientific instruments, including astrolabes, hourglasses, and water clocks. Weapons were widely produced, by techniques for making steels that were both tough and flexible (certain skills were kept secret and handed down from father to son). These methods, taken mainly from India, were used to particular effect in Damascus (already renowned for the quality of its weapons) and soon afterwards in Toledo. Breastplates and coats of mail were made in the Caucasus, where there were iron mines. Weapons were also imported from the West, swords made by the Franks and Slavs being greatly respected.

Gold and silver workshops, some belonging to the caliph, were to be found in several places. They produced objects of great value: cups, dishes, filigree work, enamels, jewels of all kinds (inspired partly by those of Hellenic antiquity but even more by Sassanid art), and the chandeliers, musical instruments, and statues of wild animals and birds that could be found in the palaces in big towns. Less precious, although they too were often embedded with gold and precious stones, were the leather goods worked in Baghdad, Morocco, the Yemen, and especially Cordoba: saddles, harnesses, belts, chests, and satchels.

The scent and perfume industry was growing. A major producing region was western Iran, where different flower essences were extracted — narcissus, lilac, jasmine — and sent to Baghdad and other big cities to be mixed with violet and rose. Rose water was produced in quantity for use both as a perfume and as a cooking ingredient. Scents were also used in ointments and cosmetics and in drinks. A whole pharmacopoeia, of Indian derivation, was created from plants, flowers, and certain minerals like borax and alum (either extracted locally or imported). Medicines, narcotics, scented waters, and aphrodisiacs were the main products of an industry of small enterprises whose collective share of total commerce was far from negligible.

Among other industries employing many workers were the sugarcane plantations in Egypt, which exported to the whole Muslim world and beyond. The ceramics industry was one of the very biggest in terms of output and of the number of workers and artisans employed. Factories scattered throughout the empire, but concentrated in Syria and Mesopotamia, made millions of the glazed tiles used to decorate the walls of houses, and vases, dishes, jars, and ewers for everyday use, as well as finer pieces. Glassware, already long established, was heavily produced in the workshops of Egypt and Syria; and factories were soon to appear in Iran and Andalusia. Glass exports went as far as China.

Another major employer was the building industry, with its masons, bricklayers, plasterers, carpenters, and other specialists. In some towns, including Baghdad, shipbuilding was the dominant industry; it produced everything from cargo lighters to the decorated state barges used by the caliphs and princes to warships, some of which were fireproofed against Byzantium's flamethrowers and explosive missiles. Yakubi tells us that in Ubulla, a large port near Basra, boats were constructed "by sewing pieces of wood together". He adds that they "can go as far as China".

Many other trades produced goods for use and for export. Basket makers, blacksmiths, tanners, wood turners, carpenters and joiners, shoemakers, wheelwrights were all represented, even in quite small villages. They used the technology handed down by previous generations: wheel, bellows, hoist, irrigation systems. But, through development of the exact sciences and the ingenuity of their specialists, the Arabs were able to modify these methods and thus increase output and offer new products. The import of hitherto unknown raw materials — alum, indigo, saffron — encouraged the creation of other branches of industry, and the provinces that produced their wares became suppliers to the rest of the empire. Technology and knowhow were shared. The silk industry of lower Iraq was influenced by the Persian industry; linen textiles from the shores of the Caspian were Egyptian-influenced; Syrian glass was imitated in Mesopotamia and Egyptian glass in Samarra.

The new needs of an ever-growing population gave rise to an enormous development of industrial production, and this led in turn to the rapid expansion of commercial exchange, at first only within Islam but soon in increasing volume with every region of the known world.

The Prodigious Expansion of Trade

Basic necessities and luxury goods moved about the empire along land routes and, to a lesser extent, rivers. The sea carried the products of Islamic countries to the ends of the earth and brought back raw materials. What are the underlying reasons for this commercial expansion, comparable only to the great industrial and communications revolution of the nineteenth and twentieth centuries?

The concentrated demand of great cities does not wholly explain it; nor does the unification of hitherto separate territories by language, religion, and the central power of the caliphate. There are other reasons, starting with the astonishing dynamism that seized the peoples of the empire soon after the Arab conquest and persisted in the decades following the Abbasid revolution. The speed with which the legions of Islam, actually an incredibly small number of people, had conquered such vast territories, and the subsequent glorious rise of Baghdad, inspired the Arabs with an enthusiasm that would not be seen again until the age of the great discoveries several centuries later.

The conquest also put the peoples of the empire in touch with new regions and seas and opened their eyes to cultures remote in time or space. The Mediterranean revealed the Egyptian and Hellenic civilizations and provided a route to the West, giving access to new riches and modes of thought (especially those of Spain).

In the southern part of the empire, the occupation of the countries along the Persian Gulf improved access to Asia. The Arabs now had an easier and more direct route than the Red Sea, through

Mesopotamia and the valleys of the Tigris and Euphrates to Syria, Anatolia, and northern Persia. Access to Egypt and the Mediterranean was equally easy, as all the old frontiers had vanished. The Red Sea and the Persian Gulf now formed two parallel routes towards Southeast Asia and the Far East. Soon heavily travelled, especially by Arabs, Persians, Jews, and Copts, these routes contributed to the prosperity of Iraq, Egypt, and the entire world.

Situated at the heart of the ancient world, the Arab empire also had the privilege of finding its cradle lined with enormous quantities of precious metals. This enabled it to base its currency on solid foundations and thus obtain easily all the products necessary for economic development.

For centuries — millennia in Egypt's case — the Orient had been amassing gold: pharaohs of every dynasty, Sassanid emperors and princes, bishops, and many others had been piling up treasures in their palaces, tombs, monasteries, and churches. It has been calculated that the gold found in the tomb of Tutenkhamun alone was worth twice as much as the gold reserves of the Bank of Egypt in 1925.[10] How many tons of it must have been buried in the tombs of great kings! In Persia, where the currency was silver, gold was made into jewels, furniture, and decorative objects for the king of kings and his entourage. In Syria and Mesopotamia, following the expansion of Christianity, churches and monasteries had accumulated enormous wealth in the form of ornaments, statues, and religious objects either bought or donated. Byzantine emperors had already plundered these treasures in moments of monetary crisis. But an immense store of gold remained for the Arabs, who used it first in Damascus, then in Baghdad, to strike a currency — the dinar — which made its own solid contribution to their international trade.

From about the end of the eighth century the mass of precious metal was renewed with gold from the Sudan, sent by caràvan across the Sahara to the coastal towns and then exported to Egypt, Syria, and Mesopotamia. Backed by these great and continuously renewed resources, the dinar (with the Byzantine *nomisma*) long remained the only currency in general circulation in the Muslim world, Russia, and the West. Slightly lighter in weight at 4.25 grams than the nomisma (4.55 grams), its purity was excellent — 96 to 98 per cent — as a result of new smelting methods used by the Arabs. Silver from the numerous mines within the empire (in Iran and central Asia) was also used to support the currency. The silver dirham weighed 2.97 grams and its value during Harun al-Rashid's reign was about one-fifteenth of a dinar. At that time it was used principally in Mesopotamia, as gold was preferred in Syria and Ifriqiya. Both were in use in Baghdad. Silver gradually fell out of favour until, after the tenth century, gold became almost totally dominant.

In the late eighth and ninth centuries the Persian Gulf was the main trade route to the Indian Ocean, Ceylon, Malaya, the Indochinese peninsula, and China. During the tenth century, under Fatimid Egypt, a rival route via the Red Sea would be established; but in the time of Harun al-Rashid and his successors the great Gulf ports were still supreme.

Basra, described by Yakubi as "the world's greatest city and first centre of commerce and riches", was by far the most splendid Muslim emporium of the age. Founded in 650, it grew rapidly from the beginning of the eighth century to become a thriving metropolis. A financial centre thronged with Christians, Jews, Persians, Arabs, and Indians, and an industrial town whose shipyards built most of the vessels for the merchant fleet and whose sugar factories and spinning mills supplied large areas of the empire, Basra was also a great intellectual centre. But all these activities were insignificant compared to those of its port. With its river port at Kalla and the neighbouring port of Ubulla, which was closer to the sea, the city had the most vital harbour complex of the whole empire. It was situated on the Euphrates estuary, and ships had to make a long journey through tidal flats to reach it, but this did not prevent the extraordinary development of large-volume trade. Basra handled the greater part of trade between Muslim countries and the Orient.

Siraf, the port for southern Iran's trade with the Indian Ocean area and beyond, developed a few decades after Basra, but was already an important trade centre. Its merchants were reputed to be the richest in Iran and were thought to live in houses several storeys high built of teak — an unheard-of luxury. They were also thought to be the best and hardiest sailors of the entire Muslim world.

Most of the Chinese ships load and unload their cargoes at Siraf [we read in *The Marvels of India*]. Goods are brought there from Basra, Oman and elsewhere to be loaded onto the Chinese ships:

this is because of the heavy swell in that sea and the shallow waters in certain places. The distance from Basra to Siraf by sea is 120 parasangs. When the cargo has been loaded at Siraf, they take on fresh water and set sail for a place called Muscat which is at the tip of Oman.

By comparison with these great ports, Aden was relatively unimportant; its principal trade was in the products of the African coast, and it served as a staging post between Africa and the distant Orient. Oman, with its towns of Muscat and Sohar, was a transit market for spices, ivory, and rare products from India. Jeddah was the port for Mecca and a staging post on the Red Sea.

The first actors in this permanent traffic along the highways of the world were the Jews. The unification of the Muslim empire enabled them to restore links between their scattered communities from Spain to Egypt, Syria, Palestine, Mesopotamia, and as far afield as India. They were especially active in Baghdad, where they had a political leader (the Resh Galutha), a spiritual leader, and schools of theology (from which the Babylonian Talmud was to emerge). All of these communities, well organized in a network of associations and connections, owned trade houses that supported one another and shared responsibility for their common commercial operations. At about the end of the eighth century a group of Jews called Rahdanites[11] took up large-scale commerce and travelled far and wide, dealing in a comprehensive range of products — grain, spices, fabrics, slaves, precious materials. They were to dominate international trade for two centuries.

The Christians, taking advantage of their own widely dispersed communities, concentrated most of their efforts on overland trade. They were leading participants in banking operations, in which Armenians were the acknowledged experts; but they were not wholly absent from international commerce. The same was true of the Muslims, who controlled most of the great fortunes of Baghdad and Basra in the ninth and tenth centuries and held a virtual monopoly on exchanges with Ifriqiya and the Maghreb.

Representatives of all these different groups tirelessly travelled the roads, rivers, and seas of the known world, but without penetrating far into the Christian Occident. Muslims never crossed the Spanish frontier and set foot only in the Italian ports where business was conducted, principally Pisa and Amalfi. Even the Jews and Christians of the Orient rarely travelled to the West. The Orientals may have thought the business possibilities too limited to justify the effort, but it also seems probable that in order to protect their own markets, the Italians prevented Oriental traders from going beyond certain limits.

There were several ways of doing business. One could either go to other countries in person to buy and sell products, or entrust goods to a traveller who would then sell them and buy others. Sinbad, the famous hero of the *Thousand and One Nights*, made his first four voyages in the company of other merchants: "I provided myself with a greater quantity of precious merchandise than I had ever carried before and had it conveyed to Basra. There I embarked upon a great ship, in company with some of the best known merchants of the city."[12] After extraordinary adventures, Sinbad returns home with large profits, and for his fifth voyage, he hires a ship and its captain for his sole use. Although he has become extremely rich, his love of adventure persuades him to undertake a sixth voyage, this time in company with other traders. On his seventh voyage he travels on the caliph's own ship

Obviously the hire of a large ship was a very costly undertaking, and the usual system was for a group of co-religionists to share the cost. This custom gradually fell into disuse and was replaced by another commercial system, that of trading "to order". The investor would provide goods to be transported and sold by freelance traders, who would share in any profits but were not liable for the investor's losses. The system had been practised by caravan traders in the pre-Islamic epoch. Jurists had declared it lawful under Islam and the system spread through the Muslim world during the tenth century, then through the Mediterranean basin and into Europe.

How were transfers of money arranged for these great commercial transactions? Muslims had long used the *sakk* (cheque), a method of payment which quickly became popular. Money changers issued letters of exchange, letters of credit, and so on; settlements were also worked out on paper. Bankers would advance the funds to finance one or several operations by big merchants whose reputations guaranteed a measure of honesty and competence. And new forms of credit were devised in the period of commercial dynamism that occurred during the ninth and tenth centuries;

adaptable to every situation, they go a long way towards explaining the economic superiority of Islam in the Middle Ages. Theologians and jurists placed few obstacles in their path despite the formal Koranic prohibition of *riba* (literally "accumulation"), or usury.

Great Highways of the Empire and of the World

Navigable rivers were few in the Muslim world of the Middle Ages. The tenth-century geographer Muqadassi lists twelve, but of these only three — the Nile, the Tigris, and the Euphrates — could be used reliably in all seasons for the transport of passengers and goods. Egypt and Mesopotamia were thus privileged regions. Apart from the Tigris and Euphrates, which were navigable over long distances, canals linking the two rivers gave the Baghdad region and lower Mesopotamia a whole network of waterways. Timber from Armenia and olive oil from Syria came down the Euphrates on rafts, goods for the capital being trans-shipped at Anbar onto smaller barges that then reached Baghdad through the Isa canal. Barges and rafts from Samarra, Takrit, Mosul, upper Mesopotamia, and the Djezireh sailed down the Tigris to Baghdad itself. The rafts, usually very large, were assembled by skilled operators and carried heavy cargoes through the rapids. In Baghdad they were dismantled and the timber, a rare and expensive commodity, sold.

An enormous fleet travelled the Nile, barges with the traditional square sails, as well as the modern triangular, so-called lateen rig borrowed from Indian Ocean ships, which made it possible to sail closer to the wind. Feluccas swarmed in the innumerable branches of the delta and the many canals. One of the canals, built by Trajan, linked Fostat to Kolzum on the Red Sea, where products destined for the capital arrived by ship; vessels supplying Mecca and Medina, via Jeddah, also called there. Upstream, the Nile was navigable as far as upper Egypt. Aswan was the great river terminus and market serving the Sudan: the Nubians brought their goods there by caravan to be shipped down the river.

Most other rivers in the Muslim world had an irregular flow and were navigable only for short distances or at certain times of the year. These included the Oxus (the Amu-Daria), the Iaxarte (the Syr-Daria), the Helmand, and the rivers flowing down from the Anatolian plateau. River traffic thus played a limited role in transport in the Muslim countries, especially when compared with the role of the great European waterways and the rivers of the Slavic countries.

Trade between the Gulf ports and Southeast Asia was a relatively recent development. A few Persian traders had ventured as far as China in the time of the Sassanids, but such journeys were rare. The Indian Ocean trade had started to expand during the Umayyad period, in 700, when Muslim merchants established themselves in Ceylon. But the removal of the empire's commercial and political centre from Damascus to Baghdad and Mesopotamia was to transform the development of trade with the Far East.[13]

India was the first objective. To reach the Malabar coast — usually the port of Mandjapur (Mangalore) — ships sailing from Basra or Siraf could either call at Muscat on the coast of Oman and from there head straight for the Malabar coast, or sail along the coasts of Sind and the Makran. On the outward journey the ships carried salt, sheets of copper and silver, silk and cotton fabrics, tiraz, perfumes from Iraq, porcelain, and Omani horses. In exchange the Indian subcontinent supplied teak of excellent quality, dye woods, ambergris, cardamom, iron, and weapons.

Ships heading towards China would call at Ceylon, known to the Arabs as Sarandib, the "Isle of Rubies", but also a source of sapphires, cinnamon, and elephants. Some ships would then sail for Sumatra, Java, or the other spice islands to buy nutmeg, cloves, pepper, camphor, sandalwood, teak, and tin. Others passed north of Sumatra to reach the Cambodian coast through the Straits of Malacca. The main ports of call were Sanf (north of Saigon) and Luquin (Hanoi), on the way to Kanfu (Canton), which some ships reached via the Paracel Islands. The Arabs hardly ever went beyond Canton; the unknown started on the other side of Korea. Arab cargoes to China included luxury textiles, carpets, copper and silver objects, gold and pearls from Southeast Asia, rhinoceros horns, and ivory. In return the Arabs received paper, medicines, musk, silks, and camphor: all these products went through meticulous official formalities before being cleared for loading. In China the export of goods considered to be in short supply was forbidden.

The return voyage usually followed the same route as the outward one. Ships would leave at the end of November to take advantage of the northwest monsoon and reach Canton six months later; they would stay there for the summer and set sail for home in November or December to get the benefit of the northeast monsoon, reaching Basra or Siraf at the beginning of the following summer. Thus the whole voyage lasted eighteen months, if all went well.

This was by no means always the case. We read in the mid-ninth century *Account of India and China*: "The products of China are rare. One of the causes of this rarity is the frequency of fires in the port of Kanfu, the port where Arab and Chinese goods are stored. Sometimes ships are wrecked or pillaged, or forced to spend long periods in port and sell their goods in non-Muslim countries. Sometimes they also have to make long stops for repairs." According to the *Marvels of India*: "All who had been to China found the voyage a dangerous adventure. Nobody has ever heard of a man going there and returning home without incident. Or if it ever happened it was a miracle." Some regions, even in the Gulf itself, were infested with pirates. Arab merchants were particularly wary of those inhabiting the coasts of northern India, whose galleys were much faster than their own slow-sailing ships. The merchants carried "Greek fire" for defence against them. Fantastic though they are, Sinbad's *Adventures* reflect the dangers faced by navigators at this time and the fear that such long voyages aroused.

Navigation itself presented formidable problems. Instruments and charts, Persian for the most part, were very approximate[14] even after the studies carried out on Mamun's orders (notably measurement of the arc of the meridian), and countless ships were lost. But these risks did not discourage Arab merchants, whose fleet virtually dominated international trade. Indians sailed the Indian Ocean as far as Indonesia, and great Chinese junks were sometimes to be seen in the Gulf ports; but the bulk of international commerce was in Muslim hands. It remained so for more than two centuries, then gradually shifted to Indian and Chinese traders. In the late fifteenth century, the Portuguese explorer Vasco da Gama — piloted by an illustrious Arab sailor, Ahmed ibn Majid — made his first visit to these waters and tried, not wholly successfully, to drive out the Muslim navigators.

Although by the eighth and ninth centuries most of the traffic with the Far East was by sea, the old Silk Road had not been abandoned and still carried limited volumes of lightweight, high-value products. Political tremors in the Middle Kingdom had left the Sinkiang route unsafe; and despite the alliance agreed upon in

798 between the Tang emperor and Harun al-Rashid, the central Asian route would take some time to resume full-scale activity.

Starting in Baghdad, the "China road" crossed the Iranian plateau by the time-honoured route through Khaniqin and Kermanshah and reached Khorasan via Hamadan and Ray. Near Nishapur a fork led towards India through Balkh, Bamyan, Kabul, and Multan on the Indus. Travellers to China had the choice of two routes: one through Tashkent and Talas, following the Ili; the other towards Kashgar and a double chain of oases on either side of the Tarim (Axum and Turfan to the north, Yarkand and Khotan to the south). The two routes then converged again and continued towards the Chinese provinces of Kansu and Chang'an.

There were dangers to be encountered in these vast steppes and these deserts of stone and sand. For protection against bandit attacks, caravans were usually composed of many merchants, who carried weapons and employed armed guards. But nothing could be done against bad weather: sudden storms that swelled rivers, cut roads and drowned animals and people; blizzards; torrid droughts that dried up springs and streams. The journey took eight to twelve months.

Although by now silk was being spun and woven in several parts of the Muslim empire and in Byzantium, the old trade had not disappeared entirely, and bolts of high-quality silk cloth would continue to be brought across central Asia and Khorasan for many years. But this route was increasingly used to bring Chinese porcelain to the Arab world: it had become fashionable in the Baghdad court, probably after the Khorasan governor Ali ibn Isa sent Harun twenty pieces of Imperial Chinese porcelain "the like of which had never been seen before". Spices that could not be found in India or Southeast Asia, jade, and the musk[15] that was so greatly appreciated in Baghdad also came from China by this route (two or three centuries later, tea would replace silk in this East–West trade). In exchange, Arab and Persian merchants exported to China perfumes and incense, pearls, coral, and certain very luxurious textiles. The Turks of central Asia bought silks and spices from them in exchange for weapons, copper utensils, felt, and, above all, slaves.

Trade Products

Slaves were essential to the functioning of Abbasid society, so much so that fluctuations in the slave market could affect the economy. Multitudes of slaves were needed to perform tasks avoided by free men, especially as the Muslims readily freed slaves in their service. They were forbidden by religion to enslave a fellow Muslim. The wars of conquest had provided the conquerors with large numbers of prisoners of both sexes, many of whom had become slaves. But once Arab expansion reached its limits, prisoners could be found only by making incursions into Byzantine territory.

During the time of the Abbasids this source too began to dry up[16] and slave traders were obliged to seek merchandise wherever they could find it, so that the Baghdad markets offered slaves from all sorts of places:

> The crier looked over the assembled merchants and saw that they had not yet all arrived. He waited until the market was full and until women of all races had been sold: Nubians and Takurians (from the Sudan), Franks, Maraghians (from Azerbaijan), Greeks, Tatars, Khirghiz, Berbers, Ethiopians, Khalandjians (of a colour between red and yellow) and many others.[17]

The African continent supplied Nubians, Ethiopians, Somalis, Bantus, even Senegalese and Chadian slaves. Bought from tribal chiefs, or captured by bands working for slave traders based in the great cities of Africa and the Arabian coast, they were moved from one centre to another overland or by sea. Those doomed to become eunuchs, usually Sudanese, were sold at much higher prices than the rest after being castrated in Egypt.

Another main source was the Slavic region of central and eastern Europe. Slavs and Anglo-Saxons were highly prized. (From the eighth century onwards they had replaced local slave labour on the internal markets of Catholic western Europe.)

A number of well-trodden routes led to the great slave markets: to the East, travellers went along the Volga (Itil, the capital of the Khazars), through Armenia (a centre for castration), to Ray and Baghdad; another route passed through the Black Sea, and a third followed the Rhine and the Danube. The busiest market in western Europe was at Verdun, another centre of castration (which was performed mainly by Jews). From there slaves were carried down the Saone and the Rhone to Narbonne or Arles, then were marched into Spain or shipped to the Orient. From the middle of the eighth century, Venice (despite the protests of successive popes) became one of the greatest centres of the trade, as did Prague. Thus, throughout Europe, men and women were being captured and sold into slavery under the Muslims or under the Christians of Byzantium. Anglo-Saxons were brought to Venice through Lyons or directly to Spain; Lombards were purchased by the merchants of southern Italy and resold in Egypt and Ifriqiya.

The Muslims appreciated the weapons forged in Catholic Europe. German superiority in sword-making was doubtless a result of that nation's contacts with the peoples of central Asia, probably with the Turks, whose metallurgical skills were already very ancient. The tough but flexible Scandinavian weapons were also admired in the Orient.

The Muslims also bought metals, timber for shipbuilding, and furs in the West. Backward and poor, Europe had little else to offer, while its imports — luxury products it was unable to manufacture, especially textiles — went to a small minority of the population. The upper clergy and nobility wore purple silk robes embroidered with gold (the clothes worn by Charlemagne and his daughters dazzled the poets). Louis the Germanic issued an edict forbidding his soldiers to dress in embroidered silk; Alcuin denounced the clergy for wasting church funds on magnificent robes for themselves. Europe also imported small quantities of spices, medicinal herbs, ivory, gold, and silver.

There were a number of trade routes between West and East. One went from England through Brittany to Lisbon and thence to the Muslim ports on the Atlantic. Another, from Germany and the countries of the Franks, reached Spain and north Africa via Narbonne. Italian ports such as Amalfi, Gaeta, and Salerno also played a role in maintaining links with the towns of north Africa — Tunis, Fostat, Kairouan. Scandinavian and Russian merchants sent to Baghdad furs, weapons, honey and beeswax, horses, and, of course, slaves; they got back fabrics, dishes, and silver coin. Transport was by caravan and, mainly, by waterways: the Don, the Volga, and the Dnieper flowed to the Caspian and the Black Sea, where exchanges took place with Muslim merchants from

Azerbaijan, Gurgan, and Kwarizm (some of whom ventured as far north as Kiev, the upper Volga, and the Baltic).

The Muslim world became the centre of a vast commercial development answering the growing demands of consumers and itself giving rise to new activities. Without this drive to consume and the material base that it provided, Islamic civilization would probably never have known such glittering success. It was this prosperity, underpinned by a strong political regime, which made the Abbasid empire a melting pot for elements from other civilizations, both near and far, and one of the essential sources of inspiration and example for medieval Europe.

9
A Thirst for Knowledge

*Seek ye after science, for which ye should
be prepared to go to China itself.*
Mohammed, Hadith

*The scholar's ink is more sacred than the
blood of martyrs.*
Mohammed, Hadith

Great builders, and nostalgic lovers of Arab and Bedouin poetry,
the Umayyads seem to have been almost impervious to the
intellectual influence of the empires they destroyed. Nevertheless,
from about the end of the seventh century some caliphs possessed
libraries: first Muawia, then Yazid I's son Prince Khalid. Ibn al-Adim
tells us that Khalid "called together a group of Greek philosophers
who lived in Egypt and whose Arabic was clear and eloquent, and
asked them to translate works on alchemy from their original Greek
and Coptic. These were the first translations made in the lands of
Islam."[1] But these works remained isolated, and the sole celebrated
author of the period, Jabir — the Geber cited in Latin treatises on
alchemy — was probably dreamed up for political reasons by Ismaili
missionaries in the ninth and tenth centuries.[2] Until the Abbasid
period there existed no specifically Arab science. It was only after
studying ancient Greek texts and those of Iranian and Indian authors
that the Arabs themselves began producing original works. Islam
assimilated the contributions of earlier cultures and then, from the
tenth through to the thirteenth century, passed this heritage on to the
West.

The Legacy of the Ancients

An outpost of Hellenic culture had appeared in the Arab Middle East in the very distant past. Following the Council of Nicaea in 325, the Church became aware that the Christians of Syria, who spoke Syriac, a language with Aramaic roots, were drifting away from Catholic theology and liturgy and stood in need of instruction. A school was founded at Nisibe, on the frontier between Syria and upper Mesopotamia, under the direction of one Ephrem, a doctor of the Church. When Nisibe was seized by the Persians, Ephrem fled to Edessa and opened another school, which quickly gained wide renown. Its language of instruction was Syriac, and Greek works were being translated into that language from about the end of the fourth century — first theology, then certain texts of Aristotle. In 431, however, the Council of Ephesus denounced the schism of Nestorius;[3] as most members of the school of Edessa were Nestorians, the emperor Xenon, who supported Monophysitism, ordered its closure at the end of the fifth century. The school returned to Nisibe, where it became the great university of the Nestorian church (it boasted a hospital and a school of medicine). The Nestorian church was extending its influence at that time; its missionaries were travelling deep into central Asia and as far as Medina in Arabia.

But the task of translating ancient Greek texts was pursued most systematically at Gundeshapur in western Iran, under the influence of the Sassanid king Khosrov I. Although fiercely hostile to the basileus, he greatly admired the culture Byzantium had inherited and offered asylum to the last Neo-platonist philosophers after the closure of the school of Athens on Justinian's orders in 529. Khosrov wanted to establish an academy at Gundeshapur comparable to the one that had made Alexandria's reputation, and it did become a very active centre of learning, predominantly of Greek culture. Logic, medicine, mathematics, and astronomy were taught (the last with the aid of an observatory). Syriac was used more than Persian, and among the works translated into Syriac were the writings of Galen, much of Hippocrates, Aristotle's *Logics*, a treatise by Porphyry, and texts on astronomy, mathematics, and agriculture. Among the translators whose names have survived were the Monophysite bishop Giorgios, who translated Aristotle's *Organon*, and a bishop called Severos, who translated the *Analytics* and is credited with introducing the so-called Arabic numerals (really of Indian origin) to Iran. Gundeshapur was close to Mesopotamia, and it is not surprising that some of its doctors and professors found themselves drawn to Baghdad and to the salaries and honours offered by caliphs. Jibril, Harun's doctor, was the grandson of one of the most illustrious medical men of the time, ibn Bakhtyashu, who had taught at Gundeshapur.

Some of the knowledge incorporated into Arab-Islamic culture came to Baghdad through other channels: from Antioch; from Harran in Syria, a centre of gnosticism where there also survived a Babylonian form of paganism based on the study of the sky; from northern India; and especially from Bactria. All these regions had retained the imprint of Greek thought after Alexander's conquests. Under the Aristotelian influence an important role was given to the natural sciences and medicine, astronomy and mathematics. But the influence of Neoplatonism and of a strongly Hellenized form of Christianity can also be discerned. These foreign, and especially Greek, currents of thought constituted the essence of what was to be called the *falsafa* and so fostered the new intellectual dynamism of the Arab-Muslim world.

The Golden Age of Arab Science
After the flood of translations made possible by contact with the Hellenized Mediterranean, a host of Arabic commentaries on the works of antiquity began to appear. The intellectual and spiritual resources of conquered territories, mostly ignored by the Umayyads, seemed to the Abbasids a rich seam of wisdom and they mined it energetically. The Nestorian school and Gundeshapur played a determining role in the birth of this new culture, but official approval was also very important.[4] Harun al-Rashid encouraged translators and men of science in systematic fashion: he sent a mission to Byzantium to search out Greek texts for translation into Arabic and Syriac — supported in this effort by the very cultivated Jaffar the Barmakid, whose father, Yahya, imported doctors and philosophers from India and protected anyone who might contribute to the advance of learning. Mamun,[5] too, would later send a mission to Constantinople with orders to bring back the complete works of Aristotle. Translators and commentators, as well as poets, could call on the patronage of courtiers and dignitaries.

The Arabs considered astronomy the noblest science because of its religious applications: finding the direction of Mecca, determining times for prayer, fixing the month of Ramadan, and so on. Thus, under the influence of the Barmakids and other men from Khorasan, the first translations into Arabic were of texts dealing with astronomy and mathematics. The Sassanids had strongly encouraged work in astronomy, and the Indians had contributed their own advances in this field. A long-established observatory was functioning at Merv; after the conquest of the surrounding region, research continued there and later in Baghdad. During Harun's reign, perhaps even earlier, work began on translating a fifth-century Indian work on astronomy, the *Siddharta*. This translation led to others — Euclid's *Elements* and Ptolemy's *Almagest* — probably on the initiative of Harun, who is said to have been told that his astronomers did not know enough geometry to understand Indian texts. During this period the Arabs compiled tables of planetary movements on the basis of Indian and Persian works. Some were done by Harun's chief librarian, Fadl ibn Nawbakt. Mamun, deeply interested in astronomy and astrology, "the science of what is ordained by the laws", ordered his scholars to compile new astronomical tables and to measure a degree of meridian so that the earth's circumference could be calculated more precisely. But Arab astronomers (and mathematicians) had initially been inspired mainly by the Greeks and remained so.

In the medical domain a translation was made of the *Pandectae medicinae*, a Greek encyclopedia by Aaron of Alexandria. Dr Jibril worked on the *Kunnash*, a Syriac text inspired by the works of Galen, Hippocrates, and Paul of Aegina, which long served as a reference work. Ayyub of Edessa produced his own Syriac versions of the writings of Galen and Simon of Taibuthe. Ali Sahl al-Tabrai, son of the translator of the *Almagest*, wrote a major medical work of his own, the *Paradise of Wisdom*. Harun al-Rashid ordered the translation of a text on agriculture, the *Vindonios Anatolios*.

Another accomplished scientific translator was Harun's contemporary Hunayn ibn Ishak, who was followed by his son Yakub and his nephew Hubays, both converted from Nestorian Christianity. Arab science owes to them a great many adaptations of Greek authors, including Aristotle, Euclid, Galen, and Ptolemy. Also worth mentioning are the three sons of Musa ibn Shakir, a former highwayman turned chief of the caliph's police. One was a talented astronomer, the second a distinguished mechanician, and the third a specialist in geometry. They left a treatise that was later translated into Latin (*Liber trium fratrum de geometria*). Individually wealthy, they founded their own school of translators and scientists.

Many other works were translated from Greek into Syriac, a language that continued to be used until the Gundeshapur school closed at the end of the eighth century. But translations from Greek or Syriac into Arabic were being made in increasing numbers; Arabic was becoming the language of scholarship in the Middle East, although Jews still wrote their books in Hebrew, Iranians in Persian, and Christians in Syriac. Scientific translators were no longer content merely to translate the works of the ancients but were increasingly inclined to adapt and verify them, repeating and checking their calculations and sometimes reaching different conclusions. Even Aristotle was looked at in a new way:

> The problem with most people is the extravagant respect with which they treat Aristotle's ideas. They receive his opinions as if they were gospel truths although they know perfectly well that he formulated theories to the best of his ability without ever claiming to be protected by God or incapable of error.[6]

Translators were no longer always simple transmitters of other people's work but often scholars in their own right; a true scientific spirit was making its appearance. Kwarizmi (d. 830), one of the greatest Arab mathematicians, introduced the decimal system and wrote a book — *Al-Jabr* — on which modern algebra is based. Al-Biruni, or Aliboron, was an encyclopedic scholar who wrote treatises on astronomy, mathematics, physics, and medicine and was also (as we shall see) a celebrated geographer. Ibn Sina, or Avicenna (d. 1037), philosopher, medical doctor, chemist, physicist, and extraordinarily prolific author, wrote on almost every subject, including music. Haytam, or Hazin (d. 1039), was another universal savant, a mathematician and physicist who wrote an *Optics* unique in the Arab world. Razi, a doctor famous for his work on smallpox, compiled an enormous medical encyclopedia based on clinical observations; he also wrote a whole series of works on philosophy, theology, and the natural sciences, including the *Sirr al-Asrar*, which formed the basis of scientific chemistry. Omar Khayyam (d. 1126), now better known for his quatrains than for scientific work, left an *Algebra* of great value.

Geographers were also achieving prominence. The powerful Abbasid economy was reaching out to China through its sailors and merchants, and the descriptions of the world left by the Greeks were by now thoroughly obsolete. By the beginning of the ninth century, observation was preferred to traditional accounts, and quickly there appeared an Arab geographical literature whose accuracy still astonishes us today.

Appearing alongside such amusing but over-imaginative travellers' tales as the merchant Suleiman's *Voyages to the Far East* were ibn Fadlan's *Journey to the Bulgars of the Volga* and the sea captain Buzurg ibn Shahriyar's *Marvels of India*, both highly accurate accounts free of romantic exaggeration. Such reports were often written by senior officials of the barid, whose work obliged them to travel widely. Ibn Khurdadbeh, in his late ninth-century *Book of Countries and Provinces*, gives minute descriptions of the countries visited and includes main distances and trade routes. Yakubi, writing in the same period, describes in his *Book of Countries* the routes leading to the frontiers of the empire on the basis of his own observations and those of other travellers he considers reliable. Masudi (d. 956) was a great traveller who sailed the Caspian and Mediterranean seas; he considered geography to be part of history and studied the influence of the environment on men, animals, and plants. His *Meadows of Gold* is a mine of information, as are the *Annals* left by Tabari (d. 923), which trace history back to the Creation.

All of these men placed Baghdad and Iraq at the centre of the world, and their descriptions look outwards from there. Their observations are restricted to the countries of Islam. The West is of no interest to them, and there are no accounts by Arab travellers of Europe in the early Middle Ages; the few pages they do devote to it reflect their contempt for its barbarian peoples, wild, pagan, and filthy. The universe of the Arabs extended only to those Oriental countries with which they traded on more or less equal terms.

For some geographers, however, like ibn Rusteh, or Balkhi, who wrote a *Commentary on Maps*, the centre of the world was in Arabia — Mecca, to be exact, as it was there that the Prophet had received

Revelation. Although these men strove to keep their conclusions in tune with the Koran, they too produced scientific works that went beyond mere observation. Muqadassi in the tenth century extended the field of geography to include the study of races, customs, languages, and weights and measures, accepting as true only what he had seen for himself. But Arab geography reached its apogee at the beginning of the eleventh century with the work of al-Biruni. He accompanied Mahmud of Ghazni to India and returned with a monumental *Book of India* containing all the available knowledge on that country. He also produced a critical examination of earlier geographical works, published remarkable observations in astronomy and physical geography, managed to perfect a procedure for desalinating seawater, and measured the specific weights of different substances.

All of these books, starting with translations that generated compilations, commentaries, and finally original works, made for voluminous, ever-growing libraries; Harun's own library employed a large staff.

The sages of Gundeshapur, Baghdad, and Basra were soon faced with the problem of reconciling all this science with the revealed faith. Was there, they wondered, a contradiction between Greek philosophy and the concept of the world, the morality and politics, imposed on the believer by the Koran? Al-Kindi, the first Muslim philosopher to be given the title "Philosopher of the Arabs", saw no fundamental disagreement between the teachings of the Prophet and Greek thought. Al-Farabi and Avicenna, treating only the social aspect of Islam, agreed with him. Al-Ghazali (1058–1111), undoubtedly Islam's supreme theologian — with an influence comparable to that of Thomas Aquinas in Christian theology — gave more weight to mystical thought.

So vigorous was the flowering of science and philosophy in the time of Harun al-Rashid and the next two centuries that the period has been called "the golden age of Arab science". Towards 830 Mamun provided an official structure for this great movement by founding in Baghdad the "House of Wisdom" (*Bayt al-Hikma*), a sort of academy responsible for translations and scientific research. Scholars were attracted to it as they once had been to the library in Alexandria. Those accepted as scholars or teachers received a salary.

Astronomers, mathematicians, doctors, geographers, philosophers, translators, and writers came from all parts of the empire to take part in this scientific and intellectual progress. They conjured from the old Orient a new civilization and a new culture — the distillation of earlier great societies of the eastern Mediterranean and the Middle East. The new learning, embracing a vast field of knowledge, would later be assimilated in turn by the West, providing the basis for Western development.

Arab Culture in the West

To reach Western scholars, who until that time had access only to Latin compilations from Byzantium, Arab culture followed three main paths. The first of these routes, primarily one for medical works, ran from Ifriqiya and Sicily to Salerno, where there was an old and famous medical school. Imported and translated by a doctor — or perhaps a merchant — who came from Carthage, converted to Christianity and took the name Constantine, these books gave the doctors of Salerno a much-needed injection of scientific thought, which they then passed on to other European schools.

Sicily and southern Italy had greater influence in Christian intellectual circles. A sort of Arabic-Graeco-Latin culture developed, encouraged by the tolerance and intellectual tastes of successive Muslim emirs, Norman kings, and, later, Hohenstaufens and Angevins. Frederick II supported Oriental sages, and Michel Scot, famous translator from Toledo, ended his life at Frederick's court. Others who spent time there were Theodore of Antioch, an eminent Arab intellectual who was one of the emperor's secretaries (as well as his astrologer); Leonard of Pisa (Fibonacci), who is reputed to have introduced "Arabic" numerals to the West; and Manfred, a man so "Arabized" that the pope denounced him as a "lord of the Saracens". Charles of Anjou, who ended Hohenstaufen dominance in Sicily, subsidized the translation of Razi's medical encyclopedia. The region became a centre for translations into Latin, Arabic, and Italian, and made classical and Oriental works available to the intellectual elites of Europe.

Still more fundamental was the role of translators and scholars in Spain and Portugal, where Christians, Jews, and Muslims of all nationalities were accomplishing an incredible amount of work. Scholars from all over Europe were instantly drawn to these new centres of learning, where they could find works from antiquity hitherto available only in extract form. One of the first to go to Spain was the mathematician and philosopher Gerbert, who later (in 999) became Pope Sylvester II. For three centuries other scholars, including the English philosopher Daniel de Morley, followed in his footsteps.

Thus, by about 1200 all the most significant scientific works of antiquity were translated into Latin. In Segovia, Robert de Chester translated Kwarizmi's *Algebra*; in Barcelona, around the middle of the twelfth century, Plato of Tivoli did the same for al-Battani's *Treatise on Astronomy*, Ptolemy's *Opus Quadripartum*, and Abraham bar Hiyya's *Algebra*. Harmannus the Slav translated the Koran and several works on astronomy. Gerard of Cremona translated the *Almagest* and works by al-Kindi, Euclid, Archimedes, Ptolemy, Hippocrates, Razi, and ibn Sina — eighty-seven books in all, so many that he is thought to have run a translators' school.

Translations into Hebrew were of secondary importance, but among Jewish scholars of the period we should mention the very productive Tibbon family that lived in Granada, Lunel, Marseilles and Montpellier. Their output over several generations included thirty-odd translations signed by Moses Tibbon and original works by Prophatius, who lived in Marseilles and whose *Almanac*, translated into Latin, was used by astronomers until the Renaissance.

The kings and princes of Christian and Muslim Spain looked favourably upon this scientific movement, with the result that in the eleventh century a remarkable scientific upsurge took place in Seville, Malaga, Cordoba, Almeria, Majorca, and, soon afterwards, Toledo.

Christian princelings, for their part, encouraged Arabic studies and translations even as they fought the Moors. In the thirteenth century their enthusiasm was overshadowed by that of the great figure of Alfonso the Wise: a scholar himself, he directed the compilation of the *Alfonsine Tables*, which were used for many years by navigators. One of his grandsons, King Dinis, followed his example on a smaller scale by having Arabic, Latin, and Spanish works translated into Portuguese. He founded the University of Lisbon, which was later moved to Coimbra.

The work of intellectuals who went to the Levant with the Crusades appears thin by comparison. Few of them showed much interest in the scientific and literary works of the peoples conquered by Christian knights. Only Adelard of Bath (an Englishman) and Stephen of Antioch settled for a time in the Orient and worked as translators. Adelard produced versions of Kwarizmi's *Astronomical Tables* and Euclid's *Elements*.

Poetry in the Century of the Well-Guided

Greek antiquity had but minimal influence on Arabic poetry, and even the influence of Iran and India was slight. The Arabs knew nothing about Greek poetry; Homer was just a name to them and they had never heard of Aristophanes. No one translated foreign poetry during the Abbasid period. In any case, says the writer Djahiz, poetry is untranslatable: "Its texture is broken, its metre is lost, its beauty destroyed... it becomes nothing more than prose."[7] The Arabs were fascinated by the philosophy and science of the peoples they had subjected, but they ignored the poetry.

In the centuries before Islam, recited lyrical poetry reigned supreme. Its language was rich and its themes simple and timeless: the valour of heroes, the love of women, the beauties of nature, animals, the nomad's solitude in the desert. Poetry of this kind still existed in the time of the Umayyads, but as the Arab mode of life changed, the sentiments expressed went through a parallel evolution. Iranian influence can be discerned in the decline of this traditional literature of open spaces in favour of something more urban and refined. As the Bedouin lifestyle faded into distant memory, a new form of poetry appeared: short compositions in a lighter metre (*rajaz*), singing in praise of wine, gardens, the chase, and passion for beautiful singers and youths.

The most celebrated poet of this school was Abu Nuwas, firmly linked in popular legend with Harun al-Rashid. "For you must know," Shehrazade says in the *Thousand and One Nights*, "that Harun al-Rashid was always wont to send for the poet when he was in an evil humour, in order to distract himself with the improvised poems and rhymed adventures of that remarkable man."[8] His formative years were passed in the great cultural crucible of Basra. Almost a Bacchic archetype, he describes debauches in the company of disreputable youths who spare neither his purse nor his feelings. He often appears as the butt of drunken misadventures in which the poet is fleeced by his young companions. From the poem "Drunkenness":

Pour wine! Come, pour and pour again
And tell me clearly: Here is wine!
Don't make me drink in secret, when
You can shout my name in front of everyone...
I woke a barmaid from her forty winks...
Who's knocking at my door? she cried.
A brotherhood (we noisily replied)
Of empty glasses. Wine is what they need;
They want adultery here without delay.
My substitute, she said, will be a man
With languorous glances, shining like the dawn.

Like other Oriental poets, Abu Nuwas bewails the passage of
time and the loss of once joyous drinking companions. Sometimes
he collapses into total pessimism:

Men are no different from the living dead,
Born of the dead, who once lived as they do.
Last of a line of heroes, stinking bones
Dissolving in the putrid swarming mass.
He who looks wisely, with a steady eye,
At all the wealth and glories of this world
Can see them for the deadly foe they are
Behind the flaunted raiment of a friend.

Although a regular and frequent sinner, Abu Nuwas was
optimistic about God's mercy and claimed to believe that so
wretched a creature might easily escape Divine notice:

Stunned by my sin in its enormity,
I took heart, Lord, and laid it side by side
With that great mercy which is Thine alone,
And measured both with yardstick up and down.
My sin is great; but now I know, O Lord,
That even greater is Thy clemency.

His ability to improvise was amazing, even for a time when
educated people were expected to be able to express themselves in
verse; he is thought to be one of the most imaginative geniuses of

Arab letters. Masudi says of him:

> Abu Nuwas sang of wine, its taste, its fragrance, its beauty and glitter, its influence on the soul. He described the splendour of banquets, the goblets and amphorae, the companions in pleasure, their morning and evening libations... and did so with such brilliance that he would have put the lid on lyrical poetry for good, so to speak, if its field were not so vast, if one could imagine any limits to its domain...

Abu Nuwas is variously said to have died of maltreatment inflicted on him by the Nawbakht (a family of scholars, one of whom was Harun al-Rashid's librarian) after he wrote scurrilous verses about them; to have perished in gaol while serving a sentence for sacrilegious poetry; and to have been found dead in a barmaid's bedroom. This last is pleasantly in keeping with his stage persona.

Harun's favourite poet and drinking companion may have far eclipsed other poets, but they were not discouraged. There were plenty of them. Minstrels of city life, "modern" in style and content, they too lived disorderly lives and liked a drop of wine. One was the very popular beggar-poet ibn Dibil, a sort of ninth-century Villon full of malice and bile. Another was Dik al-Djinn (the Devil's Cock), also a singer of wine:

> Rise now, for she begins to drink her unrelenting cup;
> so pour her liquor from a precious gem, none other
> than her wine.
> [. . .]
> Wine exercised its assured vengeance on our wandering
> steps.

Also worth mentioning is Muslim ibn Walid, a talented bohemian renowned for elegance of style and for the originality of his erotic verse. Often quoted is his:

> What is this life but loving, and surrender to the
> drunkenness of wine and pretty eyes?

Another intimate of Harun al-Rashid (and of his father, Mahdi, before him) was the poet Abu al-Atahiya, who, after a dissipated life, became an ascetic given to philosophical poetry:

> Youth, leisure and avidity are seeds
>   purpose-made for the corruption of men.
> To escape evil, we must break with it.
>
> When my allotted share of time runs out,
>   the mourner's keening will give little comfort.
> My memory will slip away; forgotten by friends,
>   my affection will leave space for newer friends.

He also had a shrewd idea of the forms of address likely to find favour with the Caliph of the Believers:

> So noble is my Emir that the people, if they could,
> Would spread a carpet of their cheeks before him on the
>   ground.
> Our steeds have reason to complain of thee!
>   they prance towards thee lightly, with empty saddlebags,
>   but go forth weighed down with thy generosity.

Bashar ibn Burd, a frequenter of Mahdi's court, belonged to the same generation. Of Persian origin, he made no secret of his sympathies for his ancestral Mazdaeism but wrote in Arabic eloquently and with passion. This ensured his protection despite the disapproval with which he was widely regarded; but when Mahdi dropped him in 738, he was immediately killed and his body thrown into the Tigris. With a sensuality sometimes close to obscenity, but in perfect form, he wrote of love:

> Yes, by God, I do
>   desire to be bewitched
>   by the sorcery of your eyes

but also of disappointment and melancholy:

> I weep on those who have given me a taste of their affection
> only to doze off as desire awakened in me...

We are old acquaintances,
sadness and I,
and always will be so, now
(unless eternity should end some day).

There are many more of these eighth- and ninth-century poets who mingle the erotic with the mystical, love of wine with love of God, the passion for young boys and beautiful slaves with the disappointments of life and the horror of death. But we should perhaps mention Abbas al-Ahnaf, the poet closest to Harun al-Rashid in spirit (and another Persian). He celebrated courtly love and later had great influence on Spanish writers.

In speaking of her to me, O Saad, you have added to my madness.
O Saad, never stop, keep piling up your chatter...
I want her with such ardour
   that my heart knows nothing else;
   a burning desire with no before or after.

This kind of verse, very much alive in the time of Harun al-Rashid and his sons, left deep traces on Arabic literature. But it aged rapidly and faded during the next century, leaving room for the re-emergence of older, more authentic forms that were closer to genuine human feelings.

The Birth of Prose
While the Greek influence on Arabic literature remained slight, the Persian heritage played a strong role. The presence of many literate Iranians and kuttab from Iran brought about the translation of works written in Persian. The best-known example was the translation, first into Persian, then into Arabic, by ibn Muqaffa, of the Indian fable *Kalila and Dimna*. Written by a Brahmin of the fourth century (Bidpay), the book tells the story of two jackal brothers at the lion's court; it was widely diffused and many later writings were inspired by it. Ibn Muqaffa also translated into Arabic a comprehensive *History of Iran*, for a long time the basis for all historiography of that country. Other Iranian works on everything from history to morals and the occult sciences helped to enrich Arab-Islamic culture.

   Simultaneously, there arose a movement of reaction against Arab culture in pro-Iranian circles; it was known as the *shuubiya*, a word which one writer translates as "Gentiles' Movement".[9] The reaction set the Persianized element in society, a worldly and sophisticated elite proud of its intellectual pre-eminence and its disproportionate strength in the upper ranks of the state bureaucracy, against the upholders of Arab tradition who insisted on fidelity to the glorious past. This conflict between traditionalists and modernists, which was not without social and even racial overtones, was present everywhere, especially in Harun al-Rashid's time.

At the very beginning of the ninth century, as poetry began to take a new direction, Arabic prose received a tremendous boost in the person of Djahiz, a mulatto polymath who came from Basra and died there after spending most of his ninety-plus years in Baghdad. His oeuvre was unequalled in his own time, and perhaps in any other: he left nearly two hundred works on science, history, ethnology, theology, grammar, and other subjects. In the *Book of Misers* he describes Arab society and contrasts its generosity with the avarice of the Persians. His *Book of Animals* is a treatise on natural history. The *Bayan* deals with rhetoric. He wrote books on the Turks, the Christians, the Jews, and other groups. His encyclopedic mind spanned the whole synthesis of contemporary knowledge. As a moralist and essayist he has been compared to Lucian, Molière, and Voltaire. According to his contemporary ibn Qutaiba, "He is the ultimate theologian, the strongest in bringing out proofs, the most skilled at enlarging what is small and reducing what is large. And so great is his power that he can argue opposites: he knows how to prove the superiority of blacks over whites and vice versa." Charles Pellat, the leading specialist on Djahiz, holds that "the observations and descriptions of his contemporaries place him closer to La Bruyère and Molière than to other Arab writers."

As remarkable for its volume as for its innovative character, the work of Djahiz occupies a central place in Arabic literature. His prolific brilliance was reflected in his formative influence on the new culture. He was the initiator of adab, which brought the Arab-Islamic culture to the point of perfection.

Adab signifies "custom" or "usage", but during the first centuries of Islam it took on the connotations of "proper upbringing", "urbanity", "courtesy". According to F. Gabrielli, it marks "the progressive refinement by Islam of Bedouin ethics and customs".

The word acquired an intellectual significance and came to designate "the sum of knowledge that goes to make up a courteous and urbane man", more or less equivalent to the seventeenth-century French *honnête homme* (gentleman).

At the beginning of Islam, a person could pass for cultivated if he knew the message of Mohammed and the refinements of the Arabic language. Townsmen used to visit the Bedouins for language tuition. As Islamic doctrine evolved, the religious sciences were added to the list of requirements, and afterwards one needed some knowledge of the cultures of conquered countries. The first adab in this broader sense was thus ibn Muqaffa, who by translating *Kalila and Dimna* achieved a synthesis of Arab and Persian cultures.

The enormous accumulation of learning taking place at this time had the paradoxical effect of threatening Arab culture. The danger was that a specializing of knowledge would make it easier for the kuttab to strengthen the influence of Persian and Indian contributions and so bring the triumph of the shuubiya a step closer. It was Djahiz who, without elaborating a doctrine as such, managed to give definition to the culture as a whole — poetry, history, rhetoric, geography, religious sciences — by emphasizing the importance of thought and the need to write clearly and without pedantry.

This concept of adab as general culture implying freedom to think changed after Mamun's reign; adab then came to mean verbal virtuosity, a sort of objectless purism. Literature was reduced, on the one hand, to treatises destined for consumption by the kuttab, and on the other, to *maqamat*, ornate pieces whose sole merit is that they describe contemporary society in a polished style. Harir and Hamadhani are both examples of this genre.

Another influential prose writer of the Abbasid period was ibn Qutaiba, whose works include a *Book of Poetry and Poets* and the *Book of Knowledge* — the earliest history manual in the Arabic language. Inferior in quality to those of Djahiz, his works are largely devoted to violent polemic against the shuubiya and to defending Arabism against those adepts of foreign sciences, the kuttab.

Myriad works by other writers of the same period could also be cited. A catalogue still survives, the *Fihrist*, which was compiled by the Baghdad librarian ibn al-Nadim. It lists numerous translations and original works in Arabic. The *Fihrist* devotes much space to works of literature, as well as to those of science.

10
From the Well-Guided to the Magnificent

The traces left on Baghdad by the civil war disappeared quite swiftly. The town was gradually reconstructed and the protracted hostilities between Harun's two sons forgotten. Mamun died in 833 and was succeeded by his brother al-Mutasim. Two conspiracies in a row made the new caliph realize that the abna was no longer trustworthy and he needed to recruit men who would be personally loyal to him. As the abna was firmly established in Baghdad, he decided in 836 to build another town for himself and his soldiers — Samarra,[1] on the east bank of the Tigris a hundred kilometres upstream from the capital. Volunteers poured in, mainly Turks, many from the east. These new troops were going to open the way to a new regime.

It did not take them long to realize that they represented the caliph's only strength and that without their support he was nothing. From there to the seizure of power was a short step, soon taken. In 861 the army chiefs assassinated al-Mutasim's successor, Mutawakil, probably at the instigation of his eldest son, Muntasir, who was immediately proclaimed caliph. The praetorians were masters of the empire.

In the future caliphs were to be chosen by the generals: still from

223

the Abbasid family, they were usually selected for their docility. Strong personalities were not wholly lacking (Muwaffak, brother of the late ninth-century caliph Mutamid, is a notable example); but despite their efforts the caliphs never succeeded in repossessing the empire. For a time, around 865, there were even two caliphs, Mutazz in Samarra and Mustain in Baghdad; both were eventually murdered. Samarra was abandoned in 892, but nothing changed. The military strengthened their grip on the state while repressing various revolts. The rebellion of the Zendj,[2] who formed their own government and occupied Basra for a time, bloodied southern Iraq from 869 to 883. That of the Qarmat[3] spread soon afterwards in almost the same area; a small Qarmat state, democratic and egalitarian, was established in Bahrain.

Another reason for the influence of the army was the cost of maintaining it — around half the total state budget. There were only two practical ways for the government to manage this: one was to award a sort of financial autonomy to regional military commanders, who would pay the army out of the local tax yield and send any surplus to Baghdad; the other was to sign over to the generals, in person, the income from specified estates. The iqta system had existed for some time, but only for the benefit of members of the imperial family and specially favoured dignitaries. Its spread to military chiefs helped weaken the central authority, as provincial governors practising iqta quickly acquired de facto independence. Once Baghdad lost financial control of these provinces, they began to slip out of its grasp in other ways. Ahmed ibn Tulun, who reorganized the army and administration in Egypt and annexed Syria, became a virtual sovereign (and was succeeded by his son). The caliph managed to restore his authority for a short time, only to see it fall into the hands of a Turkish dynasty, the Ikshid, who held on to it for more than fifty years until the arrival of the Fatimids.

Thus did the empire fall apart. Local dynasties replaced the caliph's governors in Azerbaijan, Chirvan, Kurdistan, Daylam, and northern Syria (which was taken over by the Hamanids), while Oriental mercenaries, mainly Turks, took the place of the Abbasid army. In Khorasan, which Mamun had ceded to Tahir ibn Husein — whose support had enabled him to return to Baghdad — sovereignty became hereditary; the province later fell into the hands of the

Saffarids, then into those of the Samanids. They were to be driven out in turn by the Ghaznevids, architects of a powerful empire based in Afghanistan which reached as far as the Punjab. The caliph's sovereignty was flouted everywhere; but none of the new masters would have dared to reign without his imprimatur. It was as if his presence, lurking invisibly in the depths of some Baghdad palace, was still necessary to the world order. Coinage continued to bear his effigy, and Friday prayer was still intoned in his name.

The erosion of state authority led to the formation of a new aristocracy, which gradually changed the nature of society. Extended to the army's lower echelons, iqta produced the same effects as it did on the generals who governed whole provinces. An officer allocated the revenues of an estate may not have become the landowner; nonetheless he regarded himself as belonging to a class apart. It was from this group, composed mainly of non-Arab foreigners, that members of the civil service were recruited; and from the ranks of the bureaucracy there emerged in 924 the *amir al-umara*, the emir of emirs, supreme commander of the civil administration and the army. He was above the viziers and held all power; but for what purpose? Naming a strong man had been a desperate measure that "did not save the empire, because there was no empire to be saved".[4]

Disorder was still mounting. Five amir al-umara and five caliphs succeeded one another within ten years. Radi, placed in power by the army in 932, died eight years later and was succeeded by his brother, who was deposed after his eyes had been put out. Mustaksi was then proclaimed caliph. It was one of those times when the toughest and most heavily armed have the best chance of seizing power. In 945 the Buyids came from Daylam, on the shores of the Caspian, to take over in Baghdad.

Could the Shiite Buyids coexist with the caliph, defender of the detestable Sunni faith? If not, who could they put in his place without risking a new quarrel with the Sunni principalities? Reasons of state prevailed and the caliph survived. Stripped of all authority, the Commander of the Faithful and the guarantor of justice represented no threat to the new masters of Baghdad. The head of the Buyid family called himself *shahinshah* (king of kings), a title with Sassanid overtones.

More than a century passed before the Buyid confederation

crumbled in its turn under pressure of new invaders from the East. But during that time, under the rule of those initially rather rustic warriors, the Arab-Islamic civilization echoed the time of Harun al-Rashid and the first Abbasids.

The collapse of the caliphate and its reduction to supervised status did not lead to decadence; on the contrary, Baghdad experienced a renewal of activity in all domains. The Buyid princes were great patrons of art and culture who built monuments in the capital and wherever their family had authority — in Shiraz and Isfahan, for example. New dynasties in Cairo, Aleppo, Nishapur, and Ghazni developed the country and encouraged intellectual life. No prince or rich merchant was now without his library. In Afghanistan, where Mahmud of Ghazni, the conqueror of India, kept four hundred poets at court to celebrate his exploits, Firdousi composed his admirable *Shahnam*, the *Book of Kings*, which sang of Iran's glorious past in neo-Persian, a language then making its appearance and later to be a defining element of the Iranian Renaissance. In Aleppo, Sayf al-Daula — on whose personality the storytellers of the *Thousand and One Nights* are believed to have based parts of their portrait of Harun al-Rashid — surrounded himself with versifiers, writers, and scientists; al-Farabi went there from Transoxiana to finish his oeuvre, and there al-Mutannabi composed his best poems. Central Asia and the Samanid capital, Nishapur, were having a golden age. In newly-founded Cairo (al-Kahira, "the Victorious") the Fatimids had assembled a spectacular court whose magnificence equalled that of the Abbasids.

The erosion of caliphal power had in no way reduced the enthusiasm for learning; indeed, the scattering of seats of authority multiplied the centres of culture and prosperity. Each prince concentrated his efforts on his own province. Fed by their rivalries, and even more by population growth and the appearance of new towns, the economy continued to develop throughout the Islamic world.

In 1055 the Seljuk Turks entered Baghdad. They were Sunni Muslims and their arrival transformed the political map of the Orient without altering the course of its civilization. The main result was to restore to the caliphate some of its former lustre. At the end of the twelfth century the visionary caliph al-Nasir even attempted to reconcile Sunnis and Shiites by promoting *futuwa*, associations that were half religious and half professional. Soon afterwards, however, the empire, and the caliphate, met its nemesis in the form of the Mongol invasion.

It was the end of everything. Hülagu, grandson of Genghis Khan, took Baghdad by storm during the first days of 1258. The caliph al-Mutasim surrendered on 18 February, and Hülagu had him executed along with all his family. The massacres that followed lasted eighteen days, and the eventual death toll was estimated by chroniclers at between eight hundred thousand and two million (figures that are obviously wildly exaggerated). Whole quarters of the city were looted and burned and the Great Mosque and the Shiite mosque of Khazimain were razed. It was a disaster without precedent. Baghdad would never again be the capital of Islam; it survived, but only as a provincial city at the mercy of successive conquerors. Tamerlane took it in 1393.

The caliphate survived in purely nominal form for a while longer. Mustansir, an Abbasid, found refuge in Cairo with the Mamelukes, whose sultan Baibars proclaimed him caliph in order to legitimize his own power. The new caliph had no authority whatsoever. All that was left to him was the privilege of granting investiture on request to certain far-off princes who, like the sultan of Delhi, despite everything still saw him as "God's messenger on earth". By 1517 when the Ottoman sultan Selim I (Selim the Terrible) entered Cairo, the man he captured was no more than the faintest shadow of the Commander of the Faithful. The caliph was sent to Istanbul, where Suleiman the Magnificent gave him permission to return to Egypt. He died there in 1543, and with him vanished all trace of the family of Abbas.

Notes

Chapter 1

1. The first four caliphs are known as *rashidun* (well-guided, walking the straight path) in contrast to their successors, who have been accused of exploiting the institution in their own or their families' interests. The rashidun caliphs are: Abu Bakr, 632-634; Omar ibn al-Khattab, 634-644; Othman ibn Affan, 644-656; and Ali ibn Abu Talib, 656-661. Harun was also to bear the title "Rashid".

2. Named after Umayya, common ancestor of Othman and Muawia.

3. The cycle of prophecy ended with Mohammed, Seal of the Prophets. Then began the cycle of initiation (*walayat*), the succession of those whose mission is to interpret revelation in an esoteric sense and to guide humanity in its spiritual life.

4. Abbas, brother of Mohammed's father, Abdallah, and of Ali's father, Abu Talib, played no significant part in the beginnings of Islam but was later responsible for supplying pilgrims with provisions, which probably made him fairly rich.

5. The black standards flown by the Abbasids had been used previously by other movements of religious rebellion under the Umayyads. They had thus acquired a messianic significance, symbolizing the hope that deviations and injustices would be righted. Black became the colour of the Abbasid revolution.

6. This word can also mean "the Bloodthirsty".

7. Masudi, *Meadows of Gold*.

8. B. Lewis, *The Arabs in History*.

9. Yakubi.

10. The Town of Peace was not the first in history to be built on a circular plan. Hagmatana (Ecbatane), in Iran, dated from the eighth century BC; Mantinaea had been built by Epaminondas in 370 BC; and Ctesiphon and Hatra, in Iraq, as well as Darajberd and Gur (today Firuzabad), in Iran, all predated Baghdad.

11. Koran, VI, 127: the "dwelling of peace".

12. Constructing the Round City is thought to have cost four million dinars (under the early Abbasids, a dinar was 4.55 grammes

of gold).

13. Abu al-Faradj, *Kitab al-Aghani*.

14. Umayyad supporters gathered behind red emblems.

15. According to Nizam al-Mulk, vizier of the eleventh-century Seljuk sultan Melik Shah, the Barmakids had been viziers to the king of Persia, passing the job from father to son. Kwondamir, a chronicler of the Timurid era (fifteenth century), claims that they were descended originally from Persian kings. In reality the name Barmak was originally the title of the superior of a Buddhist monastery (D. Sourdel).

16. Huang-Tsang, a Chinese monk, travelled to India to study sacred Buddhist texts.

17. Quoted in C. Scheffer, *Chrestomathie persane*.

18. Masudi.

19. Tabari.

20. N. Abbott.

21. Abu al-Atahiya.

Chapter 2

1. The call for severity and rigour is no mere stylistic flourish. Young princes were sometimes beaten mercilessly.

2. The historian ibn Tiktaka recounts that the caliph Saffah remarked one day to Khalid, "Khalid, you will not be satisfied until you have made me your servant." "How so, O Emir of the Believers?" asked the alarmed Khalid. "It is I who am your servant and your slave." Chuckling, Saffah explained, "My daughter Raitah and your daughter were asleep together in the same bed. Passing during the night, I saw that their cover had fallen to the floor, and I replaced it on the bed." "Then let the master accept payment from his servant and his handmaiden!" replied Khalid, kissing the caliph's hand.

3. The reader will encounter other quotations from the *Thousand and One Nights* in the course of this book. The famous tales are seldom a trustworthy historical source but — especially when set in Baghdad or Basra — provide a faithful reflection of the rhythm and texture of life during the golden age of Arab–Islamic civilization.

4. Principally the officials in charge of the treasury and chancery.

5. Masudi.

6. Christian heretics in the same period used doctrinal differences

as a pretext for flouting authority.

7. Cf. D. Sourdel, *Le Vizirat abbasside*.

8. Nothing survives of al-Khuld, but at Ukhaidir, some two hundred kilometres southwest of Baghdad, can be found the remains of a castle built in the latter half of the eighth century. According to the archeologist K.A.C. Cresswell, it probably belonged to Isa ibn Musa, the nephew of Saffah and Mansour. The external wall of the building, with towers at the four corners, measures 175 by 169 metres, and the palace proper covers an area of more than nine thousand square metres. The architecture of Ukhaidir mingles the traditions of the old Arab Orient with the more recent Sassanid and Umayyad influences. Throne rooms and state chambers, adapted to the complex ceremonial resulting from the quasi-deification of the caliph, became increasingly luxurious in later buildings. The new palaces built in Baghdad (Rusafa, al-Taj) only a few decades after Ukhaidir, and even more those at Samarra, were gigantic complexes (see Appendix II).

9. Although this description dates from about a century after Harun's reign, it gives us some idea of the way the court would have been spruced up for a state occasion in the time of the Well-Guided.

10. There is no record of a zoological garden in Harun al-Rashid's palace, but (like the Umayyads before them) Harun and his father, Mahdi, probably owned collections of wild animals.

11. According to al-Khatib al-Baghdadi, *Introduction to the History of Baghdad*.

12. 152nd Night.

13. A dynasty from the Caspian region which held the real political power in Baghdad from 945 until 1055 (see Chapter 10).

14. Mamun had ten sons; Mahdi had six sons and at least six daughters; Harun had fourteen sons, and the names of four of his daughters survive in records.

15. 926th Night.

16. Harun had sworn never to marry Ghadir (an oath taken at his brother's behest), and Ghadir had sworn the same oath; but they had married barely a month after Hadi's demise. Ghadir awakened one night terrified by a dream in which Hadi appeared to her, reproached her for marrying Harun, and said, "When morning comes, you will rejoin me." She was dead within the hour.

17. See the passages on textiles in Chapter 8.

18. *Thousand and One Nights.*

19. On the east bank of the Tigris, it had cost twenty million dirhams.

20. The caliph Mutawakil once gave two hundred dinars to one of his nadim who had cooked an excellent meal.

21. Harun granted pensions to good chess players; tournaments were held in the palace, and treatises on the game were published. Of Indian origin, the game reached the Arabs via Iran. Backgammon probably also came from India. A player was expected to be well-dressed and respectable, to have a good memory and a good education, and to "answer promptly when asked a question" (Ahsan). History records the names of some great chess players and of some of the palace slave girls whose play was outstanding. Sovereigns would send one another gifts of fine chess sets, with pieces carved from rock crystal, precious stones, and so on.

22. Djahiz, *The Book of the Crown.*

23. 926th Night.

24. Harun's half brother by his father, Mahdi, and a concubine called Chiklah (see Chapter 1). His sister Ulaiyah, born two years earlier, was the daughter of another slave.

25. Music made pious orthodox Muslims uneasy, as they considered it incompatible with strict observance of their religion.

26. Masudi.

27. *Thousand and One Nights.*

28. According to the *Book of Kings,* Harun never drank in public and allowed only his favourites to be present when he drank wine.

29. Ibn Khaldun.

30. Sourdel, *Le Vizirat abbasside.* (A more detailed discussion of the Barmakids' political role appears in Chapter 3.)

Chapter 3

1. See Appendix I.

2. Harun's mother, Khaizuran, owned many of these estates ("Khaizuraniyyah") in and around Baghdad, the income from which was about 160 million dirhams annually. She managed them herself with the help of her secretary, Omar ibn Mahran.

3. According to G. Wiet, *Histoire de la nation egyptienne.*

4. Members of the Prophet's family.

5. He also converted the Buddhist temple at Balkh into a mosque. He is thought to have started the custom of hanging lamps in every mosque at this time, a custom that later spread throughout the Muslim world.

6. Musa al-Kazim figures prominently in the history of Shiism. His brother Ismail had been chosen by their father, Jaffar Sadiq, as his successor, but Ismail died prematurely and some of his disciples rallied round his young son, Mohammed ibn Ismail. The Ismailis worked out a highly intellectual philosophic doctrine. Other Shiites rallied round Musa al-Kazim, the seventh imam. According to their doctrine, Musa's descendant Mohammed, who vanished mysteriously in 940, is in a state of "occultation", from which he will emerge when human beings become capable of recognizing the "perfect man".

7. The most threatening was the Azariqa revolt, which began in Basra in 684 and spread to Khorasan, Fars and Firman. It was not suppressed until 700, after a series of bloody struggles. Other uprisings immobilized large numbers of the Ummayyads' troops, and the heresy spread in Iraq, Syria, and north Africa, especially Tripolitania.

8. C. Cahen.

9. B. Lewis.

10. The first mercenaries, mostly Turks, appeared in Harun's personal guard.

11. Named after Seleucos II Kallinikos (256–226 BC), its founder.

12. According to the poet Marwan ibn Hafsah.

13. The corner of a room can still be seen there, decorated with stalactites, the earliest known example of this feature found in Seljuk and Ottoman architecture. There are no other remains of the Raqqa palace, but the general plan was doubtless similar to the layout of the palaces at Samarra, where al-Mutasim, one of Harun's sons, established his capital in 836 (see Appendix II).

14. See Appendix III for an account of the hunts organized by caliphs.

15. In *cawgan*, for which players wore special clothing with a gilded belt and red boots, a ball (generally of leather) was thrown high into the air. Mallets were used to catch and pass the ball. The object was to place it between the goal posts at either end of the ground. Each goal was defended by four players. Rather like golf

clubs, the wooden mallets had a curved end.

Chapter 4

1. *Ribat* were usually erected on the coast to repel invaders, especially Christians, and to serve as bases for the pursuit of holy war. They were garrisoned by men who might be described as soldier-monks, dedicated to war and prayer. These fortresses, with their bastions and towers, could be found all along the coast of Ifriqiya; ibn Khaldun claimed that they numbered ten thousand (a gross exaggeration). Ribat generally had an exterior curtain wall flanked by turrets; inside, porticos surrounded a courtyard opening into a room for prayer, another for ablutions, and cells arranged on two storeys. One of the external corner-turrets was built very high and was used for signal beacons. Apart from the surviving ribat at Monastir, others exist at Sousse and Sfax (all in present-day Tunisia).

2. The western part of Ifriqiya.

3. Present-day Tunisia and eastern Algeria.

4. On the same plan as the palace at Raqqa.

5. One Rostemid (quoted in G. Marcais) claimed: "We do not even have a serving-woman who does not know the signs of the zodiac."

6. It has been argued that they were Mutazilites, but this is hardly convincing. The heresy of Mutazilism is based on five principles: the Koran is not co-essential to God but was created by Him to be communicated to men; mankind has free will; the punishment of hell is eternal in all cases; any Muslim guilty of a grave sin is condemned to hell if he does not repent; the purpose of a government is to promote good and prevent evil, which implies the right to revolt against an unjust imam.

7. The Abbasid influence on Muslim Spain remained strong in many areas, however. Cordoba and Seville absorbed and imitated everything that came from Baghdad. The luxury of the peninsula's Muslims and Christians rivalled that of Abbasid society. The arrival in Cordoba, early in the ninth century, of the celebrated Baghdad singer Ziryab accentuated the process of "Orientalization". Ziryab quickly became a renowned musician and leader of fashion: he taught Cordobans of both sexes how to dress appropriately for the different seasons, how to wear their hair and make up their faces, how to make and use toothpaste, and so on. Under the supervision of this

234

man, formerly a slave of the caliph Mahdi, interiors were transformed and cuisine became more refined.

8. According to Masudi.

9. Ibid.

10. Ibid.

11. Harun's accounts included the item of ten kirat of naphtha and tow used to cremate Jaffar's body.

12. One day soon after Yahya's death, Harun sent for Dananir and asked her to sing. He told her that the Barmakids had betrayed their master's trust and deserved their terrible punishment. Dananir replied that she owed everything to the Barmakids, including the honour of entering the caliph's presence, and that she had been unable to sing since their downfall because her voice was choked with tears. Harun called Masrur and ordered him to maltreat Dananir in all sorts of ways to force her to sing. She gave way eventually and sang, while shedding streams of tears, "O dwelling of Salma! Thou art far from us now, but thine image is still graven on my heart. When I saw the house fall in ruins, I knew that the good times would never come again." Harun, touched, excused Dananir and stopped tormenting her.

13. From Quatremere, *Journal asiatique.*

14. *The Book of the Crown.*

15. Tabari, Masudi, and other historians; the storytellers of the *Thousand and One Nights*; and, more recently, G. Zaidan (*Al Abbassa* or *La Soeur du calife*) and C. Hermary-Vieille, *Le Grand Vizir de la nuit* (Paris, 1981), among others.

16. Yezdi, *Tarikh.*

17. *Prolegomena.*

18. A handsome Arab by the name of Zarara ibn Mohammed al-Arabi, a man of "eloquence and good education", was one day introduced to the palace by the Barmakids' sworn enemy, the chamberlain Fadl ibn al-Rabi. He was quickly admitted to the caliph's intimate circle and became a dangerous rival of Jaffar, who even tried to do away with him. But Zarara came out of his tomb. "I thought you were dead!" exclaimed Harun. "I was," replied Zarara, "but Allah enabled me to return to life, that I might inform the Emir of the Believers of the bad things which have been done to me." Harun showed Zarara more favour than ever and he became Jaffar's arch enemy. (Yezdi, according to Bouvat).

19. The Barmakids were of Buddhist origins and had never been Mazdaeans.

20. According to Masudi, the Barmakids possessed real-estate all over the empire. Khalid and Yahya owned a whole district of Baghdad, where they rented out houses and shops. Yahya built a palace modestly named Kasrat Tin, "Palace of Clay", but also lived in another palace, facing al-Khuld. Jaffar's palace, the one he presented to Mamun, was downstream of it, on the same bank of the Tigris. Also in Baghdad were the souks of Yahya and Jaffar, the "Fadl Canal", and "Khalid Square". They earned large sums from agriculture in the provinces; in Basra they owned the castle of Seihan; near Balkh, one of whose gates was named after Yahya, they owned the prosperous village of Raven; Bokhara had a gate bearing Fadl's name.

21. The *Thousand and One Nights* echoes the reputation of the Barmakids for being all-powerful: "There was never mention of any other house than theirs; one could not come to the royal favour save through them, directly or indirectly; members of their family filled all the highest positions at court and in the army, of the magistrature and in the provinces; the fairest properties near the city belonged to them; their palace was more encumbered by courtiers and petitioners than that of the Khalifah himself." (996th Night)

Chapter 5

1. Especially after the failure of the rebellion led by Ala ibn Mughit against the emir of Cordoba, which the Abbasids had fomented.

2. F.W. Buckler.

3. K.F. Werner, *Les Origines*.

4. According to Vasiliev, the ownership of elephants was restricted to the caliph. The animals were brought from India.

5. The cause of their deaths is not recorded, but was probably illness, as murder would have been noted by chroniclers.

6. G. Musca.

7. According to the *Annals of the Kingdom*.

8. According to A. Kleinclausz.

9. This story is almost certainly wholly invented by the pious monk, who was writing fifty years after the event and whose book,

Gesta Caroli Magni is a prolonged eulogy to Charlemagne.

10. The *Annals of the Kingdom* identify it as a clepsydra, which on the hour sounded a chime and dropped small coloured balls into a pool; at midday twelve horsemen galloped out of twelve windows in the case.

11. See Appendix IV.

12. Arculfe I, Vol. 3 (quoted in Kleinclausz, *Syria*). Bishop Arculfe (624–704) made a journey to the Holy Land and wrote a detailed description of it.

13. A Capitulary of Charlemagne in the year 810 ordered an inquiry into necessary repairs of churches in Jerusalem damaged during the civil war.

14. But in 831 Mamun did send two missions, one Muslim and the other Christian, to Charlemagne's son and successor, Louis the Pious. Their purpose was probably to sound out the attitudes of the Frankish king in the context of a new offensive the caliph was planning against Byzantium.

15. A non-Muslim subject belonging to a religion of the Book and required to pay the djiziya.

16. B. Lewis, *The Arabs in History*.

17. The town was taken in 1453 by Mehmed II, whose heavy artillery was able to breach its walls.

18. The use of incendiary liquids and compounds goes far back into antiquity; it is mentioned by Herodotus, Thucydides, and Livy. Ammien Marcellin mentions "melleoli", or missiles containing inflammable materials. These "oils" contained pitch, quicklime, wax, sulphur, and saltpetre in varying combinations. The Persians used them to impregnate tow, which was then attached to arrows. Naphtha was particularly formidable, as its flames spread uncontrollably. The Arabs also used incendiary liquids, notably during an expedition to India in 779; Harun used them at the siege of Heraclaea in 806. The name "Greek fire" dates from the import of these techniques from Syria to Byzantium by the Greek Kallinikos.

19. This concept of territorial defence dates from 625 but was applied only gradually; it is based on division of the territory into military districts, each responsible for recruiting its own troops. The strategist was virtually the absolute master of his province. Landowning families were obliged to perform military service: when

the alert was sounded, the men reported for duty fully armed and mounted. Peasants who could not afford weapons or a horse were equipped at the expense of the village. The system provided the state with battle-ready contingents at short notice. The same reforms had been applied to the navy.

20. This restrictive ruling soon evolved, however; the jurists managed to reconcile the law with economic necessity by devising an intermediate status, called "truce" (extended as well to non-Muslims travelling in Muslim territory), which covered journeys for trading and other necessary purposes. For more detail on commerce see Chapter 8.

21. In reality, castration was carried out mainly by Jews.

22. V. Grunebaum, *Medieval Islam*.

23. 46th Night.

24. The legend was that seven young people had been walled up in a cave near Ephesus, in which they had taken refuge from persecution under the emperor Decius in the third century. They had gone to sleep and awakened two hundred years later. When they finally died they were buried at the spot, and their grotto then became a place of pilgrimage famous throughout the Near East.

25. According to the official protocol laid down in the *Book of Ceremonies*, the caliph's name appeared before the emperor's in letters addressed to the Arab sovereign, while the order was reversed in correspondence with Western kings.

26. The river that has its source in the Anti-Taurus and flows into the Gulf of Alexandretta.

27. Muawia in 655, 668, and 674; Suleiman ibn Abd al-Malik in 715.

28. According to Brehier.

29. According to Theophanes.

30. Haruniya was built in 799 and still exists.

31. Towns in the interior, like Ancyre, Caesaraea, Dorylaea, Nicaea, and others, secure behind their ramparts, steadily increased in size and population until the Ottoman period, while Priene (to take one example) disappeared.

32. Its effectiveness became clear in 806 when the Arabs mounted a major raid on Cyprus.

33. In 805 the Aghlabids of Kairouan had launched seaborne raids on the Peloponnesus and given support to the Slavs besieging Patras.

34. Foot soldiers were relatively well paid (their wages two or three times those of a Baghdad worker). Cavalry troops received three times as much again. (C. Cahen)

35. Abu al-Faradj, quoted in Mercier, *Le Feu grégeois.*

Chapter 6
1. Tabari.
2. Abu al-Atahiya.
3. Koran, LXIX, 28–29.

Chapter 7
1. Yakubi, *The Countries.*
2. A parasang is roughly equivalent to six kilometres.
3. The upkeep of buildings used to be an idea wholly alien to the Orient.
4. Quoted in A. Mez, *The Renaissance of Islam.*
5. An attempt was made in the second half of the ninth century to drain the marshes of southern Iraq using slave labour imported from east Africa, but the experiment was brought to an end by the revolt of the Zendj and was not repeated.
6. "And the children of Israel took captive the women of Midian and their little ones." (Numbers, 31, 9)
7. Sura XVI, 73.
8. Mohammed also advises the believer to emancipate his slaves (Sura XXIV, 35), in which he goes somewhat further than the Old Testament, which merely recommends the emancipation of Israelites enslaved for debt.
9. Castration was sternly prohibited by Islam.
10. "He bought them wherever he could find them and they surrounded him day and night, at meals, during drinking sessions and even during working hours. He wished to see no women, whether free-born or slaves. White eunuchs he called *grasshoppers* and black ones *ravens.*" (Tabari, III)
11. 32nd Night.
12. Nishwar al-Muhadara, *The Table-Talk of a Mesopotamian Judge* (London, 1921).
13. A system still used in the countries of the Persian Gulf.
14. G. Marcais.
15. At the beginning of the Hegira the tales told by qusass were

usually designed to arouse greater piety in the faithful; on the battlefield they bolstered the troops' courage by describing the felicities of the afterlife. These popular theologians were encouraged by the authorities.

16. He gave his name to a dish, the *ibrahimiyya*.

17. See Appendix V.

18. Quoted in A. Mez, op. cit.

19. Some observed this custom to drive away evil, others to expel bad air from the house or even purify the body of the fumes of winter.

Chapter 8

1. André Miquel, *L'Islam et sa civilisation*.

2. The *Book of Land Taxation*, written by Abu Yusuf at the end of the eighth century, advises governments on reclaiming and using land: "If the Caliph is informed that there is land in such and such a place which might be cultivable if irrigated, and if the fact is confirmed on investigation, you should give orders for canals to be dug at the expense of the Treasury and not of the local inhabitants; for it is preferable in practice that they be prosperous rather than impoverished and that they become rich rather than being ruined and reduced to powerlessness." (Quoted by Sourdel, *Le Vizirat abbasside*)

3. The wheel disappeared because of the technical inadequacy of harnessing systems and the high cost of transport by cart. Wheeled vehicles were not reintroduced until the arrival of the Turks in the twelfth century.

4. Maurice Lombard.

5. Ibn Tiktaka.

6. *Prolegomena*, II.

7. Kufic was an angular script. Very simple at first, over the centuries it became more ornate, with the addition of stylized leaves and flowers.

8. Some fabrics were made waterproof by being very tightly woven or covered with a film of wax.

9. Ibn Khaldun.

10. According to M. Lombard, op. cit.

11. A word of Persian origin that originally meant "hypocrite" (not "from Rhodes") but acquired the general meaning of a trader,

not necessarily a Jewish one.

12. 302nd Night.

13. Chinese ships were still rare in Indian Ocean waters. The Chinese empire's centre of gravity was in the north and the government had little interest in developing the southern ports. It was not until the Sung dynasty of the eleventh and twelfth centuries that the rulers of China showed interest in this region and its overseas trading activities.

14. However, both Arabs and Persians had the advantage of the triangular "lateen" sail, which made it possible to sail upwind. Lateen rig reached northern Europe, via the Mediterranean, in about the fifteenth century. The magnetic compass, invented by the Chinese, was not used by the Arabs until the middle of the eleventh century. They later passed it on to the West.

15. Secreted by a particular species of deer. The best musk came from Tibet.

16. Turkish slaves were uncommon in Harun's time.

17. *Thousand and One Nights.*

Chapter 9

1. Quoted in J. Vernet, *Ce que la culture doit aux Arabes d'Espagne* (Paris, 1986).

2. On this controversy, see J. Vernet, op. cit.

3. Nestorianism, which appeared at the beginning of the fifth century, held that Christ contained two persons: a human person born of the Virgin Mary and a divine person of the Word. After prolonged discussions between Nestorius, Bishop of Constantinople and main propagandist of the new doctrine, and Cyril, Bishop of Alexandria, who supported orthodoxy, a Council held at Ephesus in 431 condemned Nestorianism; but it rapidly gained support and spread to Iran, Arabia, India, even China, and eventually had more than two hundred dioceses. The number and influence of the Nestorians declined suddenly after Tamerlane's invasions in the fourteenth and fifteenth centuries, and again after the national struggles that took place in the Middle East during the nineteenth century.

4. Mansour asked the emperor of Byzantium to send him the works of Euclid and other mathematicians. Loot from conquered towns such as Amorium and Ancyre helped swell the libraries of

caliphs. The Arabs sometimes asked the Byzantines to pay war indemnities partly in books.

5. Legend has it that Mamun understood the importance of the Hellenic heritage when Aristotle appeared to him in a dream and answered his questions: "What is beauty?" — That which is beautiful to our reason. "And what is that?" — That which is beautiful to the Law. "And what is that?" — That which is accepted by the majority. "Tell me more." — He who advises you on gold shall be as gold in your eyes. Respect the oneness of God. (Ibn al-Nadim, quoted in J. Vernet).

6. Quoted in Abd al-Salam.

7. Quoted in Charles Pellat.

8. 287th Night. See also 378th and 379th Nights.

9. C. Cahen.

Chapter 10

1. See Appendix II.

2. This movement had followers from various population groups: black Africans, Arabs, Persians, Jews, and Christians. The most widely accepted theory holds that the revolt stemmed from the inhuman conditions to which black slaves were subjected on the sugarcane plantations. But Shaban (*Islamic History*, II) thinks that the uprising, which was supported by merchants, was aimed at seizing control of north African trade routes.

3. Qarmatism, named after its founder Hamdan–Qarmat, was a form of septimian Ismailism; it was a movement of social character strongly tinged with messianism.

4. M.A. Shaban, *Islamic History*.

Appendix I
Messianic Movements

Movements claiming a connection with Abu Muslim began to appear soon after his death in 755. Messianic-type sects arose mainly among the Iranian peoples and the Turks of Khorasan and Transoxania. Their doctrines were inspired by every religion known: Mazdaeism and Zoroastrianism, Islam, even Christianity.

The first of these movements was started by Sunbad, a Mazdaean associate of Abu Muslim. He quickly gathered a large number of supporters, sixty thousand according to Tabari, by persuading them that Abu Muslim was not dead but had assumed the form of a dove and flown off to live with Mazda in a castle made of copper. Sunbad marched on Iraq but was stopped between Ray and Hamadan by the army Mansour sent out against him. He was later killed in the Jurjan. Soon afterwards another of Abu Muslim's companions, Ishak al-Turki, came up with a story claiming that Abu Muslim was an envoy of Zoroaster, that he was still alive and hiding near Ray, and that he would return.

Towards 756 the rebellion of al-Muqanna — an Iranian who, because he concealed his face behind a veil (or gold mask), was called "the Veiled Prophet" — broke out in the Merv region. He explained to his many followers that God had inhabited successively the persons of Adam, Seth, Noah, Abraham, Moses, Jesus, Mohammed, and finally himself. The peoples of Transoxania were particularly receptive to these anarchistic doctrines so different from ordinary religious laws. Al-Muqanna committed suicide while under siege in a fortress.

Later the name of Abu Muslim was absorbed into the mystical, heterodox currents found among the common people, especially among artisans and guild members. Over the years he became in legend a sort of champion of the humble and defender of the oppressed. His name and the account of his wondrous deeds spread by way of epic literature throughout the Orient, particularly among the Anatolian trade guilds and later the dervish brotherhoods. The Bektashis linked their founder, Hajji Bektash, with Abu Muslim and his companions. An extensive literature, filled with marvellous events in which the hero's prowess is infinitely embroidered, has kept the Abu Muslim legend alive among Persians and Turks to the present day.

Appendix II
Samarra

In 836, after succeeding Mamun, al–Mutasim decided to establish his capital at Samarra. The site, previously inhabited only by Christian monks, allowed the caliph to indulge his taste for the grandiose, which characterized palace architecture at that time.

Just as Mansour had brought in artisans from all over the empire to build the Round City, al–Mutasim "gave the order in writing for labourers, masons, specialists, blacksmiths, carpenters, and other artisans to be summoned, for all sorts of timber, especially teak and palm trunks, to be brought from Basra and its surrounding region, from Baghdad and the whole Sawad region, from Antioch and from the whole littoral of Syria. He also sent for specialists in cutting and laying marble..." (Yakubi, *The Countries*).

About thirty palaces were erected in Samarra by Abbasid caliphs over a period of nearly fifty years. At its height the town's population is said to have reached a million. So great were the distances inside the palaces that people moved about them on horseback. Groups of buildings separated by green spaces, courtyards, ponds, and lakes stretched along the Tigris for hundreds of metres.

The first palace, al–Mutasim's Djausaq al–Khaqani, covered 175 hectares. It was entered through a three-arched gate (part of which survives), whose vaulted arches were nearly twelve metres high and decorated with stucco work. This gave onto a terrace overlooking the Tigris; inside, one was led through large halls to a vast courtyard, around which were arranged the treasury, the armoury, barracks, mosques, and stores. The throne room, reached by crossing two further courtyards, was square and surmounted by a dome; the iwan (large barrel vaults) of other chambers opened into it on all sides. After that came the harem and, last, another domed chamber (of which part of the painted dome survives). This last opened through five doors onto an esplanade measuring 350 by 180 metres, with two fountains and a canal. Under this esplanade was an underground apartment sheltered from the heat and containing more ponds.

The complex ended in a polo ground, with a raised pavilion for watching the games, a bathhouse, and stables. Beyond this was a five-kilometres-long "paradise" (game park).

The principal material was sun-dried mud brick, with fired brick used for structures needing greater strength. New architectural forms were appearing: arches, iwan, domed chambers with iwan leading into them.

The remains of another Samarra palace, Balkuwara, built by the caliph Mutawakil (847–861), help to give an impression of the great palace complexes of the period. A rectangle measuring 575 by 460 metres, it looked out onto the river and its valley through three monumental arches; these opened onto three courtyards from which the iwan leading to the state chambers were entered. Beyond them were the private apartments; offices, harem, rooms for courtiers and troops were housed in other wings. On the east side was a large garden scattered with luxurious pavilions, streams, and waterfalls. Beyond it was a polo ground with its buildings and other small gardens. These palaces were built in the space of a few months, something that helps to explain their rapid decay.

Easy to make and apply, either by trowel or in ready-moulded slabs, stucco generally covered the lower half of the walls and the door embrasures. The doors themselves were often decorated with gold nails. Ceilings were made of wood, especially teak. Painted friezes were common and sometimes covered an entire wall; walls might also be lined with glazed tiles, carved marble, or mosaics inspired by Hellenic or Umayyad art. The windows were glazed with small multicoloured panes, probably similar to those seen today in old houses in the Yemen. In the state chambers and the caliph's apartments were precious carpets, silk and brocade hangings embroidered with gold, and wall niches displaying objects of great beauty and value: finely worked gold ornaments, glazed porcelain dishes, cups of crystal and gold.

Arab art in Samarra had lost much of its Muslim character. Iranian influences were predominant. The sovereign's glory is magnified in these paintings, in which male figures represent members of his Turkish bodyguard. Almond-eyed dancers — with kiss-curls lying on their plump Oriental cheeks, their robes falling in heavy folds, and diadems on their heads — move like priestesses before the sovereign in his majesty. The caliph's hunt is represented in the same half-frozen way, with horsewomen and huntresses taking part: here a bull bearing a Sassanid sash is put to death, there hounds and game dash between horns of plenty and vine branches.

Fragments of paintings unearthed at Nishapur show the same buxom female figures; the style became a school and was also current in Tulunid Egypt in the same period. In art, as in literature, Asia thus regained much of the ground lost to the heritage of Rome and Athens. However, the "Abbasid" style did not take hold in Syria, nor in Umayyad Spain, which used Syrian artists to build and decorate its palaces and mosques. The two artistic approaches competed for dominance over several centuries until eventually the different "provinces" of Islam — Iran and Mesopotamia, Syria and the eastern Mediterranean, Egypt and the Maghreb — each evolved its own artistic character and defined its own classicism.

Ceramics

Ceramics reached a point of perfection in Samarra. Chinese ceramic wares, the best in the world at that time, had originally arrived in Baghdad via Khorasan in Harun al-Rashid's day. Others arrived by sea. They brought celadons speckled with apricot or cream, green and brown stoneware. Mesopotamian potters, heirs to a long tradition, wasted no time in imitating these pieces. The best-known Baghdad potteries at first produced moulded and incised work, sometimes painted as well; later they made glazed vases and dishes, similar to Chinese ceramics but more highly decorated.

Mesopotamian ceramic art reached its highest expression with metallic glazes, obtained by firing pottery with a glaze containing metallic oxides. Highlights in a wide variety of colours — red, yellow, green, and brown — testify to the existence of a ninth-century technique subsequent potters have never succeeded in surpassing. Some of the effects produced by the Baghdad potteries were the results of experimenting with different combinations of metallic compounds. They are still amazing. Their design was usually of Sassanid or Abbasid inspiration, with added Kufic inscriptions. After 860–870 these pieces were no longer made.

These fine dishes, ewers, cups, and other items were in daily use in the caliph's palace and in the houses of dignitaries; but they were also for sale. In the mosque of Sidi Oqba in Kairouan, on the wall of the mihrab, one can still see tiles of this ceramic. They were sent from Baghdad in 862. Archeological digs in Samarra have turned up many fragments of this admirable pottery.

Appendix III
Hunting with the Caliph

The Abbasid caliphs were enthusiastic hunters. Mahdi, it will be recalled, died while pursuing a gazelle, and the chroniclers have left numerous accounts of the chase. Harun often went hunting, especially after moving to Raqqa, which swarmed with big and small game, including lions, tigers, ostriches, and wild bulls.

The caliph's hunting parties involved hundreds, sometimes thousands, of people, horses, camels, and trained birds and animals. When a hunt had been planned, the imperial hunt master would order the chief grooms, guides, beaters, archers, falconers, and the keepers of other animals to prepare themselves and their charges. Armed soldiers would escort the caliph and his family, who were nearly always accompanied by their doctors, secretaries, readers of the Koran, astronomers, and so forth. Beasts of burden carried an enormous amount of equipment, tents, carpets, and all the utensils of daily life, to make the caliph's desert encampment as luxurious as the apartments in his palace.

Guides were sent ahead to locate the game, which was then encircled by the hunters and beaters with drums. The hunting animals were then let loose: falcons for pheasants, partridges, and waterfowl; sparrow hawks for hares. Hounds and cheetahs would be unleashed, and when the game had been cornered or run to a standstill, the caliph and the princes would come in for the kill. Back in camp, the edible game would be roasted by servants for the caliph and his guests.

For the lion hunts favoured by Harun, specially trained horses were used to run the prey down; when it was exhausted, the hunter would try to dispatch it with lance, sword, or arrows.

These hunting parties employed large numbers of people. Officials, artisans and workers were kept permanently busy at the palace looking after the animals and equipment. Merchants imported hunting animals and sold items of equipment. And there were the guides, the beaters, and others. Under Mutawakil, half a century after Harun, the wages of this staff alone amounted to half a million dirhams a year. If the purchase of animals and equipment is added, along with the compensation usually paid in Harun's day to peasants for damage to their crops, the annual cost of this hobby rises to tens of thousands of dinars.

The purchase and training of animals used for hunting cost enormous sums. These beasts were sometimes presented by other sovereigns or high dignitaries; the emperor of Byzantium once gave Harun twelve falcons and four hounds. Among the tributes paid by Armenia were thirty falcons each year. Birds of prey were very costly: hawks, eagles, peregrine falcons; the best bird was thought to be the *baz*, the goshawk from Turkestan, Greece, or India. Other birds of prey were imported, especially those with plumage of one colour.

Hounds were also much used, and the best, which came from the Yemen, sold for very high prices. Weasels were used to dislodge foxes from their earths. The cheetah occupied a special place in the list of hunting animals; only the richest people could afford it, as it does not reproduce in captivity, its training is long and difficult, and it requires very skilled care. Caliphs often included leashed cheetahs in their official processions; court poets, including the famous Abu Nuwas, sang the animal's praises.

Appendix IV
Harun al-Rashid
and
Charlemagne

No surviving Arabic source makes any mention of relations between Harun al-Rashid and Charlemagne. Even Tabari and Masudi, who left a mass of detailed information on the reigns of the early Abbasid caliphs, say not a word on this subject. This has led some historians to deny that any contacts took place.

There are several possible reasons for the silence of Oriental writers. There was nothing unusual in relations between the caliph and a foreign sovereign; like his predecessors, Harun maintained contacts with princes of the Orient, including Indian monarchs. Arab historians never mention these meetings unless they are the occasion for some exceptional display of splendour by the caliph (as during the reception organized for the Byzantine emperor in 917). Nor were these historians especially well disposed to the Christians. They had no pressing reason to record the diplomatic relations of the Commander of the Faithful with some infidel whose dowdy little embassies passed unnoticed at Raqqa (all Charlemagne's missions having arrived after Harun had left Baghdad).

At first Charlemagne was regarded in Europe simply as the most illustrious of those making the pilgrimage to Palestine, but after the Renaissance, people began claiming that the holy places had been given to the emperor by the caliph. The account by the monk of Saint-Gall came to be considered the most reliable source, and Eginhard fell into disfavour. It was even claimed (by Mme de Genlis in her novel *Les Chevaliers du Cygne* and by at least one music historian) that Harun had sent Charles an organ as a gift. The legend continued to be embellished until the nineteenth century, when Pouqueville published a *Historical Memoir* concluding that there had been no relations of any kind between the two emperors. The Russian historian W. Barthold adopted this opinion in 1912; his argument emphasized the absence of Arabic sources and the fact that Arab geographers make no mention of Christian establishments in Jerusalem. At almost the same time, the Russian Byzantine expert A. Vasiliev accepted the greater part of the monk's account. In 1919 L. Brehier asserted, at the French congress on Syria, that Harun had granted Charles what amounted to a protectorate over Palestine: "A sort of right to give protection to the Christians which the Byzantine emperors never enjoyed, except perhaps during the 11th century." During that postwar period, with France demanding a mandate over the whole Levant, the great scholar had perhaps allowed himself to be carried away by what another Byzantinist, S. Runciman, called "the fervour of western patriotism". Brehier abandoned this idea a few years later and adopted a more moderate position (*Charlemagne et la Palestine*, 1928), while Joransen, in *The Alleged Frankish Protectorate in Palestine* (1927), resumed part of Barthold's thesis. In *Harunul' Rashid and Charles the Great* (1921), the American F.W. Buckler suggests that Charlemagne had been Harun's vassal in Palestine and his wali (governor) in Jerusalem.

The expression "Aix-la-Chapelle–Baghdad axis" employed by the historian J. Calmette is conditioned, like Brehier's thesis, by the political realities of Europe between the World Wars (cf. "Rome–Berlin axis"). Calmette certainly seems to go too far when he claims that this axis was "an essential element in the Carolingian successes" in the affair of the Spanish Glacis and in obtaining Byzantine recognition for Charlemagne's empire. Kleinklausz (*Le Légende du protectorat de Charlemagne sur la terre sainte*) is undoubtedly closer to the truth when he suggests that Charlemagne was given Christ's tomb to mark the identity of Harun's views with Charles's. Runciman accepts this opinion but limits Harun's gift to the Church of St Mary and the grant of facilities for Christian pilgrims.

Appendix V
The Table in
Harun al-Rashid's Century

"'I have five pots for you,' I answered, 'all containing admirable foods: egg-apples and stuffed marrows, filled vine-leaves seasoned with lemon, cakes of bruised wheat and minced meat, sliced fillet of mutton cooked in tomatoed rice, a stew of little onions; further I have ten roast fowls and a roast sheep, and two great dishes, one of kunafah and the other of a pastry made with sweet cheese and honey; fruits of every kind: melons, cucumbers, limes, and fresh dates.' I had a little chest brought, containing more than fifty gold dinars' worth of ambergris, aloewood, nard, musk, incense and benzoin, and had it packed up for him with aromatic essences and silver water-sprays." (29th Night)

"And there were four deep porcelain bowls: the first contained halwa, perfumed with orange juice, sprinkled with cinnamon and powder of nuts; the second held crushed raisins discreetly sublimated with rose; the third, ah! the third was filled with bakkalawah, each of whose thousand leaves was the work of an artist and had lozenge-shaped divisions of an infinite suggestion; and in the fourth were almond cakes ready to burst because of their generous provision of heavy syrup. The other half of the dish was bright with all my favourite fruits, figs wrinkled with ripeness, knowing themselves desirable, grape-fruit and limes, grapes and bananas; these were divided by intervals of coloured flowers; roses, jasmine and tulips, lilies and jonquils." (116th Night)

Asparagus

We have lances with drooping points, twisted and plaited like a rope,
But regular and unknotted; their heads are thicker than their stems.
Planted erect in the earth, like pillars, they have been clothed by
    the hand of the one and eternal Creator
In silky cloth, like the *soundous* over a cloak. Their colour is a fine

and glowing red;
One might say they were touched with red, like a cheek crimsoned
   by an angry hand.
They are interlaced like the rings of a coat of mail made from gold
   filigree.
They look like a silk mitraf [raw silk cloth with coloured edges]
   spread out for display. Would that they lasted as long!
They might be the setting for a pearl ring. They swim in appetizing
   juice,
Which flows about them; butter covers them with its foamy cloth
And, soaking their stems, forms tresses of gold and silver.
At the sight of this delicious dish, even a pious doctor of religion
   would salivate during prayer and break his fast before sundown.

(Poem by Mahmud, known as Kochadjim, quoted in Masudi,
Meadows of Gold, VIII)

Djoudabah

A djoudabah made with the best rice, golden like the face of a lover,
Admirable, shining delicacy from the hand of virtuous and
   intelligent cook,
Pure as bullion, its rosy tint is the work of the Creator.
The Ahwaz sugar that flavours it tastes sweeter than the kisses of
   the beloved.
Its quivering oil-soaked mass envelops the dinner-guest in sweet
   perfume.
It is soft and consistent like cream; its scent is of purest amber.
At the sight of it, nestling in its bowl, one would say that a star
   had risen in the dark sky;
Or that a fine yellow carnelian glittered on the neck of a slim-bodied
   young virgin.
More welcome is it than sanctuary extended without warning to a
   heart oppressed with fear.

(also by Mahmud, quoted in Masudi, *Meadows of Gold*, VIII)

Chronology
AD 570–1543

IN ISLAM		OUTSIDE ISLAM
570	Birth of Mohammed	
612	Mohammed's preaching begins	
618		Tang dynasty starts in China
622	Mohammed in Medina. Hegira	
630	Mohammed returns to Mecca	
632	Death of Mohammed. Omar becomes caliph	
634	Byzantine defeat at Adjnayn	
635	Capture of Damascus	
636	Byzantine defeat at Yarmuk	
638	Capture of Jerusalem	
640	Capture of Heliopolis	
642		Collapse of Sassanid empire
644	Omar assassinated. Othman becomes caliph	
646	Capture of Alexandria	
655	Naval defeat of Byzantines	
656	Othman dies. Ali becomes caliph	
657	Battle of Siffin. Kharidjites abandon Ali	
661	Ali assassinated at Kufa. Muawia becomes caliph at Damascus	
663–77	Arab expeditions reach Constantinople	
670	Foundation of Kairouan	
680	Husein dies at Kerbela	Pippin of Herstal takes power in Frankish kingdom
685	Mukhtar's movement	
711	Tarik reaches Spain	
716	Siege of Constantinople by Maslama. Abbasid conspiracy begins	Charles Martel
717		Leon III (the Isaurian) emperor of Byzantium
726		Quarrel over images begins
732		Battle of Poitiers

	IN ISLAM	OUTSIDE ISLAM
747	Abbasid insurrection in Khorasan. Abu Muslim	
749	Saffah becomes first Abbasid caliph	
751	Chinese defeated at Talas	Pippin the Brief king of the Franks
754	Mansour becomes caliph	
755	Execution of Abu Muslim	
756	Abderahman becomes emir of Cordoba	
762	Baghdad founded	
766	*Birth of Harun al-Rashid*	
771		Charlemagne king of the Franks
775	Mahdi becomes caliph	
778		Roncevalles
779	Harun's first expedition against the Byzantines	
781	Harun's second expedition	
785	Hadi becomes caliph	
786	Harun al-Rashid becomes caliph (14 September)	
787		Irene becomes regent and reinstates cult of images
789	Idrisids found Fez in Morocco	
796	Harun leaves Baghdad for Raqqa	
797	Harun marches against Byzantines	Irene becomes Byzantine empress. Charlemagne's first mission to Harun
800	Aghlabids in Ifriqiya	Coronation of Charlemagne
802	Convention of the Kaaba. Empire divided	Two Muslim dignitaries arrive to see Charlemagne. New embassy from Charlemagne to the caliph. Nicephoros becomes Byzantine emperor; Irene ousted
803	Tragedy of Barmakids. New expedition by Harun against the Byzantines	

	IN ISLAM	OUTSIDE ISLAM
805	Abdallah sent on mission to Charlemagne by the caliph	
806	Campaign against Byzantium by Harun. Capture of Heraclaea	
807		New embassy sent by Charlemagne to Harun
809	*Death of Harun al-Rashid* (in Tus on 24 March)	
809–13	Conflict between Mamun and Amin. Baghdad Commune"	
810	Tahirids in Khorasan	
813	Mamun becomes caliph	
814		Death of Charlemagne
825	Arabs in Crete	
831	Arabs in Sicily	
832	Foundation of House of Wisdom (*Bayt al-Hikma*)	
833	Death of Mamun. Al-Mutasim becomes caliph	
836	Capital moved to Samarra	
868	Tulunids in power in Egypt	
874	Samanids in Khorasan	
945	Buyids in Baghdad	
1055	Seljuk Turks in Baghdad	
1258	Mongols take Baghdad	
1393	Tamerlane in Baghdad	
1517	Selim I imprisons Abbasid caliph in Cairo	
1543	Suleiman the Magnificent releases Abbasid caliph, who dies	

Index

Index

Index

Index